Natural Rights and the Birth of Romanticism
in the 1790s

Natural Rights and the Birth of Romanticism in the 1790s

R. S. White

820.9384
W587n

First published in 2005 by
PALGRAVE MACMILLAN
Houndmills, Basingstoke, Hampshire RG21 6XS and
175 Fifth Avenue, New York, N.Y. 10010
Companies and representatives throughout the world.

PALGRAVE MACMILLAN is the global academic imprint of the Palgrave
Macmillan division of St. Martin's Press, LLC and of Palgrave Macmillan Ltd.
Macmillan® is a registered trademark in the United States, United Kingdom
and other countries. Palgrave is a registered trademark in the European
Union and other countries.

ISBN 13: 978–1–4039–9478–3
ISBN 10: 1–4039–9478–1

A catalogue record for this book is available from the British Library.

Library of Congress Cataloging-in-Publication Data

White, R. S., 1948–
    Natural rights and the birth of romanticism in the 1790s / R. S. White.
        p. cm.
    Includes bibliographical references and index.
    ISBN 1–4039–9478–1 (cloth)
        1. English literature – 18th century – History and criticism.
    2. Romanticism – Great Britain – History – 18th century. 3. Human
    rights – Great Britain – History – 18th century. 4. Natural law – History –
    18th century. 5. Human rights in literature. 6. Natural law in literature. I. Title.

PR447.W47 2005
820.9'384—dc22   2005047613

10 9 8 7 6 5 4 3 2 1
14 13 12 11 10 09 08 07 06 05

Printed and bound in Great Britain by
Antony Rowe Ltd, Chippenham and Eastbourne

For Julia Darling

Contents

Acknowledgements

I am grateful to the Australian Research Council for granting me a three year Discovery Award to write this book. I used the resources of the British Library in London, the Bodleian Library in Oxford, the Reid Library at the University of Western Australia, and the Robinson Library at Newcastle upon Tyne.

My colleagues in the Discipline of English, Communication and Cultural Studies at the University of Western Australia have consistently offered an amiable professional environment and a fund of expert knowledge. Judith Johnston endured the labour of reading my early drafts in full and I have profited immensely from her attentiveness to scholarly detail and from her warm encouragement at points when my faith waned. Andrew Lynch is always my first port of call for esoteric knowledge and informed insight, Gareth Griffiths generously offered the fruit of his research into the radical politics of the romantics, Kieran Dolin always comes up with the right phrase at the right time, and Gail Jones and Veronica Brady expressed infectious excitement for the subject, shared in heady conversations. Sue Lewis, Jocasta Davies and Linda Creswell have offered invariably calm and efficient administrative support, while Roger Bourke lightened my load with eagle-eyed editing. Of course, all errors that remain are my own, and usually the result of my clumsy attempts to correct an error pointed out by somebody else.

The School of English in the University of Newcastle upon Tyne gave me once again a happy home, with a visiting professorship. It was heart-warming to share my embryonic ideas with Claire Lamont, Michael Rossington and Desmond Graham. Linda Anderson and Jenny Richards even offered their own homes and domestic comfort. Ernst Honigmann was his hospitable and kindly self. It is an extra bonus to know that my dear friend Julia Darling worked alongside them, as Fellow in Literature and Health in the School. Her tragic death occurred as this book entered production.

For specific information I am grateful to Jonathan Bate, Stephanie Brown, Brian Bosworth, Deborah Cameron, Deirdre Coleman, Geoff Gallop, Carol Louise Hall, Margaret Harris, Paul Hamilton, Peter Holbrook, Alison Kershaw, Michael Meahan, Jon Mee, Rebecca Morgan, Clara Tuite, and many others whose footprints are here.

More general support came by way of timely and unstinting encouragement from an inner sanctum of friends: Hilary Fraser, John Goodridge, Philippa Kelly, David Norbrook, Sam Pickering, Emma Rooksby, Maurice Whelan, Jane Whiteley.

A book like this one takes me on average nine years from inception to publication, and during such a period there is a lot of living alongside writing, and sadly also a lot of dying. I lost close companions and my mother and my father who were always lovingly supportive. Some special people sensitively helped me through dark times: my sister Lynette Laybutt, my daughters Marina and Alana White, Davinia Costello, Rebecca Hiscock, Suzanne Montgomery, Hannah Wilkins.

1
From Natural Law to Natural Rights

Introduction

Some decades stand out as historical crucibles where ideas are forged, ferociously contested, and emerge over time as a paradigm, an orthodoxy. The struggle for and against such an idea can be observed in all aspects of philosophy, politics and culture. The 1790s in England were such a decade. Natural rights, evolving from natural law and later to become human rights, was just such an idea, and literature was one powerful forge where the idea was tested through the creative imagination and transferred to popular consciousness. Among the results were new and more egalitarian ways of thinking about society, far-reaching political reforms, and the birth of new forms of literature and the movement we call romanticism.

This book traces the reception into imaginative literature of one link in a continuous and ancient line of reasoning that seeks to show a single moral law binding all human beings for all time. It rests on the assumption that some actions are naturally right, or right according to nature, irrespective of positive law, transient beliefs, religious creeds, or opinion. It is self-evidently a powerful intellectual tradition which, I argue, has been both exemplified and amplified by imaginative writers during key periods. The long chain leads from natural law, initiated in presocratic Greek philosophy and having its heyday in the Renaissance. The weakening of natural law led to calls for natural rights, during the eighteenth century and especially around the time of the French revolution. The tradition later underwent another adaptation into human rights, most conveniently dated from 1948 when the Universal Declaration of Human Rights was signed.[1] Civil rights, expounded, for example, by black Americans in the 1960s, are a later link in the same chain. What marks all these movements is an insistence that innately, within every human being, is a knowledge that some things are right and some things are wrong, and that this knowledge 'written on the human heart' stems from the very fact of being human and part of nature. Reason, the capacity which defines the uniqueness of human beings, is at the heart of notions of

1

fundamental law and fundamental rights, since only what is reasonable can be agreed upon by all human beings. Christian thinking added to reason the capacity for conscience, an active faculty which enables us to put reason into practice. Sympathy, natural benevolence, and unforced altruism provide the emotional colouring to reason and conscience, linking the individual with broader society through the communitarianism of fellow feeling.

Some, like John Finnis, see 'human rights' as 'a contemporary idiom for "natural rights"', using the terms synonymously,[2] but it is historically important to separate the two, since the kinds of rights insisted upon as 'natural' in the 1790s are rather different from those considered 'human' after two world wars in the twentieth century and horrendous acts of genocide and atrocity into the twenty-first. Indeed, as this book will argue, the demand changed from an initially passionate but unfocused call for 'rights of man' to a set of single issues such as rights of slaves, rights of political participation, rights of women, children, and so on. Lloyd L. Weinreb points out 'the variability of specific [natural] rights from one community to another' in suggesting that human rights is a broader term: '... *all* human beings possess the rights, so that the enquiry can cross national boundaries'.[3] Peter Jones argues that there are advantages in freeing human rights from some of the features traditionally associated with natural rights.[4] Although there has been a revival of natural law, led for example by John Rawls and Joseph Raz, it is rarely suggested that the change to natural rights was a regrettable decline. In some ways this is a shame, because the theory of natural law is in itself elegant, integrated and, despite its universalist tendency, classically defined as adaptable to changing times and different societies, while rights theory is more specific to certain issues. Leo Strauss is one who has argued that the change is one from a system which taught duties, to one which is more limited in its focus on rights.[5] One could, for example, say that the latter places the onus on victims to prove their rights, or condemns abuses *ex post facto*, instead of inciting whole societies to form systems that are based on altruism and protecting the weak. The thinking of John Rawls, especially in his best-known book, *A Theory of Justice*,[6] has turned attention to measuring the efficacy of a system of justice by looking not at overall social good and liberties held by a majority, but at its protection of basic rights of the least well-off members of a community. This marks a decisive change from the classical utilitarianism of David Hume, for example, which emphasises the overall happiness of the members of a society, rather than the condition of the least well-off.

Natural rights, defined most simply, are rights that all people possess (some would say all living creatures), those which are justified by the very fact of being alive. They are inferences from one fundamental and primary right which is taken to be equal for everybody – the right that each and every individual has to preserve his or her life – and its corollary, the right to be protected from having life foreshortened. Such rights can include, for example, not only the right not to be murdered but also more positively, shelter, clothing, food, and more abstractly, an impartial legal system, equal educational and employment opportunities, and the ability to participate in the way a country is governed, so that each person is then responsible for defending the lives of all. It should be said in passing that this is what has come to be known as the 'strong' sense of rights. At the turn into the twenty-first century, we seem to live in a culture which mainly dwells on the 'weak' sense, that rights are liberties, or sanctioned by positive law, whether or not they are right in moral terms or particular situations. It might be unkind to suggest these are not rights at all, but man-made justifications for privilege or fashion.[7] How often do we hear somebody saying adamantly, 'This is my right', when their actions harm or distress others, and seem to be based on narrowly legalistic entitlement, self-regard or mere preference, rather than moral compulsion or human betterment? In this book the 'strong' sense will be our subject.

The specific part of the powerful western tradition which this book focuses on is the development of concepts of natural rights in England in the 1790s, the decade following the revolutions in America and France in the 1780s. These events shocked the British government into repressive measures but at the same time ignited radical movements whose legacy is with us still. It was also the decade in which demands for political representation and anti-slavery legislation gained direction and momentum. Many radical writers used natural rights to legitimise their social and political attitudes in these and other contexts. The book is written from the conviction that ideas, politics and literature are inextricable and symbiotic forces. Since my field of expertise is literature, this book concentrates on works by poets and novelists, but the force field that connects them is intellectual history, and as the book demonstrates, many of them wrote more philosophical or political works as well as fiction and poetry. Romanticism was conceived from political philosophy expressed in manifestoes and journalism, sometimes written by imaginative writers and sometimes influencing them. The story has been told by historians and political theorists,[8] but there are some special vantage points offered by literary history viewed alongside intellectual history, rather than the kind of diurnal history which traces political change through events. For one thing, the history of ideas breaks down the artificial barriers erected between genres of prose fiction, poetry, drama and prose polemic, and links them through ideologies and belief-systems within political contexts. For another, it allows redefinition of writing genres, right through the eighteenth and early nineteenth centuries, suggesting a philosophical preoccupation that provides a continuity and some links between writers otherwise very diverse. For example, in the course of this book, I suggest the eighteenth-century 'literature of benevolence' as a significant sub-group of the previously named 'sentimental' movement, otherwise known as literature of sensibility. Benevolence suggests a moral emphasis which is less dismissive than 'sentimentality', and less exclusively aesthetic and affective, and it explains why, in the 1790s, the novel of sensibility could turn into something far more harshly realistic and polemical than it had ever been. The Jacobin novels of the 1790s are sometimes seen as anti-sentimental, but in truth they are natural growths from the tradition of sentimental benevolence. In turn the concentration on natural rights allows us to draw links that challenge categories like 'the Jacobin (or Gothic) novel' and 'Romanticism', without resorting to artificial constructions like 'preromanticism'. For example, 'the novel of natural rights' can satisfactorily link writers who have rarely been analysed together, and the issue can place them alongside poets as diverse as Goldsmith, Cowper and Blake. When the issue of natural rights is placed at the centre of analysis, 'sentimentality' and rationality emerge as not always or necessarily antithetical, but as compatible. What is rational is also emotionally satisfying, in works by writers as different from each other as Rousseau, Paine and Blake, and even in the diverse works by one author, like Helen Maria Williams's or Charlotte Smith's. Belief in intertextuality runs through my book, and I suggest that writers could draw inspiration from philosophy, ancient and modern, and contemporary politics, as well as models from imaginative literature. But the process is not purely random and arbitrary but a focused intertextuality, as writers interrogate books with specific questions in mind. The questions will change from time to time. For example, I address the attempts to counter Hobbes's pessimistic view of human nature with a modified reassertion of the ancient natural law tradition, and to assert a practical ethic based on natural rights; and the way in which Burke's conservatism inspired many radical works.

Throughout the history of western civilisation, thought about moral behaviour has moved between two contradictory positions which seem to reflect as much antipathetic temperaments as philosophical positions. Sometimes one is in the political ascendancy, sometimes the other, but rarely is one completely eclipsed and they coexist in dynamic tension. The first is based on the view that human beings are rational and communitarian, and as such are innately and naturally drawn to virtue, and that evil is an aberration which is against reason and against the instinct for preservation of life. The second is that any tendency to goodness that people may have, or may have had, is permanently clouded over and rarely if ever revived: we are irrational and self-seeking, and perfectly capable of carrying out with equanimity actions that threaten human life and jeopardise the preservation of life. Holders of the second view maintain that it is necessary to control or curb the inclination of people to be morally careless by the imposition of strong rule by the state. The two possible views have existed from the beginnings of written records, 'the one rationalist, characterised by strategies of persuasion, and reflecting a perception of human nature as perfectible and disposed to virtue; the other voluntarist, characterised by strategies of coercion, and reflecting a perception of human nature as fallible and predisposed towards evil'.[9] Expressed as temperaments, the first position is profoundly optimistic and idealistic about human beings, while the second is at least sceptical and at most pessimistic. The one is based on belief in natural altruism and sympathy and a trust in people's ability to govern themselves, the second on a recognition of human selfishness, irresponsibility, and self-centredness.[10] Between the two poles lies a spectrum of political stances, from anarchism to fascism. The ramifications of the duality extend to virtually all realms of human endeavour: individual actions, social organisation, political institutions, religion, legal and economic systems, and preeminently, imaginative literature, which reflects the struggles in all their complexity, embedded in fictions that claim to deal with individual and social life in the broadest sense.

The story to be told in this book is of the two systems of thought in dynamic tension in one historical moment – the 1790s – as reflected in English literature. At a time when it appeared that in the public sphere the sceptical or pessimistic view had prevailed, some writers crusaded to establish that at the very least individual people and groups have rights derived from their status as human beings – natural rights – as a protection against the coercions of governments, privilege, and public law. It was the period in which the battle against slavery was being waged, among other assertions of natural rights. It was the period in which the word 'rights' appeared almost profligately in the titles of books: Thomas Paine's *Rights of Man* (Part 1, 1791), Mary Wollstonecraft's *A Vindication of the Rights of Men* (1790) and *A Vindication of the Rights of Woman* (1792), books which were as momentous for literature as for politics, among many others which are now neglected. They provoked parodies such as Thomas Taylor's *A Vindication of the Rights of Brutes* (1798), which satirised the transfer of natural rights to animals. Several great statements were enshrined in law though, alas, not in English law. The American *Declaration of Independence* (July 4, 1776) declared 'that all men are created equal; they are endowed by their Creator with certain inalienable rights; that among these are life, liberty, and the pursuit of happiness', all of which are described as 'the laws of nature and of nature's God'. The French *Declaration of the Rights of Man and of the Citizen* (1789) begins boldly, 'Men are born and remain free and equal in rights', and it aims 'to set forth in a solemn declaration the natural, unalienable, and sacred rights of man', and asserts that 'The aim of all political association is the preservation of the natural and imprescriptible rights of man. These rights are liberty, property, security, and resistance to oppression.' The American Constitution's first ten amendments, known collectively as the *Bill of Rights* (1789–91), contained a list of specific rights, including 'Freedom of Speech, Press, Religion and Petition', and at least one which has caused problems ever since, the right to keep and bear arms. Apart from these great statements of general principle, the subject came to reach many specific issues, such as those rights of women not included among 'rights of man', the right of political association, rights of slaves, children, the right to vote, the right of workers to bargain collectively with employers, and even rights of the environment, of nature, and of animals. Underneath them all lay the guiding right to equality in the eyes of God and the law.

The demand for natural rights went right through society, as one opponent noticed with ridicule. The anonymous writer of the self-evidently entitled 'No Abolition of Slavery; or the Universal Empire of Love: A Poem' wrote, dedicating his work to 'the respectable body of West-India planters and merchants',

> See in a stall three feet by four,
> Where door is window, window door,
> Saloop a hump-back'd cobler drink;
> 'With *him* the muse shall sit and think';
> *He* shall in *sentimental* strain,
> That *negroes* are *oppress'd*, complain,
> What mutters the decrepit creature?
> THE DIGNITY OF HUMAN NATURE![11]

Writers bore the brunt of such caustic satire, because so often they saw it as a central part of their art to dignify the individual human nature of their imaginative personages. Novelists and poets were at the centre of the assertion of rights and 'the dignity of human nature', as they adopted their time-honoured position to be encapsulated in Shelley's memorable phrase, 'unacknowledged legislators of the world'. They were the ones who could carry the vocabulary and concepts of rights into the popular consciousness, and move hearts and minds to identify both emotionally and rationally with their cause. However, generally speaking, writers for the theatre could not be so outspoken as novelists and poets. Whatever the intentions of dramatists and theatre owners, they were prevented from involvement in the radical movement because of the institutional repressions such as censorship applying to public performance. In fact, as John Thelwall, whose ideas will be examined in their own right in this book, recognised, theatres could be 'powerful vehicles for the suppression of every generous principle of liberty', and for social and political conformity.[12]

At the same time, although during the 1790s the struggle in England for natural rights became a practical and urgent one, for reasons to do mainly with the French revolution in 1789, yet the intellectual struggle was more than a century old. Just as Christopher Hill locates 'the intellectual origins of the English Civil War' in the sixteenth century, so writers like E. P. Thompson and Raymond Williams showed that the battle for a wide range of political rights in nineteenth-century England stretched much further back. To these two scholarly writers, who wonderfully combined deep historical scholarship with an understanding of literature, this book is pervasively indebted, in a way that any number of specific references could not do justice. It is with their emphasis on the roots of the present lying in the past, that I survey in this chapter the ancient and abiding notion of natural law and its evolution in the eighteenth century into natural rights; and in the next chapter the literary equivalent of an emerging, imaginative vehicle for the radical ideas that found vociferous advocates in the 1790s. Edward Royle and James Walvin in *English Radicals and Reformers: 1760–1848*, write with a stress on 'the significance of continuity in political issues',[13] running from the legacy of the Stuart monarchs, through periodic opposition to governments, the contribution of individuals like John Wilkes in the 1750s and onwards, and the significance of events beyond England's shores, like the American war of independence and the French revolution. Even in the single decade of the 1790s, they stress the continuity between changes from optimistic idealism, disillusionment, repression and the surviving Jacobin discontents, which surfaced later with the Chartists. It is, I argue, the emergence of natural rights as a set of intellectual but practical issues that provides an underlying continuity of material for philosophical, polemical, and imaginative writers alike, and the decade which was pivotal in the struggle was the 1790s.

Rights and Romanticism

My original project was to trace literary manifestations of natural rights through Romantic literature, but as the research progressed it became clear that this would lead to a lopsided account. The 1790s (and what led up to them in the previous 50 or so years) were the crucible in which the ideas were established and fought for, and what came after was a conflict that built upon certain intellectual positions established then. The history of constitutional reform in Britain, and the abolition of slavery, bear this out. The principles of a unified and coherent libertarian cause were established in the 1790s out of the perceived connection between many single causes, and although there was an apparent historical destiny about them, it would take over 30 long years of conservative rearguard action and backlash finally to vindicate the pioneers in at least some of their beliefs. Writing the longer story would not add enough to the conceptual and literary cause of natural rights to justify the length. Having glimpsed this fact, I realised that to call it a mainstream 'Romantic' narrative, would also be misleading. The literature of the 1790s, like the polemics, can only in hindsight be regarded as contributing to Romanticism: novels by Godwin, Wollstonecraft, Thelwall, Charlotte Smith and many others – loosely called Jacobins (or, in the case of the more radical writers, Girondistes) – mingled many aspects of eighteenth-century sentimentalism, and of the coming movement canonised by literary critics as Romanticism. But in most significant ways it is far from sentimental in tone. Some, like Wollstonecraft, reacted in fact against sentimentalism, which can itself be far from the traditionally accepted Romantic views on individualism and nature. Writers of the earlier period focus on political issues, such as the right of ordinary people to participate in government, rights of women, rights of people to be free from slavery – rather than on individual psychology, man's relationship with nature, and the creative imagination, so much a part of the development of Romanticism. The works represent very mixed modes, and in many cases original ones that did not feed directly into what we know as the Romantic movement. Paul O'Flinn, in an energetic attempt to deconstruct Romanticism as a coherent term, points out that to focus on the Romantic poets as a centre means that immensely influential writers like Tom Paine, and we could add many others who will appear in this book, who do not conform to 'the conventional connotations of Romanticism', become 'not much more than an aside in literary studies of the age',[14] whereas to the history of British politics and literature alike they are crucial, not least because their realism and contemporary engagement shattered traditional literary genres and expectations. They paved the way for Romanticism, but most were not Romantic, and it might some day be argued that they were more genuinely important to literary movements than Romanticism itself. The iconoclastic editors of *An Oxford Companion to Romantic Age: British Culture 1776–1832* complain of the 'frustratingly circular and self-limiting process' of focusing on 'a narrow set of typical aesthetic features which we label "Romantic"'. Over the years it has led some critics to equate Romanticism with a tiny, exclusive, and diminishing band of poetic geniuses'.[15] The figures who seem like 'counter-spirits – supposed misfits, throwbacks, and resisters' are in fact the very ones who take up the majority of this book, and in this sense they are guiding rather than counter-spirits, norms rather than exceptions. Furthermore, if my focus had been on natural rights in the Romantic movement, then not only would many apparently 'minor' writers such as Inchbald and Bage, Montgomery and Pratt, be neglected, but also a really central figure like Blake would be presented in the wrong 'frame'.[16] Inevitably he would be seen as a hermeneutic and isolated figure, working independently of literary movements establishing the centrality of original imagination, instead of as a man passionately involved in the debates of his time, writing political allegory at a time when any anti-government or anti-state church statement was dangerous, and drawing on polemical prose of his time, as well as on the prose and poetic writings of Milton. He was forging his own instrument of polemical prose-poems to advance the cause of natural rights in a tense political context. Another apparently inevitable danger in using Romanticism as the aesthetic receptacle of political thinking is that Wordsworth and Coleridge would, as in any such book, slide with their canonical gravity, to the centre, with a consequential inhibition because their views were later to become so conservative. Nicholas Roe's interesting book, *The Politics of Nature: Wordsworth and Some Contemporaries*,[17] for example, cannot avoid suffering such a fate. If we foreground figures like Godwin, Wollstonecraft, Paine and

Thelwall, then canonical Romantics can take a place in the gallery, but a subsidiary one, sometimes left to the reader's inference, so that the fight for natural rights itself remains central. On this issue, Wordsworth and Coleridge, among others, were followers or even doubters, rather than leaders. The change of perspective is graphically demonstrated by Jonathan Bate's observation that of the three Shakespeare lecturers in 1815 to 1820, Coleridge, Hazlitt and Thelwall, 'The presence of Thelwall, "Citizen John" of the heady 1790s when Coleridge had been "Citizen Samuel", must have been an acute embarrassment to the Coleridge who was now bowing down before "the abstract majesty of kings" '.[18] In my developing sense of the period in which natural rights were debated in literature, Romanticism had to go, as a stultifying and inhibiting model. And yet, as the editors of the *Oxford Companion* insist, the emphasis on rights *becomes* Romantic, if we can expand this term to describe more fully the radical cultural output of the period. Not only were Wordsworth and Coleridge part of the 1790s' liberal scene, and not only were the *Lyrical Ballads* radical in form and substance, but also natural rights quickly entered the assumptions of many later poets. Shelley, for example, could extend the terrain to include free love and universal suffrage, but his cradle was the 1790s radical movement, in more ways than one.

The 1790s in Britain were just one decade in one country, and merely a part of a European-wide history of ideas, which is the backdrop to this book. The larger story to be told, embracing the development of western thought, is of immense significance to the modern, western world. Many of the basic freedoms which we now cherish (or take for granted), were fought for in this period, primarily through revolutions in France and America, and by beleaguered minorities in Britain. Many specific rights, such as the right to vote for one's government, women's suffrage and equality, trade unionism, conscientious objection in time of war, and environmental awareness, owe their origins to the changes of consciousness which we shall trace back to the 1790s in England. The United Nations Declaration of Human Rights passed in 1948, however ineffectual in the short term, is a symbolically culminating point, and many nations have since then instituted bills of rights. The movement to empower blacks in the United States in the 1960s, the civil rights campaign (rights belonging to individuals as citizens in society) is a triumphant example of the ideas sown around 1800 being applied to social injustices. There is a real danger that, at least from time to time, the whole terrain of rights is either threatened, or ironically achieved, by purely economic and financial considerations, laws of 'market forces', the aspirations of dictators around the world, or war goals. But its history is now so entrenched in the popular mind that it is difficult to conceive of a world without the idealism built upon notions of natural rights. It is easy to forget that before the 1790s such ideas were dismissed as aberrations of isolated heretics and lunatics, if they were voiced at all. For this comprehensive lifting of 'mind-forg'd manacles', we can at least partially thank imaginative writers, who have acted as mass disseminators of the fundamental ideas. One more caveat should be entered at the outset. The fact that in describing the call for natural rights during the 1790s as a rather nebulous and passionate process is deliberate, since, the book will conclude, the term came to include specific, named rights only at points when the general concept had clarified.

Natural law

As I have already indicated, the whole story is much longer than the one spanning the decade of the 1790s and its immediate background. Theories of natural rights, like a phoenix out of ashes, emerged as a hard-won reaction to the apparent death of natural law. On the benign side of the divide, natural law was an elegant and tenacious construction based on the innate goodness of people and their ability to judge between right and wrong. Dating back to writers before Plato, like Heraclitus, it was first formally enunciated by pre-Christians such as Plato, Aristotle and Cicero, and repeated in the Christian Bible. It was given magisterial Christian authority by St Thomas Aquinas in his thirteenth-century *Summa Theologiae*, and was reaffirmed by English Renaissance writers such as More, Hooker and Milton.[19] As the linking of these names, pagan and Christian, ancient, medieval and early modern, indicates, natural law could survive with or without belief in a supreme God, although only Hugo Grotius amongst early thinkers was to say so explicitly. Without religious support it was grounded in human reason alone; with religion it was buttressed by an appeal to conscience.

Natural law, put simply, means that human beings have within them the capacity to make judgments about what is right and wrong, and a natural inclination to follow virtue and shun vice. The fundamental inclination is to preserve and perpetuate human existence. Every creature and every object on earth has its own unique equivalent inclination for continued existence, but what distinguishes man from everything else is reason and the capacity to understand a rationally constructed universe. Therefore, to follow reason is to follow virtue and to fulfil the most characteristic purpose of humankind on earth, its own 'natural law'. There have been writers, like John Finnis, who speaks of 'practical reasonableness'[20] and John Rawls who ponders the justice of justice,[21] who have modernised the concept for a secular world, so the debate is still alive in a very real way.

Since natural law is said to be innate, it is unwritten, and does not need to be codified. Given the situational variability determining what is virtuous in particular circumstances, the law has an eternal existence but a relative applicability. Laws which are in fact written down constitute bodies of positive law which bind the human societies making them. The classical assumption is that all positive laws by definition conform to natural law precepts, because they are passed by people governed from within by reason. Another line of thought would obviously argue that the experience of history shows this assumption to be ill-founded, and that a positive law which is clearly not in line with natural law is no law at all and can be disobeyed. This is the argument, for example, of conscientious objectors during wartime, and a more or less necessary attitude towards Nazi law in Germany before and during the Second World War. Perhaps one of the hardest things to grasp about natural law is that it is not unchanging and it is not universal. As man's only evidence of eternal law, it can change with circumstances, or vary between cultures and societies, while still remaining true to a higher abstraction of justice. What is right at one historical moment or in one situation, may not be right at another time or in another situation. For example, although it would seem that the commandment 'thou shalt not kill' is self-evidently part of the natural law, grey areas have always existed in areas like abortion and euthanasia. Some, such as the Catholic hierarchy, say these are clearly against natural law, while others argue that their very reasonableness in certain circumstances makes them natural. While the propagation of the species is also clearly central to natural law, it has been seen to be contingent in areas where choice operates, such as family planning where it can be part of the natural law, rape where it cannot. One kind of natural law theorist would argue that reason alone is capable of finding what is right in all circumstances, while another kind of theorist would argue for the necessity of a concept like conscience (which usually invokes a religious framework, but perhaps need not).

Such examples indicate that one of the strategical flaws in the model of natural law is its relativity in practice, despite its theoretical basis in universals. It could be, and has been, used to justify almost every position short of genocide, from extreme authoritarianism to extreme liberalism. Exactly what constitutes incest has always been disputed, not least so in the Renaissance,[22] and birth control has been both advocated and opposed using natural law arguments. My book, *Natural Law in English Renaissance Literature* deliberately concentrates on the liberal potential of natural law theory, to counter a view of the Renaissance which sometimes threatens to be prevalent, the notion that writers invariably bolster authoritarian ideologies like patriarchalism and political oligarchy. I tried to show that this is not necessarily so, particularly in the light of the fact that one of the most important derivations of natural law is 'a commandment to be sociable with humanity wherever it is encountered',[23] an injunction which is hard to square up with either political tyranny or right-wing individualism. But some writers at the time freely admitted, as I do, that natural law can be applied in the service of conservative and radical views, and it was this problem of equivocation that allowed Hobbes to attack it at its roots. This is not to say that thinkers of whatever persuasion could not agree in the abstract on what natural law is. They disagreed mainly on its application.

Cicero, a writer who can be seen as equally significant in the fields of literary rhetoric and law, gives classic statements in his *De Re Publica* and *De Legibus*, for example:

> Well then, the most learned men have determined to begin with Law, and it would seem that they are right, if, according to their definition, Law is the highest reason, implanted in Nature [*lex est ratio summa insita in natura*], which commands what ought to be done and forbids the opposite. This reason, when firmly fixed and fully developed in the human mind, is Law. And so they believe that Law is intelligence, whose natural function [*vis*] it is to command right conduct and forbid wrongdoing ... Now if this is correct, as I think it to be in general, then the origin of Justice is to be found in Law, for Law is a natural force [*naturae vis*]; it is the mind and reason of the intelligent man, the standard by which Justice and Injustice are measured.[24]

Cicero carefully explains that in this context Law is not 'the crowd's definition' of man-made law, but a 'Supreme Law which had its origin ages before any written law existed or any State had been established' (319). The definition of Law as a 'natural force' which is 'the highest reason, implanted in Nature', sets the terms for later debate in the context of medieval Christianity. Even more eloquently, Cicero expands on the subject in *De Re Publica*:

> True law is right reason in agreement with nature; it is of universal application, unchanging and everlasting; it summons to duty by its commands, and averts from wrongdoing by its prohibitions. And it does not lay its commands or prohibitions upon good men in vain, though neither have any effect on the wicked. It is a sin to try to alter this law, nor is it allowable to attempt to repeal any part of it, and it is impossible to abolish it entirely. We cannot be freed from its obligations by senate or people, and we need not look outside ourselves for an expounder or interpreter of it. And there will not be different laws at Rome and at Athens, or different laws now and in the future, but one eternal and unchangeable law will be valid for all nations and all times, and there will be one master and ruler, that is, God [*omnium deus*] over us all, for he is the author of this law, its promulgator, and its enforcing judge. Whoever is disobedient is fleeing from himself and denying his human nature, and by reason of this very fact he will suffer the worst penalties, even if he escapes what is commonly called punishment.[25]

Most legal systems, and certainly the Roman civil law and English equity, make appeals at some stage to the precepts of natural law, and while cynics (or hard-line positivists) may think this a mere expedience to claim universalism, and of propaganda value only, idealists have always existed who argue that the whole enterprise of setting up positive law to adjudicate daily problems must be based on some consensus on moral priorities so strongly endorsed that they are prior, unwritten laws. The whole point is that such law is grounded not in force or compulsion but in reason alone. A statement, for example, like 'judges should be fair and impartial' *should* require no written formulation, since it is so self-evidently reasonable. These days definitions of fair and reasonable are, of course, enshrined in positive law, and known as natural justice, but theorists such as Finnis argue that natural law is the realm of the *should* while positive law is the realm of *is*. We have become so familiar with scepticism about universals, and a form of analysis of situations that reveals the workings of political ideology, that it is difficult for us to see natural law as other than a human construct about a perfect world, that has little application in the 'real world'. And yet it is surprising that even in our worldly wise days there has been a genuine and global revival of natural law thinking, evident in the environmental movement, in feminist critique of positive law, and international condemnations of genocide in the name of civil wars and even 'just' wars.

The greatest natural law theorist was the thirteenth-century scholar and cleric, St Thomas Aquinas. Although the 'scholastic' movement which he inspired became increasingly dogmatic and came to be regarded by later humanists as benighted, yet Aquinas himself could be claimed as a forebear of humanism.[26] Long before the Renaissance he retrieved classical texts in a large programme of translation, mainly through intermediary Arabic texts, and he formulated natural law in such subtle and realistic ways that it could be a basis for the practical living exhorted later by humanists like Erasmus and Thomas More. Aquinas saw human beings as rational creatures participating in the divine reason of a rational universe, created according to an eternal law. While eternal law is God's purpose and providence and is not directly knowable by humans, a human equivalent, natural law, is written on man's soul. 'As though the light of natural reason, by which we discern good from evil, and which is the Natural law, were nothing else than the impression of the divine light in us. So it is clear that the Natural law is nothing else than the participation of the Eternal law in rational creatures.'[27] Reason is the essence of being human, and it can internally guide the process of ethical choice along the lines of the first precept of natural law according to Aquinas, 'do good and avoid evil'. Natural law is an 'inclination' towards morally practical action. Concepts like grace and faith thus operate only in relation to the larger, mysterious eternal law: life itself can be lived according to the much more practical faculty of reason. Some would say reason needs to be augmented by conscience, others would say they are essentially the same thing, because nothing unreasonable could be endorsed by the conscience, and equally, the impulses of conscience must be justified according to right reason. Aquinas follows ancient natural law thinking, quoting

Augustine among others, in arguing that natural law is the basis for all human justice, 'And if a [positive] law is at variance in any particular with the Natural law, it is no longer legal, but rather a corruption of law'.[28] This leads on to a contentious and important corollary – that unjust laws need not be obeyed. Aquinas himself backs away from the radical potential of this, by saying that all rulers should be obeyed if they have been correctly appointed and authorised, but his words have allowed the formulation of theories of political resistance along lines of conscience:

> Man is bound to obey secular rulers to the extent that the order of justice requires. For this reason, if such rulers have no just title to power, but have usurped it, or if they command things to be done which are unjust, their subjects are not obliged to obey them, except perhaps in certain special cases, when it is a matter of avoiding scandal or some particular danger. (*Summa Theol.* , 2a 2ae, 104, 6)

In certain cases, as d'Entrèves summarises, 'disobedience may not only be a possibility, but a duty'.[29] Natural law does hold the possibility of justifying civil and conscientious resistance to acts of state tyranny. Later humanists and liberals, again like Erasmus and More, could use natural law theory to challenge institutions like slavery and restrictive property rights, and to argue for pacifism and educational equality, anticipating the later more revolutionary attitudes which are the subject of this book. In theory, revolutionaries of the 1780s and 1790s could have used natural law in its 'pure' sense of rational, moral action, but by their time the theory had been transmuted into the more usable and less relative or subjective body of beliefs, 'natural rights'. Aquinas did not go so far, because he saw natural law as a model of harmony and perfectibility rather than a tool for social or political change, but the essence of his thought could be, and was, steadily applied in more libertarian directions.

After steeping oneself in natural law theory it is difficult not to be impressed by its simplicity and the sheer beauty of reasoning. Pico della Mirandola argues classically in the following terms, that the natural good is the foundation of all desire and the basis of all human choice:

> In the first place, there is a natural being of things, as for a man to be a man, for a lion to be a lion, for a stone to be a stone. Natural goodness undividedly follows this being ... consequently, just as all things desire the good, even so all things desire being, and first of all they desire that goodness that follows upon natural being, since this goodness is the foundation of subsequent goodnesses, which are added to it in such a way that without this goodness the others cannot be.[30]

Pico may be taking anthropomorphism to its ultimate extreme in imagining a stone contemplating its own survival, but this is done not to animate the stone but only to reflect on the contemplative human, whose unique propensity and skill is reason itself, and to extend the notion of human happiness into the moral sphere, by equating it with goodness.

Natural law after Aquinas swept across Europe and directly motivated fundamental changes in legal systems, along the lines of Roman and canon law, towards a civil law which allowed people rights within the legal system. In England, common law (based on precedent rather than reason) resisted this pressure, but so deeply had natural law taken root as an intellectual system that even advocates of common law found ways to justify its practices according to natural law. More pertinently, a new and alternative legal system grew up alongside common law. Equity was the 'court of the King's conscience', dispensed by Chancery. Formally, it could operate only in cases not covered by common law, or where common law gave uncertain answers, but in fact, since it was a less cumbersome and expensive system of law, equity began to rival its older cousin, and power struggles for jurisdiction between different courts were waged during the sixteenth century. With the radical changes of the commonwealth in the seventeenth century, equity as a monarch's prerogative could not survive, so common law appeared to 'win' the battle for jurisdiction; but the powerfully emerging estate in its own turn, was parliament, which could directly change and make law by legislation. Invariably, its members mounted arguments on an essentially natural law basis of reasoned justification, so that the doctrine influenced even statute law. In this critical period of the mid-seventeenth century, I have argued that John Milton, in particular, was guided throughout all his writings by a belief in natural law, which he sees reflected most clearly in Moses' laws.[31] However, in the first half of the seventeenth century natural law came under pressure from two antithetical directions in a way that finally discredited it in its ancient form. Calvinists, from a 'left-wing' position, had always challenged natural law for its tendency to produce conservative answers to questions of authority, and their scepticism stemmed from a belief that after the fall of man, whatever inner resources of reason he had once had, became permanently alienated from them. Calvin did not deny the validity and existence of natural law, but he maintained that only a small elect had access to it, concluding that, as a broad-based theory of moral reasoning, it was open to manipulation by authoritarian sources like the Pope. The influence of Calvinism in English culture has been disputed and may have been overstressed, but it chimed with different channels for scepticism like Descartes' and Montaigne's. They did not necessarily deny the existence of natural law but they did not trust people to live their lives according to its precepts. The more radical and ultimately influential assault came from the opposite direction, in Thomas Hobbes's *Leviathan* (1650), which almost routed natural law, but accidentally stimulated the development of natural rights thinking.

Hobbes and the demise of natural law[32]

Since most of the writers we will be meeting in this book are, either explicitly or unconsciously, refuting Thomas Hobbes, we should look in some detail at his model, most amply explained in *Leviathan*. In Hobbes's thought, the first casualty of classical Natural Law theory is conscience: 'Hobbes does not believe in freedom of conscience.'[33] He does not deny the concept of a 'consciousness' which all men hold in common and he says that it 'it was and ever will be reputed a very Evil act, for any man to speak against his *Conscience*; or to corrupt or force another so to do' (p. 132),[34] but he deplores the practice which has developed of using 'the same word metaphorically, for the knowledge of their own secret facts, and secret thoughts' in justification of individual opinions:

> And last of all, men vehemently in love with their own opinions, (though never so absurd,) and obstinately bent to maintain them, gave those their opinions also that reverenced name of Conscience, as if they would have it seem unlawful, to change or speak against them; and so pretend to know they are true, when they know at most, but that they think so. (*Ibid.*)

This is a sideswipe at contemporary Puritans such as Milton who set such stock on individual conscience against external authority, and the words echo both Calvin and Luther saying very similar things about the variability and untrustworthiness of individual consciences. There had since the Reformation been a tradition alive and available which was sceptical of natural law in Aquinas's optimistic formulations. What Hobbes did was magisterially to restate the contrary argument in its entirety, so powerfully that few chose afterwards to return to Aquinas without qualification. I should say at the outset that my understanding of Hobbes is derived from a fairly literal reading of his words in *Leviathan*, as it was read by his adversaries, to justify the proposition that Hobbes was pivotal in turning attention away from natural law and towards natural rights. I am aware of the many debates about interpretation, but it would be something of a distraction in this book to enter into them.[35]

After conscience, the second casualty in Hobbes's onslaught is reason, again as understood by earlier natural law theorists. In place of their understanding based on reason as leading us to essential truth, what is reasonable given the primal law of doing unto others only what one would have done unto us, Hobbes substituted a more restrictive sense of reason as calculation, the exercise of deductive logic, based on his beloved geometry and arithmetic. If an argument does not begin from generally agreed naming of things and proceed along the lines of '*Reckoning* (that is, Adding and Subtracting)' towards 'certainty' which will be unanimously approved, then it cannot be called rational. If Hobbes is to apply these senses of reason and conscience to the substance of Natural Law, it is bound to become very different from Aquinas's concept, and in effect, disturbingly close to its opposite.

Hobbes begins from a vision of the individual in society which, it is no exaggeration to say, is diametrically opposed to that held by classical natural law theorists, even though he claims to accept their premises. Whereas they stressed a *desire* to contribute to the public good as the major plank of Natural Law, Hobbes presupposes that although 'peace' is paramount, such a *desire* cannot be presupposed. Rather, he argues that men will not be good to one another unless either it is in their own self-interest, a line later followed by Bentham's utilitarianism, or they are compelled by a sovereign body to be so, which is Hobbes's own preference. A central passage in *Leviathan* asserts that the desire for peace can be defined only in terms of individual fears and hopes which are largely negative and without idealism:

> The Passions that incline men to Peace, are Fear of Death; Desire of such things as are necessary to commodious living; and a Hope by their Industry to obtain them. And Reason suggesteth convenient Articles of Peace, upon which men may be drawn to agreement. These Articles, are they, which otherwise are called the Laws of Nature. (188)

In his discussion, Hobbes sharply reproves those (such as Selden) who in his view confuse Natural Rights (*Jus Naturale*) and Natural Law (*Lex Naturalis*), although it is clear that he is presupposing and even originating the 'weak' sense of the word 'rights'. He squarely defines it, not by reference to the condition of living, but in individualistic terms as 'the Liberty each man hath, to use his own power, as he will himself, for the preservation of his own Nature' (189). Liberty is obviously a slippery and relative word, and would not be accepted without qualification by those who argue for the 'strong' sense of rights as guaranteeing continued survival. However, Hobbes is nothing if not clever, and just as he refutes natural law by claiming to work from its assumptions, so he defends liberty as a matter of life and death: 'the liberty each man hath, to use his own power, as he will himself, for the preservation of his own power, as he will himself, for the preservation of his own nature, that is to say, of his own life; and consequently, of doing any thing which in his own judgment, and reason, he shall conceive to be the aptest means thereunto'. This might apply when man is alone in 'the state of nature', but in a community it is merely egotism which can ignore the welfare or preservation of others. Natural law in its classical sense is inevitably seen by Hobbes as a limitation on liberty, because it determines what cannot be done ('shun evil') and binds men to its terms as to an obligation. Hovering behind these definitions is Hobbes's bleak, ruthlessly individualistic vision of the 'state of nature': 'the condition of Man ... is a condition of War of every one against every one' and as long as this is so nobody can live in security without guaranteed constraints from something outside themselves. Freedom of the individual becomes a far more effective route to the survival of humanity than reliance on fellow-feeling or altruism. His version of Law of Nature, then, is an absolute code which ensures that the preservation of one person's life is not at the expense of another's. People must be *forced* to survive mutually, since they would not do so under their own volition. It is akin to the terms of a truce or ceasefire in war. The two fundamental Laws of Nature are '*to seek Peace, and follow it*' and '*By all means we can, to defend our selves*' – again, the order-based, conservative, and individualistic attitude of those who today argue that citizens should have the right to carry guns. For Hobbes there is no potential conflict between these two maxims, given his overall metaphor of life as a state of war and of men engaged in constant competition. Rather, the one is a check on the other and vice versa. These precepts enable Hobbes to redefine the traditional golden rule as 'That a man be willing ... to be contented with so much liberty against other men, as he would allow other men against himself' (190). He then goes on to tabulate, with far more precision than anybody before, the other Laws of Nature: Justice '(*That men perform their Covenants made*); Gratitude (*That a man which receiveth Benefit from another of mere Grace, Endeavour that he which giveth it, have no reasonable cause to repent him of his good will*)'; 'Compleasance' '(*that every man strive to accommodate himself to the rest*)', and so on, to the requirements of equality and equity. There is even grudging provision for some kind of heavily qualified communalism, for the twelfth Law is '*that such things as cannot be divided, be enjoyed in Common, if it can be ...*'. Hobbes then reasserts the traditional claim of natural law to be eternal, but without the assumption that it resides in the human heart:

> The Laws of Nature are Immutable and Eternal; For Injustice, Ingratitude, Arrogance, Pride, Iniquity, Acception of persons, and the rest, can never be made lawful. (215)

All the time, Hobbes's basic aim is to justify absolute monarchy: the monarch's will is law, and there is no appeal beyond it.

Virtually every conclusion on natural law arrived at by Hobbes is exemplary and could compel only assent from all writers from Aquinas to Milton on grounds of strict logic. However, they are derived from an axiom which would be implacably rejected by many earlier thinkers, and they lead to a position justifying absolute power by a sovereign or sovereign body which effectively has as much power as the Christian God who is supposed to have handed down Natural Law. While earlier thinkers hypothesised that people living in a 'natural state' would draw consistently on *inner*, God-given resources of reason and conscience to perform altruistically for the community's good, the Hobbesian state of nature is one of vicious individualism and cut-throat murder, where Natural Law needs to be imposed from outside, through positive law, in order to compel peace:

> For the Laws of Nature (as *Justice, Equity, Modesty, Mercy*, and (in sum) *doing to others, as we would be done to*), of themselves, without the terror of some Power, to cause them to be observed, are contrary to our natural Passions, that carry us to Partiality, Pride, Revenge, and the like. And Covenants, without The Sword, are but Words, and of no strength to secure a man at all. (220)

He paints a nightmarish picture of man in a state of nature, as a cynical community without an absolute power, riven with insecurity, theft, growing inequality, cruelty, murder and invasion, a 'dominion of passions, war, fear, poverty, slovenliness, solitude, barbarism, ignorance, cruelty' [*De Cive* 10, I] No wonder 'the life of man' in a state of nature is described by Hobbes in his memorable phrase as 'solitary, poor, nasty, brutish, and short' (186). One commentator describes Hobbes's immediate influence on natural law thinking thus:

> To contemporaries and most successors Hobbes seemed to have arrived at a skepticism (what today is called relativism) even worse than the Renaissance variety that Grotius had seen as his target. Natural law seemed to have been largely emptied of meaning, and it had become exceedingly difficult for most to see how human nature, on Hobbes's account of it, would even allow the formation of social relations. In fact, Hobbes's radicalization of the subjective-rights theory made it so feared for more than a century only a few thinkers could even understand it properly.[36]

Hobbes does, however, open a small window. He uses the words rights and liberties. Although he almost certainly did not intend it, this opened a way for others to escape his conclusions. Hobbes mainly attaches the word rights to the sovereign, and such rights are as absolute as he can make them. But there is a prior process of choosing the sovereign which at least gives the people some potential power:

> A *Common-wealth* is said to be *Instituted*, when a *Multitude* of men do Agree, and *Covenant, every one, with every one*, that to whatsoever *Man*, or *Assembly of Men*, shall be given by the major part, the *Right* to *Present* the Person of them all, (that is to say, to be their *Representative*;) every one, as well he that *Voted for it*, as he that *Voted against it*, shall *Authorise* all the

Actions and Judgments, of that Man, or Assembly of men, in the same manner, as if they were his own, to the end, to live peaceably amongst themselves, and be protected against other men. (II, xviii, p. 228–9)

The fact that Hobbes goes on to spend many pages justifying the indivisibility and absoluteness of the sovereign's right suggests that his theory of a covenant based on a vote is not considered closely in the context of rights of citizens, but more to avoid the problem of arbitrary authority and to minimise power struggles. It is simply a way to create the system which then effectively takes away most rights from the people. But however unguarded, it is a concession to some popular participation in government, and clearly one that would be exploited later. Hobbes does then give some brief attention to 'liberties' of subjects, but given the wide ambit given to the sovereign, these liberties are negative rather than positive: the right to be left in peace, liberty of self-defence, the right to do anything that is not proscribed by law, 'doing what their own reasons shall suggest' (264), on the premise that 'The Greatest Liberty of Subjects, dependeth on the silence of the Law' (271). Even his definition of 'the right of nature' seems perverse, in the light of at least those writers of the 1790s whom we shall examine in this book. The right of nature is, for Hobbes,

> the *Liberty* each man hath, to use his own power, as he will himselfe, for the preservation of his own Nature; that is to say, of his own Life; and consequently, of doing any thing, which in his own Judgement, and Reason, hee shall conceive to be the aptest means thereunto. (*Lev.* 14.1.64)

This is extreme individualism in effect, especially since Hobbes goes on to say that nobody else need respect or help our right to live, and that the right applies to the guilty as well as the innocent. Life is thus Hobbes's 'war of every one against every one'.[37] Richard Cumberland, for one, 'simply found it hard to take seriously Hobbes's suggestion that from the hand of nature everyone in a sense has a right to anything he wants'.[38]

Everything in Hobbes's theory returns to the power of the sovereign, and as Jean Hampton wryly points out, if subjects threaten the king's life, no matter how justifiably, then his right to protect himself means rebellion can never happen since his tools for killing are always more ample than his subjects'. To put a hypothetical example more relevant to the 1790s, the libertarian theory of rights would mean a slave can effectively never rebel, even if his life is threatened, without ending up dead himself. It is asserted by definition that the ruler cannot do any injustice, that the subject under all circumstances must obey, and there is nothing to stop the sovereign making any laws to limit any actions whatsoever, so that civilian liberties become secondary and not self-evident. The guiding idea is that 'The end of Obedience is Protection' (272). People effectively relinquish all rights in return for the guarantee of peace in the state. For many (particularly in the ruling classes) haunted by the ever-present threat of civil war, this must have had its attractions. The only kinds of rights Hobbes concedes in *De Cive* are those which are analogous to the relationship between monarch and subject: 'Of the Rights of Lords over their Servant' (ch. viii) and 'Of the right of Parents over their children and of hereditary Government' (ch. ix). Hobbes does not concede the existence of 'natural' rights, those pertaining to human beings, simply because of their existence. None the less, by giving an initial choice to the people in entering the covenant and choosing a sovereign, he does create a point to be exploited later. In *Leviathan*, he effectively advocates relinquishment of all other rights. He argues,

> That the right of all men, to all things, ought not to be retain'd, but that some certain rights ought to be transferr'd, or relinquisht: for if every one should retain his right to all things, it must necessarily follow, that some by right might invade; and others, by the same right, might defend themselves against them, (for every man, by naturall necessity, endeavours to defend his Body, and the things which he judgeth necessary towards the protection of his Body) therefore War would follow. He therefore acts against the reason of Peace, (i.e.) against the Law of Nature, whosoever he be, that doth not part with his Right to all things.

This quotation gives a sense of how baffling Hobbes must have seemed to classical natural lawyers, both irrefutable and wrong at the same time. He seems to have the same goal in mind – preservation of the individual and the species – but by assuming that people fundamentally do not want to let others survive he makes it necessary to erect a powerful state and rule of law in order to guarantee survival. However, while allowing few if any rights to remain with the individual, yet his reasoning does suggest a shadowy cornerstone of natural rights. If men can delegate to the monarch and the state, then they have the right to do so, and if they do so for self-protection then they must desire their lives to continue.

It is necessary to stress that Hobbes did not close down natural law thinking. Its roots were too deeply embedded to be pulled up, and throughout the eighteenth century several writers, preeminently Richard Cumberland, quite specifically wrote books replying to Hobbes. As we shall see throughout this book, many if not all the writers and thinkers come from a surviving natural law tradition. Under the name of fundamental law, it was particularly strong in America, due to the emigration in the seventeenth century of dissenting Protestants from England, but it was also still meaningful to libertarian thinkers throughout Europe. However, Hobbes did expose the relativity and vagueness of natural law thought, and having done so he could not easily be ignored. What happened after him was a gradual reorientation or development into the more defensive but more intellectually compelling argument of natural rights, the doctrine that on specific issues human beings have rights which are justified by reference to their simple existence as human beings. The overall perspective was still the rational and communitarian one, that natural rights can be justified by an appeal to reason, and they necessitate ideas of 'reciprocal duties and mutual interdependence'.[39] With the breakdown of consensus over natural law, however, the emphasis had undoubtedly changed away from 'one law for all', to specific rights of individuals in their capacity as human beings.

Natural rights

Theories of natural rights were just as ancient as those of natural law, but up until the apparent discrediting of natural law, the two realms were kept separate. Natural law was the general moral and philosophical system, while rights were a branch of it, generally speaking dealing with the primary right to use or own property. Lloyd L. Weinreb puts it this way: 'Although various theories of rights, or natural rights, appear much earlier, rights are not closely associated with natural law until the seventeenth and eighteenth centuries. Even then, the association is mostly only verbal.'[40] The Latin word *ius* had its main application in the fields of property and contract, and in the broad field of legal relations, as our 'right' to expect certain actions and consequences, usually seen as more or less the same thing as a duty to provide those actions and consequences. Whilst natural law was widely accepted, there was no need for rights given by virtue of being alive, since these were guaranteed by natural law itself. However, some writers redefined the links and paved the way for natural rights to emerge later. Samuel Pufendorf, for example, asserts a cluster of rights that 'exists in a person by nature or innately, inasmuch as everyone is by nature subject to the law of nature'.[41] They are rights that do not need to be given by others or by positive laws, and we are born with them rather than acquiring them. The history of the concept has been traced in great detail by Richard Tuck in *Natural rights theories: Their origin and development*.[42] Hugo Grotius, a Dutch Protestant and humanist writing in the early seventeenth century, defined natural law, as did many others, so as to emphasise its social aspect, the 'natural' and rational desire of mankind living together to pursue 'the common good'. Tuck points out, however, that unlike other communitarian thinkers, Grotius sees rights not as subsidiary to natural law, or merely as parts of its application, but as central to its structure. A contract, he writes, is not just a promise but an action that confers a right and a duty.[43] This looks like a rather pedantic point, but in fact it led to the fundamental shift which this chapter is tracing, for it could redefine natural law in a way that avoided some of the problems exposed by Hobbes. If moral thought and action could be pinned, not to vague generalities like reason and conscience which might rely on general goodwill, but instead to a strong sense of obligation which could be legally defined and given the force of law, then it could be used as a paradigm for the application of natural law precepts in other profoundly important areas of human existence. The slave could be said to 'own' his liberty according to nature in such a way that it cannot be taken from him; people need to till the soil in order to eat, giving them some rights over the land; people living under a king or queen could define the relationship between monarch and subject as a 'social contract' in which rights and duties exist on both sides; and so on. These developments all occurred in the period which is the subject of this book, and although Grotius's work ceased to be of central importance except to theorists, his formulation came to be crucial. The high point of natural rights theorising came through the events dealt with in this book, and earlier in the discussions leading up to the American Bill of Rights (1789), underpinning which are the rights to life, liberty and the pursuit of happiness. Natural law was very much a part of the debate which led to this Bill.[44] By 1803, an insignificant but exemplary writer could take for granted some consensus on the existence of natural rights. One Dr Bemetzrieder, disingenuously confesses that his career as a musician had so suffered from his clients' influenza and his own fear of war alarms, that he had undertaken a new vocation as a writer. In his pamphlet, *A New Code for Gentlemen; in which are considered God and Man; Man's Natural Rights and Social Duties ...* ,[45] he can confidently assert that natural rights, within the context of sociability, 'must be the origin and the pact of society':

> Then man is bound to man, even for the enjoyment of his natural right. Mutual interest has brought men together; mutual co-operation has brought their works to perfection; mutual protection secures to every one the enjoyment of the necessaries and comforts of life. (9–10)

Not everybody would have agreed, but the fact that this can be written just after the turn of the century shows that the 1790s had made a difference.

Those who had the temerity to cling to a belief in natural law after Hobbes's onslaught, had, at the very least, to retire and regroup. Milton, never one to suffer from timidity, simply reasserted its claims ever more certainly, but after the Reformation in 1660 he was discredited and no longer held the moral authority that he had under the Commonwealth. Some chose literally to retire, emigrating to America, thus opening up a new chapter in natural law which was to lead to the Bill of Rights and beyond. For the rest left in England who were temperamentally indisposed to endorse Hobbes's view of humanity, the central plank of their idealism had been removed. But gradually two lines of approach were prised open. One built upon chinks opened by Hobbes himself. First, by denying that slaves in particular had rights, he had implicitly left open the possibility that some others do have rights. Second, as we have seen, by insisting on legal authority for a ruler, Hobbes had implied that the subjects have at least an embryonic right to confer authority, an opening which Locke was later to exploit, as we shall see. The other general approach was to meet Hobbes head-on, and deny two of his leading premises. The first was that, given the existence of the sovereignty of God, the notions of absolute power and of natural political and social hierarchy followed. God had given man a model by which to organise his society in a way that avoided disorder and maintained peace, and this was the model of sovereign authority. But what if God had never intended to impose His will in this way? Older natural law had said that God placed within men the innate capacity for reason, allowing them to make up their own minds about good and evil but expecting them to accept punishment if they chose evil. Even Milton asserted this, allowing himself to be outflanked in two ways: first, by the acceptance of an authoritarian, if benevolent God (which still seduces critics and students to debate whether Milton's God is a tyrant), and second, by blindness to the obvious objection that empirical observation shows that many men do not show an innate desire to follow virtue and shun vice. Only one writer, Hugo Grotius, had sought effectively to withdraw God from the model altogether, thus removing the authoritarian model. Without denying God's existence or purpose, he argued that the law of reason would operate *even if* God did not exist. This daring and rather breathtaking move allowed at least a limited subversion of Hobbes, by once again allowing human reason to take precedence over sovereign authority. Indeed, it allowed the argument to proceed (though few put it so clearly at the time) on the basis that sovereign authority might indeed be contrary to reason. History had shown duly appointed monarchs and rulers turning into tyrants and threatening lives rather than protecting them. The second challenge to Hobbes came gradually by way of a straight refutation of his assumption that men are naturally individualistic and pitted against each other in ceaseless conflict and competition. The counter-argument was that people are by nature sociable, cooperative and sympathetic, and disposed to respect each other's rights to peaceful existence and happiness. This approach, which will be considered in Chapter 2 in its literary manifestations, combines a return to a qualified version of natural law, augmented by an acknowledgement of the need to build in an assertion of individual rights.

Richard Cumberland and sympathy

A rather unlikely saviour of natural law who ensured its survival in a modified and tenuous way, was a mild clergyman called Richard Cumberland. This particular Cumberland (later there was another who wrote plays) has been all but forgotten, though his influence was considerable, and he has at least one modern admirer. Linda Kirk in *Richard Cumberland and Natural Law: Secularisation of Thought in Seventeenth-Century England*[46] has followed the turns of his argument in *De Legibus Naturae* (1672), a book written explicitly in rebuttal of Hobbes. Cumberland pursues two views of natural law, 'confusing, supporting and contradicting each other' as Kirk admits.[47] The first is close to the conventional approach. God as legislator gave human beings right reason 'with which they perceive that by pursuing the common good they benefit themselves and their fellows'. This is in effect a straight refutation of Hobbes's view that we need worldly authority to enforce actions leading to the common good – we have the authority already within us – and it is open to the challenges made by Hobbes to orthodox natural law. His second approach is more along the line of Grotius's, that the true authority behind social equilibrium does not necessarily require God, except as originator of a self-perpetuating system. Cumberland argues this by refusing to accept as his starting point Hobbes's debater's trick of considering as a test case the hermit and transferring the implications to a society, seen as a group of hermits. Kirk summarises thus:

> The second, 'utilitarian', theory depends upon a view of man living in *socialitas*, and its main points are these. Man never was, nor can be, solitary. Living in society is not a skill acquired at the cost of his real nature but rather the only way in which his nature can be realised. The exercise of right reason presents to the sane mature mind the perception that the good of the individual and the good of the community are interdependent. It also becomes apparent that it is part of being human to care for one's fellows, that we are 'programmed' for kindliness and generosity, and in this sense we ought to do what it is natural for us to do. Obligation, considered in this light, is not directly derived from the will of the legislator nor from the force of the sanctions he imposes. It is rather the fulfilment of the nature of our species ... by the second theory God's role is limited, virtually, to that of First Cause (24)

Cumberland did not assume the laws of nature are innate to man, but instead argues that they are learned as a result of our innate sociability and the need to live harmoniously in society. What is 'good' for the whole group is also good for the individual, who is led into actions which 'will chiefly promote the common Good, and by which only the entire Happiness of particular Persons can be obtained' (ch. 5, p. 189). In following through his argument by testing it against the traditional justification of the law of nature, that it preserves the human species, Cumberland becomes an early prophet of mutual aid as it came to be espoused by Prince Peter Kropotkin:

> [The philosopher] observes too the mutual interdependence of the different parts of an animal's body, the way species survive by co-operation and by caring for their young, and the vast beneficial order of the system of the heavens ... The good of the whole species ... is best preserved by each member's acting benevolently and living in co-operation rather than competition. (26)

What distinguishes man from animals is reason, and therefore reason is the fundamental nature of mankind, the ground of the human natural law. The destined end that human beings perforce follow as the central part of their nature is the common good, which entails cooperation and all its benefits. Once again, Kirk's summary is clear and concise:

> What Cumberland has attempted, albeit by starts and with no great conviction, is to discover a measure of right and wrong within ordinary existence rather than in some unchanging criterion set up outside space and time; he has rejected outright Hobbes's solution of a sovereign state whose authority creates a small artificial parody of that situation. Cumberland himself believed in God, but in his utilitarian version of the law of nature he outlines a system of morality which is binding upon a man not because he is a Christian or even a deist, but simply because he is human ... he reminds his readers that the single phrase 'law of nature' can conceal both an innate disposition for man to act in a certain way, and an obligation on him to do so. (37)

Cumberland hit a sympathetic nerve. His massive Latin tome could have gathered dust and been forgotten, but it was read, and translated in 1727 and then again in 1750. The reasons for its survival may have as much to do with the English national self-image and cultural shifts, as to its own force of logic. Cumberland may have been seen as a saviour from the cold and ruthlessly logical authoritarianism and rationalised greed of Hobbes. The English have always had an ambiguous, if not downright contradictory relationship with sympathy and social conscience. During wartime in the twentieth century, no community was more mutually supportive, whereas in the 1980s continued majorities of voters were persuaded by Margaret Thatcher's assertion that Hobbes was right and that greedy individualism is nature's way. The kindest interpretation might be that social benevolence oscillates with social indifference like a type of thermostat-controlled cycle, depending on circumstances. Whatever the truth on this matter, it is true that Cumberland, either personally, through the influence of his book, or more symptomatically, by his tuning in to a new *zeitgeist*, ushered in a general spirit of altruism and sentiment, manifested at least in fiction if not in political life. The literary manifestation was the novel of sensibility, which was immensely fashionable in the eighteenth century. In Chapter 2 we shall examine its political and philosophical underpinning, which connected it with the movement based on natural rights. But it is significant that the full argument for natural law was not again put forward in England. It had been permanently gored, and its successor was much more a set of defensive strategies and an idealised wish, than a settled conviction about the natural inclinations of human beings in society. Somehow sympathy and benevolence have the ring of weak and passive qualities, easily swallowed by the

Leviathan, even though, as reactive appeals to conscience and social cohe-
siveness, they proved remarkably resistant to being swallowed altogether.
They benefited by the bolstering given by two other thinkers, again no
friends of Hobbes, who gave separate and independent arguments for the
existence of natural rights, Locke and Rousseau.

We encounter words like sympathy, sensibility, sentimentality and benevolence at every turn in eighteenth-century politics, poems and novels, and to try
to define them satisfactorily leads us into a soup of casuistic distinctions. John
Mullan[48] picks his way through the usages amongst philosophers of the
'Scottish enlightenment', Hume, Shaftesbury, Hutcheson and Adam Smith,
noting that for some the passions themselves link humanity into sociable
knots, while for others they simply provide the motivation for such linking,
which itself depends on circumstances. Ann Jessie van Sant,[49] traces the physi-
ological and medical uses of the words. For the purposes of this introduction,
the broadest and most inclusive point is enough. Emphasis on the 'benevolent'
feelings is used in arguments which generally oppose or retreat from Hobbes
and swing to Cumberland's view. People are linked together by their feelings far
more fundamentally than they are divided into competitive individuality, thus
laying the groundwork for the possibility of selfless altruism, rather than allowing the pre-eminence of selfish action as Hobbes had argued. The existence of
such an argument implicitly allows the generation of a political model which
emphasises the divisive and competitive nature of institutions which deny
human needs. Left to their own devices people will be naturally benevolent,
but authority and its worldly offices can sway or persuade people against their
natural inclinations. Since we do inescapably live within authoritarian systems,
the natural impulses have room to bond together sociably, only in asserting
rights that can resist the more coercive and unreasonable demands of governments. Rights theories can then focus on clarifying the grounds on which
authority is conferred, and the limitations on its power. The model allows the
generation of an ethic of resistance to command structures, sectarian law, political repression and to the kind of conservative allegiances represented by, for
example, the *ancien regime* in France, British rule in America, and the reactive
political philosophy of Burke in England itself. Opposition could coalesce
around the call for 'rights' which are themselves justified by appeal to the 'contagious' (Hume's word) quality of 'natural' feelings of sympathy and shared
benevolence. By the time we get to this stage of the argument we have almost
reached the positions of Rousseau and Paine, but there is one more link in the
chain, the notion of consent between governed and governor which lies
behind Rousseau's 'social contract'.

Locke's influence

The link was supplied by one who ironically did not, at least early in his
career, believe in innate feelings at all, John Locke. To literary scholars, Locke

is best known, unfortunately, for his argument in *Essay on Humane Understanding*, that in infancy the human mind is a *tabula rasa*, having no pre-existing or innate knowledge, a position contrary to classical natural law and to the later romantics, pre-eminently Wordsworth. However, Locke did contradict himself in his later writings, where he seems to argue from a nat-ural law basis. In particular his *Two Treatises of Government* (published 1690, but composed probably in 1679–80) at least lays down the groundwork for a theory of natural rights. Because the books were potentially so dangerous, Locke refused to acknowledge authorship until his death-bed, although it seems to have been commonly assumed. This work was implicitly an argu-ment against Hobbes, but its immediate occasion was the refutation of a more recent Hobbesian, Sir Robert Filmer, the writer of a book entitled *Patriarcha, Or the Natural Power of Kings* (1680) which was immediately despatched into oblivion by the sheer persuasiveness of Locke. Locke's view of the 'state of nature', unlike Hobbes's and Filmer's, is at times anarchist. People without a ruler do not turn destructively on each other but find natural ways of cooperating to achieve the ends of natural law, by obeying moral laws. Locke's initial argument is that we are all free and we are all equal, although not free of God's rule and not equal to Him: 'The state of nature has a law of nature to govern it, which obliges every one, and reason, which is that law, teaches all mankind, who will but consult it, that being all equal and indpendent, no one ought to harm another in his life, health, lib-erty or possession' (II, 6). It is a radical position because it allows the basis for equality between men and women, children and adults. His guiding metaphor for society seems throughout to be a harmonious family based on 'a voluntary Compact between Man and Woman'.[50] Furthermore, perhaps under the influence of his friend, the Earl of Shaftesbury (to whom Locke was physician), Locke argues that co-operation between people is a universal goal and that its instrument is reason, 'the common bond whereby humane kind is united into one fellowship and societie'.[51] The next stage of the argu-ment is that, because we are equal and cooperative, no one person has power to rule over others except by their consent. This hones in on the loophole in Hobbes, and it is a crucial link in the chain leading to natural rights. Humankind collectively has a natural right to protect itself against 'trespass against the whole species', and this fundamental right can be enshrined in a judicial system giving the power of ruling to one person. But there must be the underpinning legitimation of consent by those ruled – a 'social contract' with reciprocal rights and obligations on both sides. If this consent is missing, then revolution may be justified. This is the basis for the kind of 'popular sovereignty' espoused by Locke. His book was once regarded as a rationalisation of the 1689 settlement in England, but now it is seen as a prophecy and even a cause of the 'Glorious Revolution'.

The *Treatises of Government* deal most fully with the issue of property, the material evidence of a consensual basis for community, since property cannot be taken away without consent, and it was this part of the book that Locke himself valued most highly. But the argument has room for the asser-tion of some natural or human rights which were to become significant nearly a century later. Slavery, for example, is condemned, because slaves by definition cannot give consent to their condition. It was Filmer's defence of slavery (and his underlying assumption that we are all born slaves) which particularly roused Locke's ire, at least in print:

> Slavery is so vile and miserable an estate of Man, and so directly opposite to the generous Temper and Courtesy of our Nation; that 'tis hardly to be conceived, that an *Englishman*, much less a *Gentleman*, should plead for't. (*First Treatise*, Book 1, chapter 1, Introduction)

Unfortunately, as critics of Locke have always emphasised, he himself actively supported the slave trade by investing in slave-trading companies and hold-ing administrative positions that bolstered the slave trade in America.[52] However, this embarrassing fact will not prevent him re-entering this book in several contexts alongside Rousseau, to whom he bequeathed the title of his book, *The Social Contract*, as the two prime influences on radical thought in many contexts in the 1790s. Many of the natural rights that were later demanded stemmed from Locke, not always from his specific pronounce-ments on issues, but from the general coherence of his philosophy. He has been described as the intellectual father of the American Constitution, and we shall see his influence initiating debates on rights of slaves, children, and animals, as well as political rights of association and religious tolerance.

Locke's sturdy philosophical style can hardly be compared with that of a sentimental novelist or poet, but a direct bridge between his thought and the later benevolent movement exists through his close ties with the Shaftesbury family. Locke became almost a family member to Anthony Ashley Cooper, the Earl of Shaftesbury, and he wrote *Two Treatises of Government* while living on his estate. There is clear evidence that the influ-ence upon the two men was mutual, and in fact Shaftesbury was charged with high treason and imprisoned in the Tower of London for changing alle-giance from King Charles, while Locke was writing the *Treatises*. Locke also tutored his son, the Third Earl of Shaftesbury, who went on to write *An Inquiry Concerning Virtue, or Merit* (1699), later to be incorporated into the immensely influential *Characteristics of Men, Manners, Opinions, Times* (1711). He repeatedly equated sympathy and altruism with moral action, and he followed the line of natural law in asserting that the sense of right and wrong is 'implanted in our heart'. Janet Todd summarises his impor-tance in this way:

> Shaftesbury achieved an extraordinary aestheticizing of morality, so that in his writings the good and virtuous became synonymous with the

beautiful. To philosophise was 'to learn what is *just* in society, and *beautiful* in Nature, and the Order of the World'; to be good was to see the beauty of virtue. (25)

Michael Meehan in *Liberty and Poetics in Eighteenth Century England*[53] considers this Shaftesbury, with his plea for the extension of liberty in all walks of life, to be an important figure in the development of a 'whiggish' aesthetic which developed alongside politics, leading eventually to Wordsworth's stance. More specifically, G. J. Barker – Benfield argues, Shaftesbury provided a conceptual basis for the development of the rise of sensibility, by criticising the male-dominated social culture from a position that stressed harmony and sympathy.[54]

Causes aplenty: political and social contexts in the 1790s

Obviously literary and philosophical developments occur alongside the political and social events happening at the time. In the 1780s and 1790s, there were enough issues and causes to focus the minds of writers on radical, rights-based structures of thought. Since this is not a history book, it is inappropriate to give a detailed chronology, but we need at least to have firmly fixed in our minds the major precipitating affairs of the time. Although the Magna Carta in 1215 is often hailed as the originating document for 'rights' in England, it was essentially an agreement between the major barons and King John, curbing the monarch's power. Its significance lies in its power as a symbol or myth rather than a reality, for it hardly established rights for ordinary people, but more political rights for the ruling classes, against the reigning monarch. The origins of demands for more popular rights stem from the English civil war and the commonwealth period (1642–60).[55] Although the republic was defeated, it had lasted long enough to establish certain expectations among a Protestant, artisan and rising middle class, concerning their political involvement in affairs of state. The Restoration set them back, but the so-called Glorious Revolution of 1688–89 recovered some ground by enforcing the abdication of James II and establishing a Protestant line for the monarchy through William of Orange and James's daughter, Mary. In 1689, crucially, the Bill of Rights was passed, ratifying the Revolution, built upon a 'Declaration of Rights' presented to William when he took the throne, and imposing limitations on the monarchy. In effect the king now had to rule with parliament rather than against it as had been the case under the Stuarts. The English Bill of Rights in 1689 does speak of 'the right of the subjects to petition the king', and of the 'undoubted rights and liberties' of 'the people'. One suspects that in practice some subjects and people were considered more significant than others, but none the less the Bill remained as much a talisman as Magna Carta for those, who a century later, argued for rights. Ironically, it also served as precedent for conservatives like

Burke, who argued that this Bill could not be improved upon. At the very least, a small window had opened towards rule by the people, and the whole sequence spanning the century provided a political education for a wider section of the population than ever before. Although the events of the French revolution a century later are seen as monumentally significant for the campaign for rights in England, it was in fact only one factor, and the seventeenth-century roots were of more permanent significance. Writers in the late eighteenth century continually hearkened back for their inspiration to 1689, and to great radicals like Algernon Sidney and John Milton. Many poems were written with titles like D. Deacon's *The Triumph of Liberty. A Poem, Occasioned by the Centenary Commemoration of the Glorious Revolution* (1790). This rather forgettable work sings of 'BRITANNIA's Triumph o'er Oppression's sway' and expresses gratitude to those who risked fortune and life for the cause of 'rights of man', 'native rights', and 'the flame of FREE-DOM' which was taken by the poet to be an Englishman's 'Birthright'. The gathering movement for reform on many fronts, drawing on appeals to extra-parliamentary pressure for change, represented a bringing 'to the surface of British life a subterranean tradition of political radicalism'[56] now embraced by middling classes, 'primarily urban merchants, minor professionals, shopkeepers, and master artisans'.[57] The figures who emerged as leaders were men like John Wilkes, Dr Joseph Priestley, Richard Price and others who were invariably of a Protestant Dissenting background which emphasised liberty, and first of all religious liberty, as their watchword. Generations of the official persecution and intolerance that had driven many of them to America had hardened their hearts against oppression and steeled their resolve to fight for natural rights.

Another quieter but equally important factor, was the colonisation from the early seventeenth century of America. Emigrants had always been from a generally dissenting background, and many were periodically forced to fly from religious intolerance in Britain, so that inevitably the population was considerably more radical than their counterparts at 'home'. It is fair to say that natural law in its most unadulterated and communitarian guise was transported to America and became a founding notion, under the names fundamental law, and then natural rights. 1776 was the year in which the colonists passed their Declaration of Independence, to be followed by the successful war of independence where, significantly, the French actively supported the Americans against their colonial masters. The Declaration publicly enshrined equality as the heart of natural rights and as the basis of the country's constitution:

> We hold these truths to be self-evident, that all men are created equal, that they are endowed by their Creator with certain inalienable Rights, that among these are Life, liberty and the pursuit of Happiness. That, to secure these rights, Governments are instituted among Men, deriving

their just powers from the consent of the governed, that whenever any form of Government becomes destructive of these ends, it is the Right of the People to alter or to abolish it, and to institute new Government.

The later Bill of Rights (1789), whilst more specific in its provisions, reinforced the acknowledgment of 'Rights' which were by no means available in Britain. Events in America provided a very important issue in England, since writers represented the struggle, in novels like Charlotte Smith's *The Old Manor House* (1793) and Samuel Jackson Pratt's *Emma Corbett* (1781), as one that could tear families apart. They brought to popular consciousness not only the argument that the British government was not an inevitable ruling institution forever, but also the rhetoric of independence and rights. They provided a radical and apparently successful model for the basis of government which could not so easily be dismissed as 'foreign' because European Americans were very clearly of British descent. In some ways the American war could be seen as even more important than the French revolution in preparing public sympathy for radical demands, since the struggle was between British people. It should be added, however, that not all supporters of American independence argued on the grounds of natural rights. Edmund Burke, obviously a passionate opponent of the French Revolution, supported the American cause, but in D. D. Raphael's words, 'for less high-flown reasons than the claim of natural rights'.[58]

One of the most specific areas in which rights theory played a significant part was the right to vote for one's government and parliamentary reform in general. While the right to own property was an unceasing argument, the right to have a say in electing governments even if one did not own property was the more significant issue. The story of how corrupt and unrepresentative the whole parliamentary system was in the mid-eighteenth century has been told many times,[59] and obviously its driving force was wealth and property rather than an acknowledgment that people have any rights about how they are governed, let alone equality as a general issue. What was represented was not people but property, and especially land. John Wilkes, M.P. for Aylesbury, in 1763, lit the torch for parliamentary reform in an article in what became the notorious 'Number 45' of the *North Briton*, a publication which was becoming more and more popular. Wilkes was a volatile and contradictory character, whose audacious and politically brilliant manoeuvres dominated English politics for a decade, as he single-handedly forged an alliance between merchants and common people, supported crucially by printers and publishers, united against the corrupt purchase of political representation. They even brought London to a state of insurrection. His colourful interventions sometimes had the qualities of tragicomedy and near-farce. In the short term, long-lasting change was not secured in this period, and in some ways the beneficiaries were the aristocracy who not only demanded greater 'law and order' provisions which were to stand the government in good stead for repressing dissent when the French revolution ignited, but also were enabled to use the situation further to weaken the position of the King. Wilkes's own personal excesses steadily alienated him from his more serious followers, who were genuinely committed to reform and who were to become increasingly significant. But as a catalyst for popular forces, Wilkes was central, and the causes and factions which he represented marched steadily onwards, despite massacres such as those at St Georges Fields (1768) through to Peterloo (1819), and the repression and victimisation, towards at least partial victory in the Reform Bill of 1832. That it took 70 years to run its course shows that the movement for parliamentary reform was bigger than any individual within it and its momentum was sustained by a combination of courageous persistence, the politics of non-cooperation and martyrdom immortalised in Shelley's *Masque of Anarchy*, and the increasing entrenchment in the popular mind of a philosophy of natural rights. The events, trials and vociferous polemics in the 1790s, although faced by a high point of government repression, also marked a turning point in the political tide, towards change.

The French revolution of 1789, and the events leading up to it and its consequences, of course, provided the most spectacular cause for the debate over natural rights in England. While successive English governments, the nobles and their most eloquent apologist, Edmund Burke, sensed the dangers that the revolution posed to England and became increasingly reactionary and restrictive, so libertarians and imaginative writers took inspiration from it, and steadily increased their demands in the 1790s and beyond. This book is not the occasion for charting in any detail the tense and dramatic events of the decade, nor the longer struggle for parliamentary reform. The immensity of that task is demonstrated in John Barrell's *Imagining the King's Death: Figurative Treason, Fantasies of Regicide, 1793–1796*, which documents the events of just four years in terms of one issue, the law of 'constructive treason'.[60] The historically minded should consult this major work of scholarship for an almost daily chronology of what happened between 1793 and 1796 in this crucial decade, and also the breezier but equally erudite and massive book, *Poisoning the Minds of the Lower Orders* by Don Herzog. My aim at this stage is to sketch the context in which natural rights were discussed, and in later chapters to trace the debates through literary works. Hundreds of reform societies grew up all over England to discuss the implications of the French revolution for their own kingdom. The societies became increasingly clandestine as government suppression became tighter, but their continuing existence demonstrated the integrity of those who wished for reform. They were small or large, and ranged from the moderate Whig position taken by Friends of the People, which was relatively conservative, through the Society for Constitutional Information founded by Sheridan in the 1780s and revived by Horne Tooke, which was middle-class and influential, to the London Corresponding Society which was large, working-class (artisan) and visible through its pamphlets and meetings. It urged universal suffrage and annual parliaments. It was on November 4, 1789, when Dr Richard Price, a Unitarian minister, addressed two societies, the Revolution Society and the Society for Commemorating the Revolution in Great Britain, that Burke was goaded into his polemic on the iniquities of the French Revolution. Price delivered twice the same 'sermon' entitled *A Discourse on the Love of our Country* and its theme was the 'general rights of man':

> I have lived to see the rights of men better understood than ever; and nations panting for liberty, which seemed to have lost the idea of it. – I have lived to see Thirty millions of people, indignant and resolute, spurning at slavery, and demanding liberty with an irresistible voice; their king led in triumph, and an arbitrary monarch surrendering himself to his subjects ... I see the ardor for liberty catch and spreading ... Behold, the light you have struck out, after setting America free, reflected to France, and there kindled into a blaze that lays despotism in ashes, and warms and illuminates Europe![61]

The sermon ended stirringly: 'Restore to mankind their rights; and consent to the correction of abuses, before they and you are destroyed together.' It was published immediately, augmented by an appendix demanding liberty of conscience, trial by jury, freedom of the press, and freedom of election. The point at issue between Price and Burke was not directly the events of the French revolution but the significance of the English 'Glorious Revolution' in 1689. Price and his societies believed that all their principles had been established by the English revolution and that a century of governments had unpicked the settlement. Burke (if not all conservatives) equally revered 1689 as the year which had enshrined principles of government which encapsulated the best of tradition and should apply in perpetuity, but he turns this against the radicals. He argues that its existence proves the case for maintaining tradition and the ruling class status quo at any one period of history. Pope's sublimely conservative 'Whatever is, is right' hovers behind Burke. He was committed to the view that the fundamental constitutional safeguard is not popular election but heredity. His real allegiance was not to the aristocracy but to the Whig cause, which he saw as being perverted by popular pressure and leaders like Fox.[62] It is unlikely that the opposing parties actually understood each other on this issue, so implacably different were their readings of the English Revolution.

At least one consequence of the reception of the French revolution in England was that, since it was generally supported by some poets and fiction writers in its early days, it acted as a galvanising issue which enabled writers to find each other and communicate in circles. Those who went to Paris, for example, fraternised with revolutionaries, and the incomparable biographer of romantic poets, Richard Holmes, in his book *Footsteps: Adventures of a Romantic Biographer*, evokes the exciting and dangerous times for at least three key writers:

> [In 1793] the revolutionary Terror was now absolute, and guillotinings took place daily. Almost the first act of Committee within its new powers was to order the arrest of all British citizens, and on the night of 9–10 October, with ruthless efficiency, some four hundred people (the bulk of these being nuns and clergymen who had stayed in the English convents and communities in Paris) were picked up in closed carriages and taken to a special prison established at the Luxembourg. No one seems to have escaped the police sweep, organised by the notorious Fouqier-Tinville. Helen Williams, together with her sister and mother, was arrested shortly after midnight; Tom Paine – with the proofs of *The Age of Reason* in his pocket – was brought in by dawn; even Joel Barlow, vigorously protesting American citizenship (with more success than Paine), was temporarily arrested as a precautionary measure. But Mary Wollstonecraft escaped, and this was thanks to Imlay.[63]

All liberal, English visitors seemed to arrive with a letter of introduction to the redoubtable Helen Maria Williams, including Wordsworth who came in 1791. There were other factors that made writers form groups – geographical proximity, sharing the same publisher, like Joseph Johnson (see below), sharing a single issue like slavery, or more pervasively supporting the same radical beliefs. The French revolution, however, became the most prominent single issue based on natural rights that could bond certain writers in professional comradeship, and it has always been acknowledged as the crucial event for the Romantic movement.

Slavery was another issue which acted as a rallying call for natural rights advocates. Slavery had existed at least since the Roman empire and was so deeply embedded in the European culture that it seemed immovably naturalised, almost a 'natural right' of ruling classes (particularly if we include unpaid servants as slaves) everywhere. There had been lone voices amongst the humanists who questioned slavery, like Sir Thomas More in *Utopia*, but it was not until Quakers and Unitarians took up the cause in a systematic way that resistance began to swell into a movement for repeal of the slave trade. Quakers, in particular, had campaigned against slavery in America from the 1680s. By the 1780s Dissenting clergymen were preaching against slavery, a fact which must have popularised the issue and provided grassroot support for the prominent figures who took up the cause: John Wesley (*Thoughts upon slavery*, 1774), William Pitt, Thomas Clarkson, William Wilberforce (who became a Quaker by conversion), and Hannah More. 1788 (the year of Hannah More's *Slavery, a Poem*) to 1790 (More's *The Slave Trade*) was the period of most intense activity by abolitionists which turned the tide. Women writers were at the forefront of the campaign, and some, such as Mary Wollstonecraft, were drawing parallels with their own status, in subjection to fathers and husbands. Judge Mansfield ruled in 1772 that there was no legal basis for slavery in England (extended to Scotland in 1778). At least by 1791 two bills could be introduced by Wilberforce and debated in parliament, although they were defeated with decreasing majorities, and in 1793 his next bill was passed by the Commons but defeated by the Lords. Also in 1791, 100,000 slaves and ex-slaves in the French colony of San Domingo in the West Indies revolted against their masters. In 1792 a mass petition was presented for the abolition of slavery and even Burke in his *Sketch of a Negro Code* advocated gradual emancipation. By 1796 the House of Commons resolved by a large majority (230 to 85) to gradually abolish the slave trade, and although the bill was delayed by the Lords, the battle on principle had been won by abolitionists. The slave *trade* may have been stopped, but the battle for the end of the *institution* of slavery took many more years, and the story forms a later chapter, in which Blake and Marat are seen as two writers who saw slavery as the paradigm case for all natural rights.

Not all advocates pursued the abolitionist debate on the basis of natural rights, at least by name, yet the presentation of the case, depending inevitably on a rejection of cruelty and on the right of slaves to independent existence, made the campaign implicitly a natural rights issue. Indeed the anti-slavery movement provided a pattern for other reformist movements in rooting the argument in the fact that people are born free and cannot alienate or be stripped of this fundamental right. A person cannot be sold like a chattel, or forcibly removed from family relationships because such actions are 'unnatural' in treating a person like property instead of a member of the human race. Although Justice Mansfield seemed to contradict his earlier judgement when he presided in the notorious case of the slave ship *Zong* whose captain in 1781 threw overboard 133 slaves into shark-infested waters in order to collect insurance, and ruled in favour of the captain, yet he could claim a consistent basis. He justified his various decisions on the basis that 'The state of slavery is of such a nature, that it is incapable of being introduced on any reasons, moral or political, but only positive law ... it's so odious, that nothing can be suffered to support it, but positive law' – and he then applied positive law in different circumstances. He is by implication accepting that slavery is against natural rights, but equally he is finding that natural rights do not have status in jurisdictions governed by positive laws, and strongly suggesting that the correct procedure is not to invoke unwritten laws but to change positive laws by legislation, a common stance by judges of all ages in the English system, when dealing with morally abhorrent laws. Second, the plight of slaves as a natural rights issue was rapidly taken up by writers and thus entered the field of literature which could reach a mass reading audience.

Some revolutionary causes were perennial. Ever since England subjugated Ireland and turned it into a colony there had been many patriots who wished to regain sovereignty. From the 1770s the struggle was maintained by the United Irish Society, with the goal of political independence for the country, usually accompanied by the call for republicanism. Some advocated reform, others revolution. Locke was one of the intellectual forebears, and at least one English writer, Percy Shelley, was actively engaged in the struggle by distributing pro-Irish pamphlets. The United Irish looked with eagerness and some envy towards America as it liberated itself from Britain, and then towards France as it established a republic. The 'Irish Question' will not be dealt with in this book since it turns not primarily on natural rights but the political rights of a subjugated and colonised country, but it certainly had a natural rights dimension which had been highlighted, for example, in Swift's *A Modest Proposal* published as early as 1730. More relevant here is the second perennial issue, the ongoing problem of women's inequality, as they were forcibly domesticated or exploited as low-paid labour in the textile industry. The development of theories of natural rights became significant and even decisive in this particular struggle, and many writers, as we shall see, reflected the growing debate. Finally, other issues for which natural rights became a justification were, for example, children's rights, in a time of enforced labour for the poor, and more amorphously, rights of nature, both of which found their way into literary works. In general terms, the rise of natural rights allowed claims to be made on behalf of specific groups or classes of people, and allowed the focus to be on equality. In this sense of its stimulation of 'single-issue' politics, the independent focusing on particular rights was to prove much more politically effective than had the broad-based principle of natural law.

Meanwhile, positive law in England in the eighteenth century offered no encouragement or support for rights crusaders or those who believed in natural benevolence. The rights which appeared so 'natural' to radicals, appeared quite unnatural to lawmakers. As successive governments became more alarmed by developments abroad, the legal system was increasingly used as a tool for civil control and repression, particularly as parliaments realised their long-anticipated supremacy over common law, and used statutes to make law, and to overturn the precedent-bound common law. E. P. Thompson has drawn attention to the existence of 'customary laws' which gave at least a symbolic presence of a 'libertarian ideology' based on plebeian rights,[64] but in practice common right usages had been largely ignored by legislators and common law alike. They existed at least in folk memory, so that radicals could nostalgically invoke them, but several centuries of enclosures had eroded their actual existence. It is strange and dismaying to see how deeply entrenched in English legal thinking are property rights above rights of people, and this silent ideology was the most powerful institutional resistance to notions of natural rights. The standard work on history of law is still Sir William Holdsworth's *A History of English Law* in fourteen volumes,[65] published in its entirety as late as 1952, and yet the section on natural rights in the 1790s is deeply conservative. Paine is condemned for the 'patent defects' in his book, his 'ignorance of the rules of English law', his many 'fallacies', so that there is an underwriting of Bentham's near-contemporary critique: 'Natural rights is simple nonsense ... nonsense upon stilts.'[66] Similarly, Godwin is editorially dismissed for 'the absurdities of his conclusions', while Burke is praised for his acuteness. Nowhere is it acknowledged that the problem may not have been ignorance of the law, but the law itself, in its tacit prioritising of property rights over natural rights. Alan Harding, writing *A Social History of English Law* in 1966, does not feel the need to be so judgemental, since he does not even mention the struggles for rights in the 1790s.[67] Of course, legal scholarship has been rewriting its history, at least since the 1970s, but such books, the one authoritative and the other symptomatic, show how tenaciously opposed to natural rights English positive law has been. While the body of law concerning property and institutions has always been immense and complex, law regarding persons and their rights have been, in comparison, crudely simple and scarce.

Certainly in the eighteenth century, parliamentary law reflected the politically conservative interests of the propertied elite who passed it, and the common law, despite its proud claim to equal access for all, essentially evolved to protect the same constituency. This is largely to be expected, since all the institutions of justice, from Parliament down to the courts of King's Bench and Common Pleas, were entirely controlled by men [sic] of property, who had everything by way of privilege to lose and nothing to gain from demands for the natural or human rights of other classes.[68] The one partial and apparent exception was the system of trial by jury which, although not immune to the potent attraction of property rights over human, did at least serve principle well, in leading to the acquittal of those in the Corresponding Societies like Tooke and Thelwall, prosecuted in the 1790s for 'constructive treason'.[69] No matter how morally compelling are appeals to rights, they have never been magnanimously and freely extended to populaces by ruling classes recognising the power of principle, in England or elsewhere, and they have always been surrendered only under duress, after bitter struggle and bloodshed. Even in the twentieth century, constant calls for a bill of rights in England were ignored until 1998 (and even then accepted only in a highly qualified fashion), on the argument that they would erode or weaken common law and statute law.[70] Similarly, appeals to natural law as a way of arguing that positive laws violate conscience, have never been regarded with anything but ridicule and contempt by lawmakers and lawyers alike. One could be forgiven for thinking that at least in the eighteenth and nineteenth centuries and probably beyond, property rights were considered more sacred than human rights. To make stringent laws protecting property allowed enforcers to limit human actions and effectively to suppress potential insurrection. One could also be forgiven for thinking law itself was used nakedly as an instrument of political aims by ruling parties, despite lip service paid to the 'separation of powers' and the indpendence of the judiciary. The seventeenth-century Commonwealth's 'fundamental law' based on the law of Moses had long since been swept away, and even the safeguards of Elizabethan equity, which was supposed to establish fairness over legalism, were steadily diminished by statute law. By the time *Bleak House* was written, equity as dispensed by the Court of Chancery had reversed its sixteenth-century status. It was notoriously slow, expensive, inequitable, and existed more for the profit of lawyers than the rights of citizens. Law, then, gave no comfort to radicals, and in fact it was more often used to deny their rights than to safeguard them.

Joseph Johnson: A congenial publisher

Before moving into the works of writers, we should spare a thought for at least one of their often long suffering midwives, the publisher. At no time in the eighteenth and early nineteenth centuries was it a road to a life of comfort to publish radical or politically sensitive texts. The publisher was threatened by not only bad reviews, felt as keenly by the publisher as the author because his money was being risked, but also government pressure of censorship and the constant spectre of prosecution and imprisonment for sedition. Some, like Keats's publishers Taylor and Hessey, may not have faced such draconian threats, but at least they have been vindicated and celebrated for their patient support.[71] One publisher in particular was remarkably constant in his patronage of radical writers in the 1790s, and although he has not gained much attention and remains a somewhat shadowy figure, his contribution is heroic. It is no exaggeration to say that without Joseph Johnson (1738–1809), many of the works on natural rights detailed in this book would probably have never seen the light of day until long after the authors' deaths. Johnson has had some champions in recent times, but his significance for literature and ideas is rarely acknowledged,[72] despite having been called 'Father of the Book Trade'.[73] Johnson drew to his publishing stable a remarkable group, and they came to know and meet each other, to such an extent that we can speak of a loose circle, 'a sort of Menagerie of Live Authors' in Thomas Campbell's phrase[74]: William Cowper, Tom Paine, William Blake, William Godwin, Dr Richard Price, Joseph Priestley, George Dyer, Mary Hays, Anna Barbauld, Erasmus Darwin, John Horne Tooke, Joseph Cartwright, William Beckford, Henry Fuseli – even the youthful Wordsworth and Coleridge – and Mary Wollstonecraft. He agreed to publish Paine's *Rights of Man* but mysteriously pulled out after the first dozen copies were printed bearing his name. A part of the mutual appeal must have been that he was a dissenter and a humanitarian, who was called to give evidence during the treason trials in 1794, and personally imprisoned for six months in 1798 for publishing regularly the liberal pamphlet, *Analytical Review*.[75] Many liberals, including Fox, were worried by this precedent, but *The Anti-Jacobin; or, Weekly Examiner*, loyal to tories and King, was of course delighted.

Johnson published a remarkable range of books from his shop at No. 72, St Paul's Churchyard. There was a general emphasis on 'safe' subjects like theology and scientific works, which, generally speaking, established him on the side of 'reason' in the kind of debate waged by Blake against 'Urizenic mechanism',[76] and explains his interest in the rational radicals like Paine, Godwin and Wollstonecraft, as well as a host of lesser lights. At the same time, he did use Blake regularly as an illustrator and published some of his works, as well as Coleridge's, Cowper's and Wordsworth's. At the more radical end, as Claire Tomalin points out,

> there were not many oppressed groups among his contemporaries who did not find a champion under his imprint: slaves, Jews, Dissenters, women, victims of the game laws and press gangs, little chimney sweeps, college fellows barred from matrimony, animals ill-used, the disenfranchised and the simply poor and hungry.[77]

To these one can add proponents of other causes like the right to self-determination of Ireland, 'regarded by many as potentially England's "France" ',[78] and the campaign in defence of the English Bill of Rights and against the 'Gagging Bills' (Thomas Beddoes, 1795). The relationship between Johnson, a small, asthmatic bachelor, and the mercurial Wollstonecraft has excited speculation, because immediately on meeting her he became an unusually solicitous patron, setting her up in a house of her own for the indefinite future. Claire Tomalin in her readable biography of Wollstonecraft suggests there were good business reasons for his patronage, given the expanding market for female writers, although she equally admits some mystery in his motives. She suggests that a veiled homosexual affinity with Johnson's best friend Fuseli, who became Wollstonecraft's lover, may have been a factor (a suggestion regarded by Tyson as fanciful). Whatever the truth, Johnson provided Mary with not only a publishing outlet and financial security but also the opportunity for meeting and conversing with radical dissenters at Johnson's regular three o'clock meetings and dinners at St Paul's Churchyard. It was through this group, in fact, that she met Godwin in 1791, soon after he had begun *Political Justice* and he was to become her future husband. Even after his death, the circle still met and expanded to include Leigh Hunt and Shelley, thus linking the older radical tradition of writers directly with the younger romantics.[79] In general, it is no exaggeration to say that the unsung Johnson must have at least accelerated the movement for radical reform in England, since without him the publication of many works would have been delayed for decades, or even prevented altogether.

2
The Social Passions: Benevolence and Sentimentality

> The conscious heart of Charity would warm,
> And her wide wish Benevolence dilate;
> The social Tear would rise, the social sigh;
> And into clear perfection, gradual bliss
> Refining still the social passions work.
>
> Thomson's *Seasons*, 'Winter', lines 354–8[1]

Sentimentality and benevolence

An unexpected bridge linking philosophy, politics and romantic literature is the body of eighteenth-century works known to literary historians as 'sentimental'. Indeed, it is hard to underestimate the importance of sentimentality in its eighteenth-century literary guise for the rise of romanticism, although the links relating to natural rights have not often been drawn. It is equally important to acknowledge that at least one strand of sentimentality had a strong connection with a general political stance, what G. J. Barker-Benfield calls 'A Culture of Reform', associated particularly with the articulation of women's consciousness.[2] Because the 1790s did not occur in an historical vacuum, this chapter looks backwards to the eighteenth century and forwards to the younger romantics, tracing the changes which increasing consciousness of reform under the pressure of a demand for natural rights, made to the genre.

The first literary reference to the word, which came to dominate the later eighteenth century, appears in the Postscript to the novel which gave the movement a powerful model, Richardson's *Clarissa Harlowe* (1748):

> it is hoped, good use, has been made throughout the work, by drawing Lovelace an infidel, only in *practice*; and this is as well in the arguments of his friend Belford, as in his own frequent remorses, when touched with temporary compunction, and in his last scenes, which could not have been made, had either of them been painted as *sentimental* unbelievers.[3]

41

This use of the word, as Erik Erametsa shows in an exhaustive history, adds to the original meaning, 'of thought, opinion, notion' an unambiguously moral gloss,[4] and Richardson's passage as a whole reveals that his intention was didactic. This was not true of those sentimental works in which, we feel, the primary aim is the heightening of pathos, and it is not consistently true in the most famous work, Sterne's *A Sentimental Journey* (1768), which is as much satirical of the genre as exemplary. But the didactic and political scope of at least some sentimental literature in general is stressed in recent books like Markman Ellis's *The Politics of Sensibility: Race, Gender and Commerce in the Sentimental Novel*[5] and John Mullan's *Sentiment and Sociability: The Language of Feeling in the Eighteenth Century*.[6] The word which is insistent in the works which have a didactic purpose, is 'benevolent', and indeed the whole genre of sentimental literature could without distortion be distinguished into two groups, the literature of pathos and the literature of 'natural benevolence'. The latter term is often more appropriate than 'sentimental' to describe the reformist works, and in fact 'sentimental' is limited, since virtually all recent critics emphasise that many major works in the genre are not entirely or unabashedly sentimental, but contain irony and self-ridicule, as well as political messages. I would argue that this is because the writers' longer aim is not primarily affectivity and emotional indulgence, but rather the didacticism that teaches broad social sympathy and benevolence of action. It is this which explains the paradox that in the 1790s the sentimental novel appeared to turn into the 'Jacobin' novel, which is decidedly unsentimental in its view of social iniquities. It is a further paradox that those who opposed natural rights, and paradoxically some who supported a more revolutionary approach, gradually managed to change the connotations of the words we are examining, from their didactic emphasis to their ineffectuality. 'Sentimentality' nowadays has come to be considered a negative trait, sympathy is seen as weak and sometimes self-seeking, benevolence as smacking of aristocratic philanthropy and charity, but none of these glosses would have been accepted by some eighteenth-century practitioners, whose eyes were fixed on social change. They saw themselves as involved in reform, often based on recognition of natural rights.

The original, progressive political emphases in the 'benevolent' grouping in the sentimental movement were both simultaneously recognised and deliberately obscured even in the romantic period itself, by unsympathetic critics. The devastating force of the attacks on *Endymion* and Keats's early poetry by Lockhart and other Tory reviewers was made possible because they could claim to be attacking a harmless but degraded and outmoded aesthetic stance, which is basically that of sentimentality. Such an aesthetic could, after 1800, be derided as mawkish and immature because of its language, the emotional states it depicted, and its narrative conventions. The adverse critics did not need to reveal their political biases, because they could use sentimentality as a 'stalking horse' to attack writers who belonged to a certain school which superficially avoided engagement with the practical politics of the day. In fact, the history of sentimentality, which by Keats's day had been effectively consigned to amnesia by its opponents, was often political in orientation, and was based on the philosophy of social benevolence which had grown in reaction against Hobbes, and had been developed most systematically by the 'Scottish rationalists' such as Hutcheson, David Hume and Adam Smith. *The Wealth of Nations* has been so influential that it has overshadowed Smith's work of twenty years before, *Theory of Moral Sentiments* (1759), in which he argued that moral judgements are a psychological consequence of the kind of sympathy that allows us by projection to feel what the victim is feeling, a theory of humanitarian advocacy as old as Aristotle and as new as Martin Luther King using rhetoric to advance civil rights:

> True altruism is more than the capacity to pity; it is the capacity to empathise. Pity is feeling sorry for someone; empathy is feeling sorry with someone. Empathy is fellow feeling for the person in need – his pain, agony, and burdens.[7]

Henry Mackenzie, writer of the archetypal work in the genre, *The Man of Feeling*, came out of this Scottish ethos, while Thomas Spence, no great poet but an undoubted political radical, was of Scottish descent and numbered amongst his limited books were authors such as Paine, Ogilvie and Godwin, Dyer's 'Complaint of the Poor People of England' and *Poems*, and Goldsmith's *A Citizen of the World*.[8] Behind all these lay thinkers like Cumberland, Shaftesbury and Adam Smith's teacher, Francis Hutcheson.[9] The sentimental literature of benevolence was in origin close to the philosophical development of natural rights.

Francis Hutcheson and Adam Smith

Hutcheson's *An Essay on the Nature and Conduct of the Passions and Affections* (1728), sometimes regarded as an important work in the history of psychology, was built upon a belief in the naturalness of 'General Benevolence toward all', modified by individual circumstances.[10] Hutcheson, one of those who wrote to refute Hobbes's philosophy of egotism and state sovereignty, is a largely unacknowledged pioneer of the kind of thinking which lay behind sentimental literature. Thomas Mautner, in introducing a lecture by Hutcheson, *On Human Nature*, is adamant that the debate against Hobbes 'was not merely a matter of speculative conjectural history' but one with 'strong political overtones. The Hobbesian view could be taken to favour tyranny: the anti-Hobbesian anarchy.'[11] Hutcheson wrote for example: 'But we must not hence conclude, as some have rashly done, that the very worst sort of polity is better than the best condition of anarchy.'[12] He concludes that the most natural kind of social life for man is one without civil authority at all. What Hutcheson regards as the basis for 'natural' behaviour is 'benevolence, and with it the trusting, unsuspecting expectation of reciprocity of benevolence'.[13] In his essay on the Passions and Affections, Hutcheson generates a philosophy (or rather psychology) of the senses, under which he lists four 'Classes of Perceptions': Imagination, 'Publick Sense' (by which he refers to sympathy and compassion for others), 'Moral Sense' and 'Sense of Honour', all of which underpin at least some sentimental works of the eighteenth century. He argues that people are governed by 'desires and affections':

> There is in Mankind such a *Disposition* naturally, that they desire the Happiness of any known *sensitive Nature*, when it is not inconsistent with something more strongly desired; so that were there no *Oppositions of Interest* either private of public, and *sufficient Power*, we would confer upon every Being the highest Happiness which it could receive.
>
> But our *Understanding* and *Power* are limited, so that we cannot know many other Natures, nor is our utmost *Power* capable of promoting the Happiness of many: our Actions are therefore limited by some *stronger Affections* than this general Benevolence. There are certain *Qualities* found in some Beings more than in others, which excite stronger *Degrees of Good-will* ... The ties of blood, *Benefits conferred* upon us, and the Observation of *Virtue* in others.[14]

While not a creative writer himself, Hutcheson uses literary examples of how our 'Passions' are activated by the representation of good and evil actions in affective works. Here, for instance, he explains why apparent violations of poetic justice which see virtuous characters die, can be morally instructive:

> Hence we see how unfit such Representations are in *Tragedy*, as make the perfectly Virtuous miserable in the highest degree. They can only lead the Spectators into *Distrust* of Providence, *Diffidence* in Virtue; and into such Sentiments, as some Authors, who probably mistake his meaning, tell us *Brutus* expressed at his Death, 'That the Virtue he had pursued as a solid Good, proved by an empty Name.' But we must here remember, that, notwithstanding all the frightful Ideas we have inculcated upon us of the *King of Terrors*, yet an *honourable Death* is far from appearing to a generous Mind, as the greatest of Evils. The *Ruin of a Free State*, the *Slavery of a generous Spirit*, a *Life upon shameful Terms*, still appear vastly greater Evils; beside many other exquisite *Distresses* of a more private nature, in comparison of which, an honourable Death befalling a favourite Character, is looked upon as a Deliverance.[15]

The emphasis on plots and situations that make 'the perfectly Virtuous miserable in the highest degree' and on 'exquisite *Distresses* of a more private nature' which touch the reader, but allow the characters to die honourably as Christ-like sacrifices to a right to live virtuously, all form the central psychological and philosophical and political stances of sentimental writers. Readers are meant to be not just saddened by depictions of 'virtue in distress', the phrase used as a book title by R. F. Brissenden in writing of this genre.[16] They are meant to feel indignant, and to enquire more deeply into the reasons for injustice and violated rights in their own societies.

Brissenden makes it clear that words like 'sensitive' and 'sensible' have changed their meanings from the eighteenth century through to our own age, and indeed they were in a process of change during the eighteenth century. Today we tend to draw a sharp distinction between reason and the emotions as though they are opposites, whereas writers like Hutcheson and the sentimental writers assumed a rational structure behind feelings, just as Renaissance concepts of natural law as stemming from reason, need to be defined now as excluding the drier, logic-centred connotations of 'reason'. 'Right Reason' was not logic, but closer to 'reasonableness', an innate awareness of the interconnectedness of the world and human society, both clear-headedness and an emotional state of active desire for justice, fused into one. Nowadays it is a rather backhanded compliment to be described as 'sensible' as if it is a dull virtue, but right through to its redefinition by Jane Austen in *Sense and Sensibility* it had resonances of an understanding and love of people in all their complexity: a genuine 'moral attribute of man',[17] combining both reason and passion. It could make people spontaneously weep for the miseries of others, and as such it was the part of the human mind that established a principle of equality which was to lead in the related directions of claims for political rights and social concern for the fate of economic, class and sexual victims. As Janet Todd emphasises, sensibility was a part of the more socially minded religions of the time, and it spread into debate on general humanitarian issues:

> The hymns of Methodism, like Charles Wesley's 'Jesu, Lover of my Soul, are a kind of sentimental dramatic poetry reaching out to the singers and taking them into the religious theatre. Like sentimental fiction and drama, they teach and provoke emotion. With its emphasis on the loving kindness of Jesus and the charity of the individual heart, the emotional Christianity of Methodism fed the sentimental concern for the victim and the dispossessed. The humanitarian movement was couched in religious terminology, and its various causes were prosecuted with crusading zeal. These humanitarian concerns also produced an immense quantity of literature, and slavery in particular became a fine subject for treatment. As the dramatist Richard Cumberland unkindly expressed it, the slave was 'fair game' for poets, an absolute 'mine of sentiment'.[18]

Many of these 'humanitarian concerns' involved natural rights, and slavery, for example, is the one mentioned as a prime issue. Chris Jones draws a direct link between Hutcheson and the radical novel of the 1790s: 'For Godwin the disposition towards benevolence is as natural to the mind as it is for Shaftesbury and Hutcheson.'[19]

Adam Smith was Hutcheson's most famous student. Smith nowadays is known mainly to economic historians for his *The Wealth of Nations* (1776), and he is credited with amplifying the notion of the 'invisible hand' guiding market forces in capitalist activity. All this would have surprised Smith. He did not think of himself as an economist. As professor of Logic and Rhetoric and then professor of Moral Philosophy (1752–64) at Glasgow University he can be claimed as one of the first professors of literature, philosophy or humanities. His ultimate aim was to write 'a connected history of the liberal sciences and elegant arts', a project which, in the words of Tom Campbell, 'probably grew out of his studies at Balliol and his lectures on rhetoric and *belles-lettres*, which were delivered in the first place at Edinburgh in 1748–49 and elaborated in his Glasgow lectures':[20]

> I have likewise two other great works upon the anvil; the one is a sort of Philosophical History of all the different branches of Literature, of Philosophy, Poetry and Eloquence; the other is a sort of Theory and History of Law and Government.[21]

Furthermore, it is clear that Smith regarded *The Wealth of Nations*, substantial as it is, as only a specific and limited part of his overall social theory, and he is reported to have valued more highly his earlier *Theory of Moral Sentiments* (1759), the work which is relevant to this study. What would have dismayed Smith most keenly was to see the idea of the 'invisible hand' used to justify inhuman and mechanical processes of an economic market. It was, rather, one who was antagonistic to notions of natural rights, Jeremy Bentham, who proposed an ethical system based on a calculation of the utility of many particular, self-interested and hedonistic actions, which will, he argues, lead to the greatest happiness of all. Smith's 'invisible hand', far from being simple market forces based on self-seeking action, is proposed in a way that is closer to the human analogue of God's purpose, trying to explain how rationally based actions by individuals can work cumulatively towards the prosperity of all. In his theory he was developing Hutcheson's teaching on benevolence. Smith's economic application of his ideas was generated at a time when business was local, limited and small, so that 'millions of acts of mutual accommodation between agents and spectators'[22] could have a self-righting effect in producing overall benefits. When transferred to the modern capitalist world of trans-global financial institutions and international companies, it arguably has no relevance except a perverse one of achieving exactly the opposite result from the state of social justice and overriding of selfish or monopolistic interests which Smith envisaged.

Sympathy lies at the heart of Smith's overall theory, but he uses the word in a sense which is subtly different from his contemporaries'. For him, sympathy is more than pity and compassion, rather a form of fellow-feeling, a sharing of feelings *with* someone rather than *on behalf of* another.

> Pity and compassion are words appropriated to signify our fellow-feeling with the sorrow of others. Sympathy, though its meaning was, perhaps, originally the same, may now, however, without much impropriety, be made use of to denote our fellow-feeling with any passion whatsoever.[23]

Neither is it empathy (Hume's meaning of the term), or a pre-existing passion (Shaftesbury's understanding), or a 'contagion or infection' from others (Hutcheson). The key to Smith's use of the term lies in sympathy being a felt response to a *situation* witnessed by an impartial and reasonable 'spectator', with the assumption that all impartial spectators would share particular feelings of pain, resentment, anger, or pleasure. According to Smith's theory, 'sympathy ... does not arise so much from the view of the passion, as from that of the situation which excites it', 'by conceiving what we ourselves should feel in the like situation'.[24] David Marshall has traced the development of this usage 'from the original Greek sense of participation in the suffering of another ... [to] a general sense of fellow feeling', traced through the works of Marivaux, Diderot and Rousseau and Smith.[25] The coincidence of sentiments is explained not by the feelings of the viewer but by the proprieties required by the situation. The notion finds unexpected anticipation in Shakespeare's *The Tempest*: Miranda says, 'O, I have suffered With those that I saw suffer' (I.i.5–6), Prospero describes his daughter's response as 'the very virtue of compassion in thee' (I.2.27), while even Ariel, the spirit without feeling, can imagine human suffering:

> *Ariel.*　　　... Your charm so strongly works 'em
> That if you now beheld them, your affections
> Would become tender.
> *Prospero.*　Dost thou think so, spirit?
> *Ariel.*　　Mine would, sir, were I human.
> *Prospero.*　　　　　　And mine shall.
> Hast thou, which art but air, a touch, a feeling
> Of their afflictions, and shall not myself,
> One of their kind?[26]

Smith's impartial spectator does not forfeit warm human feelings in the interests of what he calls 'cool reason': rather the reverse, for the morally aware spectator can find through mutual sympathy the appropriate feelings which would be stirred in any reasonable person by a situation. A simple and apparently banal example might indicate the right nuance: a murdered person, of course, feels nothing. But the *situation* of the murdered person would provoke feelings appropriate to the circumstances, such as anger, shock, resentment, regret, forgiveness, or many others. Such feelings can be imagined by, and replicated in, Smith argues, the 'impartial spectator' in the light of the full circumstances, and seeking agreement from other reasonable and impartial spectators. In this sense sympathy is a moral tool, just as, in classical and Renaissance rhetorical theory, it could be a forensic tool for achieving justice. Sir Thomas Wilson, following Aristotle's version of affective poetic justice, describes the process:

> In moving affections, and stirring the judges to be grieved, the weight of the matter must be so set forth, as though they saw it plain before their eyes. ... Now in moving pity, and stirring men to mercy, the wrong done must first be plainly told: or if the Judges have sustained the like extremity, the best were to will them to remember their own state.[27]

That is, imaginatively to identify in sympathy with a reasonable eyewitness.

The hinge of Adam Smith's argument, and the point at which an 'invisible hand' of logic enters, lies in his assertion that 'mutual sympathy, the awareness of sharing sentiments with others, is one of the chief pleasures of human life, whereas to be aware of a lack of sympathy with our own feelings is extremely unpleasant'.[28] In anticipation of modern psychological practices of positive and negative reinforcement, Smith believes that there is an understandable tendency to seek approval and 'approbation' of others through mutual sympathy and shared moral sensitivity of spectators to some situation. It might be pointed out that this theory is, if anything, counter to classical natural law, since Smith argues that moral understanding through sympathy is not innate to the private individual, but is, rather, a socially refined and even collective process. In this he differs from Hutcheson and others of the time. There is a coincidence of agreement between impartial spectators which avoids the charge of individual subjectivity, and the theory allows for moral relativity, since right and wrong become situational rather than a priori rules. It might also be pointed out that herein lies the analogy with the 'natural' equilibrium of wages and prices through market forces – the 'invisible hand' is equivalent to the social expediency of mutual sympathy sustained by the desire for approval.[29] Smith explains the workings of individual conscience by using the same reasoning. If conscience is the principle by which an individual assesses and conducts his own behaviour, it is discovered by standing back and adopting the point of view of a spectator wishing to gain the approbation of others: 'We endeavour to examine our own conduct as we imagine any other fair and impartial spectator would examine it.'[30] We can each, therefore, carry two viewpoints, one as the person acting and the other as the spectator of the person acting. Thereby, any preference for selfish pleasure is overriden by altruism, which in turn gives the higher pleasure of the approval of others. Benevolent action elicits 'not only approbation but warm praise and enthusiastic reward':

> Generosity, humanity, kindness, compassion, mutual friendship and esteem, all the social and benevolent affections, when expressed in the countenance or behaviour ... please the indifferent spectator upon almost every occasion.[31]

Once again, Smith is not so much refuting as sidestepping those natural law precepts concerning innate goodness which had been discredited by Hobbes, although he is tacitly assuming that people do have an inbuilt desire to do good and avoid evil, the central plank of natural law theory. His argument is absorbing something of the utilitarian concept that choosing between right and wrong can be a social agreement rather than the product of an inner struggle of conscience. He is also, however, building his own justification for natural rights.

Smith's theory of sympathy extends to provide a comment on the 'rights of man' debate, and his thoughts are recorded in his *Lectures on Jurisprudence* which presuppose 'the doctrine of the *Moral Sentiments* that the gravity of the crime depends on the extent of resentment naturally felt by the person affected, modified by the various laws of sympathy as they apply to an observer'.[32] Rights correspond to perceived wrongs: injuries to the body, reputation or estate of a person which cause resentment, indicate the existence of a prior right not to have body, reputation or estate violated. These are rights which, Smith asserts, belong to every person 'as a man' (which we would rephrase, 'as a person'). Through the imagined negative or wrong, the positive or right can be deduced. Smith almost certainly intended at some stage to pursue his reasoning into more contentious areas where some abstract liberty has been infringed, but it is a part of his massive task which was not completed. He gives enough, however, to demonstrate his belief in natural rights, and to clarify his consistent style of reasoning from the standpoint of the impartial, sympathetic spectator. While Smith's philosophical language seems a world away from the political struggles of the 1790s and the emotivenes of the didadactic body of sentimental literature, yet he is in fact providing a conceptual basis for both.

Oliver Goldsmith

I am not suggesting that imaginative writers followed with close interest the philosophical niceties of social thinkers like Hutcheson and Smith, but I do argue that they were aware of the broader psychological and political models, and that they were reflecting them more or less consciously in their poems and novels. 'Sentimentality' in literature was derived from, and contributed to, larger contemporary debates in which social justice and natural rights were at stake.

Since I am dealing with a broad sweep of literary history as it was influenced by intellectual currents, I do not pretend to be anything like thorough, especially since this account is offered only insofar as it relates to the 1790s. There are figures along the way who are obviously influential and significant to the argument, but they have attracted so many specialised commentators on aspects of their work that I could not hope to add much. Fielding, for example, places at the centre of his celebrated novels the archetype of the man of benevolence (one of his favourite words): mature, good natured, instinctively virtuous, seeking to heal social ills and divisions – and withal so innocent that he can be naively deceived by the wiles of the more cunning. Amongst his other major characters, he divides the world into roughly two types; those like Tom Jones born with innocent and spontaneous instincts but who are outmanoeuvred and tricked by the world of convention and circumstances into false positions that lead to moral misunderstandings, and those like Blifil who are adroit at manipulating public opinion to their advantage, using not a little hypocrisy.[33] Richardson, Fielding's great contemporary, focuses on the female equivalent, the victim who stirs benevolence, and suffers through her innocent virtue and whose victimisation at the hands of the more worldly and deceitful are used to create feelings of pity and outrage in readers. As Janet Todd shows, 'In his three novels Richardson tries to portray fictionally the sentimental fellowship of benevolence and sympathy'.[34] Sterne is regularly seen as central to the line of sentimentality (often in resistant ways), but with my redefinition of the territory as literature of benevolence he moves to one side as an astonishing but very individual, playful, and idiosyncratic figure. His presence reminds us of the necessary qualification to be made, that by no means all sentimental writers are consciously didactic, and even fewer succeed in building a progressive ideology into their works, as distinct from glibly building in the obligatory genuflections to benevolence. I concentrate in this study on some eighteenth-century writers who are central to the argument concerning the influence of the benevolent intellectual and political tradition on literature which carries through into romanticism and works focusing on natural rights in the 1790s.

Oliver Goldsmith is a writer whose works have worn a little better than those of his contemporaries. At least part of the reason is because he uses the aesthetic of sentimentality to achieve more social ends than just pity for the distressed heroine. The dominant note is benevolence in the sense of the word used by Cumberland and Hutcheson. As the persona of 'the good natur'd man' reflects a view of people as naturally altruistic, so the underlying political stance is one that regrets and denounces the stripping away of ordinary people's access to common lands, and the consequent erosion of their natural rights. It was perhaps the example of Thomas Gray's tremendously popular 'Elegy Written in a Country Churchyard' (1750) which gave impetus for poems fusing the sentimental and the political. Gray extols the 'destiny obscure' of the rural poor, which could produce a humble but heroic figure to assert his class's rights against tyranny and wealth:

> Some village Hampden, that, with dauntless breast,
> The little tyrant of his fields withstood,
> Some mute inglorious Milton here may rest,
> Some Cromwell guiltless of his country's blood. (57–60)[35]

Gray condemns those who 'shut the gates of mercy on mankind' (68). Goldsmith's 'The Deserted Village' (1768–70) is a powerful and important poem in the same vein. Its nostalgia for an organic community could easily have been mawkish and unrealistic to modern eyes, and certainly there is an element of retrieving a lost innocence which may have been more of a wish than an actuality:

> Dear lovely bowers of innocence and ease,
> Seats of my youth, where every sport could please,
> How often have I loiter'd o'er thy green,
> Where humble happiness endear'd each scene. (5–8)[36]

But the word picked out from this truly sentimental vision is the initially insignificant 'humble' which is developed with all its associations of a disenfranchised underclass. The idealising descriptions of Auburn[37] in the past, 'Sweet smiling village', are not the end of the poem but its means:

> Amidst thy bowers the tyrant's hand is seen,
> And desolation saddens all thy green:
> One only master grasps the whole domain,
> And half a tillage stints thy smiling plain. (35–8)

What has destroyed the village and its community is the individualistic drive towards greedy acquisition that lay behind the movement of enclosing land. Although the specific complaint in the poem is the building of 'pleasure domes' by the wealthy, the argument must extend to the widespread historical change taking place in agricultural England. Goldsmith was living through the second ruthless bout of enclosures in England's history, a movement that was to last through to the time of John Clare. The major historian of the 'lost' English landscape, W. G. Hoskins, notes that 'The replanning of the English landscape affected nearly 2.5 million acres of open fields, most of it accomplished between 1750 and 1850. On top of this more than two million acres of commons and "wastes" were enclosed ... A whole parish, a complete and ancient landscape, could be transformed in a couple of years.'[38] The movement was legally endorsed by Enclosure Acts and by the creation of Enclosure Commissioners to oversee the process. George Crabbe described the impoverished, gipsy-like denizens pushed further out onto barren heathland:

> Here joyless roam a wild amphibious race,
> With sullen woe display'd in every face;
> Who far from civil arts and social fly,
> And scowl at strangers with suspicious eye.[39]

John Clare was to record much more subjectively the psychological alienation that enclosure could cause. Although the straight lines, hedgerows and larger fields of enclosure undoubtedly led to more efficient farming, the only ones who really benefited were the large landowners who could claim ever more extortionate rents from the small farmers who had less and less land (and time) for subsistence growing.

Goldsmith does more than just observe the loss of communities that was occurring throughout the countryside. He explains it in such a way that the deprivation of natural rights is highlighted by reference to human values, by portraying a countryside 'Where wealth accumulates and men decay' (51–2). Vincent Newey,[40] following to some extent the lead of Raymond Williams,[41] argues that Goldmsith's vision is in fact not radical but deeply conservative, in refusing to accept change and arguing 'for stasis'. But this may overemphasise the twentieth-century Marxist view, such as Williams's, above the social inequities of enclosure as it happened. In this sense the changes happening to England were reactionary rather than progressive, an accumulation of wealth into the hands of the landed aristocracy, and to argue for 'stasis' may in the circumstances be a more liberal stance. The level of political indignation emerges from an analysis of 'The Deserted Village' which focuses on the issue of natural rights rather than the undoubted, sentimental attachment to old-fashioned social hierarchies. At his level, Goldsmith speaks like the Diggers before him and Thomas Spence after, in asserting the historical commonality of land: 'A time there was, ere England's griefs began, When every rood of ground maintain'd its man', and attacks the changes wrought by 'the tyrant's power':

> But times are altered; trade's unfeeling train
> Usurp the land and dispossess the swain;
> Along the lawn, where scatter'd hamlets rose,
> Unwieldy wealth, and cumbrous pomp repose;
> And every want to opulence allied,
> And every pang that folly pays to pride. (63–8)

It may be asking too much of a writer in 1770, before Rousseau was known in England and before Paine had written, to assert, as Wiliams wants Goldsmith to, a 'practically available world' of genuine egalitarianism rather than futilely harking back to an imagined golden age. Conceding something like this, Newey acknowledges a 'profoundly seminal' quality in Goldsmith's work, which enabled Cowper in turn, and later the romantics, to present sharper and more pointed political critiques.

The system of capitalism that uses men and property to make the conspicuous monuments to profit is generalised by Goldsmith in a passage anticipating Keats's attack on capitalists in 'Isabella', to include its victims, 'wretches, born to work and weep, Explore the mine, or tempt the dangerous deep'. He attacks the root cause of greed – 'O Luxury! thou curs'd by Heaven's decree', and moralises the human consequences for whole communities:

> Even now the devastation is begun,
> And half the business of destruction done;
> Even now, methinks, as pond'ring here I stand,
> I see the rural virtues leave the land. (395–8)

Benevolent qualities like 'hospitable care' are casualties, but the root cause is the violation, in the interests of increasing the wealth and visual prospects of the wealthy, of the natural rights of peasants to live on common lands. As John Barrell emphasises, the assault is not only on the living conditions of the rural poor, but also their right to work.[42] The poem concludes its political argument by asking poetry to do its work in changing minds if not landscapes:

> Teach erring man to spurn the rage of gain;
> Teach him, that states of native strength possest,
> Tho' very poor, may still be very blest;
> That trade's proud empire hastes to swift decay; (424–8)

The losses are not confined to the insecurities of enforced depopulation. Goldsmith throughout 'The Deserted Village' uses as his sentimental touchstone 'the rural virtues' of common people, not only the male toilers on the land but women forced into prostitution in cities. He evokes a picture of the 'innocence distrest' that would herself have wept over a sentimental novel:

> – Ah, turn thine eyes
> Where the poor houseless shivering female lies.
> She once, perhaps, in village plenty blest,
> Has wept at tales of innocence distrest;
> Her modest looks the cottage might adorn,
> Sweet as the primrose peeps beneath the thorn;
> Now lost to all; her friends, her virtue fled,
> Near her betrayer's door she lays her head,

> And, pinch'd with cold, and shrinking from the shower,
> With heavy heart deplores that luckless hour,
> When idly first, ambitious of the town,
> She left her wheel and robes of country brown. (325–36)

The 'sad historian of the pensive plain' is a different kind of victim, a solitary widow who is, 'wretched matron, forced, in age, for bread, To strip the brook with mantling cresses spread ... and weep till morn' (1314). The village preacher is the conscience of the poem, an authorial projection, sadly hearing the tales of woe from his parishioners, and a man in the true benevolent mould: 'His pity gave ere charity began ... He watch'd and wept, he pray'd and felt, for all.' His manse is now deserted, empty and neglected, like the rest of the sad village. What saves Goldsmith's vision from the charge of nostalgic conservatism is that he has provided a context by observing a political process and its human results. The land is 'by luxury betray'd' so that as 'The rich man's joys increase, the poor's decay', and the betrayal reaches deep into the lives of people whose diurnal agricultural and rural lifestyle has been irrevocably destroyed in less than a generation.[43] His poem, 'The Traveller, or A Prospect of Society', contains a brief and trenchant condemnation of the same social and political ills:

> Have we not seen, round Britain's peopled shore,
> Her useful sons exchanged for useless ore?
> Seen all her triumphs but destruction haste,
> Like flaring tapers brightening as they waste;
> Seen opulence, her grandeur to maintain,
> Lead stern depopulation in her train,
> And over fields where scattered hamlets rose,
> In barren solitary pomp repose? (397–404)

Goldsmith's work contains a natural law subtext and an implicit plea for the violated natural rights of the rural poor.

Not that Goldsmith was a political radical by nature. Without equating him with his fictional character Dr Primrose, he gives the authority of a kind of 'golden mean' to the vicar's view that a monarchy is the best form of government, that the rich need to be curbed, and that 'In the middle order of mankind are generally to be found all the arts, wisdom, and virtues of society'.[44] Not that we can ever be quite sure of the author's position in *The Vicar of Wakefield* (1766), apart from detecting a general likeness in circumstances between the vicar and the biblical Job, since both spend their lives in adversity.[45] For most of the novel, we could be forgiven for thinking Goldsmith is giving endorsement to the full vision of a Hobbesian society where virtually everybody is rapacious, deceitful and hypocritical. Unlike Job, Dr Primrose is persecuted not by his God but by very human and plausible rogues, in a society lacking in strong rule or consistent justice. Within the novel we hear the players saying that the age is one of a revival of Jonson's plays, and Jonson could be seen as one who, as a dramatist, is reflecting the view that came to be associated with *Leviathan*, that only absolute sovereignty can curb the excesses and tendencies to vice intrinsic to man. Goldsmith's happy ending is so strained and incredible that it need not shake this impression. Second, the Vicar is time and again undone by his own innocent gullibility, as though the wholeheartedly benevolent man, far from being a touchstone for humanity's innate instinct for doing good, is an aberration who is ripe to be gulled.[46] Only to the most ardent reader of sentimental novels could his own inconsistencies, self-righteousness and almost idiotic naivety be ignored, surrounded as he is by more colourful and vital villains. This reading would make *The Vicar of Wakefield* a satire on sentimentalism and an exposure of the tenuousness of its philosophical basis.

But there is a third way of reading the novel, and it seems the most satisfactory. It is noticeable, for example, that few if any characters are incorrigibly wicked. People feign honest benevolence in order to gull and cheat, but two extra rules apply in this world. The first is that they come to see the error of their ways and repent. Mr Jenkinson who is the first to rob the Vicar by taking his horse without paying for it, repents in prison, and he is exemplary of others. The ending, however unbelievable, turns not on a *deus ex machina* but on revelations and changes of heart from characters who have either been dissembling or are misunderstood. Only Primrose, for all his ingenuous contradictions, remains true to a principle of charitable judgment and living, and he is ultimately vindicated after all his adversities. Second, and more crucially, villains are inevitably revealed as victims of their own upbringing in some way or another, rather than naturally evil. Again, Jenkinson is typical: 'I was thought cunning from my very childhood; ... at twenty, though I was perfectly honest, yet every one thought me so cunning, that not one would trust me. Thus I was at last obliged to turn sharper in my own defence, and have lived ever since, my head throbbing with schemes to deceive, and my heart palpitating with fears of detection' (147). He observes that those with material means like his 'honest simple neighbour Flamborough' can afford to be honest. whereas, as he says of himself, '[I] was poor, without the consolation of being honest'. At many points in the novel Goldsmith shows that any innate honesty or goodness a person may have is either compromised or, as in Primrose's case, the swiftest path to ruin. The kind of competitive acquisitiveness and survival of the fittest is not in Goldsmith's novel a vision of the norm of human behaviour, but rather a form of behaviour forced on men by the spectre of poverty and ruin, by a denial of their natural rights.

Goldsmith does not speak by name of natural rights in the novel, although in a sense his 'hero' embodies an indomitable resistance to corruptibility which is a conscious choice based on an inclination and religious conviction. However, he does more than once expose scathingly the appeal to 'liberty' as an aristocratic strategy, a way of maintaining inequality between the rich and the poor. The vicar is given hospitality by one who, representing himself as a man of property (who turns out to be the butler and a victim of false consciousness), maintains that 'liberty is the Briton's boast' (98). When Primrose asserts the 'sacred power' of the monarch, he is attacked as 'an enemy to liberty, and a defender of tyrants', and as one who is an advocate of slavery. He replies haughtily that 'I would have all men kings. I would be a king myself. We have all naturally an equal right to the throne: we are all originally equal' (99), aligning himself with 'a set of honest men who were called Levellers'. (Rather confusingly, he blames divisions within the Levellers for creating the present state of inequality.) He then goes on at such length, without internal irony from the novel, to attack the inequities created by the accumulation of wealth which leads to a tyranny of the rich over the poor far more malign than any ruler could exercise. It is at this point that he extols the virtues of 'the middle order' as defenders of 'the real liberties of the subject' (103). 'This order alone is known to be the true preserver of freedom, and may be called the People.' If we probe we find flaws in Primrose's logic, and a glaring structural contradiction in the novel in that it is the wealth of Sir William Thornhill which finally guarantees the happiness of all (he even gives fourty pounds to be distributed amongst the prisoners), but there is a warmth and passion about the general argument that lends it authorial approval. The advice to his daughters offered by Primrose, 'but learn to commune with your own hearts' in order to resist 'elegance and splendours of the worthless' (135) is projected onto the political stage as a defence of the social contract. Finally, in a novel which subjects its totally innocent hero to undeserved miseries throughout, another episode shows that Goldsmith is making a point about severe inadequacies in England's system of justice. When Primrose ends up in prison, he unsurprisingly meditates upon the system which has placed him there. He formulates a scheme for reforming rather than punishing wrongdoers, on the natural rights basis that ' "these people, however fallen, are still men" ' (148).

> And it were highly to be wished, that legislative power would thus direct the law rather to reformation than severity. That it would seem convinced that the work of eradicating crimes is not by making punishments familiar, but formidable. Then instead of our present prisons, which find or make men guilty, which enclose wretches for the commission of one crime, and return them, if returned alive, fitted for the perpetration of thousands; we should see, as in other parts of Europe, places of penitence and solitude, where the accused might be attended by such as could give them repentance if guilty, or new motives to virtue if innocent. And this, but not the increasing of punishments, is the way to mend a state.

He goes on to suggest that the priorities in English law are wrong by 'questioning the validity of that right which social combinations have assumed of capitally punishing offences of a slight nature' (149). While 'Natural Law gives me no right to take away his life', it is not natural law but a social contract, an agreement, that prevents one from taking away a horse or any other sort of property. The principle of punishing offences against property just as severely, or more so, than murder, is creating 'a great penalty for a very trifling convenience, since it is far better that two men should live, than that one man should ride' (150). In an extension of the argument behind the economics of 'The Deserted Village', Primrose (or, fairly transparently Goldsmith) condemns any community where 'penal laws, which are in the hands of the rich, are laid upon the poor' (150). Goldsmith, adopting the benevolent stance, is a writer who lays the foundations for using the novel form as a vehicle for espousing natural rights.

Henry Mackenzie

If Goldsmith is a 'sentimental' writer then he is certainly one with a social conscience and an ideological purpose, and he demonstrates that moral purpose is a central characteristic of sentimental writing in general. The same applies to a novel which is often taken to be a kind of benchmark for the genre, Henry Mackenzie's *The Man of Feeling* (1771).[47] As I have mentioned, Mackenzie was a lawyer in Edinburgh, who was so close to the so-called Scottish rationalists like Hutcheson, Hume and Smith that he could be regarded as virtually a part of their circle. A cursory reading makes it unsurprising that this tough substratum has rarely been claimed for the novel, since it manifests all the extreme misery of situation, lachrimosity and pathos which came to make the genre more mocked than respected. But there are strong and explicit links that have encouraged John Mullan at least to associate not only Mackenzie but his fictional work with its context:

> Hume found his particular social identity, and a model for the operation of 'humanity, generosity, beneficence', in the associations of the educated and the enlightened in eighteenth century Edinburgh. In its clubs and its groups of enquiring men of letters was a kind of paradigm of sociability itself.[48]

As Hume sought in his *Treatise of Human Nature* to make passion the motivation to moral action, supported secondarily by reason, and seeks to connect benevolence, comprehensive sympathy and the desire for another's welfare,[49] so Mackenzie presents his pictures of virtue under threat with a didactic intention. This shows at particular points in the novel where opinions ('sentiments' in its original meaning) are offered as a gloss on the poignant and tragic situations, and these opinions characteristically focus on the general issue of natural rights of victimised individuals and classes in an uncaring society. Feeling comes first, but the reasoning capacity follows, as the novel's hero Harley muses:

> The world is ever tyrannical; it warps our sorrows to edge them with keener affliction. Let us not be slaves to the names it affixes to motive or to action. I know an ingenuous mind cannot help feeling when they sting. But there are considerations by which it may be overcome. Its fantastic ideas vanish as they rise; they teach us to look beyond it. (51)[50]

Even 'the man of feeling' rises above pure sensibility in order to find moral lessons in affecting circumstances, and there is an element of Smith's notion of the sympathetic man's feelings being close to 'the sentiments of the supposed impartial spectator'.[51] Mackenzie does use an elaborate technique of multiple narrators, but since the didactic intention is always clear I shall not deal here with formal aspects of the deliberately fragmentary novel. Its main formal property is its use of episodic narrative, where the 'man of feeling' (Harley) observes and becomes implicated in affecting situations, listens to the stories of others, and is himself observed by a narrator who does not claim omniscience over the material which he presents as 'found'.

Very early, 'benevolence' is mentioned as a touchstone, and it is even conveniently defined in natural law fashion as '[that] which ye deduce immediately from the natural impulse of the heart' (28). In an episode reminiscent of those read by Goldsmith's 'poor houseless shivering female' who, 'once, perhaps, in village plenty blest, Has wept at tales of innocence distrest', the corrupted, abandoned and desperately ill Miss Atkins tells Harley her story, on the assumption that 'to the humane, I know there is a pleasure in goodness for its own sake' (37). She charts her fall into prostitution in a way which absolves her from direct responsibility and portrays her as a suffering victim who is representative of a whole class of social casualties robbed of their natural right to dignity and self-determination. Her lament is, 'Oh! did the daughters of virtue know our sufferings' (45). She is gratefully saved from the miserable brothel (and reunited with her father) through the good offices of Harley, who acts upon 'an exertion of benevolence which the infection of our infamy prevents even in the humane' (45).

Among those who are not wholly benevolent but somehow seem redeemable, are those who have caught 'the infection of our infamy' for personal reasons such as being 'softened to the admonition of friendship or soured into the severity of reproof' (2). This characterisation is applied by Mackenzie to a 'strange creature' who seems too close in his theorising to Bentham's (or Mandeville's in *The Fable of the Bees* [1714–18]) to be quite coincidental or entirely fictional. This is the voice claiming that even acts which are benevolent in the outcome are driven by selfish motives. The philosophy of utilitarianism is sketched by a corrosive misanthrope who suspects even poets of being hypocritical or misguided:

> In short, man is an animal equally selfish and vain. Vanity, indeed, is but a modification of selfishness. From the latter, there are some who pretend to be free: they are generally such as declaim against the lust of wealth and power, because they have never been able to attain any high degree in either: they boast of generosity and feeling. They tell us (perhaps they tell us in rhyme) that the sensations of an honest heart, of a mind universally benevolent, make up the quiet bliss which they enjoy; but they will not, by this, be exempted from the charge of selfishness. Whence the luxurious happiness they describe in their little family-circles? Whence the pleasure which they feel, when they trim their evening fires and listen to the howl of winter's wind? Whence, but from the secret reflection of what houseless wretches feel from it? Or do you administer comfort in affliction – the motive is at hand; I have preached to me in nineteen out of twenty of your consolatory discourses – the comparative littleness of our misfortunes. (28)

It is rather daring for Mackenzie to insert such a headlong attack on the very kind of novel he is writing, and he does not seem to know quite how to handle it by way of direct refutation. Its logic is in a sense unanswerable by the benevolent man of feeling who simply notes that the remarks are not 'of the pleasant kind': he can by definition have no way of retaliating because such anti-benevolence is beyond his comprehension.[52] It would appear that Mackenzie is trusting his readers to see the philosophy as flawed in comparison with the overwhelming evidence produced by the fable, that people at least *can* be selfless if they are not warped by bitterness and cynicism in the daily fight against adversity and institutional persecution. He reinforces the emphasis by socially isolating the speaker, who is presented as a ruined man of wealth grown cynical and preferring to be left to his own meditations rather than testing his theories in company. He is a kind of man of feeling in his own right, but one who has let his personal feelings overwhelm him without interposing analytical reason or empathy with others, in order to understand his position. Mackenzie also presumably expects a tug to the reader's own feelings in the images of moral comfort uttered with an inadvertent envy by the embittered utilitarian: the sentimental lure of the cosy family circle trimming their evening fires, listening to 'the howl of winter's wind' outside. This man, one feels, is lost in the winter's wind, unable to retreat into the comfort of well-based morality.

Like Goldsmith, Mackenzie chooses as his target for condemnation, those who are adept at 'getting rich at the expense of [their] conscience' (65) and Harley expostulates on the desecration of rural England by the wealthy:

> 'Alack a day!' said she, 'it was the school-house indeed; but to be sure, sir, the squire has pulled it down because it stood in the way of his prospects'.

'What! how! prospects! pulled down!' cried Harley.

'Yes, to be sure, sir; and the green, where the children used to play, he has ploughed up, because, he said they hurt his fence on the other side of it.'

'Curses on his narrow heart,' cried Harley, 'that could violate a right so sacred! Heaven blast the wretch!' (67)

The 'villains' who violate such a 'sacred right' to live comfortably are not presented to our view, and the general implication is that they are not acting as human beings but have been alienated from human feelings. In other circumstances the evil in the world is located not in individual humans, who usually turn out to be reformable, but in social institutions, the existence of poverty which drives men to desperate deeds, and people acting as collective groups rather than as feeling individuals. In fact the economic jargon which was fashionable in the late twentieth century ironically and unintentionally illuminates the nature of such alienation. Appeals to 'economic rationalism' place an almost holy faith not in human agency but in the conveniently disembodied but presumably inexorable process of 'market forces'. Casualties are inevitable and not to be regretted. because their fate is vaguely seen either as their own fault for not somehow utilising these 'forces', or else they are necessary sacrifices to the need to 'reward the wealth creators'. R. F. Brissenden uses words from the writer of *The Whole Duty of Man* ... (1659) to establish that in the sentimental movement, 'society, "the world", was inherently and necessarily cruel and inhumane – [but] it was also widely maintained that man was by nature benevolent'.[53] Mackenzie is just as prophetic when he comes to analyse the nature of imperialism. The chapter heading 'The man of feeling talks of what he does not understand' is clearly meant ironically, as Harley expatiates from his naive but morally centred point of view on England's conquest and annexation of India:

You tell me of immense territories subject to the English: I cannot think of their possessions without being led to inquire by what right they possess them. (72)

The English, he argues, were initially accepted in India in good faith on terms of traders in 'friendly commerce' with 'equitable' rights, paying for commodities, but that to go further, conquer the country, appoint 'their own petty princes', 'draining the treasuries' and 'oppressing the industry of their subjects' is tyranny without legitimate right. Harley asserts that the fundamental motive was simply 'wealth', to which even 'the fame of conquest' is secondary. Nor is the colonisation of India seen as unique: 'Could you tell me of some conqueror giving peace and happiness to the conquered?'. Harley clinches the underlying logic, which ties this episode in with the others in the book:

> however the general current of opinion may point, the feelings are not yet lost that applaud benevolence and censure inhumanity. Let us endeavour to strengthen them in ourselves; and we, who live sequestered from the noise of the multitude, have better opportunities of listening undisturbed to their voice. (73)

It is Mackenzie's clear intention that the community of readers, listening undisturbed in the necessarily 'sequestered' activity of reading, are the 'we' who are appealed to in this passage.

Women writers

It is rather unfortunate that the examples I have given so far are by male writers, since the more general cult of sensibility was identified as targeting women readers, the audience which Sterne almost unctuously addresses. There were celebrated female writers in the genre, but the general impression that emerges in the eighteenth century is that the earlier women writers tended to yoke sensibility with fiction dealing with passion and romance, rather than with contemporary social issues or moral concerns presented didactically.[54] Towards the end of the century, however, this pattern changed and increasingly women wrote more realistic novels of benevolence. When we reach the 1790s, we find amongst the most notable exponents of novels of natural rights, women like Mary Wollstonecraft, Charlotte Smith, Elizabeth Inchbald and Mary Hays, all of whom in many ways were influenced as much by Rousseau and the precipitating events of the French Revolution, as by earlier eighteenth-century sentimental fiction. Rival explanations have been advanced for this development. Janet Todd sees the more abrasive and pessimistic novels of Jacobins in the 1790s as a reaction against sentimental novels, while Nicola J. Watson assumes they are a straightforward development from the sentimental novel, and that reaction against the movement came later with a 'conservative backlash' opposed to the shared political views.[55] Watson advances the 'rather startling contention' that the sentimental novel and the Jacobin novel are interfused and have a common family tree leading back to Rousseau, that 'revolutionary politics were understood crucially in terms of sentimental fiction – and in particular the plot of a single novel, *La Nouvelle Héloise* ... so it was that the "novel of sensibility" came to serve as such an important matrix in the period'.[56] Chris Jones provides a slightly different gloss on this approach, arguing that there were 'conflicting trends' within the sentimental movement, 'which became, for short time in the 1790s, a site of contention between radical and conservative discourses'.[57] The ambiguity hanging over sensibility as a political response was present even at the time, since unsympathetic critics like Burke and reviewers for the *Anti-Jacobin*, saw excessive emotion as a cause of what they regarded as the horrors of revolution, while others, like the novelists themselves presumably, saw feeling as a moral faculty awakening readers to the social ills which made revolution desirable and necessary. In this book, I argue the latter position, and suggest that writers like Godwin, Wollstonecraft, Smith and others are in effect writing benevolent, sentimental novels but from a point of view which recognises that benevolence is not likely to be achieved on a mass scale and that something like revolution is required to reverse the bleakly horrifying social and political realities of the 1790s.

Divergence of critical opinion over eighteenth-century women novelists may find its origins in ambiguity of the evidence itself. A mid-century novelist, Sarah Scott, demonstrates the ways in which pre-1790s women writers predominantly linked sentimentality and romance, while also giving anticipations of the novels of social purpose. *The History of Cornelia* (1750) is one among many eighteenth-century female picaresque novels. The beautiful Cornelia, after fleeing from her uncle's incestuous designs and finding herself, like Marina in Shakespeare's *Pericles*, inadvertently lodging in a brothel, is assailed in her travels through France and Spain by dashing Lotharios, gangs of ruffians, and the jealousy of other women. She remains immovably true to her initial virtue and to the love of her life, Bernardo, with whom she is eventually reunited and married. Her 'angelic compassion and goodness'[58] make her the recipient of many melancholy confidences and she becomes a wise counsellor to those in trouble or grief. The story is a straightforward sentimental romance. All that distinguishes *Cornelia* from the 'plays, romances, and poetry' given to the heroine by her cunning uncle is that it is not calculated to inflame the passions but to extol 'the virtue founded on reason, true religion, and benevolence' (8) in which her father had raised her. It is this moral aspect that the book's 'Advertisement' stresses, claiming it as a work of imagination that has 'a tendency to inculcate, illustrate or exemplify morality', innocently amusing the fancy of the reader 'while the sentiments interspersed may, if not instruct in the knowledge, yet animate in the practice of, virtue'. Scott seems to have made this kind of novel her specialty, for *Millenium Hall* (1762; sometimes attributed to Lady Barbara Montagu and even Oliver Goldsmith) presents a set of sentimental stories which, the title page announces, 'May excite in the READER proper sentiments of Humanity, and lead the Mind to the Love of VIRTUE'. Her *The Man of Real Sensibility; or, The History of Sir George Ellison* (1765) places a man on the high moral ground. Again, edifying claims are often advanced for these novels, making it possible for them to be interpreted either as unashamed sentimental romance or as novels of benevolence. Readers can at least enjoy the affectivity and sensibility with a free conscience. However, the one thing that could not be claimed for *Cornelia* is that it turns on a point of natural rights or that its 'benevolence' is more than a superficial justification. Much the same could be said of many novels written at the time by women.

A veneer of moralism overlays or frames a largely sentimental romantic fiction which broadly depicts the triumph of virtuous womanhood over social evils. Margaret Doody argues that such a formula was later to be amplified into a new form in which the compassionate heroine engages more realistically with her society,[59] and we shall look at some examples later in this book. Certainly, the evidence compiled by Cheryl Turner in *Living by the Pen: Women writers in the eighteenth century*[60] confirms the hunch expressed by many, that the number of professional women writers escalated dramatically after 1780, but at the same time shows surprisingly that the actual number of novels written in each five year period from 1700 to 1800 was relatively stable, with a sudden jump in the 1720s. Turner provides an invaluable list, spanning nearly 70 pages, of all women's fiction published in book form from 1696 to 1796, and 'improving' sentimental novels preponderate. However, my sampling of the output suggests that it was not until the 1790s that women novelists began to contribute with a social purpose to the literature of benevolence, and to raise questions of fundamental natural rights. The figure of Mary Wollstonecraft will soon loom large. These days the eighteenth-century woman whose novels are most often recuperated is Frances Burney, but it is difficult without strain to argue that she contributed to socially or politically progressive ideas in her novels. Her characters aspire not to acquiring natural rights, but social advancement.[61] Some women poets from the 1770s onwards, such as Hannah More and Laetitia Barbauld, adopted the viewpoint of benevolent literature, in dealing with the increasingly central issue of slavery, and this further legacy of the field of sentimental literature will be considered in a later chapter.

Robert Merry

As in prose, so in poetry, sensibility and benevolence were linked in ways that led to the 1790s and the romantics. Although the broad genre of sentimental literature was ridiculed by writers of a later generation like Coleridge, Scott and Byron, it is not true that romanticism spelt an end for all its conventions. For one thing, sensibility has continued unabated to the present day in popular romances. More importantly for the present book, although the excesses of affective aesthetics became insipid in the sterner climates after 1790, the core values of appealing to the reader's sympathies, celebrating benevolence in its philosophical and political senses, passed directly into romanticism itself as a way of asserting natural rights through literature. In this development, Jerome McGann argues for the pivotal importance of the Della Cruscan movement, the poetic equivalent of the sentimental novel:

> The romantic movement thus keeps splitting into numerous variant forms. One critical point of departure is the so-called Della Cruscan poetry of sentiment. Launched with The Florence Miscellany (Florence,

1785, privately printed), Della Cruscan writing soon found its way back to England, became a great force in the 1790s, and had a signal influence on later writing as well, especially the work of Keats, Shelley, Byron, and the poets of the 1820s. A distinctly urban project, it was committed to extreme displays of stylistic artifice. (In an important sense, Keats is the greatest representative of the Della Cruscan movement, as the attacks and criticisms of John Wilson Croker, Wordsworth, Byron, and later Matthew Arnold show very well.) The contrast of this work with Burns, and ultimately with the programme of Lake School poetry, is striking – even though, in all these cases, 'sensibility' is an important shared element.[62]

McGann has been one of the very few critics to keep alive the name of Robert Merry and his Della Cruscan school, but perhaps not entirely for the right reasons. By the particular choice of poems in *The New Oxford Book of Romantic Period Verse*, McGann makes the movement seem somewhat self-congratulatory and innocuous,[63] confirming the impression given by his book, *The poetics of sensibility: a revolution in literary style*,[64] that Merry and his cohorts were interesting only for their language of 'sensibility' and 'extreme displays of stylistic artifice'. There was, however, a strong political edge to the work of Merry, if not that of the other Della Cruscans, and his radicalism arguably deserves to be seen as his most abiding quality. A Chorus from *The Picture of Paris* (1790) condemns slavery, war and 'tyrannical sway' in Britain, and has the refrain, 'Oppression's heavy hour is past'.[65] *The Laurel of Liberty: A Poem* (1790), is dedicated to the National Assembly of France, and in the Preface Merry says he visited Paris and sees France as 'a new Land of Liberty', where 'Oppression is no more'. He asserts that tyrants can never prevail because 'THE CAUSE OF FREEDOM IS THE CAUSE OF ALL MANKIND', and in a footnote he supports the struggle for natural rights:

> Though the enemies to the French Revolution despise the idea of *the Rights of Men*, yet they are very strenuous to support the *Rights of Nobility*; it is therefore evident that they suppose *some* men to have Rights, though not *all*! The *few* are entitled to *every thing*, the *many* alas! to *nothing*!

The poem is a celebration of 'IMMORTAL LIBERTY!' which is allegorised as a woman who comes to Britain. Merry's phrase, 'and binding reason in a chain of fears' sounds like Blake, as does his general procedure of creating myth and allegory out of contemporary events. He attacks despotism, inequality and subjection, and celebrates equality and revolution to overturn corruption, hoping for reform in Britain along the lines of the French example, 'in emulous delight', but anticipating resistance from the

British government:

> Alas! destructive of the rising joy,
> Still Europe bleeds, and maniacs will destroy.

A footnote explains, 'By Kings, is here only meant that species of oppressive authority which knows neither humanity nor restraint'. *The Laurel of Liberty* ends on a note of quiet optimism, hoping that 'Benignity's soft gale' will prevail.

'Ode for the fourteenth of July, 1791, the day consecrated to freedom' (1791), celebrating Bastille Day and the French Revolution in 1789, is a poem so central to the theme of this book, and so little reproduced or anthologised, that it deserves lengthy quotation. It begins with an anti-invocation banishing the bondage of tyranny:

> A myrtle wreath upon the fetter'd mind,
> And force degrading Prejudice to please.
> But hence – far hence be themes like these,
> Tyrannic infants, fools of state,
> And such as Ignorance deem'd the great,
> Have now their tinsel lustre lost.

Liberty and equality become the poem's themes:

> Have Kings and Nobles Rights alone?
> Is this prolific globe their own?
> And is the mingled mass beside,
> Form'd as the creature of their pride?
> Not so, – the dire deception o'er,
> Mankind can now mankind adore;
> Nor bauble crowns, nor regal toys,
> Shall cheat them of their natural joys,
> Nor shall they more, by artifice subdued,
> Kiss the Oppressor's rod, 'A swinish Multitude.'

The 'Health of Humankind' is toasted, as revolutionary freedom is instated:

> The Angel Freedom, from celestial wing,
> O'er ev'ry clime new bliss shall fling,
> Dissolve the mental frost that reigns
> On silent Lapland's dark domains;
> Cheer the black Natives of the burning zone,
> And bid to All the Rights of All be known:
> Till from his height each Despot shall be hurl'd,
> And Reason bear aloft the Fasces of the World.

The chains of hereditary privilege usurped by 'the titled Sons of Earth' are condemned in favour of equality:

> And has not kind, impartial Heav'n,
> To ev'ry rank an equal feeling giv'n?
> Virtue alone should vice subdue,
> Nor are the Many baser than the Few.

'Justice and Benevolence' are hailed as 'the common share':

> And has not kind, impartial Heav'n,
> To ev'ry rank an equal feeling giv'n?
> Virtue alone should vice subdue,
> Nor are the Many baser than the Few.

Merry's poem ends with a call to freedom which amounts in Britain to a call to revolution:

> Then Britons think, that, chains to bear,
> Is but to linger in despair;
> Think on the blood your fathers shed,
> And venerate the mighty dead:
> Or should contending Factions e'er presume,
> By smiles, or frowns, to fix your doom,
> Assert the hallow'd Rights which Nature gave,
> And let your last, best vow be Freedom or the Grave.
>   CHORUS.
> Assert the hallow'd Rights which Nature gave,
> And let your last, best vow be Freedom or the Grave.
>   THE END.

Such a poem, published in 1791, is a far cry from the ineffectual poetry of sensibility now associated with the Della Cruscan movement, and it is representative of other poems by Merry and of his general political stance. His long poem, *The Pains of Memory*, written later in 1796 when some zealous radicals had retreated from their earlier position, indicates that Merry is still prepared to use 'meek philosophy' and 'sympathetic tears' to support natural rights, even as he nostalgically sees the possibility of their victory slipping away:

> And from the faded promises of youth
> Retain the love of liberty and truth.

The poem recalls Goldsmith's 'The Deserted Village' in its tone of painful recollection, youthful hopes disappointed, but hard-won ideals still in place.

Once again, in poetry as in fiction, 'Benevolence', sympathy, sensibility are as much political as emotional qualities. 'Pity' for Merry is a political projection: in the early *Diversity: A Poem* (1788) he glosses in a footnote, 'Pity' ('* i.e. Active pity') is a response to 'the pressure of a World's offence'. Merry, with his adherence to the language of sensibility, the morality of benevolence, and his political commitment to natural rights, is centrally important in stitching eighteenth-century forms into the revolutionary demand for natural rights in the 1790s.

Sentimentality and romanticism

As McGann intimates, all the romantics, as part of their central purpose, resorted to the affective didacticism of sentimental literature from time to time, as it suited their purposes. Blake's *Songs* drew as much from this genre as its related form, children's poetry. The respectively 'innocent' and 'experienced' versions of 'The Chimney Sweeper' and 'Holy Thursday', and poems like 'London', 'The Little Vagabond', 'The Little Girl Lost' and 'The Little Girl Found' draw on the repertoire of benevolent feelings stirred by the sight of innocent children being exploited or placed in jeopardy, in order to attack institutions like the church. Others about adolescent sexuality and about jealousy such as 'The Sick Rose', 'My Pretty Rose-tree', 'Never seek to tell thy love', 'The Garden of Love' and 'Ah! Sun-flower' employ the psychological strategies of feeling used by novelists, in order to enforce moral points about the inhibiting power of adult restrictions motivated by jealousy and bitterness. At heart, these are lyrics which are both sympathetic in its eighteenth century meaning and didactic, and they require and teach an empathy which Blake sometimes makes explicit:

> Can I see another's woe,
> And not be in sorrow too?
> Can I see another's grief,
> And not seek for relief?

> And can He who smiles on all
> Hear the wren with sorrows small,
> Hear the small bird's grief and care,
> Hear the woes that infants bear,

> And not sit beside the next,
> Pouring pity in their breast;
> And not sit the cradle near,
> Weeping tear on infant's tear;

> And not sit both night and day,
> Wiping all our tears away?

> O, no! never can it be!
> Never, never can it be!
>
> He doth give His joy to all;
> He becomes an infant small;
> He becomes a man of woe;
> He doth feel the sorrow too.

The capitalised 'He' is not only God in his least vengeful and most non-conformist roles, but also the familiar literary figure, the sentimental man driven by benevolent feelings of respect for the natural rights of children as representatives of all humanity. Even Coleridge, for all his public disavowals of the earlier movement, builds its central values of community, the awakened conscience and the healing power of sympathy with all living creatures into poems as diverse as 'The Ancient Mariner' and 'This lime tree bower my prison'. In fact barely a poem of his escapes a substratum of thought which yearns for connectedness through mutual benevolence. The satires on romanticism by Peacock could not have been written in the way they were, unless romantic writers still exhibited a substantial legacy from sentimentalism.

Despite the poetic revolution he helped to usher in, Wordsworth carried over many traces from sentimental literature.[66] Many of his early narrative poems and 'lyrical ballads' invite and even require well practised and familiar readers' responses. Here is the denouement to 'Peter Bell', composed in 1798:

> Beside the Woman Peter stands;
> His heart is opening more and more;
> A holy sense pervades his mind;
> He feels what he for human-kind
> Has never felt before.
>
> At length, by Peter's arm sustained,
> The Woman rises from the ground–
> 'Oh mercy! something must be done,
> My little Rachel, you must run,
> Some willing neighbour must be found.
>
> 'Make haste – my little Rachel – do,
> The first you meet with – bid him come,
> Ask him to lend his horse to-night,
> And this good Man whom heavens requite,
> Will help to bring the body home.'
>
> Away goes Rachel weeping loud: –
> An infant, waked by her distress,

Makes in the house a piteous cry;
And Peter hears the Mother sigh,
'Seven are they, and all fatherless!'

And now is Peter taught to feel
That man's heart is a holy thing;
And Nature, through a world of death,
Breathes into him a second breath,
More searching than the breath of spring.

...

And Peter Bell, who, till that night,
Had been the wildest of his clan,
Forsook his crimes, renounced his folly,
And, after ten months' melancholy,
Became a good and honest man.[67]

No matter how unmistakably 'Wordsworthian' this is, it reveals clear connections with the kind of literature we have been analysing: the tableau of the woman weeping over the corpse clearly intended to affect the reader as powerfully as it affects Peter Bell, the melodramatic situation, the conversion of Peter into one who can 'feel That man's heart is a holy thing', his emotions based on sudden and profound sympathy with other human beings, the social connectedness, and the 'improving' didacticism signalled in the last stanza. More generally he presents his female characters and 'solitaries' as products of nature but they are just as recognisably products of eighteenth century literature, set up to evoke feelings of social responsibility and benevolence which leads to 'charity'. And although his poetry is presented as almost documentary in its charting of 'the growth of the poet's mind' and of the relationship between the external world and the imagination, we can still detect a solid residue of the philosophies of Shaftesbury and Hutcheson, and a didacticism that lies close to the surface. 'Nutting' (composed 1798–99) is on one level a statement of pantheism and a depiction of the solitary poet's violation of nature, but on another level its initial language of 'voluptuous' emotions and the dismay of its climax pitches it as a poem with a moral. Nor is the influence limited to Wordsworth's early poems. 'Humanity', composed in 1829, presents human justice as a reflection of the kind of 'eternal laws' that had marked the rhetoric of natural law:

Not from his fellows only man may learn
Rights to compare and duties to discern!

On this basis the poet condemns slavery which, although formally banned in England lives on in the circumstances of those who 'Groan underneath a weight of slavish toil', sacrificing their health for somebody else's wealth.

Whether we claim as primary influences Wordsworth's politicization in the French Revolution or his communion with nature, there is a direct line leading from Shaftesbury and Goldsmith to such sentiments. And just as perceptibly the idea of an original innocence in 'Intimations of Immortality' (composed 1802–06) is an implicit rebuke to the philosophy of Hobbes and an argument that evil is learned as a response to institutional forces and experiences that lead us away from innate goodness, 'high instincts'. The line of influence includes Mackenzie and his like. The child, even the youth, is 'Nature's priest', but as he grows through the 'endless imitation' of the world around him, he also grows away from the original contact with 'the eternal deep' into a dulled maturity. However, the poem is optimistic insofar as it envisages that this contact is never quite lost and can be reconnected by 'the philosophic mind', 'Thanks to the human heart by which we live, Thanks to its tenderness, its joys and fears ...'. The unstated but everpresent model is that of natural law which lies within the human heart, and can be schooled into moral judgment by the sympathy with suffering that is the constant didactic refrain in literature of benevolence:

> Though nothing can bring back the hour
> Of splendour in the grass, of glory in the flower;
> We will grieve not, rather find
> Strength in what remains behind;
> In the primal sympathy
> Which having been must ever be;
> In the soothing thoughts that spring
> Out of human suffering.

If literature of natural rights in the 1790s had its origins in eighteenth-century sentimental benevolence, we find a later and unexpected legacy as well amongst the younger romantics. Almost the full force of benevolent literature using the aesthetics of sensibility, resurfaced with the second generation of romantics. Leigh Hunt, the contemporary of Keats who was (and still is) blamed for the young poet's lush style which owed something to the sentimental movement, was an avowed political radical and republican. William Hazlitt, who was to become one of Keats's wider circle, first set himself the task, at the age of 14 in Hackney College, of writing 'a system of political rights and general jurisprudence', a project which eventually led to his first published work, *An Essay on the Principles of Human Action: Being an Argument in favour of the Natural Disinterestedness of the Human Mind* (1805, printed anonymously). Its title immediately places Hazlitt among the thinkers who appeared earlier in this book, and the first sentence places his book squarely in the sentimental or benevolent line and the tradition of Adam Smith:

> It is the design of the following Essay to shew that the human mind is
> naturally disinterested, or that it is naturally interested in the welfare of

others in the same way, and from the same direct motives, by which we are impelled to the pursuit of our own interest.[68]

Unlike some of the earlier writers, however, Hazlitt is quite aware of the danger of judging simply by benevolent actions, saying that they may spring from self-interest. Equally, disinterestedness is not *'indifference'*.[69] He is equally careful to stress that there is no abstract, primary concept that people work from, 'either of an original principle of general comprehensive benevolence, or of general and comprehensive self-love'.[70] His whole philosophy is rooted in particularity, and his notion of benevolence is situational, springing from 'many actual pleasures and pains'. It is connected with personal experience and memory: 'a sentiment of general benevolence can only arise from an habitual cultivation of the natural disposition of the mind to sympathies with the feelings of others by constantly taking an interest in those which we know, and imagining others that we do not know'. The 'other feeling of abstract self-interest' leads to 'a long narrowing of the mind to our own particular feelings and interest, a phrase which Hazlitt came to apply to the retreat from radicalism he saw in Wordsworth and Coleridge. The imagination is central to the development (Keats's "schooling") of the benevolent heart, since it is the means by which we are stirred and motivated to moral action 'by the prospect of future good or evil.'[71] Hazlitt's approach was to be significant to his contemporaries, the younger romantics, such as Keats, who directly had Hazlitt in mind in formulating his own distinction between 'negative capability' and 'the egotistical sublime' and his thoughts on the 'disinterestedness' of Socrates, Jesus and Shakespeare; and it led also to Shelley's eloquent statement of the same position:

> The great secret of morals is love; or a going out of our own nature, and an identification of ourselves with the beautiful which exists in thought, action, or person, not our own. A man, to be greatly good, must imagine intensely and comprehensively, he must put himself in the place of another and of many others; the pains and pleasures of his species must become his own. the great instrument of moral good is the imagination; and poetry administers to the effect by acting upon the cause. Poetry strengthens the faculty which is the organ of the moral nature of man, in the same manner as exercise strengthens a limb. (*Defence of Poetry*)

Shelley's application of the idea of benevolence to poetry is his own, but the language he uses is so similar to Hazlitt's phrases that it sounds like an echo. His poems, such as 'The Sensitive Plant' and the general tenor of *Prometheus Unbound*, exemplify Shelley's debt to benevolent sentimentality, as redefined for his age by Hazlitt. In fact, so significant for at least Keats and Shelley is Hazlitt's 'Argument in defence of the Natural Disinterestedness of the Human Mind', developing as it does eighteenth century benevolence and sentimentalism, that it is surprising its influence has not been generally acknowledged or studied.

The assumption of disinterested, moral benevolence lies behind almost all Hazlitt was to write thereafter, whether in fulminating against corrupt governments and the monarchy, praising the great actors of his day, analysing the ventriloquial skills in character creation of Shakespeare, or the representational powers of the old painting masters, tracing the rise and fall of Napoleon, or just whimsically reminiscing or ruminating on life and books. On the many occasions when he was to praise Shakespeare for being 'naturally disinterested', he did not mean that Shakespeare maintains a poetic stance of non-aligned neutrality, the 'aloofness' described by Coleridge, but that he mirrors a philosophy that humanity is actively benevolent, altruistic and sympathetic rather than passively selfish and self-seeking.[72] It is as if the dramatic characters have a 'natural right' to exist which is just as inalienable as a living human being's. The equation Hazlitt draws between disinterestedness and self-interest reflects the Christian 'golden rule', and also echoes Cumberland's fusion of benevolence and utilitarianism. Hazlitt leaves no evidence that he had read Cumberland's book, but in the *Essay* he refers to its legatees, Adam Smith's *Theory of Moral Sentiments* (1759) and others such as James Mackintosh's 'On the Law of Nature and Nations' (lectures delivered in 1799) and Rousseau's *The Essay on the Inequality of Mankind* (1755). He was to write on the same theme in 'Self-Love and Benevolence' published in *The Spirit of the Age* and 'On Good-Nature' in *The Round Table* where, drawing directly on Shaftesbury's writing, he points out that benevolence is not a superficial appearance of 'good nature' which 'costs nothing' and can hide a mean-minded and selfish attitude, but an attachment to justice and 'a passion for truth' which can be hidden beneath the 'disagreeable' personality of the 'good hater' (with himself in mind):

> If the truth were known, the most disagreeable people are the most amiable. They are the only persons who feel an interest in what does not concern them. They have as much regard for others as they have for themselves. They have as many vexations and causes of complaints as there are in the world. They are general righters of wrongs, and redressers of grievances. They not only are annoyed by what they can help, by an act of inhumanity done in the next street, or in a neighbouring country by their own countrymen ... but a piece of injustice done three thousand years ago touches them to the quick. They have an unfortunate attachment to a set of abstract phrases, such as *liberty, truth, justice, humanity, honour*, which are continually abused by knaves, and misunderstood by fools, and they can hardly contain themselves for spleen ... They have a fellow-feeling with all that has been done, said, or thought.[73]

So prevalent is the legacy of sentimentality with its underpinning of natural benevolence in the poems and letters of John Keats, that it is surprising it has received so little critical attention.[74] Keats himself was to pick up the word 'disinterestedness' from Hazlitt[75] and to develop his ideas independently, but behind both romantics lay thinkers like Cumberland, Shaftesbury, Hutcheson, as well as the spirit of Rousseau. In the poetry of Keats the elements of what Christopher Ricks singles out for critical attention as 'embarrassment' are often relics of fullblown sentimentalism.[76] The ease with which Tory critics attacked his first volumes of poetry was almost invited, if not entirely anticipated, as much by Keats's revival of the sentimental style as by his political affiliations with the *Examiner* circle – the two, in fact, ran together.

'Isabella; Or The Pot of Basil' and 'The Eve of St Agnes' are narratives which have affinities with earlier sentimental literature. The repressive family context, the necessary secretiveness of lovers, the female victim, may well be perennial romance themes, but their particular fusing mark these poems' legacy from novels like Charlotte Smith's *The Old Manor House* (1793) as well as the gothic works of Ann Radcliff. Keats worried that 'Isabella' was 'too smokeable ... too much inexperience of life, and simplicity of knowledge in it – A weak-sided Poem ... There are very few would look to the reality'.[77] He feared it would be laughed at. While it may not be easy to pinpoint precisely what he meant, the general impression is that he was worried about its closeness to the outdated sentimental movement, since these are the negative qualities of the genre ridiculed by critics of Keats's time. However, there are reasons to think Keats has intellectually understood a level of contradiction within the genre of sentimental benevolence that he is drawing on, and that he has not managed to resolve the two impulses of emotiveness and social justice. The latter is not integrated with the former. His curious phrase is 'There are very few would look to the reality', which might almost mean 'realism', or at least a political purpose behind the poem. One aspect of 'the reality' in the fullest sense is the startling condemnation of slavery and capitalism which, if we did not detect more generally the generic influence of didactic benevolence which fuelled works against aristocratic 'pleasure-domes' and the slave trade, would seem to be hardly part of the same poem.

14
With her two brothers, this fair lady dwelt,
  Enriched from ancestral merchandize,
And for them many a weary hand did swelt
  In torched mines and noisy factories,
And many once proud-quiver'd loins did melt
  In blood from stinging whip; – with hollow eyes
Many all day in dazzling river stood,
  To take the rich-ored driftings of the flood.

15
For them the Ceylon diver held his breath,
  And went all naked to the hungry shark;

For them his ears gush'd blood; for them in death
The seal on the cold ice with piteous bark
Lay full of darts; for them alone did seethe
A thousand men in troubles wide and dark;
Half-ignorant, they turned an easy wheel,
That set sharp racks at work, to pinch and peel.

16

Why were they proud? Because their marble founts
Gushed with more pride than do a wretch's tears? –
Why were they proud? Because fair orange-mounts
Were of more soft ascent than lazar stairs? –
Why were they proud? Because red-lin'd accounts
Were richer than the songs of Grecian years, –
Why were they proud? again we ask aloud,
Why in the name of Glory were they proud?[78]

The most apt reference is to Goldsmith's general attitude towards wealth, as for example, in this passage from 'The Traveller':

Laws grind the poor and rich men rule the law;
The wealth of climes, where savage nations roam,
Pillaged from slaves to purchase slaves at home;
Fear, pity, justice, indignation start,
Tear off reserve and bare my swelling heart;
Till half a patriot, half a coward grown,
I fly from petty tyrants to the throne.

...

Have we not seen, round Britain's peopled shore,
Her useful sons exchanged for useless ore?[79]

But where Goldsmith's didactic observations arise out of an essentially landscape poem, Keats's angry lines do not mesh with the romance fable. The links traced by Goldsmith between wealth and exploitation, commerce, empire and human slavery, are equally powerfully expressed in 'Isabella', but it might be objected that such sentiments are more appropriate in the context of a poem on foreign travel than in a romance. But they are in place, if the poem is intended not as a simple romance, but as a work in the benevolent sentimental genre, for they point to a concern of the poem with issues of natural rights. The link with the rest is the statement that Isabella herself is, like her brothers, 'Enriched from ancestral merchandize', and living off the proceeds of exploitation and financial extortion. However innocent and beautiful, she is trapped by her situation, and one could explain her imprisonment ultimately by reference to the alienating and corrupting nature of the accumulation of wealth. Timon of Athens may respond in a different way, but the obduracy he finds in others is that faced by Isabella and Lorenzo who, significantly, is not a suitable marriage-partner for her because of his lack of wealth,

> When 'twas their plan to coax her by degrees
> To some high noble and his olive-trees. (XXI)

Both Isabella and her lover are the victims (like the seals and the 'hunted hare' in Stanza 18) of 'money-bags' and the commercial world of merchants who are accustomed to treat people as commodities. Such an approach to the poem might explain the problems of tone created by the strange co-presence of beauty and ugliness, the diseased self-indulgence of the heroine, the omnipresent feeling of corruption and decadence in a story of essentially innocent love. It would explain the easily missed 'reality' of a didactic element which clearly reproves Isabella for her unnaturally prolonged and somewhat gruesome devotion to 'Selfishness, Love's cousin' (XXXI) leading her to neglect the world around her:

> And she forgot the stars, the moon, and sun,
> And she forgot the blue above the trees,
> And she forgot the dells where waters run,
> And she forgot the chilly autumn breeze;
> She had no knowledge when the day was done,
> And the new morn she saw not, but in peace
> Hung over her sweet basil evermore,
> And moistened it with tears unto the core. (LIII)

The tough-minded note that Keats injects into his 'smokeable' narrative is the one given him by Hazlitt, that self-destruction is a result of turning away for disinterestedness, that benevolence is also a true regard for one's own welfare. The same 'moral' runs through *Endymion*, although 'Isabella' marks a more decisive stance by Keats in rejecting the dream-lover, than the earlier poem's easy denouement where the moon and the Indian maid, each dream and reality symbols, merge. Unlike Endymion, Isabella is left in the amber suspension of her tears, 'And so she pined, and so she died forlorn'. The benevolent undercurrent uses her simultaneously to condemn the 'cruelty' (LXIII) of her capitalist brothers but also to indicate a more bracing suggestion that she has been culpable in her emotional incarceration. In Charlotte Smith's *The Old Manor House* a similar suggestion guides the plot, as the heroine spends the first half of the novel trapped not only in a house but by her love, and the second half liberates her into a world of active, 'disinterested' political involvement. 'The Eve of St Agnes' almost forcibly ejects Madeline from the seedy, deathly and corrupt familial home out into the wide world, just as Lycius in 'Lamia' must be shown the delusiveness of his serpentine love-object by the brutal but necessary intervention of his philosophical tutor. These poems not only reflect sentimental benevolence, but also develop the genre, as one would hope so long after its heyday, into a less illusioned territory. If something like this analysis is what Keats meant in saying 'There are very few would look to the reality', he was right, at least in predicting contemporary reactions which intuitively detected the barb but interpreted it as 'offensive' and unnecessary to the poem:

> There are some stanzas introduced into his delicious tale of 'Isabel – poor simple Isabel', in this volume, which, we think, dreadfully mar the musical tenderness of its general strain. They are no better than extravagant schoolboy vituperation of trade and traders; just as if lovers did not trade, – and that, often in stolen goods – or had in general any higher object than a barter of enjoyment! These stanzas in Mr. Keats's poem, when contrasted with the larger philosophy of Boccaccio, and his more genial spirit, as exemplified with reference to the very circumstances in question, are additionally offensive[80]

The anonymous reviewer has got it right and wrong at the same time.

Despite its rally amongst the later romantics, the days of benevolent sentimentality as a serious literary and moral force were numbered by 1790. Its eighteenth-century trappings of ready tears and trembling hearts made it too easily ridiculed by friend and foe alike in the new political climate. Ever since 1789 the events surrounding the French Revolution and authoritarian responses by the English government rendered such a gently sociable and philanthropic movement ineffectual. The 1790s saw it condemned by anti-Jacobins for its radical associations, distanced by Jacobins themselves like Godwin and Wollstonecraft for its failure to engage directly in real political struggles for rights, and simply ignored by the vast majority of the reading public who had sustained it in its heyday of the 1760s and '70s, because it no longer addressed their economic concerns at the inception of a new and ruthless metropolitan and industrial monopoly.[81] Blake saw 'pity' as an ineffectual hindrance to social change. By the 1790s, more assertive approaches were being used to advance in literary forms the struggle for natural rights. The time provided new models, in the works of Jean-Jacquues Rousseau and Thomas Paine.

3
Rights and Wrongs

Jean-Jacques Rousseau

Sentimental belief in the socially corrective power of benevolence gave way during the 1780s to a more urgent and polemical expression of natural rights. The subject of the rights (or wrongs) of man (and woman) came to be a powerful genre which dictated the terms in which political change were expressed by both commentators and creative writers. The essential bases of this form were established by the Genevan Jean-Jacques Rousseau, whose works came to be enormously influential in revolutionary France and in England. At the heart of his approach in a variety of fields is a belief in 'the natural goodness of Man', the phrase chosen by Arthur M. Melzer as the title for his book:

> By nature, man lacks a specific desire to harm others, and, even more important, he lacks all the needs, passions, and prejudices that now put his interests in essential and systematic conflict with others. He is naturally self-sufficient and content, and therefore strife with others is never intrinsically pleasant, it is rarely useful, and it troubles his inner repose.[1]

By glossing 'nature' in 'natural', and giving such a human face to natural law's 'reasonable man' with his innate predilection for doing good and avoiding evil, Rousseau opens up the terrain of natural rights in many different areas of application, and gives those who follow, a powerful tool of analysis. Despite the tradition of natural law, such a belief in 'natural goodness' flouted the orthodox Christian Church's teachings on original sin, and thus drew its ire. Since Rousseau wrote novels as well as polemics, his influence readily asserted itself in English imaginative literature as well as political discourse.

Rousseau laid down his fundamental approach to the question of natural rights in his early work, *A Discourse on Inequality* (1754–55).[2] He wrote it for an essay competition announced by the Academy of Dijon which proposed the subject 'What is the origin of inequality among men, and is it authorised by Natural Law?' The epigraph from Aristotle's *Politics* (I.v.1254a) announces his orientation: 'It is not in depraved beings, but in those who act in accordance with nature that we must seek what is natural.' Like other writers, Rousseau's chief target of antagonism is Hobbes. He mentions him by name (82) aligning himself with Hobbes's earlier refuters, Cumberland, Pufendorf, as well as Montesquieu, and explicitly rejects the idea that men in the state of nature are dominated by ' "need", "greed", "oppression", "desire" and "pride" '. These qualities Rousseau associates with 'civilized man' rather than 'savage man'. The latter is his own creation and has been canonised since Rousseau's writing as 'the noble savage', while the notion that civilisation (and growing away from childhood) is what corrupts, was very influential over romantics like Wordsworth and Blake. Human society, rather than humans in a natural state, displays 'the violence of powerful men and the oppression of the weak', and creates the 'shifting sands' of riches and poverty which account for most human misery (71). Rousseau respects Hobbes's reasoning but rejects his conclusions:

> Hobbes saw very clearly the defects of all modern definitions of natural right, but the conclusions he drew from his own definition show that his own concept of natural right is equally defective. (98)

Rousseau argues that 'original man' shares with animals the instinct for survival, but he has the added advantage of 'freewill'. This is equivalent to natural law's reason, although Rousseau rejects the enlightenment version of reason as 'civilised', which specifically motivates him towards 'self-improvement' (88) under the pressure of needs such as pain and hunger. Language was born from the common interests shared in the acts of survival and self-improvement. The mother teaches her child language in order to express personal needs: 'it is the child who has all his needs to express and hence has more things to say to his mother than she has to say to him' (93). Given the need for self-preservation, neither killing, self-killing, nor dwelling on miseries are in the mental horizons of man in the original state. The opposite occurs when, in a phrase whose spirit resounds through all romantic writers, Rousseau argues that just as 'pity becomes all the more intense as the perceiving animal identifies itself more intimately with this suffering animal' so in man, the 'feeling that puts us in the place of the sufferer' (100–1) becomes an 'obscure but strong' feeling in savage man, 'but weak in civilized man'.

> It is therefore very certain that pity is a natural sentiment which, by moderating in each individual the activity of self-love, contributes to the mutual preservation of the whole species. It is pity which carries us without reflection to the aid of those we see suffering; it is pity which in the state of nature takes the place of laws, morals and virtue. (101)

In this passage, and its longer, eloquent context, Rousseau is grafting the literary idea of benevolent sensibility onto philosophical natural law reasoning, and from there preparing the ground for political change. Natural rights stem from a recognition by the sympathetic and compassionate spectator that people have been placed in 'civilized' misery which is neither natural nor justifiable.

In Part Two of the *Discourse on Inequality*, Rousseau pinpoints as the source of civilized misery 'the bonds of servitude' (106) created through the unequal distribution of wealth and privileges. His position is analogous to that of Raphael Hythlodaeus in Thomas More's *Utopia*.

> The first man who, having enclosed a piece of land, thought of saying 'This is mine' and found people simple enough to believe him, was the true founder of civil society. How many crimes, wars, murders; how much misery and horror the human race would have been spared if someone had pulled up the stakes and filled in the ditch and cried out to his fellow men: 'Beware of listening to this imposter. You are lost if you forget that the fruits of the earth belong to everyone and that the earth itself belongs to no one!'[3] (109)

He quotes Locke's epigram: 'Where there is no property, there is no injury' (115), an anticipation of Proudhon's 'Property is theft'. Once again Rousseau argues from the natural state, where man lives by instinct and sensation doing everything that ensures self-preservation, then into early social bonding where 'mutual commitments' are acknowledged, once again for the species' survival, through the 'mutual affections' satisfied in the smaller unit of the loving family. Interestingly for a writer, Rousseau locates the beginning of the end in the increasing sophistication of speech and language. At first used as an instrument of benign communication, it came to express the negative aspect of social interdependence – dependence itself, with its necessary implication of superior and inferior, 'mine' and 'thine', and corrosive distinctions between people: in a word, inequality. From the development to the cultivation of land to the beginnings of industry, distinctions hardened into 'master' and 'slave', and they came to operate in all spheres of life. Summarising Grotius, he asserts that division of the earth had produced a new sort of right: that is to say, the right to property different from the one derived from natural law' (118). A set of 'bogus rights' based on the 'right' to property and privilege replaced 'natural right' based on the right to live, because the latter was 'disadvantageous' to the rich. In his wonderful phrase, Rousseau summarises the process: 'All ran towards their chains believing that they were securing their liberty.' Rousseau relentlessly traces 'the progress of inequality' through the establishment of the body politic, the assertion of positive law based on property rights over natural law, loss of human bonding through feelings of pity, the rise of competitive nation states, massacres, wars fought as legitimised atrocities, and so on in an ever descending spiral towards self-destructiveness and away from the 'primitive' assumption of the right and instinct to self-preservation.

> it is manifestly contrary to the law of nature, however defined, that a child should govern an old man, that an imbecile should lead a wise man, and that a handful of people should gorge themselves with superfluities while the hungry multitude goes in want of necessities. (137)

Rousseau's *A Discourse on Inequality*, for all its eloquent power, could have gathered dust as the work of a bookish and unworldly scholar pursuing an argument as an academic exercise. Antagonists could say that the construction of primitive man living according to peaceful natural law does not reflect contemporary realities closely enough to carry force. But one can also see the glimmerings of a current that would gather swell both in his own writings and in the ideas of those around him: the description of the savage inequalities and denials of natural rights that characterise savage but 'civilised' society, was all too accurate to contemporary reality. It was this recognition that eventually was to light the fire of revolution in Europe and America, and to make Rousseau's name synonymous with violent social upheaval and change. Seven years later, two of his books, *The Social Contract* and *Émile*, which said little more in essence than the *Discourse*, were publicly burned in his native Geneva, and a warrant for his arrest was issued.

The importance of *The Social Contract* lay in the timeliness of its message. In a Europe whose ruling classes had in all countries implacably set themselves against any concession to 'the will of the people', Rousseau gave eloquent expression to the model of government which saw the body politic as an act of association between all its members, each of whom deserved the right to have their person and goods defended by the collective force of all. Echoing Locke, Rousseau argued that this could be achieved by the notion of a social contract, where all agreed to unite under the terms of a contract, by which all take on reciprocal commitments to guarantee the rights to others, which they themselves expect to be extended to them. In terms of the development of civil society, justice as a rule of conduct is raised above instinct, 'duty has taken the place of physical impulse, and right that of desire'.[4]

> Suppose we draw up a balance sheet, so that the losses and gains may be readily compared. What man loses by the social contract is his natural liberty and the absolute right to anything that tempts him and that he can take; what he gains by the social contract is civil liberty and the legal right of property in what he possesses ... We might also add that man acquires with civil society, moral freedom, which alone makes man the master of himself; for to be governed by appetite alone is slavery. (65)

In following through the reasoning to political organisation, Rousseau creates the concept of 'the general will' which guarantees certain freedoms while limiting other freedoms. The consent of the people becomes paramount in defining sovereignty in the state, which in turn confers the capacity to make laws which are equally binding on all. While such claims were like a bombshell in the world of eighteenth-century systems of government, they have now become so familiar that they are virtually taken for granted in western society. Rousseau's most important contribution may not have been to political theory, since all his important concepts were available already, for example in the works of Locke, but rather in his incentive to political action which led eventually to what we now accept as democracy. However, *The Social Contract* did this work so successfully that almost every other aspect of the book can now be seen as dated and flawed.

Even at the time, writers like Mary Wollstonecraft noticed that the theory as presented did not include women amongst the 'general will' (although, to be fair, one could say that the *theory* itself held the potential for inclusion). Rousseau's constant reference to the family as the prototype of political organisation leaves intact a structure which is built on patriarchal power, thus undermining his rejection of the doctrine of 'might is right' in civil society – might seems all right if it is exercised by a benign father or a benign king. Rousseau systematically canvasses different systems of government which satisfy his own criteria for consensus, but work so much within the context available to him that many of these systems seem to us to be intrinsically flawed with a prior inequality. He seems happiest, paradoxically, with monarchy that makes concessions, rather than with a genuine republic, and indeed his use of the word 'republic', which he emphasises and repeats over and over again, seems now to be rather tame. He makes some references to the commonality of land, but then focuses his attention not on opening up a more equal division, as we would expect from the writer of *A Discourse on Inequality*, but rather on how to entrench the individuality and right to ownership which one would think threatens the very notion of the general will. Nowadays, as one reads through *The Social Contract* and its commentators, one feels unease and reservations about the generally conservative caste of mind behind the presentation of a generally radical programme. This peculiar combination might well be close to the mark: for example, as we read Rousseau's more personal work, *The Confessions*, it is hard to see the origins of a genuine social or political radical. He seems to have a privileged outlook and addiction to at least one individual pursuit – male sexual satisfaction at the expense of female autonomy – but is sufficiently an eccentric outsider and brilliant writer to express in language the aspirations of those denied privileges. To some extent, everybody reads what they are predisposed to find in books, and Rousseau's *Social Contract* at least is roomy enough to galvanise radical political instincts, while the parts of the book which lack this drive fade into the background of consciousness. It would probably surprise Rousseau himself, who reserved his most orderly and careful reasoning for *The Social Contract*, that at least to this reader the earlier *Discourse on Inequality* has the more genuinely radical capacity to unsettle assumptions and to continue to challenge political theory with the force of, for example, More's *Utopia*.

There is one underlying strength to *The Social Contract* which must have redeemed its limitations and allowed for its mass appeal. This stems more from the imaginative writer's passion rather than the cool analysis of the would-be political analyst. It is the very powerful and recurrent revulsion from the condition of slavery, a subliminal message which sometimes is consciously expressed, which allows anybody deprived of social or political rights to endorse the overall idea of the social contract itself. Most well-meaning people can find their emotions engaged on the specific issue of the inhumanity of slavery, and on the more general objections to the bully who relies on 'The Right of the Strongest' (title to chapter 3), and certainly poets have traditionally been acutely sensitive on these scores. Rousseau argues that 'might does not make right', and that the duty of obedience is owed only to legitimate powers. Any powers that rely on might are not legitimate: 'If I am held up by a robber at the edge of a wood, force compels me to hand over my purse. But if I could somehow contrive to keep the purse from him, would I still be obliged to surrender it? After all, the pistol in the robber's hand is undoubtedly a *power*' (53). The bond of slavery is taken as the paradigm for all relationships of subjection built upon the presumed right of might, since the idea of trading one's own body and freedom for no return except a spurious and delusory kind of 'tranquillity' is shown to be no fair trade since it has no reciprocal covenant. The despot may offer civil tranquillity but the cost is lack of freedom for his subjects: 'There is peace in dungeons, but is that enough to make dungeons desirable?' We see the real power of Rousseau's writing in these casually anecdotal but telling examples. It is the power of metaphor. He assumes that people are 'born free' and simply cannot give away their liberty irrevocably and unconditionally. 'To renounce freedom is to renounce one's humanity, one's rights as a man and equally one's duties. There is no possible *quid pro quo* for one who renounces everything; indeed such renunciation is contrary to man's very nature (55). Even at times of extremity, in war for example, surrender to the conqueror does not give the conqueror the right to take away fundamental freedom simply in return for sparing life, since this argument for enslavement depends on nothing more than power and 'is an argument trapped in a vicious circle'. Only at this point in his argument does Rousseau actually use the example of the slave, in a ringing passage:

> Even if we assumed that this terrible right of massacre did exist, then slaves of war, or a conquered people, would be under no obligation to

obey their master any further than they were forced to do so. By taking an equivalent of his victim's life, the victor shows him no favour; instead of destroying him unprofitably, he destroys him by exploiting him ... An agreement has assuredly been made, but that agreement, far from ending the state of war, presupposes its continuation ... The words 'slavery' and 'right' are contradictory, they cancel each other out. (57–8)

This argument takes only a couple of pages to advance, but so strong is its appeal to feelings of moral indignation that in many ways it outweighs the rest of the sober reasoning in *The Social Contract*, providing the fuel of conscience that established in the popular mind the sanctity of natural rights. Whatever they thought of Rousseau's suggestions for political organisation in the state, it was this sentiment that could inspire writers and revolutionaries, giving point and substance through metaphorical intensity to the most memorable sentence in the book, the very first in Chapter 1, 'Man was born free, and he is everywhere in chains'.

Rousseau is the first we shall encounter in this book of a group of writers who present a theory in a discursively philosophical fashion and also write works of the imagination designed to illustrate and develop the theory. Others appear in a later chapter. *Émile* (1762), however, has only the slightest narrative structure to qualify it as a novel. It is like a pedagogical manual of the best way to educate a child up to manhood, following the process as a fiction. We see Émile guided by the fatherly narrator through each stage, until by the end the child is considered mature enough to be introduced to the theory of the social contract based on the general will of the people. The drift of the educational programme is to be age-specific, to introduce lessons only when the child is ready for them, and if possible grounded in real situations that he encounters. At first, and for well on into his journey, the child is seen to be the product of nature that Rousseau had described as man in the natural state, governed by passions and desires which can be channelled into worthy pursuits. Without protection from the world, the narrator makes clear, the child would rapidly find his passions straying into undesirable actions, and the damage would be done for a lifetime and cannot be undone. Appeals to reason and conscience and the training of these faculties come very late in the process, just before (and as a necessary prelude to) Émile falling in love with his rather token female equivalent, Sophie. They are essential to the condition of full adulthood and to the capacity to make moral judgments. Once again, in words reminiscent of the sentimental novel, Rousseau locates the inception of a moral sense in 'the first stirrings of awakening sensibility in the heart of a young man',[5] and it operates through empathetic sympathy for the weak and suffering:

So pity is born, the first relative sentiment which touches the human heart according to the order of nature. To become sensitive and pitiful the child must know that he has fellow-creatures who suffer as he has suffered, who feel the pains he has felt, and others which he can form some idea of, being capable of feeling them himself. Indeed, how can we let ourselves be stirred by pity unless we go beyond ourselves, and identify ourselves with the suffering animal, by leaving, so to speak, our own nature and taking his. We only suffer so far as we suppose he suffers; the suffering is not ours but his. So no one becomes sensitive till his imagination is aroused and begins to carry him outside himself. (184)

In order 'to stimulate and nourish this growing sensibility, to direct it, and to follow its natural bent' we should remove circumstances that reinforce selfishness and vanity: 'that is to say, in other words, we should arouse in him kindness, goodness, pity, and beneficence, all the gentle and attractive passions which are naturally pleasing to man' (184). Through an understanding of the sufferings of the poor, the child is educated into the principle of equality. A respect for the natural rights of individuals follows almost without the need for conscious tuition. Eventually the educational programme reaches questions of politics and government, and Rousseau takes the opportunity to repeat his idea of the sovereignty of the 'general will' of the people through a 'social contract'. By this stage the process is complete, Émile is fully educated and is ready to marry Sophie. The book ends with the birth of his own child, allowing the whole cycle to be carried through again.

Thomas Paine *versus* Edmund Burke

Thomas Paine in his *Rights of Man* (1791–92) pays eloquent but reserved tribute to Rousseau:

> we find in the writings of Rousseau ... a loveliness of sentiment in favour of Liberty, that excites respect, and elevates the human faculties; but having raised this animation, they do not direct its operations, and leave the mind in love with an object, without describing the means of possessing it.[6]

What strikes us in the work of Paine is not 'loveliness of sentiment', but unyielding audacity and clear thinking. He wrote at a time when England was imposing its own version of 'the terror' in systematic persecution of people espousing all colours of radical views. He did not write on a general, abstractly pitched level like Rousseau about principles, but he named names, commented with ferocious specificity on particular contemporary events, and fearlessly took on the highest in the land. For this, and after playing his part in the American revolution and then supporting the French revolution, he narrowly escaped certain death by prosecution for sedition by removing himself to France, and for the rest of his life he was officially outlawed from England, and declared a wanted man. What lay beneath his willingness to take on powerful adversaries head-on may have been the fact that in different times he had been their friend and he saw himself as merely keeping up correspondence in the vain hope that he might bring people back to their senses. The main influences on Paine's thinking were the English Whig and republican tradition, stretching back to Algernon Sidney, dissenting Protestantism and especially Quakerism, with which he grew up, and natural law which, according to Gregory Claeys, has been 'gravely neglected' in all studies of Paine.[7] However, it is remarkable also how clear his mind was on central contemporary issues, so deeply had he assimilated the past. Not only was he straightforwardly in favour of the revolutions in America and France, and parliamentary representation in general, at a time when even radicals could be complicated, but he was also one of the first to proclaim, in his own first publication, that slavery violated natural rights and should be abolished. This latter would have been more familiar to him than many others because of his Quaker upbringing, but he was among the first to turn the issue into one of mass public debate. Even if he does not base his arguments on religion, Paine seems to have lived his life by the 'inner light' which is at the heart of Quaker beliefs.

His particular target in *Rights of Man* is Edmund Burke, and the book reads like an open letter which scathingly berates his former acquaintance for his inconsistencies, like a friend or pupil disappointed in the errant and treacherous behaviour of his turncoat teacher. Paine does accurately diagnose a particular weakness in Burke which must have been especially damaging. From his published writings, Burke emerges as like some of the figures in the English establishment during the late 1960s when various freedoms were proclaimed as loudly as in the 1790s: the type of aristocrat who is happy to be liberal and progressive so long as power remains firmly in the hands of his own class and concessions can be made as charity or magnanimity rather than as responses to demands. Before the events of 1789 in France steeled his will against revolution, he was a supporter of benevolent meliorism, a sentimentalist, no less. His *Enquiry into the Origin of our Ideas of the Sublime and Beautiful* (1757, 1759) stressed the affective nature of literature, and the primacy of sympathy in human psychology. When, 30 years later, a revolution took place in France based on principles of natural rights as the product of sympathy, Burke found that his benevolent views on literature did not extend to life.

Paine points out that Burke had come from a time when despotic government was unquestioned as a system, and individual opinions existed within it irrespective of personality: 'The despotic principles of the government were the same in both reigns, though the dispositions of the men were as remote as tyranny and benevolence' (71). However, he argues, the French revolution was 'generated in the rational contemplation of the rights of man, and distinguishing from the beginning between persons and principles' (71) so that no amount of 'benevolent thoughts' could excuse tacit support for a corrupt regime. Burke may use 'the language of a heart feeling as it ought to feel for the rights and happiness of the human race' in the service of aristocrats, while forgetting the victims of governments, 'whether sold into slavery, or tortured out of existence'. Burke's words against the revolution are said to draw on imagery that intends to produce 'through the weakness of sympathy, a weeping effect', but does not engage with facts: 'Mr Burke should recollect that he is writing History, and not *Plays*; and that his readers will expect truth, and not the spouting rant of high-toned exclamation' (72). In one of his most memorable phrases, Paine nails on Burke the accusation of using the language of sympathy for the wrong people, forgetting the real victims of despotic government: 'He pities the plumage, but forgets the dying bird' (73). He goes on: '[Burke's] hero or his heroine must be a tragedy-victim expiring in show, and not the real prisoner of misery, sliding into death in the silence of a dungeon' (73).

Even allowing for the exaggerations of polemical rhetoric, Paine has put his finger on a genuine inconsistency, not only in Burke but in the sentimental movement as a whole, before its transformation into the Jacobin novel in the 1790s. It could never become more than a vehicle for mild social criticism because its strategies of evoking sympathy could be deployed on behalf of anybody facing temporary tribulation instead of focusing so centrally on victims of injustice that the need for political change would be irresistible. Pity can be an impotent feeling beside social anger. For Burke himself, the French revolution was a critical test case of his fundamental principles, which in some ways was unfortunate for him as a writer. If he had been allowed to stay in the realms of fiction, under a benign authoritarian system, he could have remained loyal to an intellectual affinity with the Scottish enlightenment, a latterday McKenzie or even a milder version of Rousseau. His *A Vindication of Natural Society* (1756) pointed towards the philosophical territory occupied by Hume. The sheer factuality of bloody revolution, and Burke's position of some political authority within England, turned him away from these roots. In another sense, as Mary Wollstonecraft shrewdly (or mischievously) suggests, if Burke had lived in the quite different circumstances of pre-revolutionary France his temperamental tendency to passion and moral indignation might have galvanised in him revolutionary fervour:

> Reading your *Reflections* warily over, it has continually struck me, that had you been a Frenchman, you would have been, in spite of your respect for rank and antiquity, a violent revolutionist ... Your imagination would have taken fire.[8]

There may be some evidence for this view in light of the fact that despite his class interests Burke ironically supported the aims of independence behind the American revolution.

Burke's real concern is to stifle the demands for change in England which were becoming more strident and focused, for example, in the Revolution Society. He is contemptuous of these people who he implies are driven by petty envy because they themselves are not franchised and 'have not a single vote for a king amongst them, either individually or collectively'.[9] (Of course his logic refuses to acknowledge that this is exactly the point behind demands for change.) Burke's argument is summed up early and with cryptic force as he fulminates against Richard Price's *Discourse on the Love of our Country* (1789):

Lest the foundation of the king's exclusive legal title should pass for a mere rant of adulatory freedom, the political Divine proceeds dogmatically to assert, that by the principles of the Revolution the people of England have acquired three fundamental rights, all which, with him, compose one system and lie together in one short sentence; namely, that we have acquired a right

1. 'To choose our own governors.'
2. 'To cashier them for misconduct.'
3. 'To frame a government for ourselves.'

This new, and hitherto unheard-of bill of rights, though made in the name of the whole people, belongs to those gentlemen and their faction only. The body of the people of England have no share in it. They utterly disclaim it. They will resist the practical assertion of it with their lives and fortunes. They are bound to do so by the laws of their country, made at the time of that very Revolution, which is appealed to in favour of the fictitious rights claimed by the society which abuses its name. (99)

Paine was to have a merry time driving cart horses between the contradictory logic (why should Englishmen with no vote give up their lives to prevent them from ever having a vote?), but as a piece of political rhetoric Burke's prose is masterly. It contrasts the solid-sounding 'foundation of the king's exclusive legal title' with 'a mere rant of adulatory freedom', it satirises Price as 'the political Divine' who 'asserts dogmatically' rather than logically argues. The 'bill of rights' is set up to be self-evidently extreme, violent ('cashier') and self-interested, and supported only by the shabby-gentility of a few 'gentlemen' supported by a more sinister 'faction'. Burke then with crashing confidence speaks for the entire, reasonable population, the body of 'the people of England'. Lest there might be disquiet, he adds a clear threat of the sanction of 'the laws of their country' and cleverly attaches himself to the so-called 'Glorious Revolution' of 1688, which was held in reverence as at least a minimal step towards limited monarchy rather than autocracy. While espousing a deeply conservative attitude that nothing can ever change, Burke at the same time claims to be the true revolutionary. This position is maintained throughout the *Reflections*. The Declaration of Right in 1688 is claimed as the real bedrock of revolutionary thought in England, and it is a statement of '*principles*': 'In that most wise, sober, and considerate declaration, drawn up by great lawyers and great statesmen, and not by warm and inexperienced enthusiasts, not one word is said, nor one suggestion made, of a general right "to choose our own *governors*; to cashier them for misconduct; and to *form* a government for *ourselves*" ' (100). Even the italics are placed to highlight insubordination and irrational selfishness of the claims. He claims that the basis of government in England is not 'right', despite the use of the word in the Declaration of Right, but rather on rule of law and historical precedent: 'Government is not made in virtue of natural rights, which may and do exist in total independence of it' (150). It is pure arrogance, Burke argues, to change time-honoured traditions on the basis of natural rights, and to tie up in perpetuity future generations along the sectarian lines suggested by revolutionists. He speaks eloquently of the rights of the dead to dictate the present, and of the rights of the unborn to inherit the world of the dead.

Burke's argument is advanced along familiar Hobbesian lines. He establishes the need for supreme authority in the state, vested in a monarch, in order to guarantee a secure and harmonious state. He is all in favour of those 'people of England' who fight to resist being given the freedom of voting, but for the unwittingly paradoxical reason that he would not trust their judgement if they were given political voice. They must be represented indirectly by those who have 'the stability of property' under their feet, as though this would establish stability in the state. Propertyless men (women do not enter even the most extreme nightmare that Burke can envisage) are simply 'not taught habitually to respect themselves'. They have no experience in exercising power with 'moderation' and 'discretion' and all in all would be 'intoxicated with their unprepared greatness' if 'snatched from the humblest rank of subordination' and given supreme authority. Throughout his argument Burke walks a tightrope of maintaining the sympathy of ordinary readers by respecting their sobriety and general trustworthiness, while constantly suggesting that their virtues would be useless and dangerous if they were given powers. He was aiming at the conclusion that they should be grateful and relieved that they are being saved by wise seniors from their own most unpredictably wild potential. The book is a remarkable document in that it is not addressed to the politically great but to something like the reasonable common man. By the end Burke sums up his qualifications by saying that he has spent a lifetime exercising 'long observation and much impartiality', resisting tyranny and struggling for the liberty of others, acting the part of 'one who has been no tool of power, no flatterer of greatness' (376). His last word is 'equipoise' which gathers into itself his vision of the perfect state and of himself.

Paine's *Rights of Man* is a reply to Burke's *Reflections on the Revolution in France*, and it begins provocatively by directly addressing Burke as an old friend who has lost his principles and is acting 'as if he were afraid that England and France would cease to be enemies', like 'those men in all countries who get their living by war, and by keeping up all the quarrels of Nations'.[10] Paine picks up straight away Burke's glaring flaw, that the 1688 settlement, far from proving that the English constitution is unchangeable, proved that in fact the Declaration decisively *changed* the constitution:

> There never did, there never will, and there never can exist a parliament, or any description of men, or any generation of men, in any country, possessed of the right or the power of binding and controlling posterity to the *'end of time,'* or of commanding for ever how the world shall be governed, or who shall govern it ... Every age and generation must be as free to act for itself, *in all cases*, as the ages and generations which preceded it. The vanity and presumption of governing beyond the grave, is the most ridiculous and insolent of all tyrannies. (64)

His style is straightforward and trenchant, demonstrating the rationalism that had made his *Common Sense* (1776) such a powerful intervention in favour of the American revolution, and it is a part of his strategy to expose Burke as employing a rhetoric that conceals through its flourishes and elegance a hollowness of logic. He exposes the falsity of sentimentality when it is not underpinned by experience of genuine suffering. When he comes to advance his own reading of the French revolution, making comparisons along the way with the American situation from where he is writing, Paine radically challenges the repression of the English government for setting up exactly the situation that made the French revolution necessary: 'Lay then the axe to the root, and teach governments humanity. It is their sanguinary punishments which corrupt mankind' (80). He builds his broader argument on the basis of equality through natural rights, arguing 'consequently that all men are born equal, and with equal natural right ... and consequently, every child born into the world must be considered as deriving its existence from God. The world is as new to him as it was to the first man that existed, and his natural right in it is of the same kind' (88). Paine provides a direct definition of natural rights, by distinguishing them from civil rights, although he emphasises that 'every civil right grows out of a natural right; or, in other words, is a natural right exchanged' (91).

> Natural rights are those which appertain to man in right of his existence. Of this kind are all the intellectual rights, or rights of the mind, and also all those rights of acting as an individual for his own comfort and happiness, which are not injurious to the natural rights of others. – Civil rights are those which appertain to man in right of his being a member of society.

Every civil right has for its foundation, some natural right pre-existing in the individual, but to the enjoyment of which his individual power is not, in all cases, sufficiently competent. Of this kind are all those which relate to security and protection. (90)

Paine is surprisingly general in his description of natural rights, but in some ways this marks his innovativeness. Others, like the Levellers, had used the phrase 'the rights of man', but 'only with Paine, it has been emphasized, was the "fully *universal*"character of rights revealed'[11] with examples such as the right to one's own religion and 'rights of the mind' such as 'a right to judge in his own cause'. In his Conclusion he adds as natural rights to be preserved by the state, 'liberty, property, security, and resistance of oppression', and looking to both France and the reconstituted America, Paine mentions 'UNIVERSAL RIGHT OF CONSCIENCE, AND UNIVERSAL RIGHT OF CITIZENSHIP' (110). He sees the new constitution of the National Assembly in France as being 'founded on the Rights of Man and the Authority of the People, the only authority on which government has a right to exist in any country' (131), and against this he attacks Burke's desire to maintain hereditary rule as a principle. The reason Paine does not go further in exemplifying rights is because he has one in particular which is his central target – the collective right of a people to change their country's constitution to guarantee both individual and civil rights – the capacity denied by Burke in his condemnation of the demands made by Price in his sermon in 1789, to choose governors to cashier them for misconduct, and 'To frame a government for ourselves'.

The importance of Paine's *The Rights of Man* for this book is not to spell out in detail the content of natural rights, but boldly to bring the general ideas and the phrase itself into the practical arena in England, giving them a topicality that infectiously led to controversy and strong political debate in polemical and imaginative literature. Paine was himself never free to return to England without fear for his life, but his book's title became a clarion call, and its effect extended to the reforms of 1832 and beyond. His book, deliberately written for a wide audience, encourages its readers to define themselves as equal to Burke and his aristocratic tribe, and as republicans,[12] and judging from its astonishing publishing success, *The Rights of Man* politicised and radicalised a whole class which would press harder and harder for the rights he demanded on their behalf.

Mary Wollstonecraft

If Rousseau stood behind the general call by writers for natural rights, Burke was the one perversely responsible for generating more than fifty books in some way espousing exactly what he had condemned. Paine's was the most famous and influential of the immediate responses, but the first was Mary

Wollstonecraft's *Vindication of the Rights of Men* (1790). The book is short and fiery, written in apparent haste and probably not as complete as its author intended, but some commentators have compared it (in the context of Wollstonecraft's output) favourably with Rousseau's work, for its philosophical originality.[13] By honing in on Burke's defence of primogeniture as a key plank in an hereditary system, she forecasts her own point of entry in a way that led on to the more famous and complete *A Vindication of the Rights of Woman*.[14] Clearly, that system threatened women's rights in a very basic way, but it also denied the 'birthright' of 'liberty, civil and religious' to anybody other than the wealthy.[15] Wollstonecraft argues that the reliance on heredity as a form of governing 'was settled in the dark days of ignorance, when the minds of men were shackled by the grossest prejudices and most immoral superstition' (11), making its basis in 'might as the fittest' inappropriate in more enlightened times. Interestingly, Wollstonecraft moves through the argument by continually returning to the touchstone of Burke's own aesthetic, his credentials as somebody who had attached himself to the movement of sensibility and benevolence, and she exposes contradictions in his views. 'Where was your sensibility when you could utter this cruel mockery?' (25). In particular, on several occasions she evokes the sentimental herself as a morally educative faculty. The poor are described with a pity designed to tug at the feelings:

> your respect for rank has swallowed up the common feelings of humanity; you seem to consider the poor as only the live stock of an estate, the feather of hereditary nobility. When you had so little respect for the silent majority of misery. (16)
>
> But, among all your plausible arguments, and witty illustrations, your contempt for the poor always appears conspicuous, and rouses my indignation. (56)

On several occasions she points out that under Burke's view slavery would be acceptable and benign. Wollstonecraft goes further and attacks the sentimental movement as contributing to the cauterising of moral feelings: 'Benevolence is a very amiable specious quality' (53). It is capable of mistaking 'the pangs of hurt vanity' for 'virtuous indignation', and she constructs the image of the sentimental female reader:

> Where is the dignity, the infallibility of sensibility, in the fair ladies, whom, if the voice of rumour is to be credited, the captive negroes curse in all the agony of bodily pain, for the unheard of tortures they invent? It is probable that some of them, after the sight of a flagellation, compose their ruffled spirits and exercise their tender feelings by the perusal of the last imported novel. – How true these tears are to nature, I leave you to determine.

But these ladies may have read your Enquiry concerning the origin of our ideas of the Sublime and Beautiful, and, convinced by your arguments, may have laboured to be pretty, by counterfeiting weakness. (45)

Wollstonecraft is less forthcoming than Paine in specifying the particular attributes of what she reverences as 'the rights of men. – Sacred rights!' (33). However, she does give a general approach which is not only very close to ancient natural law, but also becomes an important statement to be set beside William Blake's early poetry:

> Children are born ignorant, consequently innocent; the passions are nei-
> ther good nor evil dispositions, till they receive a direction, and either
> bound over the feeble barrier raised by a faint glimmering of unexercised
> reason, called conscience ... if virtue is to be acquired by experience, or
> taught by example, reason, perfected by reflection, must be the director of
> the whole host of passions. (31)

This passage, as it goes on, is confusingly written, but it seems that its general drift is to attack Burke's reliance on 'inbred' aristocratic instincts for good and evil, laid down long ago and unlikely ever to be improved upon. This, Wollstonecraft, argues, is a recipe for complacency in which 'reason' becomes mere rationalisation. True reason is something which is 'arduous' (30), continually requiring exercise, and superior to the 'passions'. It is the bedrock of any society purporting to be based on 'the rights of man', and Wollstonecraft locates true political authority, as Wendy Gunther-Canada puts it, 'in the democratic reason of ordinary men and women instead of the divine right of kings. In arguing for the "sovereignty of reason" Wollstonecraft calls for the creation of a government founded on rational discourse to replace monarchical rule.'[16]

However, the truly original step taken by Wollstonecraft came in 1792, when she challenged the universally accepted but gendered phrase 'rights of man' itself, in *A Vindication of the Rights of Woman*, which will be examined later in this book. Whereas all writers, including herself, had taken 'man' to include 'woman', she argued that in practice women were not extended the same rights as men, in an iniquitous system,[17] whose reliance on unequal hierarchy had permeated law, religion, the family, schooling, and indeed every aspect of organised life in Britain.[18] Nor were women able to exercise true reason when the educational institutions denied them proper knowledge.

Thomas Spence

Not all treatises on natural rights came in response to Burke, the French revolution or the American, nor were they all written by professional writers. Thomas Spence (1750–1814) was a working-class man from Newcastle upon

Tyne who went to London in the 1790s. In 1775 he delivered a lecture to the Philosophical Society in Newcastle, 'for printing of which', he ironically writes, 'the Society did the Author the Honour to expel him'.[19] It was reprinted four times, the last in 1793 when its application to contemporary events had changed. Spence became best known for his weekly paper, *Pigs' Meat; or Lessons for the Swinish Multitude ... Collected by the Poor Man's Advocate* (1793–95). Spence's ideas come not from France or America or abstract principles like Godwin's, but from a tradition of working-class radical politics in the north-east of England[20] which had links with the seventeenth-century radicals such as Winstanley, the Levellers and Diggers. Spence 'was the first to argue unambiguously for democratic republicanism, common ownership and popular revolution',[21] and he created a fictional utopia called Spensonia, based structurally on the literary work *Oceana* by the Jacobean James Harington, and influenced also by Defoe's *Robinson Crusoe*, to show his revolutionary schemes in operation. He was also amongst the first to write a work explicitly on 'The Rights of Infants' (1797), to which we shall return.[22] With an admirable integrity he worked from his own childhood perceptions: one of his early biographers writes that 'As a child he was oppressed with a sense of injustice. He could not understand why his parents should toil so hard and be so poor, whilst others who did not deserve it had plenty.'[23]

Spence's basis for his vision of an 'empire of right and reason' (66) in *The Rights of Man* has an admirable simplicity. Rather than claiming political rights as an origin, or kings and rulers as the enemy, he sees them as consequences of a far more radical position – a belief in 'natural and equal rights of property in land and liberty.' (59)

> That property in land and liberty among men in a state of nature ought to be equal, few, one would be fain to hope, would be foolish enough to deny. Therefore, taking this to be granted, the country of any people, in a native state, is properly their common, in which each of them has an equal property, with free liberty to sustain himself and family with the animals, fruits and other products thereof ... Surely, to deny them that right is in effect denying them a right to live. (59)

Apparently without knowledge of Rousseau's *A Discourse on Inequality*, he argues also from the edenic 'state of nature' before private landowning, asserting that 'Thus were the first landholders usurpers and tyrants' (61), and that they never had the right to deprive others of life. And to Spence, land is life: 'mankind have as equal and just a property in land as they have in liberty, air, or the light and heat of the sun ... those common gifts of nature' (62). (Spence is not a true anarchist theorist, for he excepts ownership of 'movables' from common ownership of land.) In his lecture, Spence proceeds to sketch out the political implications of this theory of rights. On an appointed day, he says, there should be what amounts to a revolution, 'on which the inhabitants of each parish meet, in their respective parishes, to take their long-lost rights into possession, and to form themselves into corporations' (62). All these corporations become self-governing with representative, decision-making committees elected by secret ballot. Since there is no private ownership of land, suffrage can be theoretically universal and equal, and there is no cause for corruption in this process, since there will be no point in being greedy. Each person pays a rent to the corporation, according to the means to pay, for essential services. 'Freedom to do anything whatever cannot there be bought; a thing is either entirely prohibited, as theft of murder; or entirely free to everyone without tax or price' (65). There will no longer be a handful of 'haughty, unthankful landlords' who can be bribed and who exercise unwarranted political and economic power in Spence's own England. The brief but forthright lecture is written with an audacious joviality which, despite its adopted stance of common sense and reason, suggests that Spence anticipated it would be too radical for the Philosophical Society, who duly (and to Spence's ironic gratitude) expelled him from its membership.

By 1793 Spence could bring the argument up to date by publishing with the lecture 'An Interesting Conversation, between a Gentleman and the Author, on the Subject of the foregoing Lecture', in which the 'Gentleman' challenges the 'strange Lecture' by saying that not even 'the Revolutionists in either America, France, or England, or any where else, ever disputed or attempted to invalidate the rights of landed interest' (67); even Paine, he says, who seems to please the most ardent revolutionists, does not claim a right to common ownership of land. 'The Author' responds, 'I hate patching and cobling' and continues: 'Let us have a perfect system that will keep itself right, and let us have done; for what is radically wrong must be a continual plague' (67). He is quite right in saying that most of the reformists of the 1790s, like Paine himself, still defended the monopoly of land. The Gentleman turns out, not surprisingly, to be a landholder, and he politely argues that there can be no return to a forgotten and ancient age of common ownership. But the Author cites a string of natural law theorists including Pufendorf and Locke, to suggest otherwise. He quotes the scriptural Leviticus, chapter 25, where it is predicted that on a jubilee day in the world's history, liberty will be proclaimed throughout the land: 'and ye shall return every man unto his possession, and ye shall return every man unto his family ... The land shall not be sold for ever; for the land is mine; for ye are strangers and sojourners with me.' Spence ironically adds 'Thus you see god Almighty himself is a very notorious leveller, and certainly meant to stir up the people every fiftieth year, to insist upon liberty and equality, or the repossession of their just rights' (69). In 1782 he had printed a song, 'Hark! how the Trumpet's Sound' based on this biblical passage. He then reiterates and develops the socially beneficial consequences of his 'simple, easy, practicable scheme' (70). Landlords will become obsolete and remembered in the same way as highwaymen. Spence once again emphasises that he is more radical than Paine, by making the Gentleman praise that writer's caution. Several times in the 1790s he returns to the comparison with Paine and other reformists, who, he says, 'level all their Artillery at Kings, without striking like Spence at this root of every abuse and of every grievance' ('The End of Oppression' [1795], another dramatised dialogue between a 'Young Man' and Spence's mouthpiece, an 'Old Man'). Spence continued to contrast Paine's view against his own, even when the former addressed the question of land ownership in *Agrarian Justice* (1797). In publishing *The Rights of Infants* which was written in 1796 but published in 1797, Spence adds a Preface and Appendix to take account of the work which he says he read 'before it was published'. He congratulates Paine for at last acknowledging the Psalmist's '*God hath given the earth to the children of men, given it to mankind in common*' (111), but he goes on scornfully to deplore the concessions and compromises suggested by Paine to placate the aristocracy. He returns to his own programme of root and branch removal:

> All dominion is rooted and grounded in land, and thence spring every kind of lordship which overtops and choaks all the shrubs and flowers of the forest. But take away those tall, those overbearing aristocratic trees, and then the lowly plants of the soil will have air, will thrive and grow robust. (112)

The Appendix tabulates in two columns the contrast between the two systems, Paine's 'Under the system of Agrarian Justice' and his own 'Under the system of the End of Oppression', using this to argue that Paine's will lead to a worse state of injustice than the present, while his more radical scheme will genuinely change the system and return it to a basis in natural rights.

William Laurence Brown

Having canvassed the more radical social critics who built their arguments on natural rights, it is useful to add that more conservative and scholarly people did so too in the 1790s. His very insignificance might qualify William Laurence Brown for exemplary status as a proselytiser for a moderate version of enlightened thinking on natural rights.[24] In his day he had some celebrity as Professor of Moral Philosophy at Utrecht and then Professor of Divinity at Aberdeen, and although his published works seem 'unincendiary' (vi), and he openly opposed Paine, yet they fell foul of the paranoid British government of the early 1790s. Aberdeen as an intellectual environment was neither revolutionary nor reactionary, but it had welcomed the French revolution, supported the abolition of slavery, and generally as a burgh agitated for 'the natural rights of mankind' (vii). But open disputes against authorities, and calls for revolution, met with disapproval. Brown himself saw Jacobin calls for revolution as little better than the despotism they sought to over-throw, and he supported constitutionalism and gradual change. On the political map he was on the progressive side, belonging with the Scottish enlightenment writers, but a moderate within this group. While he does not specifically address the rights of particular groups like women, labourers, and the poor, his philosophy of sympathy is broad enough to defend the idea of fundamental rights for all members of humanity. His *An Essay on the Natural Equality of Men*, published in Edinburgh in 1793, provides a conservative blueprint, but one which has enough latitude to allow us to inspect the natural rights content of Jacobin novels, and especially those like Robert Bage's, which assert natural rights, but close with the conventional reassertion of inherited wealth which leaves hero and heroine to a comfortable-ever-after existence.

Brown challenges the assumption that all men are a priori equal and that differences emerge through relative opportunities. He points out that people have different aptitudes: some have benevolence, some fortitude, others ambition, avarice, voluptuousness, indolence, vanity, and so on. In itself this seems to be close to a novelist's view of humans, each one bearing an individual 'character'. 'Nature herself, then, has evidently established unambiguous distinctions among men, and produced a very remarkable *inequality* among the individuals of our species' (20). Moreover, all the talents have not, and cannot be, united in one individual – for example, a lively and bright fancy is not found with dour patience in one person: 'Variety of talents is, therefore, more applicable to the species than to individuals'. Brown finds that equality lies in the notion of mutual dependence: 'however paradoxical it may seem, an *equality* the most exact and perfect, in respect of every moral and social obligation, springs from *inequality* itself' (31). A man can 'neither begin, nor proceed without the co-operation of his fellow men' (35), since each individual is insufficient for happiness on his own and must depend on the assistance of others. Again, it is not difficult to foresee the usefulness of such a social model to the little world of a novel. Through a view of society as based on mutual dependence, he posits the existence of 'equality of obligation' – the mutually sustaining duties one owes through one's talents to help others – and 'in this view, no human creature is more or less worthy than another' (57). The real enemies, as in novels of the time, are pride and tyranny, which destroy the very structure of mutual obligation and equality. Brown does acknowledge the existence of subordination and hierarchy, but it is moral rather than based on riches or position. Those at the top are wholly benevolent, those at the bottom despots, tyrants, and those who take '*licentiousness* for *liberty*'.

Brown goes on to elaborate on what he himself calls a 'moderate' set of 'Rights resulting from the natural Equality of Men' (heading, Book II). Since his official job description when he wrote the book was 'Professor of Moral

Philosophy, and the Law of Nature, and of Ecclesiastical History' (title page) it is appropriate that he should revert to some natural law assumptions about the innate and rational desire of people to follow virtue and shun vice:

> there seems annexed to every natural *desire* and *propensity* of the heart, a certain feeling of a *right* to its indulgence. The original propensities and desires spring up spontaneously in the soul, and impel it to action. (95) ... Reason, recollecting the past, and anticipating the future, establishes such rules of action and enjoyment as unite the perfection and happiness of the individual with the general interest of the species. (97)

He then goes on to deduce 'certain *natural rights*, which cannot be infringed without overturning the foundations of human society ... the original conditions of the social compact' (99), distinguishing these from consequential rights which are 'necessary for the general felicity'. Both flow from 'the idea of equality of obligation'. The first are 'the inherent and original *rights* of human nature, which equally belong to all men without exception', while the second are 'those adventitious *rights*, which belong only to particular descriptions of men, as characterised, whether by particular talents, or by particular functions in civil life' (102). Again, the distinction has relevance for the societies depicted in contemporary novels. Brown lists the 'original and inherent Rights of human Nature as follows:

I. Every innocent member of society has a *perfect right* to life, and to the integrity of his body. No principle is more deeply engraved in the constitution of all animals, than that of self-preservation. This right arises from an obligation – 'Nothing excites the detestation of mankind more than an unprovoked attempt on life, or even violent assault' (103) [and the rationale for the 'sacred and inviolable' right to life is to enable the person] 'to discharge the most important social duties. The preservation of individuals supports the preservation of society.'

II. 'Every man has a *perfect right* to the full fruits of his own honest ingenuity and labour' (104). By this Brown does not mean anything like a workers' collective, although by implication he could include fair wages. His real interest lies in giving each person proper incentive to work hard, which 'best promotes his own private happiness, and, in the same manner, he contributes most to the public good' (107). Again, mutual dependence and the interrelatedness of society are his prime concerns. Accordingly, Brown regards 'the Utopian system of a community of goods' as not conducive to social good: 'it is undoubted that both public and private happiness require that the right of property should be sacredly maintained' (107). However, Brown is careful to separate inheritance from these primary rights. Since 'the foundation of all property is the common *right* to the earth, and its productions, which God has granted to mankind' (109) the only primary rights are ones derived from use.

III. All men have an equal *right* to a fair and honest character, till it has been proved that they have justly forfeited it. The love of character is deeply implanted in the human breast ... The loss of reputation, wounding one of the most lively feelings of the human heart, is one of the greatest calamities in life (110).

Once again, what bothers Brown is not just the loss of private happiness at the loss of reputation, but the frustration of 'his public utility'. What he calls 'the character of honesty' (111) as a primary right has been a central motif in novels from *Tom Jones* to *Great Expectations*.

IV. 'Every man has a *perfect right* to *liberty*, or to act in whatever manner he pleases, provided he offers no injury to others, and violates no law enacted by the public authority of the civil society to which he belongs' (113). All happiness and all virtue rests on this foundation, and it in turn is based on reason and the power of regulating one's actions. 'In short, liberty and human nature are inseparable; to destroy the former is to annihilate the latter' (116). Brown deems slavery 'the greatest of human evils' (117), and he takes it as an example of servitude in general which the love of freedom abhors. However, once again Brown is circumspect in distinguishing the love of genuine freedom from the false freedom of exercising personal oppression, placing it firmly within his overall pattern of mutual dependence. 'Whoever injures others is not a free man, but a tyrant, and, if he is free, others are slaves' (121). Perfect liberty is subject to the limitations of the law and of 'the collective power of the whole community' (121). Obviously this right to liberty is to be contested by radical novelists in the context of perceived injustice within legal restrictions. Brown devotes much space to defining liberty, which he classifies as 'first, personal liberty; secondly, liberty of action; thirdly, liberty of conscience; fourthly, liberty of communication of sentiment' (139). He argues that it is in the interests of governments to preserve inviolate the right to liberty, and as usual he takes the opportunity to berate despotism and arbitrary rule. However closely he may try to hedge the right to liberty, it is clear from his presentation that Brown accepts, as do novelists from their different perspectives, that it is the most difficult, relative, but fundamental right of all.

Having covered the primary rights which belong to all, Brown describes the secondary or 'adventitious' rights held by 'those who are placed in the higher stations' either by government or wealth. They are entitled to their privileges and to their place in the social hierarchy, so long as they respect the 'equality of obligation' which requires them to discharge their powers justly and to use their riches, 'acquired by honest industry' (151), 'to relieve want, to sooth affliction, to diffuse around them a spirit of improvement, to encourage industry, and to make their superfluity circulate through the general mass of the community' (151). At the same time, 'the inferior ranks of society' have a right to demand that all delegated authority be exercised for the general good (152). These distinctions are reflected in novels which have a benevolent squire or justice, who is usually wealthy. Finally, Brown asserts that 'All men have an equal, though imperfect, *right* to those offices of humanity which, while they cost the performers of them little trouble, are the sweeteners of social intercourse; and to the compassion and relief of others, proportioned to their condition and circumstances, when they are overpowered by distress and calamity' (154). We hardly need reminding that virtuous characters in novels, no matter what their social standing, always speak and behave with perfect decorum, and they are constitutionally predisposed to relieve distress and calamity. While only relating to an 'adventitious' right or obligation, this characteristic completes Brown's scheme of rights, which can stand as a calculus of moral structure in some novels of the 1790s, explaining both the core of radical demands for rights while simultaneously preserving certain aspects of social subordination within the status quo.

4
Manifestoes into Fictions

The most philosophically systematic accounts of natural rights emanated from the group of writers generally known as members of the 'Scottish Enlightenment' – in particular, Hume, Hutcheson and Adam Smith. A slender but tensile thread connects the armchair with the hustings, urbane, idealistic philosophy with revolutionary rhetoric and fervour. Nowhere is this unexpected connection more visible than in the 'Jacobin' novels of the 1790s. Since novelists need to be culturally literate at least in their own genre, writers like Wollstonecraft and Godwin show that they know the traditions of novels written along 'enlightened' lines in the eighteenth century, but they are equally stirred by contemporary debates about revolution in France and its significance for England, and the rights of women and slaves. Equally, it is clear, as we have seen, that a novel like Mackenzie's *The Man of Feeling* or Goldsmith's *The Vicar of Wakefield* could hardly have been written without influence, whether at first- or second-hand, from the philosophers who emphasise benevolence as a social glue, with natural rights as a set of ground rules. The circle is closed when we note the cultural omnivorousness of somebody like Adam Smith, who aspired to write 'a connected history of the liberal sciences and elegant arts', and of his teacher Hutcheson. They would certainly have been aware of those developments in the novel which were compatible with their own social, moral, and political philosophies. It is not necessary and perhaps not possible to ascertain whether philosophy guided novels or whether philosophers generalised as much from literature as from observation. Even today it is a moot point whether thinkers like Foucault, Lacan and Derrida have in a self-vindicating way generated theories of signification from life in order to illuminate literature, or from literature in order to illuminate life. Some are unashamed intertextualists, believing that all the world's a text and all the men and women merely readers. And it seems clear that Freud 'found' the oedipal complex in *Hamlet* and the medusa complex in *Macbeth*.[1] It is, however, very clear that philosophy and certain kinds of novels from 1750 to 1800 ran alongside each other and worked mutually from a similar theory or model of social justice.

One of the central arguments I pursued in *Natural Law in English Renaissance Literature* is that literary models of 'poetic justice' found analogy and justification in natural law theory. If theory pronounced that people have an innate desire to follow virtue and avoid vice, then plays were written to endorse virtue and punish vice. Even when the simple rule does not apply, as in the case of victims, like most of Shakespeare's tragic heroines who have done no conspicuous wrong and are innocent in the legal or moral sense, it seems clear that audiences are expected to recognise the violation of natural law in their unjust fates, and feel it keenly enough to learn something from it in quasi-didactic fashion. It is my contention here that something similar happens in novels of the 1790s. Their underlying paradigm of social and psychological and legal morality is basically the same as that advanced by natural rights theorists. Both groups are concerned with diagnosing ills and pointing the way towards a more just and egalitarian future, and it is at least arguable that both create little fictional worlds to demonstrate their social analysis. Natural rights, either in the foreground or the background, provide a moral reference point for the judgements implicitly made in the narrative.

William Godwin

Nothing could be further removed from the sentimental novel than William Godwin's *Caleb Williams* (1794), a work which, both in its bleak first version in which Williams dies, or in its more optimistic revision which gives Williams a moral victory, anticipates with an original force novels by Dickens, Dostoyevsky and Camus. Quite deliberately, Godwin misleads the reader by setting up Falkland as a sentimental hero coming to the rescue of the wronged maiden, a man of entirely benevolent caste, only to proceed by showing him to be a hypocrite and nasty persecutor. Godwin is making the point that the novelistic conventions of benevolence are not reflected in 'Things as They Are', the novel's subtitle. What we get is a narrative of unrelenting psychological terrorism perpetrated by a clandestine murderer over the man who knows his guilty secret. At a literary level the fable imitates Milton's *Paradise Lost*, where it is Williams's (Adam's) overreaching curiosity and prying that gives him knowledge of Falkland's guilt, and where such knowledge in its own right becomes a terrible burden and loss of innocence. Williams says of himself 'I had an inquisitive mind', which was made even stronger in subsequent editions: 'The spring of action which, perhaps more than any other, characterised the whole train of my life, was curiosity.' The structure of the novel has an overarching sense of Milton's 'fortunate fall', indicating the terrible burden of knowledge acquired by an innocent man.

The case of Godwin is a convenient one in this book, which deals with the way ideas bear upon literature, as is that of Wollstonecraft, because both wrote lengthy polemical treatises and also novels which are consistent with, and exemplify, their philosophies. Godwin's *Enquiry Concerning Political*

Justice (1793) is especially apt since it immediately predated *Caleb Williams*, which was published the year after, and can be assumed to follow in its wake.[2] Almost all critics, in fact, read the novel as a fictional representation of some strand in *Political Justice*, although each focuses on a different issue. Given that the *Enquiry* is over 800 pages long, there is considerable scope for using it as a source and quarry in this way.[3] Godwin signalled clearly in his original 'Preface', suppressed by publishers for fear of prosecution in the period of 'The Terror', that he would comment on radicals and conservatives in his own age, and also represent 'things passing in the moral world'. Although an historical novel, the subtitle (or, in fact, title), *Things as they Are*, indicates that there is a contemporary reference to the 1790s. Gary Kelly develops the idea that the central parts of the novel 'are clearly related to Book seven of *Political Justice*, entitled "Of Crimes and Punishments" the right of the state to punish, and to enforce its "contract" by the sanction of the law'.[4] He equally finds vestiges of Book two, 'The Principles of Society' and Book four, 'Of the Powers of Man Considered in his Social Capacity', and he draws on John Middleton Murry's reading of *Caleb Williams* as The Protestant Dream'[5] to propose that the novel is 'an allegory of Protestant, not to say Dissenting history' (208). Pamela Clemit finds 'a psychologically complex fable' which is used by Godwin to expose and attack eighteenth-century power relations, in an answer to Burke's hierarchical politics.

> In foregrounding the political undercurrents of Gothic romance, he projects on to this starkly representative opposition of master and servant the contradictory pressures of all human relationships.[6]

In the context of this book, I also want to argue that *Caleb Williams* reflects preoccupations expressed in *Political Justice*, but I choose to focus on a different issue from these writers, the way Godwin reflects on natural rights. He takes up a different angle from Paine's political account, and from Locke's version which Godwin thought too individualistic and concerned to give people the right to do what they like. His approach is communitarian, and closer than his contemporaries' to classical natural law. I argue that the novel, *Caleb Williams*, can be satisfyingly read as a fable exploring in its three volumes three different aspects of Godwin's understanding of natural rights. To make the point graphically, I suggest the three volumes can be subtitled without severe distortion, respectively, 'the book of tyranny' (as the enemy to natural rights), 'the book of justice' (showing the imperfections of positive law and human punishment when measured against natural law and reason), and 'the book of conscience' (the natural right to hold and openly express knowledge gained by the moral conscience). All three themes are consistent *leitmotifs* running through *Political Justice*. In *Enquiry Concerning Political Justice*, Godwin's account of rights lacks Paine's populist clarity and confidence, mainly because Paine generates his theory from a sense of political oppression whereas Godwin is creating a more self-consciously philosophical model of the individual's place in society. For him, rights are inextricably interfused with issues of equality, justice, and moral conscience. The way he expresses this interconnectedness sounds surprisingly like modern chaos theory. His equivalent of the butterfly which flutters its wings in Rio and causes a storm in Sydney, is the birth of Shakespeare which depended on both accident and rigid determinism. 'If any man asserted that, if Alexander had not bathed in the river Cydnus, Shakespeare would never have written, it would be impossible to prove that his assertion was wrong' (193). Or again,

> It has been observed by natural philosophers that a single grain of land more or less in the structure of the earth would have produced an infinite variation in its history. If this be true in inanimate nature, it is much more so in morals. (192)

Morality itself, Godwin defines as 'nothing else but that system which teaches us to contribute upon all occasions, to the extent of our power, to the well-being and happiness of every intellectual and sensitive existence' (192). In pursuing this end, there is available in every circumstance a mode of proceeding which will be more reasonable than any other – this, Godwin says, is the principle of justice – and it sounds close to the heart of classical natural law. Only after discussing the principles of equality, morals and justice, does Godwin invoke rights, and then it is first in a hedging way, cautioning against those who maintain that individual liberty is built on rights, and who justify any impulsive action. His version of rights begins rather with duties: 'as ... it cannot be their duty to do anything detrimental to the general happiness, so it appears with equal evidence that they can have a right to do so. There cannot be a more absurd proposition than that which affirms the right of doing wrong'. Where this marks a significant difference from political activists like Thelwall, Paine and others who came to distance themselves from Godwin, comes on issues like revolution, where Godwin in a coded way condemns as ridiculous the idea that the voice of the people is ' "the voice of truth and of God" '. Just as strong as his mistrust of the masses is his detestation of any form of government, since inevitably it will have coercive and repressive elements. It is this aspect of Godwin's argument that gives Godwin an honourable chapter in any history of philosophical anarchism.[7] Rational discussion, equality and free enquiry should, he argues, be the basis for political and social change, not violent action which risks life and which is simply the assertion of 'might is right'. Godwin stands on the non-violent side of debate about revolution, and he accords only contingent status to 'the active rights of man' since, he says 'all of them [are] superseded and rendered null by the superior claims of justice' (197). A 'passive right' like 'a right to life' is less controversial, but the right to 'personal liberty' is limited to not having another person's will imposed on one, and if such a right exists it must conform to reason and conscience in a social situation. When Godwin argues that another man may advise him 'but he must not expect to dictate to [him]', he draws the active and passive rights into a unity, since both come down to a rejection of tyranny of one over another – positively expressed as the assertion of equality and justice. Equality itself lies at the heart of Godwin's whole theory, as it explains the nature of justice: 'By moral equality I understand the propriety of applying one unalterable rule of justice to every case that arises.' Inequality, and its consequential injustices, is central also to *Caleb Williams*. Godwin's section on rights in *Political Justice* is almost minimal (it had also been rewritten between 1794 and 1798), but it does consistently argue for the interconnectedness of rights, justice, morality, and conscience, and systematically opposes tyranny and violence. This interconnectedness is exactly the point of *Caleb Williams*.

In volume I, Caleb Williams is more an observer than a participant in the plot. The central action presents very clearly and schematically a series of acts of tyranny by the presumably allegorically named Tyrrel, a local tyrant in every way. He is a wealthy landowner who is condemned by his actions, first in victimising his tenant, Hawkins, then in depriving of her liberty his niece, Miss Emily Melvile, out of jealousy and also because she will not marry the man of his choice. Emily, presented as the victim heroine of a sentimental novel, escapes her imprisonment with the help of the central character, Ferdinando Falkland, a landowner who is the social equal of Tyrrel and hated by him for his initially manifest benevolence. Re-arrested on the writ of her uncle, Emily dies, and Tyrrel is loathed as 'the most diabolical wretch that had ever dishonoured the human form' (79). The volume ends with the discovery of his body, violently murdered. This bears out Falkland's prediction:

> Very well, sir, I have done. I have only to tell you beforehand that such tyranny as yours will make you the universal abhorrence of mankind. You may hug yourself in your wealth and impunity, but be sure the genuine sense of the world will pierce through all your intrenchments, and fully avenge those for whose blood you so cruelly thirst. Good day to you. (44)

This passage, one among many expressing its gist, clearly expresses the theme of the first volume: inequities of wealth and social power directly cause tyranny and injustice, and create victims like Emily and Hawkins's family:

> It was mere madness in [Hawkins] to think of contesting with a man of Mr Tyrrel's eminence and fortune. It was a fawn contending with a lion. Nothing could have been more easy to predict, than that it was of no avail for him to have right on his side, when his adversary had influence and wealth, and therefore could so victoriously justify any extravagancies that he might think proper to commit. Wealth and despotism easily know

how to engage those laws, which were perhaps at first intended (witless and miserable precaution!) for the safeguards of the poor, as the coadjutors of their oppression. (40; see also 43)

All that is left to the victims is dignity and liberty of mind, rights that come from being human. In an echo of the Lady in Milton's *Comus*, Godwin puts into the mouth of his heroine the line 'But I am not so helpless as you may imagine. You may imprison my body, but you cannot conquer my mind' (62), while Hawkins says, 'Though I am a plain working man, your honour, do you see? yet I am a man still' (39). Both statements raise the book's concentration on the tyranny of privilege to the significance of natural rights.

In volume II, Caleb becomes a character in the story in his own right, as a man persecuted for his knowledge. The mysteriously moody Falkland changes his status from saviour of Emily and moral spokesman, to a dark villain. Because of Caleb's innate curiosity, he discovers evidence that Falkland in fact murdered Tyrrel, and stood by while the innocent Hawkins was convicted and hanged for the crime. Falkland's erratic behaviour is seen as stemming from a guilty conscience, and when he finds out that Wiliams knows of his guilt he turns all his wrath on him. In collusion with a rich relative, he has Williams incarcerated on false charges. Presumably Godwin's points in making Falkland such a villain after initially setting him up as a benevolent figure of sympathy, are first that he is genuinely corrupted by covering up his guilt, even if everybody in fact would secretly see the death of Tyrrel as poetic justice; and second that even at their most apparently benign the rich are never to be trusted because of the basic inequality of their status. Volume II, 'the book of justice' deals with the way justice is perverted by the existence of inequality between rich and poor, and various vignettes are shown of people wrongly imprisoned. The degrading conditions of prisons in his time are clearly another target for Godwin. In more ways than one the inmates of the prison system are deprived of natural rights and human dignity.

Volume III, 'the book of conscience', proceeds from two statements made in volume II: of Falkland Williams says, 'he had the guilt of blood on him ... his conscience would reproach him as long as he lived' (116), and of himself, 'You may cut off my existence, but you cannot disturb my serenity', and again: 'in this forlorn condition ... I was superior to all my persecutors. Blessed state of innocence and self approbation. The sunshine of conscious integrity pierced through all the barriers of my cell' (165). But Williams's conscience is not entirely clean either, for although he vigorously protests his own innocence, he does not publicly condemn Falkland. In this sense he sees himself as compounding an injustice against the memory of Hawkins. The fact also that he actively sought evidence of his master's guilt, rather than stumbling over the secret, adds another subtlety to his moral position.

He escapes from prison, likening the moment of freedom to his rights: 'Ah, this is indeed to be a man! ... Sacred and indescribable moment, when man regains his rights!' (187).

He falls in with a gang of thieves who protect him and turn out to have a stronger moral sense and code of conduct, more 'kindness and humanity' (194) than any other group in the novel. Satirically, Godwin draws them as the real justicers: 'Our profession is the profession of justice ... We undertake to counteract the partiality and iniquity of public institutions' (192). Obviously their analysis coincides with the earlier depiction of the law as a profession favouring the rich and privileged over the poor. The one lesson Caleb can teach his new friends is the inner reward of having 'an approving conscience', which is the faculty that gives himself strength. The section concludes when he is forced to leave them, with the words, 'This is the form in which tyranny and injustice oblige me to seek for refuge; but better, a thousand times better is it, thus to incur contempt with the dregs of mankind, than to trust to the tender mercies of our superiors' (208). Ruthlessly hunted like an animal by Falkland, who offers large rewards and uses a kind of personal secret service, Caleb adopts various disguises, in particular that of a Jew, indicating his identification with the marginalised and victimised race. He also chooses to become a writer, using a pseudonym, and the printer is impressed by his stories: 'he writes them all to my mind extremely fine, and yet he is no more than a Jew. (To my honest printer this seemed as strange as if they had been written by a Cherokee chieftain at the falls of the Missisippi)' (233). His choice of profession is clearly meant by Godwin to signal the status of outsider and critic occupied by writers and Jews alike.

In writing first one ending to the novel and then another, Godwin demonstrates his determination to avoid easy or sentimental solutions. He ostentatiously raises a novelistic convention, only to seep it away: Caleb accidentally meets his dead father's friend, Mr Collins, a man of 'calm and benevolent philosophy' who had known Caleb as a child. We expect autumnal reconciliation and a new advocate for him – but the surrogate father simply dismisses Caleb in his vagabond state, as incorrigibly vicious. (In fact, one reviewer at the time regretted not only the absence of a happy marriage but also 'no fondly absent parent', since Caleb's father dies at the beginning of the book.)[8] Williams does, however, write to Mr Collins, using 'this little engine, this little pen' to record the truth in a form which has become the novel we are reading. The final triumph of wronged innocence is in vindication through the written word, and stripped of all other rights to freedom and life itself, Williams retains the right to write – the pun on writes/rights is never quite made by Godwin but it is close to the surface.

These papers shall preserve the truth: they shall one day be published, and then the world shall do justice on us both. Recollecting that, I shall not die wholly without consolation. It is not to be endured that falsehood and tyranny should reign for ever. (267)

Inevitably there must be a final confrontation between persecutor and victim, and by this stage Falkland is being likened to historical tyrants like Nero and Caligula. The nightmarish descriptions of Williams' being stalked from region to region by Falkland's brutal functionary, 'the infernal Gines', evoke the very sense of hounded persecution that was described by a political radical like John Thelwall who was dogged by government spies wherever he went. They describe the paranoia of a man deprived of the natural right of freedom from persecution. Caleb decides to precipitate the inevitable confrontation by formally demanding a summons to make Falkland answer the charge of murder. The magistrate at first remonstrates and refuses, but eventually is driven to grant the summons. It comes as a relief to Williams's tortured conscience at last to make a clear accusation based on the truth, without concealment or fear of intimidation. In some ways the very decision is his moral reward. When Falkland is brought before the court, it is clear to all that he is a broken man. Whereas formerly he was 'haggard, ghost-like and wild, energy in his gestures and frenzy in his aspect', now he has 'the appearance of a corpse' (271). As the mirror-image to Caleb, Falkland also shows signs of encountering the consequences of conscience – in his case, guilty. Williams, in seeing the case as 'a mere piece of equity and justice', implicitly recalls the older natural law tradition enshrined in English equity. Equity was 'the court of conscience' in the renaissance, and although it could not either punish or order reimbursement for wrongdoing, its assumption was that conscience would do the rest. Indeed it does in this case. Williams presents such a masterly and understanding view of Falkland as somebody who was once honourable and deserving of 'reverence', yet led by circumstances and his own impulsive virtue, into a vicious action. The worse crime lay in concealing the murder and allowing the Hawkinses to hang for it. Williams confesses that his own 'imprudence' in not publicising the facts was also culpable, and the time spent 'manacled like a felon' was in some measure a punishment. After his 'plain and unadulterated tale', Caleb has clarified the complex moral issues, and has moved even Falkland to the point of tacit confession. Three days later Falkland dies, and Caleb must live with yet another guilty part of his conscience, having 'murdered' him, however 'innocent' he was of the surrounding events. As at the end of *Romeo and Juliet*, 'All are punishéd', and the overall moral of the fable leads us back to Godwin's point in *Political Justice* about the interconnectedness of equality, justice, and conscience, and how initial violation of equality and natural rights leads in time to implicate and incriminate even the most virtuous souls in a kind of social evil. The official system of justice and the prisons, corrupt as they are, abidingly demonstrate and perpetuate the deep-rooted inequalities.

It is really this last point that sharpens the difference between Godwin's original manuscript ending and the revised denouement which he published. His manuscript ending makes the published one look too optimistic and even 'happy' to eventuate from such an implicitly compromising society as Godwin has presented. The manuscript is totally pessimistic. In it, Godwin does not show Williams's generous eloquence and makes him much more directly accusatory. The effect on the court is to make him appear hysterical and vindictive. Falkland by contrast is dignified and plausible in denying all charges. The magistrate eventually curtails the proceedings:

> Having spoken for some time with incredible eagerness, and at length gasping and panting for breath, the magistrate sternly interposed. Be silent! said he. What is it you intend by thus continuing to intrude yourself? Do you believe you can overbear and intimidate us? We will hear none of your witnesses. We have heard you too long. Never was the dignity of administrative justice in any instance insulted with so bare faced and impudent a forgery! (337)

Williams goes insane and has as his 'keeper' the very man who was Falkland's agent of persecution, Jones. Falkland improves in health while Caleb goes to his grave unvindicated and mad. His final written words are 'all day long I do nothing – I am a stone – a GRAVE-STONE! – an obelisk to tell you, HERE LIES WHAT WAS ONCE A MAN!' (338). The words encapsulate the situation of one who has had all the rights pertaining to his status as human being – freedom of expression, freedom of conscience, equality before the law – systematically stripped from him until he is less than a man. Why did Godwin replace the misery and conspicuous lack of any resolution in his manuscript with the relatively resolved 1794 ending? Two answers suggest themselves. The first is that Godwin as a novelist realised that resolved endings can strengthen the intended didactic purpose and suggest that the evils of inequality can eventually be dismantled within the existing judicial system, once prejudice is attacked and rooted out. This goes against everything we have seen of the system in the novel, which presumably made Godwin keen to make his original message as bleakly unambiguous as possible. Second, in writing a novel originally entitled 'Things as They Are', Godwin, faced with the deterioration of natural rights in the period of the mid-1790s, and the state's use of the judicial system to repress still further free speech or dissident action, may have regarded pessimism as hopeless fatalism. He had declared himself in 1793 a meliorist in *Political Justice* – Keats described Dilke as 'a Godwin perfectibil[it]y Man'[9] – one who believes the world can improve, and he may have felt the need to show that such optimism can still be sustained. If so, he relied on the continued existence of the human quality which fuelled the sentimental novel, and which still lies, besieged and battered by circumstances, beneath the philosophy of *Political Justice*:

> The system of disinterested benevolence proves to us that it is possible to be virtuous, and not merely to talk of virtue; that all which has been said by philosophers and moralists representing impartial justice is not an unmeaning rant; and that, when we call upon mankind to divest themselves of selfish and personal considerations, we call upon them for something they are able to practise. An idea like this reconciles us to our species; teaches us to regard, with enlightened admiration, the men who have appeared to lose the feeling of their personal existence, in the pursuit of general advantage; and gives us reason to expect that, as men collectively advance in science and useful institution, they will move more and more to consolidate their private judgment, and their individual will, with abstract justice, and the unmixed approbation of general happiness. (387–8)

Mary Wollstonecraft

While Godwin can be said to have transmuted the philosophical material of *Political Justice* into the fictional mode of *Caleb Wiliams*, a unified and self-sufficient novel, the same cannot be said of the relation between Mary Wollstonecraft's *Vindication of the Rights of Woman* (1792) and *The Wrongs of Woman: or, Maria. A Fragment* (posthumously published 1798). The *Vindication* is polemical philosophy while *Maria* is a novel, but in many ways they are indistinguishable in terms of the author's relation to the material. Whole sections of the one could be transported into the other without great indecorum, for both works are infused with the same passionate didacticism and habit of providing powerful vignettes as examples of general principles. Both works could be described as 'fictional autobiography'. Even if the titles declare that the one work is on 'Rights' and the other on 'Wrongs', this also does not define a noticeable difference, because both present us with images of wrongs and statements of rights. To some extent it might be argued that, since *Maria* existed in fragmentary form and was only lightly pulled into shape by Godwin after his wife's death, she may well have envisaged a more free-standing and crafted novel than the one we have. But even this argument, aside from being unprovable, is not convincing on stylistic grounds, since the voice adopted in both works is so similar. All these points are made not to suggest that Wollstonecraft's accomplishment was any less than Godwin's – in many ways she has changed the world more decisively than Godwin ever did – but to justify treating the two works as rather like parts of a single, larger work, powerfully unified by a consistent preoccupation with equality between the sexes.

Wollstonecraft takes for granted the existence of natural rights, and her purpose is to build upon the basis of such rights, equality, to expose a limitation not only of European institutions but even of enlightened male philosophers like her husband. Equality is equality, and should not be limited to men. If women are equal to men then they should be given exactly the same rights as men. It is a measure of the entrenched ideological mindset which she was rebelling against that, despite the perfect reason and persuasiveness behind her arguments, advances were steadily made during the nineteenth century towards equality between *men*, while the rights of *women* did not really gather strong support until the twenteith century, and can still be said to be lagging behind. It is, for example, an irony that Wollstonecraft's publisher, Joseph Johnson, had in 1777 published a book, anonymously authored, which is essentially a summary of the laws of England concerning women's status, and this book alone would have given Wollstonecraft ample ammunition. Contrary to its title, *The Laws Respecting Women, As they regard their NATURAL RIGHTS* ... [10] illustrates the fact that in general women were not granted natural rights at all, despite the author's complacent eulogy:

> England has been stiled the Paradise of women; nor can it be supposed that in a country where the natural rights of mankind are enjoyed in as full an extent as is consistent with the existence and well-being of a great and extensive empire, that the interests of the softer sex should be overlooked. (vi)

The chivalric tone owes something to the sentimental movement, but the nitty-gritty of law detailed in the book demonstrates that outside royal families the legal position of women was entirely subservient in every respect to men, and it is obvious that the reforms hailed by the writer are minor and insignificant. It was in this context that Wollstonecraft took up the issue.

Wollstonecraft at the outset of *Rights of Woman* summarises 'The rights and duties of man' as flowing from certain 'axioms':

> the perfection of our nature and capability of happiness must be estimated by the degree of reason, virtue, and knowledge, that distinguish the individual, and direct the laws which bind society: and that from the exercise of reason, knowledge and virtue naturally flow, is equally undeniable, if mankind be viewed collectively.[11]

Her aim in the book, however, is not to prove or explore these 'natural rights' (92) as such, but to take them for granted and measure how far women have been denied them. 'Rights of man' should also, she argues, be 'rights of women', based on the same premise as Godwin's, equality, and she invokes the support of Milton's Adam who extols the 'harmony and true delight' of 'mutual' equality which leads to '*fellowship* ... fit to participate All rational delight'. Wollstonecraft had been deeply influenced by Rousseau but had come to hold reservations about his imagined 'state of nature' as an inappropriate model for the contemporary world,[12] and she also distances herself from writers who, in her own time, like Paine and presumably Godwin, claim certain rights. She is writing for the future: 'Rousseau exerts himself to prove that all *was* right originally; a crowd of authors that all *is* now right: and I, that all will *be* right' (95). In chapter 2, she reaches full momentum as she begins to describe and analyse 'the tyranny of man' over woman. She continually draws the analogy between the position of women and that of slaves, a comparison which had been regularly used by writers ever since *The Hardships of the English Laws in relation to Wives* (1735), which proclaims that 'the estate of wives is more disadvantagious than *Slavery* itself'.[13] Wollstonecraft's central point, however, is not so commonplace, as she argues that men have knowingly kept women in a state of ignorance, unable to exercise 'reason', deprived of 'knowledge', and in many cases stripped of 'virtue'. Such is the vicious circularity of the tactics, that even women come to collude in the deprivation of their daughters' full rights:

Women are told from their infancy, and taught by the example of their mothers, that a little knowledge of human obedience, and a scrupulous attention to a puerile kind of obedience, will obtain for them the protection of man; and propriety, will obtain for them the protection of man; and should they be beautiful, everything else is needless, for at least twenty years of their lives. (100)

Without education, women can easily be exploited and enslaved, because they will always be 'prey to prejudices', to vanity and unrealistic expectations, and they will submit to authority. They will always base their lives on an unconsidered commitment to the body, the emotions and 'manners' before reason and morality, and their best and most generous impulses of cooperation and loyalty will entrap them into submission to tyranny. With the underdevelopment of reason, 'the simple power of discerning truth' (142), women will lack 'the power of generalising ideas, of drawing comprehensive conclusions from individual observations' (143). Even the most apparently natural and emotional feelings of love, Wollstonecraft suggests, are dangerously untrustworthy to the uneducated and 'disorderly' mind of a woman who cannot foresee consequences or consider a future with a man who, after the flush of first romance has inevitably faded, may by chance and with luck turn out to be a friend but more likely to be indifferent.

Wollstonecraft places some blame for the enslavement of women on writers of fiction, and she savages the constructed heroine of the sentimental novel, 'the fanciful female character, so prettily drawn by poets and novelists, demanding the sacrifice of truth and sincerity' (139). Equal education is the fundamental agency for the goal of universal independence and for claiming natural rights, for women as well as men. And the agency and goal of education is also the key to natural law, reason:

> Let us then, as children of the same parent, if not bastardized by being the younger born, reason together, and learn to submit to the authority of Reason – when her voice is distinctly heard. But, if it proved, that this throne of prerogative only rests on a chaotic mass of prejudices, that have no inherent principle of order to keep them together, or on an elephant, tortoise, or even the mighty shoulders of a son of the earth, they may escape, who dare to brave the consequence, without any breach of duty, without sinning against the order of things. (201)

This theme is not inconsistent in Wollstonecraft's output, since her first book published was entitled *Thoughts on the Education of Daughters* ... (1787), and the first paragraph of that work announces her intentions:

> Indolence, and a thoughtless disregard of every thing, except the present indulgence, make many mothers, who may have momentary starts of tenderness, neglect their children. They follow a pleasing impulse, and never reflect that reason should cultivate and govern those instincts which are implanted in us to render the path of duty pleasant – for if they are not governed they will run wild; and strengthen the passions, which are ever endeavouring to obtain dominion – I mean vanity and self-love.[14]

Given her own background of climbing from educational deprivation to being a schoolteacher, Wollstonecraft clearly had a strong commitment, and perhaps claimed educational reform as her most radical and far-reaching emphasis, and as she claims, the way to 'reform the world'. In fact, so clear, fundamental, and insistent is the emphasis that education is the key to her thinking, it is surprising that there seems to be no close study of this strand in her thought. One reason for this scholarly deficiency may be in the prevailing view of Wollstonecraft as an advocate for narrowly 'women's rights' rather than the more comprehensive 'natural rights' with their origins in the rationality of natural law. Certainly one finds on every page evidence of keen indignation at the ways in which women are enslaved, but Wollstonecraft does not remain on the level of angry denunciation of specific instances, preferring to trace each example back to its source in educational deprivation, and secondarily in social inequalities. She quite specifically says that the problems are caused not by 'sexual character' but by lack of understanding caused by defective education (144). Perhaps also, in repeatedly insisting that men and women should be entirely equal in knowledge, reason and virtue, she does not suit at least one modern feminist paradigm, that reason is a defective emphasis of men, while emotion and corporeality are the wholly admirable provinces of women. This assumption she herself anticipates and attacks as merely the result of prejudice stemming from ignorance, and a way of further compounding and rationalising the inferior position of women.

Two other related reasons present themselves for the relative lack of attention to Wollstonecraft's adherence to rational education. One is the appeal of seeing her works as autobiographical and as allegorising the emotive chaos of her life. The other, more psychologically and equally auto-biographical, is the strong possibility that she saw reason and a focus on nat-ural rights as a willed counterweight to her own neuroses which impelled her to two suicide attempts and constantly threatened to overwhelm her. Many readers have found something paradoxical in her emphasis on reason, when her language is so emotive. Syndy McMillen Conger suggests that Wollstonecraft was a 'prisoner of language', and that although she spent her life consciously trying to escape the belief system of the cult of sensibility yet her language betrays her inability ever to do so.[15] Conger draws on philoso-phers like Gilbert Ryle and Eva Kittay who argue that, at least in some people, metaphoric language *is* their version of reality: an approach summed up in the title of the book by George Lakoff and Mark Johnson, *Metaphors We Live By*.[16] In another variation on a similar paradox, it might be argued that Samuel Johnson placed so much emphasis on reason and stylistic balance as bulwarks against his well-documented fear of madness.

Chapter 4 of *Rights of Women* gives examples of 'The State of Degradation to which Woman is Reduced' anticipating many situations in her novel, *The Wrongs of Woman*, and in Chapter 5 she attacks 'Writers', whether of phi-losophy, religion, novels, or poems, 'Who Have Rendered Women Objects of Pity' in an attempt to 'guard the mind from storing up vicious associations' (226). Her particular target, again, is Rousseau, who even in *Émile*, his book on education, does not extend its advantages to females. Chapter 7 takes the example of what is considered a quintessentially feminine characteristic, modesty, and systematically undermines it as 'Not a Sexual Virtue' but as a socially constructed way of subjugating women:

> Modesty! sacred offspring of sensibility and reason! – true delicacy of mind! ... Thou that smoothest the wrinkles of wisdom, and softenest the tone of the sublimest virtues till they all melt into humanity; thou that spreadest the ethereal cloud that, surrounding love, heightens every beauty, it half shades, breathing those coy sweets that steal into the heart, and charm the senses – modulate for me the language of persuasive reason, till I rouse my sex from the dowery bed, on which they supinely sleep life away! (227)

In these chapters she is staking out her own anti-sentimental and anti-romantic, novelistic aims. But the overall aim of the book, according to the argument pursued here, is summed up in the penultimate chapter, 'On National Education', where Wollstonecraft, without speaking of gender

divisions, says that inequalities, ignorance and misuse of power will continue to prevail, 'till education becomes a grand national concern'. (273) The
consistency with which she pursues this preoccupation throughout *Vindication
of the Rights of Woman* might be considered her most substantial and radical
contribution, at a time when very few writers saw education as an aspect of
the context for natural rights. Some followed in her wake: Maria Edgeworth
published *Practical Education* in 1798 and Hannah More wrote *Strictures on
the Modern System of Female Education* in 1799, but their campaign was not to
be taken up seriously for more than a century.

The unfinished but fitfully powerful novel, *The Wrongs of Woman; or, Maria*
is as much about pursuit and incarceration as Godwin's *Caleb Williams*, but
the prison here happens to be an asylum, and the central figure is a woman.
It presents a series of women telling their distressing tales of how they ended
up classified as mad, and each history reveals an aspect of the oppression of
women, as each one has been debased into 'a slave, a bastard, a common
property' (109)[17] by vindictive men. As Eleanor Ty writes, '*Wrongs of Women*
illustrates the universality of sexual oppression through the use of multiple
voices and echoing narratives'.[18] Jemima, the serving girl, was forced into
demeaning labour as a child, then into begging, stealing, selling her body, in
order to stave off poverty. Wollstonecraft attributes a great part of her misery
'to the misfortune of having been thrown into the world without the grand
support of life – a mother's affection' (106), and she explicitly draws the
analogy with slavery:

> I was, in fact, born a slave, and chained by infamy to slavery during the
> whole of existence, without having any companions to alleviate it by
> sympathy, or teach me how to rise above it by their example. (106)

The novel's power partly comes from 'the literalization of metaphors'[19] such
as slavery or the prison: she even coins a verb in saying that 'marriage had
bastilled [Maria] for life' (155). At the other end of the social scale, Maria has
been privileged in a wealthy family, and loved, but from an early age has
been treated as inferior to her favoured brother. Wollstonecraft puts into her
mouth virtually the same words she used in *Thoughts on the Education of
Daughters*, 'My mother had an indolence of character, which prevented her
from paying much attention to our education' (126). The context of her
other works suggests that Wollstonecraft links this deficiency with the fact
that Maria naively falls in love with George Venables, only to discover after
marriage that he is a boorish fortune-hunter intent on ruining her. She finds
herself a victim of her own 'goodness of disposition' and 'extreme credulity'
(143), both of which one imagines Wollstonecraft feels would have been
trained into discrimination by rational education. A similar pattern emerges
in Elizabeth Inchbald's *A Simple Story* (1791) where an 'improper' education
threatens the welfare of the heroine, Miss Milner, while she later in the novel

takes care to give her own daughter, Matilda, a 'proper' education:

> He has beheld the pernicious effects of an improper education in the destiny which attended the unthinking Miss Milner – On the opposite side, then, what may not be hoped from that school of prudence – though of adversity – in which Matilda was bred?
>
> And Mr Milner, Matilda's grandfather, had better have given his fortune to a distant branch of his family – as Matilda's father once meant to do – so he had bestowed upon his daughter A PROPER EDUCATION.[20]

The theme common to all Wollstonecraft's works, the untrustworthiness of the untutored emotions, is emphasised in the novel:

> A sense of right seems to result from the simplest act of reason, and to preside over the faculties of the mind, like the master sense of feeling, to rectify the rest; but (for the comparison may be carried still farther) how often is the exquisite sensibility of both weakened or destroyed by the vulgar occupations, and ignoble pleasures of life? (80)

Maria's marriage turns into a loveless prison, and she is eventually confined to the asylum so that Venables can appropriate what is left of her fortune. The heartfelt cry from Maria which ends Volume 1, 'Why was I not born a man, or why was I born at all?' (139) is repeated in various forms of words throughout the 'memoirs', as is the equation between women and slaves.[21] The issue common to these groups is the denial of the natural right to exist as a human being. A wife is 'as much a man's property as his horse, or his ass, she has nothing she can call her own' (158), laments Maria, who has been certified by her husband so that he can claim her legacy. In fact, the madhouse is one image in the book for the state of matrimony itself, from the dispossessed woman's point of view, 'the most insufferable bondage' (187). The injustice is enshrined in state law:

> If I am unfortunately united to an unprincipled man, am I for ever to be shut out from fulfilling the duties of a wife and mother? – I wish my country to approve of my conduct; but, if laws exist, made by the strong to oppress the weak, I appeal to my own sense of justice, and declare that I will not live with the individual who has violated every moral obligation which binds man to man. (197)

Like passages in *Rights of Woman*, these words show Wollstonecraft's adherence to the principles of classical natural law: a positive law which offends against conscience and shared moral obligations, is no law at all. And the repeated denials of liberty and full human status are represented as breaches of specific natural rights that can reduce women to either 'monsters' or of less than human intellect:

> By allowing women but one way of rising in the world, the fostering the libertinism of men, society makes monsters of them, and then their ignoble vices are brought forward as a proof of inferiority of intellect. (137)

Godwin's summary of the projected direction of the novel shows Wollstonecraft's strong denial of the happy ending characterising the senti-mental novel which, however well-intentioned in its social and political critique, does, according to Wollstonecraft, falsify 'the way things are'. Although a romantic hero exists for Maria in the person of Darnford, another persecuted victim in the madhouse, the notes make clear that he, like all the other men, will be unfaithful, and her own end is unsentimentally tragic: 'Divorced by her husband – Her lover unfaithful – Pregnancy – Miscarriage – Suicide' (202). Godwin labours the point of Wollstonecraft's rationalism and social realism:

> It was particularly the design of the author, in the present instance, to make her story subordinate to a great moral purpose, that of 'exhibiting the misery and oppression, peculiar to women, that arise out of the par-tial laws and customs of society.' – This view restrained her fancy. (204)

'Fancy' in this context refers to the falsifying and irrational distractions of imagination when natural rights are under consideration, and Wollstonecraft's example points toward Blake and later romantics like her posthumous son-in-law, Shelley: imagination may have been their creed, but it is rational imagination concentrated as much on bleak social realities as on hypotheti-cally ideal worlds, on actual wrongs as much as future rights – a world away from the sentimental imagination of earlier eighteenth-century writers, though linked by a common social purpose to reform the world upon foundations of natural rights.

John Thelwall

While Godwin and Wollstonecraft influenced the debate on natural rights solely through their writings, John Thelwall's impact was more immediately through political action. His writing remains as witness to his position, and is, in the contexts of this book and of modern democratic rights in general, more significant than theirs, yet his name is largely forgotten and certainly his published works are left unread. An admirer, E. P. Thompson, who planned to write a biography of Thelwall, satirically characterises the neglect: 'He also had the misfortune to be a mediocre poet – a crime which, although it is committed around us every day, historians and critics cannot forgive.'[22] At least one of Thelwall's editors tends to confirm this evaluation:

> The place of Thelwall in the Romantic context is clear enough. He was, besides being the friend of Coleridge, Southey, Wordsworth, Lamb, Hazlitt, and most London middle-class literary liberals, a central symbol of the victory of the pen and intellectual attainments over the power of established political power and tradition. He was never regarded as primarily a literary figure and certainly not as a poet.[23]

The conclusion was not 'clear enough' to Thelwall, who obviously regarded himself as a professional poet primarily. Admittedly, if the ripples and storms from across the Channel had not ignited Thelwall's political imagination to indignation at the abuse of natural rights in England, he would, probably deservedly, be given a minor role at best in the development of 1790s' fiction and poetry in its mingled use and rejection of sentimentalism, but the French revolution did stir him to his greatest prose. I shall place his political speeches, published though not often republished, as complements, extensions and adjuncts to his career as an author.[24]

Thelwall provided a kind of retrospective account of his work when, after purchasing in 1818 the weekly newspaper *The Champion* (which had published both Hazlitt and Keats), he published a volume of his own poetry which had first appeared in that forum, under the name *The Poetical Recreations of The Champion*[25] (1822). In the opening 'Advertisement', Thelwall in the third person calls this collection 'as much a Literary as a Political miscellany', saying he hopes to occasion 'intellectual refinement to go hand in hand with political enquiry', and adding 'nothing soothes the turbulent emotions of the human mind more than a taste for the elegancies of art and literature'. He says that 'poetry, in particular, was the first passion of his soul ... he is a votary of the Muses, from elective and natural propensity – a politician, only from a sense of duty' (v–vi). It was 'the peculiar circumstances of the times' which 'entangled him much more exclusively, in the mass of politics, than was consistent with his original plan or intention'. The poems in this volume are diverse in subject-matter, demonstrating that for him, in fact, poetry and politics can manifest self-consistent but different aspects of 'the structure of his own mind'. There are translations from the classics, prose disquisitions on pastoral scenery, lyrics on the nightingale, spring, and the wintry oak – alongside sonnets on 'The source of slavery' (the 'source' being 'Luxurious Pride' of the rich), 'To tyranny', 'To luxury', and so on. Most pertinently, there are short ballads: 'Stanzas on hearing for certainty that we were to be tried for high treason' (28 September 1794) and 'Stanzas written on the morning of trial, and presented to the four prisoners liberated on the same day' (dated 'Newgate, Dec. 1, 1794'). In both he clearly foresees how close he was to martyrdom, taking courage from the fact that his fate may 'benefit mankind'. Without comparing himself explicitly to Jesus Christ he does in *The Rights of Nature* say that Christ was crucified for 'preaching a great reform ... the spirit of a great reformer, martyr'd for a glorious principle, will rise again' [Claeys, 423]. However forgettable is the quality of the verse, we cannot fail to be impressed by the poetic commitment that drove him, more doggedly than most, to write for his very life.

Elsewhere, Thelwall characterises himself as a benevolent romantic, and if left alone he would happily have written on the customary romantic subjects forever. Nostalgia and pastoral loom large in his self-consciously literary works. His books of poetry and the ambitious work *The Peripatetic* bear out this judgement, however ironic and distressing he found the experience of being so hated by the government:

> Every private feeling has been belied; and every fact misrepresented; and the individual who for years has been remarked, by *all who knew him*, for carrying the principles of humanity to an extent which the world in general is disposed to consider as romantic – with whom the life of the meanest insect, not immediately hostile to the existence or comfort of man, is regarded as sacred and inviolable, has been publicly upheld, by name (that he might be deprived of all chance of an impartial trial) as a ruffian insatiable of blood, and to whom every crime was indifferent that might lead to the gratification of his ambition.[26]

Thelwall was first and foremost a professional writer, with almost sixty published works to his name, and a writer of rare consistency and integrity. The times – and personal danger – brought out the best in him, and his verbal manifestoes portray the same authorial persona as his poems and fictions, inspired to a higher degree of imaginative pressure, clarity and timely urgency. Hazlitt said that the written speeches do not convey such power as the spoken occasions:

> The most dashing orator I ever heard is the flattest writer I ever read ... sit down yourself, and read one of these very popular and electrical effusions (for they have been published) and you would not believe it to be the same! the thunder-and-lightning mixture of the orator turns out a mere drab-coloured suit in the person of the prose writer.[27]

But reading them now, one feels the reason behind Hazlitt's words can only be comparative, based on the sheer force of Thelwall's presence and rhetoric, since the written versions *do* now read as stirring defences of natural rights in the pre-democratic period. Also Hazlitt, a 'plain speaker' himself and a somewhat curt writer may not have appreciated that the rhetorical source of Thelwall's speeches is the long, Miltonic sentence building towards its crescendo. Thelwall often quotes Milton, and it is reasonable to assume that the prose strategy in his speeches was based on Milton's answer to Salmasius in *A Defence of the English People,* or perhaps even more pertinently, *Areopagitica.* The latter was Milton's defence of freedom to publish, while Thelwall's most memorable passages are those advocating freedom of association and of speech. His eloquence was all the more remarkable in light of the fact that he had overcome a debilitating stammer to become able to sway tens of thousands of listeners with his speeches. But irrespective of his oral persuasiveness, I argue that his works of fiction and poetry convey the same messages in different media.

In the mid-1790s it is no exaggeration to say that Thelwall was public enemy number one for the British government, and national laws were made for the single purpose of silencing him. That a jury acquitted him in late 1794, along with John Horne Tooke, Thomas Holcroft and Thomas Hardy, of a conviction under the law of constructive treason specifically passed to convict (and hang) him, is testament to his understanding not only of the forces against him but of the appeal to ordinary people's taste for exactly the natural rights he was espousing. In his defence, he indignantly turned the accusation of treason upon his accusers, arguing in most of his political speeches that the government was blatantly undermining the accord of the Glorious revolution in 1688, and thereby acting as traitors to the duly appointed king and the national constitution. Life was made hell for him by those whom he accused of the real treason, as they invaded not only his privacy but also his own natural right to live peaceably:

> every tavern and coffee-house has been haunted, into which (rare visitant as I have been to places of that description) I may occasionally have put my head. My hours of conviviality have been attended by spies and sycophants, my doors beset with eavesdroppers, my private chambers haunted by the familiar spirits of an infernal Inquisition, and my confidential friends stretched on the rack of interrogatory, in order to extort from them the conversation which in the unsuspecting hours of social hilarity may have been uttered at my own table.[28]

In his widow's memoir of Thelwall, she writes movingly of what happened to his life when he became involved in politics:

> the channels of vital sustenance have been dried up; and Friendship (the last stay of the human heart) – even Friendship, itself (a few instances of generous perseverance alone excepted) wearied and intimidated with the hostilities to which it was exposed, has shrunk from its own convictions, and left him in comparative insulation.[29]

Whether we describe Thelwall's writings positively as self-consistent or negatively as repetitive, there are clues to his thought that run through them all unwaveringly. He was on strong ground in asserting respectively his abhorrence of violence as an agency of change, his constitutionalism based on the 1688 agreement reinforced by Magna Carta, and his unashamed monarchism, since he saw the king as an essential court of appeal and as politically indifferent to the class structure. In these points he disagreed with Paine, who supported violent revolution, changing rather than supporting constitutional conventions, and republicanism, and these differences made Thelwall a far more insidious threat to the establishment. While Paine could be accused of simple treason and forbidden entry to Britain on pain of death, his works could be banned, and his ideas magisterially dismissed by Burke as contrary to 1688 principles, Thelwall's challenges could be met only by devious changes to the law prohibiting words that might hypothetically incite violence, anti-constitutionalism, or regicide, even though these are consequences overtly and carefully and consistently rejected by Thelwall himself. His further strength lay in his assertion of natural rights, the terms of which rise above party politics and ephemeral concerns – centrally, the right of every Englishman to speak his mind, rightly or wrongly, on contemporary issues, the consequent duty of parliament to represent the diversity of legitimate views, and the right of labouring people to be protected from exploitation by capital and from human indignity. His most constant themes were universal suffrage, annual elections, and a fairer distribution of wealth. All are justified by appeals to natural rights theory, and none of them were calculated to endear him to the English establishment of the 1790s.

Like many of the writers in this book, Thelwall replied to Burke in a work he entitled *Rights of Nature against the Usurpations of Establishments* (1796), and in it he indicates his own approach to natural rights. He describes Burke as 'a very desultory and excentric [sic] writer. His combustible imagination fumes, and boils, and bursts away, like the lava from a volcano (as bright and as destructive) in a thousand different directions; apparently without art or design' (395). In the book, Thelwall describes his own spirit as, 'unsubdued by persecutions, unawed by the daggers of assassins, unchilled by the cold neglect of an unsocial world, and forgetful of his own misfortunes ... [he] with the warm enthusiasm of conviction, proceeds to advocate the cause of man against the usurpations of establishments' (435). He contrasts Burke, for whom 'everything is natural that has the hoar of ancient prejudice upon it ... Nay, with him, that detestable traffic in blood and murder – that barter of groans, and tortures, and long lingering deaths, the *Slave Trade*, is also natural!!!' (405). Whereas Godwin had espoused the centrality of equality as an abstract principle, and Wollstonecraft had pursued the specific right of women to education, Thelwall sees political association and the removal of economic oppression as the central rights of man. He is more detailed in his description of natural rights than Godwin, and compared to the overtly political approach of Paine, he defines the '*First Principles*' (447) in more physical terms:

Thus, for example, *Man has naturally an equal claim to the elements of nature*; and although earth has been appropriated, by expediency and compact ... light, air, and water (with some exceptions) still continue to be claimed in common. (452)

This basis may be laid in the following axiom – *Man, from the very circumstances of his existence, has an inheritance in the elements and powers of nature, and a right to exercise his faculties upon those powers and elements, so as to render them subservient to his wants, and conducive to his enjoyments ... and to know the natural rights of others, it is only necessary to know our own.* (458)

When other individuals infringe such rights, they commit a nuisance which must be abated (452), and when institutions like governments infringe them, a revolutionary situation is created, since, Thelwall observes, 'in all the pages of history I have perused, there is not a single instance ... of a great, popular revolution taking place, till grinding, and long-continued oppression, had rendered it absolutely necessary; – till groaning Nature called for dire relief' (430). He sees the French revolution as a clear example of this rule, and he foresees the day when 'seven millions of enlightened Britons, all conscious of their natural and civil equality; all asserting their equal share in the common inheritance of *rights*, and producing "(in their persons)" their title deeds' (395).

Since his 'First Principles' are so elemental, Thelwall's special interest lies in those living closest to the land, labourers, and this attachment runs through all his writings, fictional, poetic and polemical. In replacing 'the Rights of Property' and 'Rights of the Peerage' with 'RIGHTS OF LABOUR-ERS', he defines their natural rights as grounded on the assumptions first, that 'As man [the labourer] is joint heir to the common bounties of nature' and is therefore owed a share of its benefits, and secondly that since 'out of common labour' have grown education, knowledge, intellectual refinement and so on, the labourer is equally entitled to a share of these mental fruits for himself and his family (478). It follows from both assumptions that the 'common interest' which underpins a civil society requires the political participation of all citizens through free speech and civil association. It is the first of these twin emphases in Thelwall's *Rights of Nature* that allows E. P. Thompson to argue that he 'took Jacobinism to the border of Socialism',[30] and the second, we might add, took him to the border of democratic theory.

Of special importance to the development of socialism was Thelwall's argument that the labourer has a right to a proportion of the employer's profits.[31] 'Origin and Distribution of Property' is the title of the third of the three 'Letters' making up Thelwall's *Natural Rights*.

The rights of man, thus considered, are simple in their elements. They are determined by his wants and his faculties; and the means presented by the general system of nature (that is to say, by the frame and elements of the material universe) for the gratification of the former, and the improvement of the latter. I repeat it, the natural rights of man, considered as an individual, are determined by his wants, his faculties, and his means. They have no other bounds. I care not upon what hypothesis of man you proceed: whether of creation, or eternal succession, of chance, of necessity, of inherent laws of matter and motion, or what not ... All lead to the same conclusion.[32]

Property is, then essentially for the benefit of all, employers and labourers, and is social in its origins and should by right be distributed for social rather than individual welfare.

Unlike revolutionary Paineite Jacobins, Thelwall stresses that violence cannot be used 'to equalize and secure the natural rights of man', because it was violence which had suppressed these rights. 'Moral arbitration' is to replace 'physical force', and the source of the moral arbitration is 'aggregate reason' (460). 'It is upon these principles only, that a multitude of individuals can be melted and organized into one harmonious mass' (461). For Thelwall, community equilibrium, 'the welfare and happiness of all' is the result of securing and protecting the natural rights of individual people, and what he envisages is the fair distribution of economic resources. If society does not fulfil this condition, then, he argues, 'the people (all gentler means having been found ineffectual) have a right – a firm, inalienable right, to renounce the broken compact, and dissolve the system' (461). He does not specify how this right can be effected without force, so despite his repeated statements of pacifism, he may leave as one last resort, revolution. He never, however, renounces or challenges universal adherence to the English constitution (which he especially locates in the 1688 settlement), to the monarchy, and to the cause of non-violent protest.

> For, whatever speculative opinions I may entertain, no *speculation* was ever yet presented to my mind which I would attempt to advance by crimes and violence. I respect the peace – I respect the happiness of society – that peace without which virtue can never flourish – that happiness without which Liberty itself would be but an empty name.[33]

The fact that he did not threaten violent revolution was the aspect of Thelwall's reformism which most maddened his adversaries, since it preempted simple measures that could have silenced him. Behind his firm adherence to peaceful change based on open discussion, lies a belief in natural law's 'Reason and the pure spirit of philosophy' (Claeys, 57) and its equivalent in the world of the novels Thelwall would have read, 'Benevolence!'.

The assertion of the right to civil association which was to be of special significance to the call for democratic principles, is most powerfully voiced in Thelwall's more personal statements, and in particular his 'Vindication', the defence speech in the trial against him for high treason, significantly entitled *The Natural and Constitutional Right of Britons To Annual Parliaments, Universal*

Suffrage and the Freedom of Popular Association ... (1795), and his short speech to the jury congratulating them on acquitting him. The charges levelled against Thelwall and the others, created by new and virtually *ad hominem* laws, were variously called 'constructive treason', 'sedition', or 'subverting the monarchy', and they effectively attempted to stifle all public criticism of government actions.[34] Here is Thelwall in full, scathing flight against the laws, and his appeal is to the natural rights of free speech and assembly:

> It is more to my purpose to shew you the precipice to the brink of which these legal sophisters have conducted you: for if it be true, that to seek to alter or ameliorate the laws and constitution of your country is high treason, because the people may *possibly* become unreasonable in their demands, and the government may *possibly* oppose their wishes, and a context may *possibly* ensue, in which the King may *possibly* be deposed or slain, then farewell at once to every boasted exercise of reason! – farewell to political improvement! – farewell even to the hope of regenerating the venerable institutions of our ancestors, or preserving the mouldering fragments that yet remain! – if it is high treason for the people to lift up their voices when they conceive themselves oppressed by partial and arbitrary laws – If it is high treason to seek for political amelioration by impressing the legislature with an aweful sense of the collective wishes of the people, in what but in name consists the difference between the *free-born Briton* and the *Asiatic slave*? (11)

Thelwall is here ridiculing the specific crime as against the natural law basis of reason, and also linking the cause of free speech to the other leading libertarian cause of the day, abolition of slavery. Such a potent set of linkages, expressed alternately with defiant sarcasm and Miltonic grandeur, was calculated to stir the national dignity of a jury of 'free-born Britons'. It is significant that before the trial, the prosecution had attempted, unsuccessfully, to exclude the right of trial by jury in this case, a particularly inflammatory move hardly calculated to endear the prosecution case to the twelve good men and true. Trial by jury had always been cherished as a symbol of English justice, so entrenched that it was regarded as virtually a natural right. Thelwall skilfully, and with an apparently instinctive consistency, weaves his whole defence around an appeal to the jury to recall and preserve such fundamental rights:

> Peaceably to meet in such assemblies [corresponding societies and similar political discussion groups], and compare their sentiments on the proceedings of Government is, I contend, an absolute right of the people and every part of the people of this country – the *constitutional right* of non-electors as well as constituents – of those who have no particular representatives as well as those who have. (35)

Nowadays such claims may seem self-evident in a democracy (although perhaps they are taken for granted with a dangerous complacency), but in the 1790s they were far from accepted by governments. The right of association, Thelwall argues, is a fundamental one:

> The political freedom of the people – their habits of public intercourse, and voluntary association, have hitherto been the root of all the blessings, and all the virtues they could ever boast. If you love the fruit, lay not the axe to the vital fibres. (46)

Beneath his argument for freedom of speech, participatory politics and the right to association, lies Thelwall's characteristic economic preoccupation with a more fair distribution of profits between employers and workers, based on his perception that labour is a form of property in its own right:

> Let us not deceive ourselves! – Property is nothing but human labour. The most inestimable of all property is the sweat of the poor man's brow: – the property from which all other is derived, and without which grandeur must starve in the midst of supposed abundance. And shall they who possess this inestimable property be told that they have no rights, because they have *nothing* to defend? Shall those who toil for our subsistence, and bleed for our protection, be excluded from all importance in the scale of humanity, because they have so toiled and bled? (31)

Throughout the 1790s, and indeed up to 1817, the government passed a series of laws, increasingly more repressive and ugly, in an attempt to curb radical political activity or criticism of the government. The specific Bills introduced in 1795 by Pitt and Grenville, opposed in parliament by Fox and Erskine, were to become known as 'gagging Acts' (or alternatively, 'The Two Acts'). The first, the Treasonable Practices Act extended treason to include not just acts but also intentions, expressed by word of mouth or written. The second, the Seditious Meetings Act, made illegal public meetings of more than fifty people, and gave discretion to magistrates to ban meetings. They were opposed publicly by William Godwin in *Considerations on Lord Grenville's and Mr Pitt's Bills* and by the various Constitutional Societies around Britain, most notably the London one. These and other Bills attempted, for example, to suspend habeas corpus (dating from 1679, a prisoner had the right to be informed of his crime and tried immediately), to criminalise outspoken criticism of the government, to prevent extra-parliamentary political meetings, to tax publications in order to put their price beyond ordinary readers, and so on. Conservatives even attempted to abolish the right to trial by jury. Thelwall spoke against each of these measures, which lent them a circularity based on the fact that they were specifically designed to gag *him*. As an example, he addressed the London Corresponding Society on November 12, 1795 on a field near Copenhagen

House, the third of increasingly multitudinous mass meetings in five months, and judging from accounts truly massive, numbering some 200,000.[35] Thelwall, who had only recently joined the London Corresponding Society for tactical reasons, published the speech with an opening 'Advertisement' signed by the chairman and secretary of the Society. Thelwall attacks the politicians who had passed the act criminalising 'constructive treason', saying they have tried to destroy 'Liberty of Speech' and 'the rights of the nations'.[36] As usual, he carefully distances himself and the Society from violence, expressing 'abhorrence of all tumult and violence' (3), and from any hint of criticising the king, arguing that the 'errors and misconduct' were perpetrated by ministers alone. He also claims 'the constitutional right of resisting oppression, as our ancestors resisted it of old' (4). He then, in a spirit of triumphalism, turns all the charges of treason on the ministers proposing the bill, and presents for endorsement by the Society a petition to the king, a right allowed by the Bill of Rights (1689), accompanied by petitions to the Lords and the Commons, basically arguing that the bills illegally repeal the Bill of Rights itself. Thelwall's tactics in the petition are very straightforward. He rests the case entirely on 'British Constitutional Liberty, as established by the principles of the Revolution in 1688', augmented by the terms of the Bill of Rights and the Act of Settlement (1701) which established the line of the royal family. To remain silent in the face of Lord Grenville's latest bill to circumscribe free speech would be, Thelwall argues, 'in reality one of those acts of *constructive treason* which it is the apparent intention of this bill once more to naturalise among us! It would be, in fact, joining in the conspiracy against the Constitution established at the REVOLUTION in 1688, and by virtue of which the House of Brunswick was seated on the British throne' (iv).

> We then are the loyal men; the framers of the present Bill, according to their own new-fangled doctrines of constructive treason, are the traitors. (8)

Thelwall firmly places the issue of suppression of free speech in the territory of natural rights: 'I will reverence the *peace of Society* – but I will never relinquish the *rights of man*' (16), and he emphatically declares, '*the voice of the People is the voice of God!*' (18). The crucial 'right' is the opportunity of subjects, either directly or through government, to advise the monarch along the lines of 'reason', and if this right is taken away then reason itself is abandoned as a basis for the monarch's policies:

> Let us then make use of our reason, as long as they will permit us to reason; and when they will not suffer us to reason any longer, why then you know we reasoning beings can no longer advise you what measures to pursue. (19)

Commentators, like Gregory Claeys, base Thelwall's historical importance on his contribution to socialist thought in terms of redistribution of profits in a more equitable way, shared between employers and labourers, but for the purposes of this book his contribution lies in standing firm against an increasingly repressive government, on what he regards as the central natural rights: the right of labouring people not to live in poverty; the right to free speech; and the right to free association so that people could gather to discuss and debate public issues. He was more dangerous to the government than Paine because he repeatedly declared himself against violent revolution and against republicanism, swearing allegiance to the monarch as the duly constituted authority in the state, over and above governments. He was also more dangerous than Paine because he was in the country (Paine was banished on pain of death), irrepressibly speaking and writing (Paine's *Rights of Man* was officially banned), acquitted by juries when attempts were made to imprison or hang him, and by dint of all these conditions he was actively, on a daily basis, reaching and influencing many thousands of people. No other radical, not even Richard Price, Horne Tooke or Holcroft, withstood such sustained threats and still remained politically active. Eventually he was effectively banned from lecturing or publishing on overtly political issues, but this meant first that his cause could now be public martyrdom to the right of free speech, and secondly he happily continued lecturing, giving the same messages in coded form about tyranny and natural rights, but in the context of apparently innocuous subjects on classical history and literature and Shakespeare, while he continued to make a modest if reclusive living by giving elocution lessons.

Thelwall's political speeches and pamphlets are certainly where his prose takes fire and rises to memorable heights. His fiction and poetry, like his lectures on the Roman empire, often display in imaginative modes the beliefs he held most dear in his political expressions, and like Godwin's and Wollstonecraft's novels, they are to some extent 'fictionalised manifestos'. Even in writing an historical ballad, 'John Gilpin's Ghost' (1795), he manages to insert his brand of egalitarianism and rights of man:

> 'He tells them, *common folks are men,*
> *And should like men be treated;*
> *Nor, like a swinish multitude,*
> *By wealthy knaves be cheated.*'

However, it must readily be admitted that a revival of Thelwall's popularity as an imaginative writer is unlikely. Despite the sheer bulk of his output, his work is not to modern taste. However, this is not to diminish the historical importance of his writing, not just because of his political significance but because it contributes to the development of romantic literature. *Lyrical Ballads* has rightly garnered the attention of romantic commentators, but in many ways Thelwall's contribution, in its time, was just as important.

One would be hard-pressed to confine *The Peripatetic* (1793) within a single genre, as a glance at its full title suggests: *THE PERIPATETIC; OR,*

SKETCHES OF THE HEART, OF NATURE AND SOCIETY, IN A SERIES OF POLITICO-SENTIMENTAL JOURNALS, IN VERSE AND PROSE, OF THE ECCENTRIC EXCURSIONS OF SYLVANUS THEOPHRASTUS; SUPPOSED TO BE WRITTEN BY HIMSELF.[37] It is, quite literally, a rambling book, following the travels around Britain and the conversations of the narrator and his amiable friend, Ambulator. Beyond that generalisation, we can find a loose but original structure which builds in many of the literary modes popular in the day. Travel and topography are provided, to attract a certain readership, the new middle-class English tourists, and regularly we are given descriptions of towns, villages and countryside written in the style of the later Baedeker series of travel guides. Descriptions of landscapes rise into the rhetoric of the romantic sublime, and Salvator Rosa's name is invoked. Friendship literature is represented since the two 'ambulators' cross paths with other friends who discuss issues of the day, and there are two romantic love stories woven around the sentimental Belmour and the unsentimental but eccentric Ambulator. Political satire on judges, lawyers and government officials frequently occurs. Finally, the prose is punctuated by flights of poetry – epic, lyric and ballad – written and read by the narrator, an undisguised version of Thelwall himself. His literary favourites are poets like Milton, who is copiously quoted, Gray (ii, 117), and 'the elegiac sonnets … of Charlotte Smyth' (i, 123), and there is an intriguing coincidence with Blake who, in the same year wrote his poem 'Visions of the Daughters of Albion', when Thelwall offers a poem beginning, 'Daughters of Albion's gay enlighten'd hour!' (i, 35). The mixture of genres sounds chaotic but in fact works to provide a consistent reading experience that draws us along in the unobtrusive way of the geographical ramble which gives the book its core. However, the degree of consistency is undoubtedly provided not by structure but point of view, since in this 'politico-sentimental journal' Thelwall's running commentary gives a set of social and political attitudes characteristic of his more embattled speeches and pamphlets, and his vocabulary is recognisably that of natural rights. The central focus is on 'the neglected terms HUMANITY! EQUAL JUSTICE! and GENERAL HAPPINESS!', and 'the imprescriptible Rights of the oppressed and lower orders of the community' (1, 172–3). '*Labour*', as Thelwall says elsewhere, 'as must be admitted, constitutes the real wealth of the community' (ii, 45), while 'sympathy and benevolence' are social and religious imperatives (ii, 91). He states in this book, as elsewhere, that not only the suffering but the 'profligacy' of the poor '*is the greatest evidence of a* VICIOUS GOVERNMENT': 'it is impossible for the tree to be good, whose fruit is rank and vicious' (iii, 130–1). Still indignant at inequalities and erosion of natural rights, he is more relaxed and imaginative in exposing them in this book than in his speeches. The main preoccupation is with poverty amongst rural workers, a fact which in itself distinguishes the book from middle-class tourist accounts which carefully hide this grim fact of life. The counterweight is a ferocious attack on decadent privilege, often imaged as in Shelley's *Ozymandias* by the 'ruin'd pile' which is all that remains of some vain, 'savage lord' (i, 183).

Everything in *The Peripatetic* is coloured by Thelwall's provocative analysis of English social and political life, and even places become politically charged: Dartford is celebrated as the town where Wat Tyler's insurrection began (ii, 24). 'Professional beggary' (i, 2) is attacked as a class betrayal of the industrious poor by the idle, who hypocritically exploit 'Powers of sympathy' (i, 34) and help to obscure the genuine needs and rights of poverty-stricken labourers and their families. A poem beginning unpromisingly 'Commerce! thou doubtful, and thou partial good!' (i, 38) introduces the attack on wealth, ambition and avarice which 'fatten'st a few upon the toils of all' (i, 39). It is shortly followed by an 'Ode to the American Republic' (i, 41), contrasting Britain with the recently liberated republic which is free of class distinctions and 'Privilege's tyrant chain', a land free of oppression and, as Thelwall sees it, marked by *'genuine* liberty'. A short poem on 'fair Reason's golden ray' (76) takes Thelwall into the regions of natural law and allows him to launch an attack on 'hereditary prejudice' which interestingly, at some points, he links up with romantic sentimentality. 'Darkness and unoccupied solitude might have led to madness', he writes, contrasting 'the pure and simple form of a milder persuasion, whose universal benevolence smiles endearment to the heart of Sensibility' (i, 77). The character who epitomises romantic solitude is Belmour the lover who, although presented as a friend to the narrator, is also reproved by him as showing a 'sullen melancholy' (i, 179) which lacks the 'lucid focus' (179) of reason and is 'deranged' to the point of 'mental insanity' (180). More pertinently, Thelwall considers this kind of romantic love to be just as destructive as hereditary wealth, in their common commitment to extreme individualism and self-indulgence. At his worst, Belmour is seen as 'steeled by his own particular sorrows against the interests, or the miseries of mankind' (i, 102), but he has the promising capacity, at least temporarily, to be stirred by the narrator's passionate social conscience. In Thelwall's eyes, 'enthusiasm' both in its religious connotation of fanaticism and its secular romantic equivalent of inward inspiration, is dangerous. By contrast, Ambulator also falls in love and eventually marries, but his love is more prudent and open-eyed. A sympathetic character called Wentworth advises young people to 'consult their Reason, as well as their Senses, in their choice of a partner: and (the delusions of romantic expectation being cha[s]ed away) by not expecting *more*, they might attain *all* the Happiness which Human Nature is capable of enjoying' (iii, 9).

The most insistent refrain in *The Peripatetic* is a demand for equality based on the humanity and natural rights of the individual. Ambulator, for example, is introduced as the exemplar, as one who is 'no enthusiast' and a defender of 'the Rights and Liberties of Mankind!' (i, 55–6):

– yet is Ambulator a steady and determined advocate for *the genuine principles of* LIBERTY *and* EQUALITY; since, while he *regards as sacred the rights and possessions of every individual,* he esteems the distinctions of *Nature* superior to those of *Fortune,* and (paying his *obedience,* only to the LAWS) proportions his *respect* to the *virtues* and *abilities* of men, and not to their *rank* and *opulence.* (i, 56)

In every social dealing he behaves 'with the respect that is due from one *Human Being* to another'. Thelwall elsewhere gives many examples of the hypocrisy of those who assert '*that the law of England is equally open to the rich and to the poor*' (i, 120). 'The necessities of the poor' are at the mercy of 'Grandeur and Opulence' which, in the person of 'the imperious lord' demean and destroy the 'poor peasant (by the sweat of whose brow he eats)'.

> Whatever be the cause, the poor inhabitant is driven from his cottage, from his little garden, and his bubbling spring, to seek, perhaps, a miserable habitation within in the smoky confines of some increasing town. (i, 135)

Thelwall is describing the consequences of enclosures of common land by aristocrats, consequences which include rural unemployment, ill-health and personal misery. 'Shame upon thee, unfeeling grandeur!' is his verdict (i, 136). Poor people, deprived of access to common lands, and driven by need and hunger to steal, are hanged by an act of 'wanton Tyranny' (i, 140): 'And are they thieves, then? – Are these poor wretches thieves?'. An old peasant vehemently expresses his outrage at the state of England:

> Detested villains! – Proud parochial tyrants! – And are these violators of all that endears society the objects who are to monopolize your generosity, while the oppressed mechanic groans in our streets unpitied, and the aged and infirm, whose strength has been exhausted in the labours most important to the community, feel the oppressions of want and sorrow accumulated to the infirmities of years, and apply for relief in vain! – (iii, 137–8)

Like Milton and other radicals, Thelwall blames the steady deterioration of England on 'the *Norman,* that *enslaved the English nation*' by oppressing 'the root, or scion of the *Saxon colony*' (ii, 73). In analysing the disturbing social implications of class difference and disrespect for natural rights, Thelwall, through Ambulator, contrasts the persecution of 'associations' of spokesmen for the poor with the lack of public acknowledgement of 'the association' of 'the wealthy few, at the expense of the entire depression of the many' (i, 146). The narrator warns his friend to 'Hush! hush! ... suppress this freedom of speech, and remember ... confederated placemen invite us to turn informers' (i, 147), a reference to the attack on free speech in the 1790s and to Thelwall's personal experiences. In an explicit reference to bribed and

perjured informers, the pun is made contrasting 'loyal' and 'royal' associa-
tors, the latter relying on the *'slavish* principle of *implicit obedience to the
arbitrary wills of kings and ministers'* (iii, 134).

In the many other 'effervescences of political enthusiasm' (ii, 99) which
pepper the three volumes, Thelwall unrelentingly flays privilege and tyranny
while extolling the virtues of honest toil and defending the natural rights to
subsistence and political representation of the labouring class. However,
sometimes with conspicuous incongruity, the tone switches when concentration returns to description and history of English towns and landscapes, and
the more 'romantic' side of Thelwall re-emerges. In an image that recurs, he
subliminally likens the poor of England to small birds who do not even
realise they are trapped. Early on the skylark is the tuneful victim of two bird-
catchers and the narrator observes 'a heap of little captives, placed in cages
around, or fixed to ductile springs at apparent liberty, [which] were pouring
forth to allure their unsuspecting fellows into similar bondage' (i, 33). Later it
is the thrush: 'Poor little captive! he had not lived, indeed, to draw out a lingering existence, and flutter his little hopeless wings against the bars of an
inexorable cage. The prospect of endless slavery had broken his little heart'
(ii, 13). This seems his abiding, poignant image of a once-proud English people trapped into degrading poverty by economic exploitation and outright
tyranny, living without even knowing that natural rights to comfortable existence, to a portion of the nation's wealth built on their labour, and to a voice
in the governing of the country, had been systematically stripped away.

An exception proves the rule: Thomas Holcroft

The three professional novelists, each of whom wrote a self-consistent,
parallel 'manifesto' of some sort, developed different aspects of natural law
theory. Thelwall was the one who most steadily based his output on a direct
appeal to 'the rights of man', carving his niche as a non-violent equivalent
of Tom Paine, working in fictional modes. Godwin, the most substantial
theorist of all, in his novels internalised natural law as a powerful moral
imperative whose social outcome could be a rationally organised, egalitarian
and harmonious community, and whose violation would lead the errant
individual into a nemesis of conscience equivalent to madness and far more
terrifying than any punishment society could mete out. Wollstonecraft took
the inevitable and important step of extending the rights of man to apply
also to women, particularly the right to equal education and equal freedom
from ignorance, which would, she argued, lead to freedom from patriarchal
institutions. But lest it appear that all libertarian novelists based their works
on an explicit 'rights of man' model, and lest it appear that this model itself
was a convention amounting to a cliché, it is worth looking at the example
of Thomas Holcroft. He is another who, like Thelwall, wrote a 'manifesto' in

the form of a personal defence, and who also wrote novels as well as many plays. He espoused radical positions on particular issues, but shows few signs of embracing an overall theory of natural rights. He arrives at these positions through the application of pure reason, and it is not surprising that his personal contribution was acknowledged by Godwin as an important influence on *Political Justice*. Holcroft lies at the 'dry' end of rationalism, seeing no need to appeal, like Paine, to revolutionary enthusiasm or, like Godwin in *Caleb Williams*, to the terrors of conscience. There is some evidence in the novel *The Adventures of Hugh Trevor*, at least, that this stance was motivated neither by extreme scepticism nor temperamental intellectualism, but instead by recoil from some personal experience with uncontrolled emotionalism: so many of his negative characters are what we would describe as manic-depressive or adult sufferers from attention deficit disability that a strong reference back to solid factuality and the touchstone of social stability seem to be his constant refrains. The result in the case of his various 'defences' is a stolid and imperturbable literal-mindedness which makes theorising seem a luxury, while in the case of his fictions he emerges as a natural satirist.

Holcroft must have driven his antagonists and official persecutors to distraction with the kind of micro-logic he applied to his own situation. He was one of the group including Thelwall and Horne Tooke of 'acquitted felons' (an unfair phrase coined by William Windham, violating English common law presumptions of 'innocent until proved guilty'), placed on trial in 1794 for 'constructive treason' on the basis of their contributions to the Society for Constitutional Information. After the first arraigned, Thomas Hardy, was acquitted by the jury, the government realised it could not successfully prosecute the rest, and tried to extricate itself from the judicial mess. But Holcroft for one was determined to extract maximum embarrassment to the impotent prosecution. At the outset, when his name was included amongst those to be prosecuted, he did not await the indignity of arrest but presented himself to the police as Thomas Holcroft of the designated address, but not as *the* Thomas Holcroft alleged to have committed treason. In this way he avoided incriminating himself, while equally avoiding the entrapment of arrest, and it is amusing to see the prosecutors trying lamely to identify him as the person named to be convicted as a traitor to the country. It is equally amusing to trace the attempts by the frustrated Chief Justice to silence him, when, even after acquittal, Holcroft persistently claimed the right to read one of the defences he had so fastidiously prepared. It is not hard to discern his triumphant relish as he demands just half an hour of the court's time, knowing full well that it will not be granted and that his written statements will be published for all to read. Where other defendants were soberly engaged with the procedures of prosecution, or patently frightened, Holcroft manages to ridicule the institution of political prosecution.

In the 'narrative of facts' which constitute his published defence(s), Holcroft refers to no overarching theory of the rights of man, but instead constantly returns to simple statements reiterating the corruptness and absurdity of an electoral system that allows 161 rich males to monopolise the entire decision-making machinery of England. Holcroft has simplified the situation to clarify the issue of injustice, but his point is clearly justified in the light of the figures supplied by a modern commentator:

> Only 5 per cent of a total population of 8 million in 1790 could vote in England and Wales. In the 1780s 6000 electors, or a majority of the voters of 129 boroughs, returned 257 MPs, or a majority of the Commons. Fifty MPs were elected by a mere 340 voters. *In the early 1790s, 162 people (71 peers and 91 commoners) secured the election of 306 MPs.* Moreover, 43,000 electors selected 52 MPs for 23 cities and two universities, while 41,000 chose 369 MPs for towns and boroughs. The boroughs and a few towns were thus grossly over represented, and the commercial cities correspondingly neglected. Old Sarum was uninhabited but returned two members[38]

In all but name this is clearly rule by a tiny inherited oligarchy rather than anything like 'the consent of the people' which Locke and others had argued was the spirit behind the 1688 settlement. Holcroft makes no more extravagant claim than the one that this is clearly not a system based on fair representation, and by limiting his logic to this simple fact he makes his position unassailable. There are no grandiose statements of rights, or vulnerable complaints of wrongs, just a myopic concentration on a simple fact which contains within itself a revelation of breathtaking institutional injustice. At the same time, he repeats many times that he abhors violence and therefore cannot be guilty of constructive treason since that 'crime' involves contemplating violence in imagining the killing of the king. As an 'opponent of all violence, and a determined friend to the publication of truth' (4), described by others as 'a kind of Quaker', he relies entirely on 'the Powers of the Human Mind', the 'more powerful operation of Philosophy and Reason' (55) to persuade his fellow-countrymen that peaceful change to a more representative parliamentary system is possible and necessary. Such change, he says, is being hindered by the government of the day, which has employed violence and provocation, which has created an unjust and unenforceable law to suppress freedom of speech, and which has invaded traditional rights by, for example, suspending the habeas corpus acts. The government, Holcroft asserts, is acting in the interests of nobody but the beneficiaries of the status quo, the handful of rich landowners who are overwhelmingly favoured by the corrupt electoral system. Holcroft does not approach the issue as one of rights, but as one of a logical absurdity that any reasonable person will acknowledge and seek to rectify. His deeper spring of motivation, he says, is a belief in 'enlightened benevolence': 'Yes, from deep rooted long meditated principle, Benevolence has been my system' (second defence, 23). Whether by conscious strategy or temperamental caution, Holcroft avoids the righteous indignation and anger which could be seen as steps on the way to violence, by avoiding an assertion of rights that have been violated.

In his novels, too, Holcroft focuses on some specific things which are wrong in the world as manifestations of an abdication from human reason, rather than claiming that a world based on natural rights would be a better one. In this sense he certainly belongs amongst the radical, Jacobin novelists of the 1790s, but not amongst those considered in this book, novelists of natural rights. In *The Adventures of Hugh Trevor* (1794), he points out the disastrous consequences for the poor of government tithes and excises, 'a cause that disturbs half the villages in the kingdom',[39] and he satirises the corrupt electoral system. His main targets for criticism are the English legal system, the church, universities, parliament itself and the aristocracy which it represented. All are alienated and exposed as corrupt by the prevailing point of view which normalises reason. Holcroft, in quite a modern way, builds in a meta-level of stylistic theory, as his protagonist, a would-be writer, continually has his style picked apart by the sober and reasonable Mr Turl, a literary critic who espouses the moral virtues of a prose style which is simple, unembellished, and truthful (123). It is to be assumed that Holcroft is implicitly drawing an unfavourable contrast with the style of Burke, which was notoriously fine-sounding, poetical, and – according to detractors like Paine – hollow. As in his *Defence*, Holcroft views social correction not as the outcome of revolution or the instatement of natural rights, but rather as based on inner conversion away from unreason and towards the enlightenment of reason. Everything he wrote (and is reported as saying), adds up to a genuine horror of irrationality that leads to 'error' and inequities, and an equally genuine belief in the capacities of human reason to recognise truth and virtue. Instead of the anger of Paine and Thelwall, and the psychological probing of Godwin in *Caleb Williams*, we find in Holcroft a tone of ridicule for those who abandon reason, and a palpable puzzlement as to why they should want to do so. If anything this is pure natural law theory, but he never shifts his presentation to the level of theory, just as his stance is typical of radical dissenting Protestantism (that of 'a kind of Quaker') without making the doctrines of religion itself an issue. The epistolary novel, *Anna St. Ives* (1792), whose plot is loosely based on Richardson's *Clarissa*, contrasts on the one side the altruistic, co-operative rationalists, Frank (carefully named) and Anna, who anticipate a coming utopia when reason and truth will guide people's actions, and on the other side the egotistical, cunning and passionate villain, Coke Clifton. The struggle is pitched not on issues of natural rights or corrupt political institutions, but on the level of an archetypal clash between the forces of rational virtue and irrational vice.

Godwin readily acknowledged Holcroft's personal contribution to his own *Political Justice*, regarding Holcroft as a wise corrective influence over his own tendency to become passionate in his causes, and Hazlitt, who was later to commit to writing Holcroft's *Memoirs*, saw him as one who advocated a 'gradual, calm and rational' progress towards 'political and moral improvement'. Such recognition from important representatives of radical thinking in England indicate his own central contribution to that tradition, but he helps us, by default, to group together those who espouse natural rights as a central issue of the day. He does not see the need to make such an affirmation, presumably because he believed the instatement of a worldly version of rational natural law would either inevitably and without fuss lead to natural rights, or alternatively, that such a utopia would make the assertion of rights unnecessary and irrelevant.

Helen Maria Williams

Helen Maria Williams certainly deserves a place in this book, but it is not entirely clear where she 'fits'. She has, perhaps most accurately, been called a 'radical chronicler', by Chris Jones,[40] and she is probably best known through her correspondence from France during the revolution. However, she also wrote poetry and novels. Known from early in her career as one attached to the cult of sensibility (the 16-year-old Wordsworth wrote a 'Sonnet on seeing Miss Helen Maria Williams weep at a Tale of Distress'), she also wrote strongly political poetry. Like Charlotte Smith, she gained early fame with her poetry, and then looked as though she would establish a reputation as a novelist. She did not continue in this direction, but instead followed her political enthusiasm and set up a radical, Girondin salon in post-revolutionary Paris, to be visited by political *literati* like Godwin, Wollstonecraft, Amelia Opie and Wordsworth, and she was on good terms with Fox and even Burke. Her true claim to literary fame lies in the volumes of *Letters from France*, 1790–96, and then *Letters on the events which have passed in France since the restoration in 1815*. Taken all together, the *Letters* chart a radical's progress from ebullient enthusiasm for the revolution, towards disillusionment with its excesses and with Napoleon, but still a consistent belief in its egalitarian aims. While others, like Coleridge and Wordsworth, came to feel that the revolution failed because of its own internal logic and contradictions, Williams felt it had been betrayed by individuals, like Robespierre, who had exhibited the traditional aspirations of despots: 'though tyrants and despotism will assuredly vanish before the light of reason, yet freedom and the people will be eternal'.[41] Her allegiance was to the aspirations towards equality and natural rights of individuals, which had been betrayed by the ambitions of leaders.

Although Williams wrote no 'manifesto' yet her life itself showed a commitment to a political programme, support for the egalitarian principles and natural rights represented by the spirit of the French revolution. Her poems, fiction, and letters show a mind capable of political reflectiveness, firm beliefs, and a capacity to turn these beliefs into fictions. *Sui generis*, Williams, more than any other writer, displays all facets of the interaction between literature and issues of natural rights, and even though she never wrote a sustained work of political philosophy, her actions spring from a coherent philosophy. The two sides to her makeup, the sentimentalist and the radical, are perhaps best conveyed in passages from her *Letters*:

> You will not suspect that I was an indifferent witness of such a scene. Oh, no! this was not a time in which the distinctions of country were remembered. It was the triumph of human kind; it was man asserting the noblest privilege of his nature; and it required but the common feelings of humanity, to become in that moment a citizen of the world. For myself, I acknowledge that my heart caught with enthusiasm the general sympathy, my eyes were filled with tears; and I shall never forget the sensations of that day, "while memory holds her seat in my bosom[42]

As in other works by Williams, the cause of liberty is underpinned by a broad acceptance of natural rights as defined according to 'the common feelings of humanity', and it is this which allows her, for example, to warn that before the English too quickly condemn the French 'terror' in the mid-1790s, they should look to their own barbarities: 'Ah, let us, till the slave-trade no longer stains the British name, be more gentle in our censure of other nations!'.[43]

Her interest in natural rights was not suddenly acquired through knowledge of the French revolution. In her *Poems* which were published as early as 1786, Williams aligns herself with most of the contemporary radical positions. In 'An Ode on the Peace' (1783) she commented on the American War of Independence. She not only condemns a situation in which sons, fathers and brothers are killing each other – as she was to do in the novel *Julia* – but she also writes in a powerful anti-war vein:

> IV.
> Now burns the savage soul of war,
> While terror flashes from his eyes,
> Lo! waving o'er his fiery car
> Aloft his bloody banner flies:
> The battle wakes – with awful sound
> He thunders o'er the echoing ground,
> He grasps his reeking blade, while streams of blood
> Tinge the vast plain, and swell the purple flood.[44]

The affective aesthetics of sentimentality are used here to shock the reader into a realistic understanding of the horrors of war, rather than to raise an

ineffectual tear of pity. The sheer waste of human life and the grieving of the
survivors are strongly evoked in the evocation of orphans and hysterical
widows. Williams does not actually condemn Britain or side with America,
but writes a poem condemning war itself on humanitarian grounds. By
focusing on this issue, Williams avoided the kind of official disapproval
which beset other writers who were more openly critical of England and its
government. Even when writing her *Letters* from France, she mainly
refrained from making adverse comparisons with England, and she reiterated many times in her life her allegiance to the King. 'Edwin and Eltruda.
A Legendary Tale' (1782), is a long poem which is ostensibly part of
the medieval gothic revival and certainly full of the rhetoric of 'the sympathetic heart' and the innocence of 'the uncorrupted heart'. However, its
narrative message is once again the tragedy of civil war when loved ones are
placed on opposite sides. In the Wars of the Roses, Eltruda's father, Albert,
fights for the Lancastrian king, and her lover Edwin in the Yorkist cause:

> Oppress'd with many an anxious care,
> Full oft Eltruda sigh'd;
> Complaining that relentless war
> Should those she lov'd–divide.

Williams observes that normally the bard 'who feels congenial fire, May sing
of martial strife', inspiring 'the gen'rous scorn of life', but that she cannot do
so in this tale. Inevitably, the father is fatally struck by an arrow, and his deadly
foe, touched in his 'yielding heart', turns out to be none other than Edwin.
In a tear-stained death scene, both weep for what they know Eltruda will
feel. In the end all three die in different states of grief and self-recrimination,
and the 'mournful muse' turns away from her subject:

> She wipes away the tears, that blot
> The melancholy page.

These lines, in fact, allow us to pinpoint the problem, contemporary and
modern, in the reception of Williams as a serious writer. She draws so much
on the excesses of sentimental writing that she comes close to parody, and
the danger of losing her serious, anti-war theme is real. Most of the first
volume of Williams' two-volume *Poems* is taken up by a kind of epic, *Peru*,
in six cantos. While not claiming to write 'a full, historical narration of the fall
of the Peruvian empire', Williams does trace the Spanish invasion of Peru
and the destruction of Inca civilisation by Pizarro. Her special brand of
sentimental radicalism allows her to do two things. First, sensibility leads her
to see change from a very human and individual point of view, since
episodes of victimisation dwell on the suffering of individuals, especially
women and children. Second, her radical perspective allows Williams to

focus indignantly on the degradations perpetrated over one culture by another engaged in tyrannical, imperialist invasion:

> But not in vain the beauteous realm shall bleed,
> Too late shall Europe's race deplore the deed.
> Region abhorr'd! be gold the tempting bane,
> The curse that desolates thy hostile plain. (I, 176–179)

Peru is the 'bleeding land' sacrificed for western profit in early colonisation, and once again slavery and war are condemned because of their tragic human consequences. But lest these natural rights themes are too abstractly stated, the poem's sentimental episodes force the reader to engage emotionally with the issues as events within human experience:

> Look on our helpless babe in mis'ry nurst –
> My child – my child, thy mother's heart will burst!
> Methinks I see the raging battle rise,
> And hear this harmless suff'rer's feeble cries;
> I view the blades that pour a sanguine flood,
> And plunge their cruel edge in infant blood. (IV, 87–92)

While all the radical writers of the 1790s to some extent draw on sentimental strategies, Williams' special blend of tones is more extreme and expressive than those of others. The uniqueness of this blend, finds justification when she writes on slavery, a subject which intrinsically raises questions of sympathy with victims and anger at 'the system'.[15] Her sustained poem, 'On the bill which was passed in England for regulating the slave-trade: A short time before its abolition' is in fact less sentimental about the plight of slaves than many other poems of the period, and more sharply incisive in its attack on the colonial apparatus which led to the slave trade:

> Alas! to Afric's fetter'd race
> Creation wears no form of grace!
> To them earth's pleasant vales are found
> A blasted waste, a sterile bound;
> Where the poor wand'rer must sustain
> The load of unremitted pain;
> A region in whose ample scope
> His eye discerns no gleam of hope.

By describing a geography which Britain and other countries have despoiled, Williams creates an image for the moral despoliation and denial of humanity to the deracinated slave. Colonialism is the machinery which 'Weighs agony in sordid scales, And marks if death or life prevails', and attention is paid to the mental suffering as well as physical:

> How deep a wound will stab the mind;
> How far the spirit can endure.

Pity there is, but it is at least counterbalanced by cool analysis and angry denunciation.

None the less, Williams is a part of the radical literary movement in terms of her themes, and they are pitched at the level of natural rights. Her objections to war after the American experience are pursued in the dramatic monologue 'the American Tale' and in her novel, *Julia* (1790), an attempt to emulate in English, Rousseau's *La Nouvelle Héloise*. This rather slow novel is, as one would expect, full of 'exquisite sensibility' but also its corrective, 'the influence of reason; as the quivering needle, though subject to some variations, still tends to one point' (I, 129). The heroine is pursued by a man who poses as a man of sensibility, and the novel might best be read as a portrayal of the difficulties of distinguishing true from false sensibility: sense from sensibility, in effect. True sensibility is defined with the gloss of Goldsmith and Mackenzie, since it is full of 'generosity and disinterestedness' (I, 53), benevolence and charity (I, 65) contrasted with 'the experience of the coldness and selfishness of mankind, and even the chilling hand of age itself' (I, 186). In her earlier poem 'To Sensibility', Williams had defined sensibility as the opposite of 'INDIFFERENCE' and 'apathy', linking it 'With friendship, sympathy, and love, And every finer thought'. Interpolated into the novel are several poems, including, 'the Bastille: A Vision', a dramatic monologue by a prisoner who, in imagination and through the comforts of Philosophy, gains freedom of the mind. In the vision, Nature's 'awak'ning voice' comes to avenge 'her violated laws':

> Did ever earth a scene display
> More glorious to the eye of day,
> Than millions with according mind,
> Who claim the rights of human kind?

After her experience of the French revolution, Williams tempers her benevolent sensibility and anti-war stance, with a deeper questioning of freedom in the context of just revolution. *August and Madelaine: A Real History* (1799) begins in a time when 'the French revolution had not yet happened' (206), and during its narrative 'the French nation, too enlightened to bear any longer those monstrous oppressions which ignorance of its just rights alone had tolerated, shook off its fetters, and the revolution was accomplished' (214). Madelaine, a friend to the revolution, innocently believes that the new liberty should extend to choice in marriage:

> obtaining liberty of choice in marriage was alone well worth the trouble of a revolution; and she was as warm a patriot from this single idea, as if she had studied the declaration of rights made by the consistent assembly. in all its extent and consequences. (215)

There may be a hint of intended comedy, at least in the portrayal of Madelaine ('I always loved the revolution, thought Madelaine, as she laid aside the white gown in which she was to be married the next morning' [219]), but Williams seems more seriously to be making the didactic point that the freedom offered by political revolution should have a personal dimension, and that true equality should break down class barriers between the noble and the daughter of a *roturier* (209–10). This approach does extend natural rights thinking into asking more subtle questions, even if the answers in her novel are simplistic.

5
Novels of Natural Rights in the 1790s

Thomas Holcroft, the Jacobin historical novelist and dramatist of the 1790s who was discussed in chapter 4 (and whose *Memoirs* were published by Hazlitt), wrote the following on the power of novels to influence and educate a popular reading public, which deserve to open this chapter.

> When we consider the influence that novels have over the manners, sentiments, and passions, of the rising generation, – instead of holding them in the contempt which, as reviewers, we are without exception said to do, – we may esteem them, on the contrary, as forming a very essential branch of literature.[1]

Written at a time when 'romances' were regarded as pernicious corrupters of youth and especially of women,[2] this is an interesting observation since his use of the word 'influence' can be non-judgemental, or at least it implies that they can change people's minds by working on their feelings, *for better or worse*. At the very least Holcroft is suggesting that such works can be described in Horatian terms of teaching and delighting, and thus placed in the ranks of respectable 'literature'. In his own practice, and that of the novelists covered in this chapter, it is clear that he attempted to rescue novels from accusations of escapism and aristocratic manners, and instead use them for teaching radical lessons that were relevant to a revolutionary age, in an attempt to 'influence ... the rising generation'. 'Rising' has a functional plurality of meanings: it could mean youthful, or upwardly mobile (middle class), or revolutionary – and all three are equally useful to his purpose. The other function of Holcroft's statement is that it gives us a contemporary bridge between philosophy, political events and imaginative literature which is the subject of this book, and has been emphasised in the works of Godwin, Wollstonecraft and Thelwall. He saw the novel at least, and by implication poetry (less so drama as it was more susceptible to censorship and the self-censorship of a playwright seeking a mass audience), as mediums that could carry issues like natural rights out of the study and into the streets. A belief in the power of novels to persuade, was shared by many from one end of the political spectrum to the other. To Holcroft the radical the process was one of healthy enticement, but to anti-Jacobin writers it was rather one of contagious infection, coercing vulnerable minds to 'see, amidst the blazing and red-hot ruins, the sons of Freedom and Liberty waving the three-coloured banners with the blood of their enemeies, and hailing the everlasting Rights of Man!!!'.[3]

Holcroft's passage is quoted by Gary Kelly in his excellent book, *The English Jacobin Novel 1780–1805*, and I am happy to acknowledge this pioneering work as an important 'influence' over this chapter and other parts of the current book. By focusing on a particular Jacobin circle Kelly excludes others whom I shall deal with, and by looking generally at radical thought in the 1790s his study is necessarily broader in political scope than my specific enquiry into the literary representation of natural rights, but his book leads us to the important issues of the period in a vivid and trustworthy way. Having paid this homage, I feel justified in quoting at more length from Kelly himself, as he describes the politically charged and uncomfortable situation in which radical writers of the 1790s were working. The passage reminds us of the degree of courage exhibited when, as a reference in Bage's *Hermstrong* indicates, one could be prosecuted simply for revealing that one had read Paine's *Rights of Man*:

> By the time *Hermstrong* was published in 1796 the Directory ruled France, and Pitt's policy of repression had already sent several men to Botany Bay and driven others, such as Joseph Priestley, into exile. In Ireland Richard Lowell Edgeworth found himself associated with Irish rebels by the undiscriminating prejudice of loyalists. The suspension of Habeas Corpus, the Treason Trials of 1793 and 1794, and the 'Two Acts' of 1795 had stifled English Jacobinism. The experience of Wordsworth and Coleridge with 'Spy Nosy' was soon to show that Bage was not wide of the mark when he depicted Lord Grondale trying to get rid of the troublesome hero by having him taken up as a French spy (*Hermsprong*, iii. 24–5).[4]

It should not be forgotten that novelists like Elizabeth Inchbald, Robert Bage, Charlotte Smith, no less than Godwin, Wollstonecraft, Thelwall, Blake and later Shelley (who both faced prosecution in more direct and sinister ways than did Wordsworth and Coleridge), were using literature to espouse natural rights at a time when they themselves faced the threat of their right to write freely being terminated. Their pleas for equality in the face of prevailing tyranny, both politically and domestically, take on a personal significance.

Elizabeth Inchbald: *Nature and Art*

The only work by Elizabeth Inchbald which is still available in a popular edition is *A Simple Story*. This may be justified in the light of the novel's appeal and accomplishment, but it is rather unjust to Inchbald's other works and particularly the neatly chiselled *Nature and Art* (1796), which is available only in a scholarly facsimile[5] and tends to be mentioned by critics only for its satire on the eighteenth-century clergy. While the satirical element is obvious, it also seems clear that Inchbald saw herself as contributing to a wider debate inspired by Rousseau and dealing with issues concerned with natural rights. The concept organising *Nature and Art* is very simple and signalled in the title. Two different kinds of education are juxtaposed, one based on spontaneous hedonism and the other on spontaneous altruism and the dictates of conscience. Brothers William and Henry bring up their respective sons (also William and Henry) in opposite ways. William is educated by paid tutors in an authoritarian way, never being 'permitted to have one conception of his own' (i, 45) and 'never once asked "what he thought?" '. Henry is more or less a Rousseauian *ingenu*, brought up by his father abroad, without access to books or teachers. He is taught to think for himself, to ask questions, to love his neighbour, and to condemn falsehood and frivolous vanity. Not surprisingly, they grow up to be very different characters. William gains wealth and privilege, even rising to the status of magistrate, but he is complacent, selfish, arrogant, and without conscience. Henry is verbally impulsive, absorbed in the predicaments of others in a spirit of 'sympathy' (i, 176), and although he returns to English society totally innocent of its ways, he exhibits a fundamentally moral way of thinking and behaving, even as a boy.

> "Come hither, child", said the dean, "and let me instruct you – your father's negligence has been inexcusable. – There are in society" (continued the dean) "rich and poor; the poor are born to serve the rich".
> "And what are the rich born for?"
> "To be served by the poor",
> "But suppose the poor would not serve them?"
> "Then they must starve."
> "And so poor people are permitted to live, only upon condition that they wait upon the rich?"
>
> ...
>
> [Dean] "In respect to placing all persons on a level, it is utterly impossible – God has ordained it otherwise." (i, 79)

Inadvertently shaming hypocrites and authoritarians, Henry demonstrates his 'defective' education by 'an incorrigible misconception and misapplication of many *words*': 'He would call *compliments*, *lies* – *Reserve*, he would call *pride* – *stateliness*, *affectation* – and for the words *war* and *battle*, he constantly substituted the word *massacre*' (i, 81). He adds in explanation, 'A massacre is when human beings are slain, who have it not in their power to defend themselves' (i, 83). (We are reminded that Inchbald wrote a play called *The Massacre*, which was effectively censored because it alluded approvingly to the French revolution.) For his ingenuousness he is constantly reproved and berated as a 'young savage'.

What takes this beyond topical satire on conventional social and religious attitudes lies in the subjects Inchbald deals with through her mouthpiece. As we have seen in the quotations, Henry constantly questions all forms of inequality, tyranny, and victimisation of the innocent – exactly the large moral and political issues raised by theorists of natural rights, and by Inchbald's own intellectual circle which included Godwin, Holcroft and other Jacobins. Her most consistent emphasis is on the injustice of poverty. Henry undermines his uncle the dean (William's father) for writing in his pamphlet that the world is full of natural riches, while denying the poor access to them (i, 101–2), and then hanging them if in desperation and starvation they steal (i, 127). The dean happens to be the one set up for particular condemnation for his 'rigid attention to the morals of people in poverty, and total neglect of their bodily wants', while speaking of 'good of the *soul*', but it mistakes Inchbald's intention to see this as isolated criticism of the clergy. She is surely using the dean, and later his son who becomes magistrate, as representative figures from respectable professions who express and live by conventional social mores. As a magistrate, William junior is little better than his father: while 'he would not inflict punishment on the innocent, nor let the guilty escape', yet 'he would alleviate or aggravate according to the rank of the offender' (ii, 64). Other characters are similarly tarred, including the aristocratic Lord and Lady Bendham, 'strenuous opposers of vice in the poor, and gentle supporters of it in the rich' (174).

In the schematic and dialectic structure, it is predictable that in volume ii William and Henry, now adults, fall in love. Although the subject is amorous, Inchbald does not compromise on her moral concentration on underlying issues of natural rights, especially in the treatment of the two women. William seduces Hannah, and abandons her after she falls pregnant.

> From the tenderest passion the most savage impulse may arise – In the deep recesses of fondness, sometimes is implanted the root of cruelty – and from loving William with unbounded lawless affection, she found herself depraved so as to become the very object, which could most of all excite her own horror! (ii, 5)

Henry falls in love with Rebecca, a plain but virtuous young woman. Hannah remorsefully leaves the inevitable baby in the woods where it is found by Henry. William is forgiven his indiscretion by the family, and steadily rises in society, while Hannah follows the course familiar from Wollstonecraft and sentimental novels, towards poverty, degradation, criminal companionship, and prostitution in London, in order to support her child. Eventually, with tragic irony, she comes before William as magistrate and is hanged on his verdict. Although her career seems almost a cliché beside so many other novels, Inchbald handles the theme of the violated rights of women with just as much analytical logic and perhaps less obtrusive emotionalism than Wollstonecraft, as she charts the social inevitability of the process:

> Hannah was driven from service to service – her deficiency in the knowledge of a mere drudge, or her lost character, pursued her wherever she went; and at length, becoming wholly destitute, she gladly accepted a place where the latter misfortune was not the least objection. (ii, 105)

Throughout the sequence, it is made quite explicit that the responsibility is entirely William's, although he fails to accept it. The last hundred pages of the novel, like the final Book of *Caleb Williams*, seeks to emphasise the centrality of conscience as the basis of virtuous action, if not worldly success: 'In a word, it was *conscience* which made Henry's years pass happier than William's' (ii, 119). Henry and Rebecca are separated when he goes to seek his father, but it is made clear that his heart is in the right place and that the lovers are loyal to each other. He attains moral but not social status because, as he says, 'His affectionate heart ... loved *persons* rather than *things*' (ii, 127), and he would not give up the liberty of his free conscience 'for all the wealth and finery of which his cousin William was the master' (*ibid.*). Inchbald pithily comments, 'He was right', and contrasts Henry's happiness with William's increasing loneliness and misery through his guilty conscience. When he discovers the identity of the woman he has sent to the gallows, nemesis strikes:

> Robbed, by this news, of his only gleam of consolation – in the consciousness of having done a mortal injury for which he never now by any means could atone, he saw all his honours, all his riches, all his proud selfish triumphs dance before him! They seemed like airy nothings, which in rapture he would exchange for the peace of a tranquil conscience! (ii, 157)

Meanwhile, the younger Henry has found his father and they return to the village to witness the funeral of the older William: 'The two Henrys, the only real mourners in the train, followed at a little distance – in rags, but in tears' (ii, 170), while others in the procession attend only for the sake of William's status as bishop and his wealth, knowing full well that he was hated by most of his parishioners as one who 'had no compassion for his fellow creatures' (ii, 176). The stark difference between loving '*persons*' rather than '*things*' is enacted in the scene which, Inchbald makes clear, explains why her own society is devoid of respect for equality and natural rights. The magnificence of the bishop's palace, like the ruins in Shelley's *Ozymandias*, is now seen not as a 'noble edifice' but 'as a heap of rubbish piled together to fascinate weak understandings' (ii, 180). Enforcing the same lesson, Lady Bendham, dedicated to the world of fashion, dies literally because of her commitment to trappings, clothes, *'things'*. Gary Kelly has pointed out the ideological weakness of the ending of *Nature and Art* with the two Henrys aggrandising poverty and unrewarded labour, while pitying the rich, explaining the world's muddled values as 'the fault of education, of early prejudice' (ii, 201). But to condemn this ending perhaps undervalues the real intention of the novel, which is to perform one of the functions which earlier had fallen to natural lawyers like Sir Thomas More, to clarify the enormous discrepancy between what *is* in an errant society and what *should be* according to the lights of conscience and the enlightened heart. The final words, written in the context of governmental repression in England in the mid-1790s, amount to a plea for ideological change and democratic reform based on natural rights, which must have seemed at the time unattainable:

> Let the poor then (cried the younger Henry) no more be their own persecutors – no longer pay homage to wealth – instantaneously the whole idolatrous worship will cease – the idol will be broken. (ii, 202)

Robert Bage: *Hermsprong or Man As He Is Not*

For the modern reader, Robert Bage's *Hermsprong* (1796) is a mixed bag. The stodgy dialogue recalls the sentimental novel, while its comedy of manners anticipates Jane Austen, and may even have suggested what was to become one of the most famous fiction titles in English literature: 'But the tender interest they had in each other was torn asunder by pride and prejudice' (97).[6] The narrative is familiar to the point of cliché. The spirited Miss Campinet resists the pressure for an arranged marriage exerted by her father, Lord Grondale, and insists on her own choice of partner, the oddly named, plain-speaking visitor from America, Mr Hermsprong. In an almost disappointing way, Hermsprong's claims as the democratic egalitarian are undercut by the revelation that he is the son of Lord Grondale's long-lost elder brother and therefore the true Lord Campinet and heir to Grondale's estate, and that he has always been privileged 'with a fortune that sets [him] above the necessity of employment' (96). This gives an easy dénouement to the love plot, but downgrades the undoubtedly radical challenge to aristocratic power within the novel. But Bage does not stay complacently at the level of trite plotting. His disruption of illusion by using as narrator a Gregory Glen who steps in and out of the narrative, looks back to Sterne and forward to Thackeray: 'If the careless writer of a novel closes his book without marrying, or putting to death, or somehow disposing, not only of his principal personages, but of all who have acted a part in the drama above the degree of a candle-snuffer, he creates an unsatisfactory want in the minds of his readers, especially his fair ones, and they hardly part friends' (246). All this conceded, however, there is a place in a book on natural rights for *Hermsprong*, through the novel's sporadic and almost guerilla raids on contemporary radical thought, invariably either expressed by Hermsprong himself or liberated as a voice from others through his eruptive presence. He is not so guileless as the innocent Henry in *Nature and Art*, but his position is similar, carrying an element of the Rousseauan noble savage – a traveller and outsider, having first-hand experience of the American republic with its 'simple government, without money to buy men' (134) and revolutionary France, he is the free-thinker and free-speaker challenging the antiquarian pompousness of the English class system. He does so persistently from a natural law and natural rights position:

> Man cannot be taught any thing contrary to nature. However he acts, he must act by nature's laws; howsoever he thinks, he must think by nature's laws. (41)

This gives him the moral authority (perhaps weakened by the revelation that he has a personal reason for feeling superior to Grondale) to assert his 'right' not to be bullied by an apparent social superior:

> 'Stop sir', said Hermsprong, rising; 'by what right do you presume to speak to me with the tone of master? I owe you no obedience; and despise you for your tyrannical and contentious spirit' (43)

Tyranny by 'rank and property' (74) in England are the special targets, and Hermsprong is attacked by the toady to the aristocracy, the Reverend Doctor Blick, as a treacherous reader of Paine:

> But, said the doctor, rising in energy, 'what can be expected from men who countenance the abominable doctrines of the Rights of Man? Rights contradicted by nature, which has given us an ascending series of inequality, corporeal and mental, and plainly pointed out the way to those wise political distinctions created by birth and rank ... all that is just and equitable upon earth.' (93)

Paine's book was banned in England in 1795, and for Bage to highlight its existence must have been provocative and courageous. His satire deftly exposes the ignorance of the class which would have demanded such censorship, as the conservative clergyman Mr Woodcock condemns books which were answers to Burke, without having read them:

> 'You have, no doubt, sir, read with attention the author you now so liberally abuse?'

'I, sir! – I read him! – No, sir, – nor the Mackintoshes, the Flowers, nor the Christies; – I never read a line in any of them – nor ever will.'

'It is the way, sir, to be well informed.' (50)[7]

Blick's hunch about Hermsprong is explored by a lawyer to Grondale, eager for prosecution of Hermsprong, and the reference indicates the chilling quality of the repression of free speech in the mid-1790s:

'And', said the lawyer, 'I have hints of other little circumstances. He has read *The Rights of Man* – this I can almost prove; and also that he has lent it to one friend, if not more, which, you know, my lord, is circulation, though to no great extent. I know also where he said, that the French constitution, though not perfect, had good things in it; and that ours was not so good but it might be mended. Now, you know, my lord, the bench of justices will not bear such things now; and if your lordship will exert your influence, I dare say they will make the country too hot to hold him.' (202)

On this evidence, as well as his habit of encouraging citizens to emigrate to America as a better country than England (206), Hermsprong is prosecuted for being 'a French spy' (204), which gives him a public platform for dramatically revealing his true identity as Lord Campinet. However, it is again to modern readers disappointing that Bage undercuts his revolutionary message (perhaps through the necessities of avoiding prosecution himself) in another way. Another accusation against Hermsprong is that he incited or at least encouraged miners to riot violently, threatening to pull down lords' houses, and especially Grondale's since he made his money in mining. (219). That Hermsprong 'went amongst the rioters is true' (225) and he admits giving money to some. But his motive, he explains, was quite the reverse of 'sedition': in fact he had made a speech deploring violence, suggesting that inequality of property cannot be changed except by extreme bloodshed which should be avoided at all costs, and asserting that 'civil order' (226) depends on a '*concord*' between king and citizens that sounds like Locke's social contract. The money he gives is not to encourage rioting but to alleviate suffering, confirming Hermsprong's credentials as the benevolent hero which have been demonstrated on other occasions in the novel when he helps the poor. It would appear that Bage sets up a radical potential only to back away from it – Hermsprong is cleared even of residing in France since he has 'not properly resided' there (227) but visited simply because his mother was a Frenchwoman – but in the climate of 1796 England both the author and his publishers could be excused some feelings of paranoia in fear of prosecution for sedition themselves. On safer ground, Bage begins his final sections with Hermsprong's idealistic description of religious tolerance amongst Americans, 'which, accustoming them to see difference of opinion in a matter of the greatest importance, disposes them to tolerate it on all subjects, and even to believe it a condition of human nature' (238). He describes his plans to create on his huge estate on the Potomac River a utopian 'society of friends' no doubt running in accord with laws of nature.

The radical incursions so far described in *Hermsprong* mainly centre on the natural right of equality, as espoused by Godwin. There is a second strand in the novel which is more sustained and acknowledges by name Wollstonecraft's *A Vindication of the Rights of Women* (137). The theme of rights for women is carried through by Caroline Campinet and her more assertive companion Maria Fluart, who has been described as a 'proto-feminist'. Both are supported by Hermsprong who declares that 'English women have too little liberty!' (134), but the women themselves sustain the debate. The familiar novelistic situation that stimulates the debate is Miss Campinet's spirited refusal to obey her father's wishes on the subject of her marriage, and it is significant that Bage presents it not in terms of emotions (as Shakespeare had in *A Midsummer Night's Dream*, for example) but of rights. Her father, even as he derides this view, acknowledges its existence: 'Fathers in general are accustomed to expect submission from their children, and obedience. I have a daughter who knows the rights of women, who stipulates conditions with her father' (216), while an inset story, by the satirical tone in which it is related, implies the woman's right to choose:

> Mr Rupré had drunk a good deal of Burgundy ... It had assisted him in his arguments, and had made him understand that daughters had no rights but the rights of obedience. (163)

By an act of tyranny, this character, again like the law in the *Dream*, condemns his daughter to a convent. Miss Campinet succeeds in avoiding her father's choice of a husband by a combination of her own resistance, motivated by love for Hermsprong, Hermsprong's confident irreverence to Grondale, and the support of her companion, Miss Fluart. The latter speaks most consistently for equality of the sexes, echoing the arguments of Wollstonecraft on the right to education, for example:

> that women would leave the lesser vanities, and learn lessons of wisdom, if men would teach them; and in particular, this, that more permanent and more cordial happiness might be produced to both the sexes, if the aims of women were rather to obtain the esteem of men, than that passionate but transient affection usually called love. (137)

She stands up for herself with candour and wit:

> When I look Miss Fluart in the face, I do not think of reason.
> Of what then?

Of beauty and good humour?

This will not do. I shall not be so bribed. It is the cause of my sex. Say again, if you dare, that women are not beings of reason. (138)

This expression of defiance of male patronising is directed at the relatively insignificant Mr Sumelin, but Miss Fluart is just as forthright and mocking of Lord Grondale, ending up literally playing tricks on him. She can even trade badinage with Hermsprong, by this stage of the novel Sir Charles Campinet, and expose the element of sanctimonius righteousness in him, which is not done by anybody else, nor by the novel's viewpoint:

'Patience and submission, my dear Miss Fluart, are not the qualities of a savage', Sir Charles replied; 'we allow not the language of tyranny even from pretty mouths'.

Miss Fluart. Savages are wonderful beings. You have no objection to the language of slavery from pretty mouths.

Hermsprong. I have not all the savage ill qualities. I learned to hate the language of slavery in all its forms, especially in the form of adulation. I consider a woman as equal to a man; but, let it not displease you, My dear Mis Fluart, I consider a man also as equal to a woman. When we marry, we give and we receive. (236)

In a slightly unfocused way, this exchange alludes to Rousseau, slavery and the rights of women, typical of this novel, like the early movement for natural rights, as an all-inclusive issue.

Charlotte Smith: *The Old Manor House and Desmond*

Charlotte Smith is one of the most underrated writers in the whole period from 1750 to 1830, and the reason is at least partly that she does not fit comfortably into one of the categories made available by literary historians, such as sentimental, romantic or 'the tribe of Jane Austen'. Her novels are sometimes considered in the context of gothic fiction, but this aspect is not central to her work, and in fact the gothic is as much satirised as utilised. She draws upon the sentimental tradition in her narratives, but she often undercuts its conventions in a 'tricksy' way.[8] Her poems like *Elegiac Sonnets* were extraordinarily popular in her time but have fallen away from consciousness, again because she is not identifiably a 'woman Romantic Poet' nor a follower of Wordsworth. (In fact, she was more celebrated than him in literary circles, at least in the 1790s, and she helped him by giving letters of introduction to fellow radicals in Paris. It has even been suggested that he bought Dove Cottage out of a memory of the Grasmere scenery in *Ethelinde*, and he certainly admired her poems when he read them as a schoolboy aged 14.) *The Emigrants*, which will receive attention later in this book, is a wonderful poem which deserves more admiration than it gets. At least an appreciative modern biography has appeared, Loraine Fletcher's *Charlotte Smith: A Critical Biography*[9] which may stimulate new interest. As with the other novelists examined in this book, her works reveal their strength if read with attention to the fundamental nature of the issues she raises, not just when writing about politics but in the broad range of human dealings. To be specific, she contributes to the literature of natural rights.

The violation of rights informs *The Old Manor House* (1793) and what makes the treatment significant is that Smith extends her consideration into domestic rights and political rights, also drawing connections between the two spheres. Her attitude to imaginative writing is as didactic as other writers', extending even to romances. The heroine describes a man who,

> recollecting not only his classics, but the romances he had delighted in at school, he had that natural and acquired tenderness of mind which made him sensible at once of all the discomforts of my situation. He saw in me a poor, deserted heroine of a novel, and nothing could be in his opinion so urgent as my relief –[10]

Since Smith's own novel is a romance depicting the rescue from family entrapment of Monimia by Orlando, the comment steers us towards noticing the morally instructive intention. It may be somewhat unusual for a male character to be so susceptible to romance, but Smith stresses the female influence over her virtuous men. Orlando, whose heart is 'open to all the generous sympathies of humanity' 'had lately been accustomed to associate only with women' (290, 291). Smith became effectively a single parent of nine surviving children, of whom she unashamedly favoured one son, and she often clearly reflects autobiography in her novels. The genre she is creating herself is a female inflected novel of benevolence, overlaid with the kind of political critique characteristic of the 1790s Jacobin writers. Even love is not always conventionally depicted: Orlando discovers 'that the romantic theory, of sacrificing every consideration to love, produced, in the practice, only the painful consciousness of having injured its object' (517). There are very unromantic touches that place the novel close to the tissue of life in the 1790s: for example, the pitiable character whom Smith takes from Goldsmith's 'Deserted Village', 'the "Broken Soldier" ' who has one leg, 'having lost his limb in the service of what is called his country, that is, in fighting the battles of its politicians; ... having been deprived of his leg to preserve the balance of Europe' (461). Smith's world does not contain genuine evil, since her unsympathetic characters are usually ungenerous, simply ignorant, or incorrigibly prejudiced and set in a myopic way of thinking. The real evils of war, she suggests, are created by such people alienating their humanity to institutional powers of government and petty ideals of nationalism. The heroine, of course, is marked by 'native rectitude of heart and generosity of spirit' (43), and both hero and heroine have the kind of innate access to the natural law potentially shared universally, 'the secret sympathy between generous mind [that] seems to exist throughout the whole human kind' (361).

The gothic machinery in *The Old Manor House*, far from being gratuitous, atmospheric, or to heighten suspense, is purposeful and uniquely used to present an analysis of domestic rights being violated.[11] Indeed, even though there are dark mysterious passageways, a gloomy turret and the kind of 'wild and dreary scene, where birds of prey screamed' (261), yet Smith deliberately distances her narrative from the conventions of the gothic as such, to the extent that it might be argued her novel is anti-gothic. With apparent authorial endorsement, Orlando gently chides Monimia for believing in ghosts and spirits. Instead of expressing simply 'the scepticism of the present day', he suggests that belief in 'supernatural appearances' flies in the face of the moral life itself: 'You shall fairly enquire whether any of those visits of the dead were ever found to be of any use to the living ... shall we therefore believe, that an all-wise and all-powerful Being shall suffer a general law of nature to be so uselessly violated, and shall make the dead restless, only to terrify the living?' (48–9). Monimia is undoubtedly placed in a gothic setting, but her entrapment is by an all-too-human agency in the person of her jealous and vindictive aunt, and the situation is set up to demonstrate domestic tyranny in action, depriving her of her natural right to independent movement. Again, it is Orlando, 'whose generous spirit revolted from every kind of injustice' (19) who demystifies:

> 'It is impossible to resist saying, that, like all other usurped authority, the power of your aunt is maintained by unjust means, and supported by prejudices, which if once looked at by the eye of reason would fall. So slender is the hold of tyranny, my Monimia!' (44)

Placed early in the novel, this strong statement links domestic injustice to the political injustices depicted later in the novel, where 'usurped authority' in the form of the tyranny of governments cause poverty by imposing window taxes, force people to fight their own relatives in America, and govern in a way that favours the rich and dissolute rather than the majority of English people. And in both the domestic and the political sphere, the artless words of the chambermaid, 'you'd better help Miss out of her cage' (240) suggest that deprivation of rights and the perpetration of injustices should not be allowed to remain as a permanent condition. Just as these things are done by human agents who take on the status of tyrants, so liberation and change are within the reach of benevolent human agents. Of course the fable of releasing Monimia can be read as specifically an issue of women's rights in an age when they were confined within family roles, or sent 'to market like cattle' into enforced marriages, yet Smith maintains a gaze upon the issue of rights in general. The larger programme behind the book is that not only can Miss be helped out of her cage but that England can be forced out of America and government out of coercion over its subjects. One could hardly conceive a more audacious purpose behind the use of a gothic setting, which is usually justified as a psychological and emotional space that leads inwards to the repressed and fearful workings of the mind than outwards to political action. Right at the end of the novel Smith invites the reader retrospectively to recognise how un-gothic her novel has been, by giving to Orlando a thought satirical of the genre:

> as silently they ascended the great stair-case, and traversed the long dark passages that led towards the apartment in question, Orlando could not, amid the anxiety of such a moment, help fancying, that the scene resembled one of those so often met with in old romances and fairy tales, where the hero is by some supernatural means directed to a golden key, which opens an invisible drawer, where a hand or an head is found swimming in blood, which it is his business to restore to the inchanted owner (527)

The Old Manor House, the passage is saying, is definitely *not* that kind of book.

The War of Independence in America is the preoccupation of the second half of the novel, but once again Smith makes it clear that this war, although especially unjust and unnecessary, is not different in kind from any other war, and that they all deprive people of liberty and often of life. It is an historical novel and the chronology is carefully set over three years, from September 1776 to September 1779. Early in the novel, nobody disagrees 'that the rebellious colonists ought to be extirpated' (147) and 'that the Americans were a set of rebellious exiles, who refused on false pretences "the tribute to Caesar" ' (246), that is paying taxes to England. Orlando joins the army, responding to self-righteous nationalism around him. Smith's authorial intrusiveness makes it very clear at the outset that she opposes the war, explaining the national sentiment as the product of exaggerated military reports and of the fact that even the more liberal cannot judge correctly on an issue where they have 'heard only one side of the question':

> They saw not the impossibility of enforcing in another country the very imposts to which, unrepresented, they would not themselves have submitted. Elate with national pride, they had learned by the successes of the preceding war to look with contempt on the inhabitants of every other part of the globe; and even on their colonists, men of their own country–little imagining that from their spirited resistance
>
> > The child would rue that was unborn
> > The *taxing* of that day.[12] (246)

Even Orlando's father, an image of benevolence, cannot see the political and economic injustice in this light. Orlando's own education comes gradually, beginning with misgivings based on natural law rather than knowledge of the facts. When his new army comrades drink a bloodcurdling toast to the mass slaughter of 'the Yankies', 'ignorant as he was of the nature of the contest with America, his reason and humanity alike recoiled' (294). Further doubts arise on shipboard:

> when he considered a number of men thus packed together in a little vessel, perishing by disease; such of them as survived going to another hemisphere to avenge on a branch of their own nation a quarrel, of the justice of which they knew little, and were never suffered to enquire; he felt disposed to wonder at the folly of mankind, and to enquire again *what all this was for?* (348)

Each time he tries to justify the war to himself, Charlotte Smith forces Orlando to see the contradictions. The sacred glory of his country leads him 'to enquire if it was not from a mistaken point of honour, from the wickedness of governments, or the sanguinary ambition or revenge of monarchs, that so much misery was owing'. He turns to history for precedents of heroic activity, and this time the author nudges the reader, for Orlando 'did not recollect that their being themselves so indifferent to life was no reason why, to satisfy their own vanity, they should deluge the world with human blood!' (248). As the food on board perishes and conditions become even more degrading, the economic injustices become clear. The government has contracted 'universally bad' food to last the journey, and the writer's indignation mounts to boiling point:

> it was all for *glory*. And that the ministry should, in thus purchasing glory, put a little more than was requisite into the pockets of contractors, and destroy as many men by sickness as by the sword ... the contractors were for the most part members of parliament, who under other names enjoyed the profits of a war, which, disregarding the voices of the people in general, or even of their own constituents, they voted for pursuing. Merciful God! can it be thy will that mankind should thus tear each other to pieces with more ferocity than the beasts of the wilderness? Can it be thy dispensation that kings are entrusted with power only to deform thy works – and in learning politics to forget humanity? (349)

Orlando gradually comes to the view that the war against the Americans is unjust and based on the assumption that English Americans are 'men of an inferior species', which offends against his instincts for equality. He agrees with a view being voiced in England that it is 'a war against the people' (358), and he is far from convinced by the view put by the otherwise humane fellow-soldier Fleming that 'a man who takes the King's money is to do as he is bid': 'the sword is my argument', says Fleming. Charlotte Smith now steers Orlando to recognising that the war is against principles of government because it does not rest on 'the will of the people', and that it is 'in direct contradiction of the rights universally claimed', being 'in absolute contradiction to the wishes of the people who were taxed to support it'. His anti-war education is furthered by a conversation with an American whom the British take prisoner and who puts the opposite case, and by friendship with one of 'the native American auxiliaries who had been called to the aid of the English' (360), a conscription considered quite unworthy and treacherous by Orlando. (Smith appends a long footnote on this general practice.) By this stage he is 'mortified that such brutish inhospitality as what he had just experienced could exist in British bosoms ... lamenting that there were Englishmen less humane than the rude savages of the wilds of America' (393). He sees also that without the British America itself represented a fresh start – 'whichever way Orlando looked, a new Eden seemed to be opening around him' (383). Later, having extricated himself from the conflict, Orlando reads about it in England with more informed feelings:

> when he read that the American soldiers, fighting in defence of their liberties (of all those *rights* which his campaign as a British officer had not made him forget were the most sacred to an *Englishman*), had marked their route with the blood which had flowed from their naked feet in walking over frozen ground, his heart felt for the sufferings of the oppressed, and for the honour of the oppressor. (450)

At the end of this long and evidently heartfelt sequence, Smith reveals in a footnote that her main source of information and analysis is 'the history of the American Revolution, by Ramsay', 'a perusal of [which]', she says, 'is humbly recommended to those Englishmen who doubt whether, in defence of their freedom, any other nation but their own will fight, or conquer' (450).[13]

Smith was not the only one to make it a subject for a novel, but there are various remarkable aspects to her treatment of the American revolution in *The Old Manor House*. Nowadays we are probably better placed than earlier generations to evaluate the collage of authorial opinion, reportage, historical analysis and fiction, not as a fatal violation of the novel's illusion, but as a powerful contemporary view carried by the moral passion of the writer commenting on her own times. The French revolution is not far from her concerns, by analogy. Moreover, she does present the *bricollage* within an overall pattern that might be encapsulated in the phrase 'the education of Orlando', and inevitably what she hopes is the education of the reader. However, in the context of this book, Smith's most striking quality is the ability to generalise from the particular. Rather than presenting her argument against this war solely in terms of local historical considerations and getting bogged down in detail, she constantly judges the events against a much larger range of issues that can be transferred to other similar conflicts, of which she surely expects the French revolution to be the main one. Issues of corrupt government, 'the will of the people' and, most relevantly natural rights of citizens, constantly dictate the course of the presentation. This allows the novel to rise above historical circumstance and to make effective and powerful appeals to universal, radical concerns, turning the book into one of the strongest indictments of the institution of war, based on considerations of natural rights to life and liberty and self-determination, written in the period. She has other abuses in her sights as well, and they were ones which were of special autobiographical significance to her – deliberate procrastination of lawyers in dealing with family matters, simply in order to enlarge their fees, the erosion of legal rights to inheritance by ambiguous and corruptly interpreted laws, the inhuman degradations of unjust and enforced penury 'where poverty is punished by loss of liberty' (443). Despite the fact that Smith had personal cause to complain of each of these, in her novel she manages to distance the issues by presenting them, again, in terms of an appeal to universal natural rights. Even slavery does not escape her net, as she depicts a merchant carrying a cargo of slaves from Guinea, who 'calculates the profits of a fortunate adventure, but never considers the tears and blood with which this money is to be raised ... He hears not the groans of an hundred human creatures confined together in the hold of a small merchantman' (501). All this adds up to the expression of a powerful mind keenly attuned to the central issues in the 'rights of man' campaign, and turns *The Old Manor House* into a work which is more a vigorous vehicle for contemporary, radical political thought than a contribution to the gothic novel.

Desmond (1792) had been published a year before *The Old Manor House*, but the events it depicts are those happening in France at the very time of writing. It has been part of the received wisdom of critics that this is Smith's first novel dealing with revolutionary politics, but in fact, as Rebecca Morgan, shows, *Celestina* (1791) is the novel in which she first includes reference to the French revolution, in an interpolated tale, and it is also the first novel in which the revolution is dealt with in England.[14] This novel in some ways anticipates *Persuasion* in dealing with the problems of communication between separated lovers. It is only towards the end of the third volume that political material appears, in the memoirs of Count de Bellegarde, who had spent time in the Bastille and also in the American revolution. Morgan points out that Smith introduces the revolutionary events in Europe in no less than seven of her nine works of prose fiction after 1789.[15] However, undoubtedly *Desmond* is the fullest and most sympathetic of her treatments of the French revolution. The part of the novel relevant to this book is presented as a debate over the rights and wrongs of the French revolution, as

Smith indicates in a Preface which describes her task as 'making a book of entertainment the vehicle of political discussion':[16]

> As to the political passages dispersed through the work, they are for the most part, drawn from conversations to which I have been a witness, in England, and France, during the last twelve months. In carrying on my story in those countries, and at a period when their political situation (but particularly that of the latter) is the general topic of discourse in both; I have given to my imaginary characters the arguments I have heard on both sides; and if those in favour of one party have evidently the advantage, it is not owing to my partial representation but to the predominant power of truth and reason, which can neither be altered nor concealed. (5–6)

Of course Smith is being disingenuous here, not only in claiming appropriate French experience when in fact her only visit was some eight years earlier when she was not in Paris, under terrible family circumstances, and unlikely to have heard any intellectual conversations; but also in suggesting she has not slanted the argument. That she supports the revolution and ridicules its opposition is patently clear, and it is the fact that brought controversy to her novel, forcing her to retreat into historical fiction and later into partial retraction. But it is interesting to note that she makes her appeal to the watchwords of natural law and natural rights, 'truth and reason', later 'truth, reason and humanity' (8), and she certainly would have believed this to be the case. As with other writers from the renaissance on, fictions have the convenient power to transform contemporary political debate into a fundamentalist moral discourse, under the general rubric of 'natural justice'.[17] In her Preface, Smith also asserts another right, when she attacks the opinion that 'women it is said have no business with politics' (6) by basing her argument on the right to 'female education' (6). Women, she says, have a right not only to 'acquire some knowledge of history' but to be informed and to think about events happening around them. In contemporary England, however, women live 'in a world where they are subject to such mental degradation; where they are censured as affecting masculine knowledge if they happen to have any understanding; or despised as insignificant triflers if they have none' (6).

Desmond is an epistolary novel using the form popularised by the book by Smith's radical friend Helen Maria Williams, *Letters from France*, and the first letter is dated 9 June 1790, so the political circumstances are clearly defined. The revolution has occurred in France, the *ancien regime* has been overthrown, and noblemen have been stripped of titles in favour of a more egalitarian society. The first of the three books, which is the most significant on the subject of natural rights, focuses the debate on this issue predominantly. At first Lionel Desmond views from England 'the present political tumult in France' (13). One side of the debate is voiced by English noblemen, who see the revolution as 'vulgar triumph and popular anarchy' (34), in which by 'a decree passed the nineteenth of June, these low wretches, this collection of dirty fellows, have abolished all titles, and abolished the very name of nobility' (34). This news brings the retort from Lord Newminster, ' "the devil they have? – then I wish the King and the Lords may smash them all – and be cursed to them – Now damme – do you know if I was King of France for three days, I would drive them all to the devil in a jiffy" ' (34). In her depiction of the English aristocracy, spluttering in apoplectic indigna-tion, Smith uses a repertoire of satire, ridicule and broad humour that is more evident in the first book of *Desmond* than elsewhere in her writing. She clearly enjoyed the comedy, while loathing its target, when she allows her English lords to shout that they would ' "set fire to their assembly, and mind no more shooting them all, than if they were so many made dogs" ' (34). In these representatives of 'law and order' she is clearly attacking Burke, and she links them also with an irrational hatred of the French: ' "I vote for their cutting one another's throats, and so saving us the trouble ... for, as for my part, I detest a Frenchman, and always did" ' (42). The xenophobia of 'Englishmen, free-born Britons' of the aristocracy, is comically portrayed as one in which an abhorrence of French politics is on the same level as an abhorrence of French food and wine.

Lionel Desmond himself supports the abolition of titles as birth-rights on grounds of equality, and he answers Miss Fairfax's conventional English atti-tude that this means the end of civilisation and a ' "most horrid cruelty and injustice" ' (37) by asserting that the injustice is on the other side, in a situ-ation where one group of people can, simply by possessing a name, oppress the vast majority of the population. He does not fully condemn the English aristocracy who, he says, are less numerous than those of the *ancien regime* and lacking in the power directly 'to oppress, individually, the inferior order of men', but points out that their political influence is greater in that ' "they possess, in their right of hereditary legislation, a strong, and to many, an obnoxious feature which the higher ranks in France never possessed" ' (37). Desmond deeply offends the 'beautiful aristocrat' with his levelling view that abolition of titles would be a good thing in England. He later condones state appropriation of church revenues, arguing that the church is an instru-ment or even 'property' of the state. Another issue raised is the birthright of the English nobility to indulge in hunting, while even the hungry amongst the populace cannot – a right which a nobleman asserts to be the prime symbol of English 'liberty' which is the pride of the world: ' "one of the things these fellows have done since they have got the notion of liberty into their heads, has been, to let loose all the taylors and tinkers and fris-seurs in their country, to destroy as much game as they please" ' (44–5). In general, the English ruling class's view of events in France is, 'This is the time there for beggars – they have got the upper hand' (47), and a genuinely destitute refugee, a woman with children, is advised to ' "go back to your own country" ' to ' "join the fish-women, and such like, who are pulling down the king's palaces" ' (47).

Desmond then visits Paris himself, ostensibly on a selfless errand to assist the brother of the woman he loves, who is unhappily but unattainably married (which adds an unconventional and *risqué* element to Smith's novel). He immediately realises the English perception is based solely on propaganda, 'the malignant fabrications of those who have been paid for their misrepresentations' (52). His own views are gained from conversation with an idealised French nobleman, 'the *ci-devant* Marquis de Montfleuri', who was happy to have his title taken away, and since he is a liberal employer who supports the revolution's principles, he has kept his lands. It would appear that Smith uses such a figure as spokesman because he can be claimed as impartial, appreciating as he does the higher aims of a movement that is clearly not in his own personal interests: 'Montfleuri ... though born a courtier, is one of the steadiest friends to the people' (53). He does see the issue as one of equality and natural rights, since he regards the fate of the nobility as simply one of being 'deprived of the invaluable privilege of believing themselves of a superior species', having 'to be compelled to learn that they are men' (54). In praising Montfleuri's prophetic and fair-minded approach, Desmond links him with the destiny of the nation itself, invoking Milton's words in *Areopagitica*, his argument for free speech and free publication: 'Methinks I see in my mind a noble and puissant nation, rousing herself like the strong man after sleep; and shaking her invincible locks' (55). Desmond visits Montfleuri's pleasant estate on the banks of the Loire and not only sees for himself the benefits instituted by a philanthropical lord who had agreed with and anticipated 'the predisposing causes of the revolution – and ... its effects' (65), but he also has the benefit of hearing this paragon's philosophy. The estate is run almost along feudal lines, where there is a semi-contractual relationship between owner and workers, guaranteeing advantages and rights to both sides. The peasantry have been relieved of crippling taxes and are able to afford decent subsistence for themselves and their families. All the necessities for comfortable existence – their natural rights as human beings – are taken care of. Montfleuri sees this pattern as replicated over post-revolutionary France, now a country whose newfound liberty a king would be proud to defend. Charlotte Smith even slips in one of England's rare claims to guaranteeing a particular right: 'Let the voice of common sense answer, whether the whole nation has gained nothing in its dignity, by obtaining the right of trial by jury' (64), as part of a general reform of the justice system along the lines of protecting all individuals rather than blatantly favouring the rich. The phrase is repeated later in an appeal to 'common sense, nature, and reason' (106), and it is worth pointing out that Smith's use of the term 'common sense' indicates a shift in its meaning, from the renaissance biological idea that there is a kind of 'sixth sense' which receives and synthesises stimuli from the other five senses, to a much more politically informed notion of experiential consensus – what all people everywhere regard as self-evident because it is seen as true to 'truth, humanity and reason'. Thomas Paine gave currency to this usage in his appeal to Americans to rebel against the British yoke in *Common Sense* (1776), where the term is related to 'the Commons', the British House of Commons. Montfleuri (and Charlotte Smith) turn critical attention to the ways in which England has hypocritically misrepresented the issues behind the revolution:

> when I meet, as too often I have done, Englishmen of mature judgment and solid abilities, so lost to all right principles as to deprecate, misrepresent, and condemn those exertions by which we have obtained that liberty they affect so sedulously to defend for themselves; when they declaim in favour of an hierarchy so subversive of all true freedom, either of thought or action, and so inimical to the welfare of the people – and pretend to blame *us* for throwing off those yokes, which would be intolerable to themselves, and which they have been accustomed to ridicule us for enduring; I ever hear them with a mixture of contempt and indignation, and reflect with concern on the power of national prejudice and national jealousy, to darken and pervert the understanding. (67)

As if to remind us of the lesson right at the end of the novel, Montfleuri's voice returns in a letter, pointing out that 'throughout the revolution, every circumstance has, on your side, been exaggerated, falsified, distorted, and misrepresented, to serve the purposes of party' (iii, 342). The not-too veiled threat is that 'the light of reason thus rapidly advancing ... will make too evident, the faults of their own system of government, which it is their particular interest to screen from research and reformation'.

Montfleuri gives a brief 'people's history' of French politics (70–1), and it is interesting that, as Charlotte Smith's mouthpiece, he stresses the substantial contribution to public consciousness made by writers. 'Voltaire attacked despotism in all its holds, with the powers of resistless wit: – Rousseau with matchless eloquence: – and, as these were authors who, to the force of reason, added the charms of fancy, they were universally read, and their sentiments were adopted by all classes of men' (71). Milton's *Areopagitica* is again mentioned as the English call to liberty, and it seems clear from the heightened tone of the writing that Smith would like to place her own works in this illustrious company, at least as another clarion call for liberty. From 'the liberties of mankind' Montfleuri turns to 'the liberties of America' (72), supporting the Americans' determination 'to feel and to assert their right to be themselves free', and condemning the British despotic forces 'who, in learning to call them rebels, seemed too often to have forgotten that they were men' (73). In post-revolutionary France, as in America, Montfleuri believes the landowner can be 'free among freemen, instead of being a petty tyrant among slaves' (92), and the enlightened Frenchman's own estate is shown in idyllic terms as a place where the employees and their families are cared for and contented, 'happy in a generous and considerate master; (and now more rationally happy)' (82), a microcosm of what the nation-state should be. So transparently idealised is the vision that it is hard to feel that Smith intends any kind of social realism or historical accuracy faithful to the French revolution in this whole account. Rather, she is trying to persuade through her rhetoric that the English view of events is a dishonest caricature, and attempting to give her readers an imaginative awareness of a wholly different approach to political organisation, more or less as Thomas More did in *Utopia*. She gives a political fable, in the hope that its bold simplicity and principled consistency will infect others with its intrinsic appeal. The emotional plot of the narrative barely matters to this dimension, which makes *Desmond* a less integrated, and less appealing, novel than *The Old Manor House*. At least in the first book, its contribution is primarily to the literature of equality and natural rights.

The final two books of *Desmond* have less to do with public politics in France and more to do with the complex relationships between Desmond, Geraldine, her feckless brother and brutal husband, and the plight of Bethel. The situation in France re-enters occasionally as a way Desmond finds to 'divert [his] mind' from the painful subject of love. He rejoices, for example, that the return of the king into Paris is greeted by the people with 'calmness and magnanimity':

> This will surely convince the world, that the *bloody democracy* of Mr. Burke, is not a combination of the swinish multitude for the purposes of anarchy, but the association of reasonable beings, who determine to be, and deserve to be, free. (iii, 89)

There is a digression in which Desmond parries the argument that negro slaves 'were not men', arguing 'that their physical and moral sensibility is more acute than ours' (iii, 164) and that the floggings they endure are a violation of their rights as human beings. His interlocutor virtually concedes the point by describing them as 'monkeys'. Burke is often named as the enemy of rights, for example when Desmond argues that 'common sense has told us before, that government is not for the benefit of the governors, but the governed; that the people are not transferrable like property' (iii, 210). Smith also turns her attention to women's rights. The only area in which she concedes France has not yet given perfect freedom to its citizens is to Carmelite nuns, who are seen to endure 'years of rigid confinement' (93). Her description owes much to Helen Maria Williams' report in *Letters written in France* of the Carmelite convent she had visited in 1790, and it stands in *Desmond* as a horrifying metaphor for the position of even married women.

Generally, Smith does not advocate extending political rights to women, except insofar as her concentration is on 'the general rights of mankind' (121), but she does highlight the lack of natural rights for women in her society. Later stages of the book, Lorraine Fletcher argues, turn it into 'Charlotte's most overtly feminist novel',[18] when 'the cruelty of the marriage tie is felt by Bethel [Desmond's correspondent] as well as Geraldine'. Geraldine, the married woman whom Desmond loves, forces herself even in her unhappiness to act as an exemplary and faithful wife. She slides from a defence of harmless romantic novels against moralistic attacks (and perhaps Wollstonecraft's condemnation of romance fiction), into a description of her sad plight in the 'real' world: 'I was, you see, "obedient–very obedient"; and, in the four years that have since past, I have thought only of being a quiet wife, and a good nurse, and of fulfilling, as well as I can, the part which has been chosen for me' (ii, 174–5). Like many such women in Smith's novels, Geraldine is a thinly disguised self-portrait. At another stage Smith gives vent to another of her own grievances about the absence of 'rights and liberties' in English law, as Desmond describes the ruinous problems, especially to deserted separated, and widowed women, of a suit at equity to recover property which is rightfully theirs (ii, 133–6). The description not only anticipates *Bleak House* but also accurately reflects Smith's own lifelong problem in trying to recover through legal means the inheritance rights of herself and her family.

As the 1790s developed, many radical writers either recanted or toned down their more forceful political ideas, sometimes out of increasing unease that the French revolution was betraying its principles and inaugurating a new regime of terror, but more often as a response to publishers' legitimate fears as the English government became more paranoid and repressive. Smith did retreat from the positions she adopted in 1792 and 1793. *The Banished Man* (1794) is a nightmarish account following the harrowing experiences of a Fench nobleman, D'Alonville, who has remained loyal to the 'murdered king' and discovers that under revolutionary government a new tyranny has emerged. It might be possible to argue that the novel is more anti-war than anti-revolution, but this would, I think, require some special pleading. In 1798 she returned to some of her earlier thoughts in *The Young Philosopher*, although the tone is now resigned to accepting the failure of the revolution. Here the issues are not located in a revolutionary situation, but they are tinged with the pessimism of one who still saw deep wrongs in England and can foresee no change, revolutionary or legislative, for the better.

From detestation against individuals, such as justices and overseers, [Delmont] began to reflect on the laws that put it in their power thus to drive forth to nakedness and famine the wretched beings they were empowered to protect; and he was led to enquire if the complicated misery he every day saw (a very small part of so wide an evil) could be the fruits of the very best laws that could be framed in a state of society said to be the most perfect among what are called the civilised nations of the world.[19]

Her characteristic narrative pattern of trapping a woman in a gothic building[20] is here repeated several times with not just one but three different heroines, and the added twist is that, like Wollstonecraft's heroine, they are driven to madness by the combination of physical entrapment, mental cruelty, and patriarchal oppression.[21] Progressive attitudes are expressed by characters modelled on Godwin (Armitage) and Paine (Glenmorris), but the general tone of disillusion makes them ineffective. Lorraine Fletcher succinctly sums up, '*The Young Philosopher* contains no hope for England',[22] and the hero Delmont and heroine Medora emigrate to America which is seen, at least temporarily, as offering the freedom and rights which are lacking in England. It may be telling that Smith's next novel was called *The Solitary Wanderer* (1799). The historical occasion of the early 1790s, and the youthful idealism of Charlotte Smith at that time, created the unrepeatable conditions in which she could write her two most powerful and most politically explicit novels of natural rights, *Desmond* and *The Old Manor House*.

Eliza Fenwick: *Secresy; or, the Ruin on the Rock*

One novel deserves at least passing mention, even if it is not sustained as a novel of ideas, turning on a point of natural rights. Eliza Fenwick's *Secresy; or, the Ruin on the Rock* (1795) plunges straight into the argument initiated by Wollstonecraft, that women should be treated as rational human beings, and that their education should fit them for this equal role. Sibella Valmont[23] is commanded by her tyrannical uncle with his belief in female obedience: ' "Always reasoning," he said: "I tell you, child, you cannot, you shall not reason. Repine in secret as much as you please, but no reasonings. No matter how sullen the submission, if it is submission." '[24] Sibella knows otherwise: 'But I know, and he knows too if he would but own it, that I do think; that I was born to think: – and I will think' (43). 'Born to think' is an audacious and unambiguous claim to a natural right, in directly contradicting the 'right' assumed by her uncle, of choosing for her. The epistolary form adopted by Fenwick is an effective vehicle, since it allows the intimate, if 'secret', thinking of Sibella as she writes to Caroline Ashburn, and it allows the development of a mutually supportive female relationship, while placing the third person Lord Valmont as an unsympathetic and distant figure, maintaining his 'mysterious reserve and silence' (60). Caroline explains his background, and his current scheme of educating children, 'instructing a new race, to put the old world out of countenance' (64). He has adopted Sibella and a boy, Clement, and instituted his principles, which effectively mean teaching the boy to think, the girl to feel, allowing her to do only 'what the instinct of appetite demands' [65], while at the same time denying her instincts by forbidding the burgeoning love between Sibella and Clement. The goal is to make the female wholly dependent and submissive. Unfortunately for her uncle, Sibella has an 'eager desire of knowledge' and a determination to use her 'comprehensive powers of intellect'. Equally unfortunately, Clement turns out to be characterised by 'softness' rather than the masculine rationality expected by his uncle. The common comparison between the woman and 'a fettered slave' is drawn, but as Sibella asks rhetorically, 'But where, Miss Ashburn, is the tyrant that could ever chain thought, or put fetters on fancy' (73). Isobel Grundy has pointed out that Valmont's educational principles based on gender difference are intended to mirror those of Rousseau, who, however enlightened he was in general, reveals a blind spot in wanting women to be educated to please men. Wollstonecraft had berated him for this.[25] As the novel's characters increase, a social vista emerges that is full of sexually predatory men and idle, dissipated women, a world where the weak are censured and the unfortunate 'contemned' and the book takes its place within the tradition of the novel of benevolence: 'I hope benevolence is not a novelty' (83). The wealthy, in particular, are depicted as generally hypocritical, useless and immoral. But as it proceeds, the work wanders into the lovers' intrigues signalled by its title, 'secresy', and into gothic mystery implied by the subtitle, 'The Ruin on the Rock'. The point about female education is not pursued far, except that at times blame for the tragic fates of the lovers is cast on deficiencies created by Valmont's enforced and misguided programme. The implication is that if Sibella had been allowed to develop her intellect, she would not have been so much prey to the 'diseased imagination' of infatuation.

Mary Hays: *The Victim of Prejudice*

Mary Hays, another radical dissenter in Joseph Johnson's group of writers, could have been included amongst those who wrote both 'manifesto' and fiction. Her *Appeal to the Men of Great Britain in Behalf of Women* (1798),[26] was reflected in her novel of the next year, *The Victim of Prejudice* The former work was consciously indebted to Wollstonecraft's *Vindication of the Rights of Women*, but although ideologically similar, Hays's book is very different in tone. It is written with conscious rationalism and good humour, and lacks Wollstonecraft's fire and rhetoric. The three grounds on which she bases her appeal, are, first, biblical quotation and injunction; second, rational argument for equality between men and women on the grounds that both are subject to the same weaknesses and it is only 'prejudice' that has led to assumptions of women's inferiority; and third, the conciliatory assertion that equality would be in the interests of men:

> Let them but endeavour to make women happy – not by flattering their
> follies and absurdities – but by every reasonable means; and above all by

considering them as rational beings upon a footing with themselves, – influenced by the same passions, – and having the same claims to all the rights of humanity; which, indeed, are so simple, that justice well defined includes the whole. And then 'women from being happy, will always be in good humour;' and from being happy, and always in good humor, it is but reasonable to hope, that they will at last be, what all wise, and good men wish them, and what in reality they may – and OUGHT TO BE. (293)

This passage, coming as the conclusion to the book as published (its promised second part never appeared) is a little like the end of *The Taming of the Shrew*, putting into Katherine's mouth some words that might in this case be interpreted as, 'If you treat us as equals, then we will be good company'. The conclusion comes after a lengthy and closely reasoned argument placing rights of women within 'the rights of humanity', with only occasionally glimpsed flashes of Wollstonecraft's anger. The resounding 'OUGHT TO BE' is the subjunctive terrain of natural law existing in an ideal realm, rather than 'things as they are'. The difference in tone presumably in part stems from differences in temperament between the writers, but it almost certainly reflects also the years in which the works were written. Wollstonecraft, was writing in the early 1790s and was fired by the French revolution, provoked by Burke, and given morale by the works by Paine and Godwin. Hays, in the late 1790s, faced a much more repressive and dangerous situation under the increasing legal restrictions. Anybody writing then with less than her sober rationality and concessions of good humour would not have hoped for publication. However, the very mildness of the *Address* limited its effectiveness in a period when the issue of rights of women seemed eclipsed by the more urgent task of addressing general rights of assembly and free speech. It was not until the 1820s, when John Stuart Mill and others raised the issue again, that it was placed as much in the public's consciousness as when Wollstonecraft had written.

'Prejudice' is a key word in Hays's *Appeal*. In a brief, powerful opening section, she pleads for 'unprejudiced readers' who are willing to follow her in struggling 'against the accumulated prejudice of ages!' (29). She asks them to 'come forth and look Reason boldly in the face', and to 'bring not the fiend Prejudice in your train'; to trust 'dignified, unbending, conscious Reason' and to resist 'the dear, – deluding, – long-loved, – long-chrerished, – convenient Prejudice' (30). Throughout the book, the plea is reiterated, to look at principles of equality, justice, and fairness rather than being 'guided by custom and prejudice' and carried along by unexamined, man-made 'authority'. A victim of defamatory rumour herself throughout her life, Hays understood from bitter experience the perniciousness of prejudice. The whole idea was clearly on her mind as she wrote her novel, which appeared the year after the *Appeal*.

The Victim of Prejudice (1799) could have been a sentimental story of a persecuted heroine, 'passive and helpless', eventually finding happiness with her chosen marriage partner, but instead Mary Hays chooses to make it into a fable condemning 'the injustice and barbarity of society' (I, ii).[27] It is a tale of victimisation and deprivation of natural rights every bit as bleakly unrelenting as Godwin's *Caleb Williams*, told by its heroine from her prison cell, with her didactic hope that it 'should kindle in the heart of man, in behalf of my oppressed sex, the sacred claims of humanity and justice'. The main part of the plot does dwell on injustice to a woman, as the heroine Mary is pursued, raped and persecuted by the dissolute aristocrat, Sir Peter Osborne, but its wider theme applies equally to men and women, as it applies here to Mary and in a lesser degree to the man she hopelessly loves, William. Both are victims of 'barbarous prejudice' against her illegitimate birth, which dogs her and all who shelter and love her, from the moment she is born. She is reduced from a spirited and well-educated young woman to a ravaged prisoner, her early guardian is ruined, and her lover ends up marrying elsewhere in a loveless relationship, all because of a presumed taint inherited from her equally victimised mother. Symbolically, her downfall is started by a rash, impulsive gesture in stealing a bunch of grapes, described with all the biblical overtones of Eve destroying paradise, but in truth it goes back to the accident of her birth. Mary herself is very much a rationalist by education, having been reared by a foster father, Mr Raymond, who believes that 'an enlightened intellect is the highest of human endowments' (I, 63) and who teaches her that 'right reason' is a supreme virtue. However, he is also aware that in society as it is, 'philosophers are not yet the legislators of mankind' (I, 75), and he is well aware of the power of public prejudice to cloud rational thought, turning what was 'innocent and laudable' into the 'pernicious and criminal' (I, 85). His rationalism extends to love: 'The canker most pernicious to every virtue is *dependence*; and the most fatal species of bondage is subjection to the demands of our own imperious passions.' Hays is clearly influenced by Wollstonecraft in seeing women's lack of education as a fatal limitation that makes them prey to sentimentalism:

> Few marriages are formed on what is called *love*, in its appropriate sense; it is a bewitching, but delusive , sentiment; it dwells in the imagination, and frequently has little other connection with the object. The true beauty, of which the lover is enamoured, is merely ideal; an exquisite enchantment, dissolving on a nearer approach; an intoxicating species of enthusiasm ... *virtue* (II, 33)

Mr Raymond himself may be a victim of his own prejudice in this matter, but for him infatuation is the emotional equivalent of social prejudice. He firmly believes that because of Mary's low birth neither the young man nor the world will ever accept her as a match for William Pelham who, he predicts, will turn to depravity in 'the theatre of the world'. Although in the eyes of the virtuous, 'reputation is but a secondary good; it wears the semblance of virtue', but Raymond recognises that in the eyes of the world reputation is often 'prized before the substance' and carries more weight than true virtue. (II, 44) He therefore pleads with Mary to 'distinguish, I pray you, between the dictates of nature and virtue and the factitious relations of society' and not confuse her own love for William with the social reality of how a liaison will be viewed, or whether, indeed, it is possible (II, 106). In the scheme of things, Mary is 'a victim to circumstances over which [she] had little power' (II, 116). The novel remains undecided about whether Mary should have pursued her natural feelings of love, but Raymond does seem to be correct in thinking the world will never give respectability to the relationship with her lover, and that William's inclination to spurn prejudice is unrealistic:

> Why, my sweet girl, should we suffer the prejudices of others to enslave us? Let us purchase a cottage, and hide ourselves from the world, supremely blest in each other. (I, 133)

Mr Raymond himself is unexpectedly ruined because of his wholly benevolent association with Mary, proving from another direction that the power of prejudice is just as vicious as he thinks, and the rest of the novel demonstrates in gruesome detail that there is no room to 'hide ourselves' in a prejudiced world. The assumption is that if she had married William, he too would be personally ruined by the association. There is also a strong opinion that, since she is illegitimate, she will also be depraved herself as if by an hereditary taint, and so her resistance to the advances of Osborne are described by him as 'theatrical coyness' (II, 140). Mary herself is in fact a 'poor, innocent lamb' (ii, 176), and she does everything to gain respectability by living virtuously, only to find that the prejudice of society imposes 'almost insuperable barriers' (I, 162), until 'it is too late! *Law* completes the triumph of injustice', and she ends up in prison. The rhetoric of the novel shows that Hays is not writing a lurid narrative of pursuit, rape and degradation as ends in themselves, but that she is indignantly objecting to the deprivation of 'the common *right* of a human being', who has committed no offence, to live in unmolested peace and respectability. Mary's existential cry carries great force, as she objects to ostracism, persecution and victimisation, simply because she was not born in wedlock:

> ... amidst the luxuriant and the opulent, who surrounded me, I put in no claims either for happiness, for gratification, or even for the common comforts of life: yet, surely, *I had a right to exist!* (II, 143)

Only for a very brief period does she begin 'to taste the sweets of independence, the dignity of an active, useful life' (II, 190), before being swept back into prison and sinks apparently forever beneath 'the trammels of prejudice' against which she has fought 'with dauntless intrepidity' (II, 213). The only redeeming feature of her dreadful experiences will, she feels, lie in their potential to teach readers to challenge the system of prejudicial law which has destroyed her and denied her natural rights of independent existence:

> The sensibilities of my heart have been turned to bitterness, the powers of my mind wasted, my projects rendered abortive, my virtues and my sufferings alike unrewarded. *I have lived in vain!* unless the cry of my sorrows should kindle in the heart of man, in behalf of my oppressed sex, the sacred claims of humanity and justice. (II, 231)

We presume she does not live to see her vindication, and the short, powerful novel, like others of the anti-romantic kind in the 1790s, ends in despair. Nicola J. Watson argues that this kind of novel, a set of death-bed or prison memoirs, can be linked with the female epistolary novel which could be radical and even revolutionary in spirit but consciously doomed to obscurity by the solipsism of the writing mode adopted by imprisoned victims of oppression.[28] Terence Allan Hoagwood agrees that *The Victim of Prejudice*, like other works by Hays such as *Appeal to the Men of Great Britain in Behalf of Women* (1798), is structured to call attention not to unique instances but general determining structures, to 'collective concept-formations'.[29] He describes the relevant concepts in this novel as 'prejudice, mental chains, delusions, and harmful structures of thought' (125) within institutions which include marriage, law and economic class distinction. However, he never quite reaches the point which gives this and the other novels in this chapter their special centrality: they deal with the fundamental nature of natural rights, and the profound injustices that follow deprivation of rights. Mary's call, *I had a right to exist!*, stands as a motto for them all.

6
Slavery as Fact and Metaphor: William Blake and Jean Paul Marat

In many ways, William Blake is the guiding spirit behind this book, and his most characteristic, bardic tone of 'the voice of honest indignation' (*The Marriage of Heaven and Hell*) is exemplary of those reformists who identify social wrongs and espouse natural rights. Through his poetry he comments on each of the dominant political and social causes which attracted natural law theorists: the American revolution, the French revolution, slavery, child labour and female emancipation. However, his mythological and psychological model of the states of innocence and experience is so broad-based and comprehensive that it is capable of exposing many other specific issues. In fact, his approach is intrinsically one which is uniquely based on an essential and prior theory of natural rights. His poetry graphically (and in some cases, literally) encapsulates the movement away from laws or law, which are inherently restrictive, to rights or freedoms. The tendency of natural rights thinking is away from systems and abstractions and towards the needs of individual human beings in their 'natural' state. Blake is always working from these premises, and actively opposing systems and laws, however well-meaning they may have been in origin (such as Christianity). In particular, Blake realises that one issue which provides him with a central reference point for rights thinking is slavery and its abolition, a cause which had a special topical reference for writers and politicians in the 1790s. The chains of slavery could stand as metaphor for the confinement of women in marriage laws (a commonplace in the writings of Wollstonecraft and Smith, for example),[1] for Americans before their war of independence, for the French before their revolution, and for children working in London. The state of slavery itself, of course, goes to the heart of principles of equality espoused by so many writers like Godwin and Thelwall, and although not necessarily in itself a radical issue, 'the trope of slavery', in Markman Ellis's words, 'presented a rich symbolic storehouse for articulating related issues of contemporary note, such as marriage, imprisonment, or labour'.[2] More generally, 'mind-forg'd manacles' becomes for Blake a central metaphor for the restrictive ways in which the mind itself, constricted and coerced by institutions like the law, religion and science, became blinkered to the conditions of freedom lying beyond socially accepted sanctions. By looking at Blake's use of slavery in the context of his contemporaries' views, we may not do justice to the whole of his mythology and poetic vision, but we can find a central position in his overall thinking. Other writers like Mary Wollstonecraft and Charlotte Smith link slavery with, for example, the woman's place in marriage, while some, like Thelwall, Spence and Paine use the imagery of slavery to describe the economic dependence of the poor. Helen Maria Williams witnessed a prisoner in the Bastille and described his captive state in terms evoking that of slaves: 'round his neck an iron band, bound to the impregnable wall'.[3] But Blake was virtually alone in seeing slavery as a paradigm for all injustice, as the centrally unequal relationship between people which fundamentally violated all discrete natural rights, and could stand as a metonymy for the whole conceptual field. Freedom from slavery, equally, becomes metonymic for all forms of liberation, political, sexual and intellectual. We shall find a comparable treatment in an unexpected work by Jean Paul Marat, *The Chains of Slavery*.

Slavery in fact and fiction

The history of slavery and its abolition has been written so many times from so many points of view and at such length, that it need not and cannot be fully rehearsed here,[4] but since abolitionism was the single most public and successful campaign implicitly concerned with natural rights in the period, some necessarily brief account should be given of its history and the literary reception. I hope this detail will be justified by the centrality of slavery as a metaphor in Blake's work discussed in the second part of this chapter. The main point that emerges in relation to the 1790s and adjoining decades in England was that the call for abolition was the only 'respectable' campaign sometimes presented on the basis of natural rights of the time, and its proselytisers were not persecuted by officialdom with the same zealous opposition and hostility reserved for those who wanted political rights for the English, economic independence for the poor, revolution along the lines of the French experiment, or rights for women.

Anti-slavery as a mass movement was led by the middle-classes and succeeded partly through the direct action of citizens who presented to parliament petitions with signatures in the thousands. Its seedbed was not radical politics but religious and evangelical humanitarianism.[5] It was probably the only campaign which could command the mutual agreement of figures so diverse and publicly powerful as Pitt, Fox and Burke, and before them Sir Joshua Reynolds and Dr Johnson. Its most active campaigners were hardly revolutionists or radicals. William Wilberforce, member of parliament for Hull and then Yorkshire, doggedly pursued the issue in parliament. Granville Sharp, son of the Archdeacon of Northumberland and grandson of the Archbishop of York, took to court the grievance of the slave James Somerset, leading to the celebrated Mansfield judgment, which, after 'tracing the subject to natural principles', declared slavery illegal in England (1772). Thomas Clarkson was a scholar at St John's College, Oxford, and trainee clergyman, until the cause of abolition seized his attention and his time as he trawled the south of England seeking evidence of cruelty to slaves and organising for petitions to be collected. Nor were their respective beliefs in equality based on such socially disruptive principles as Godwin's, Paine's and Spence's. Wilberforce, concerned about the evidence of cruelty to slaves on a mass scale, was persuaded by Pitt to enter the public fray, while Sharp and Clarkson were first-hand witnesses to cruelty to individual slaves in England. The pedantic Sharp also had a religious obsession to prove that black people were derived not from the biblical Ham whose dark descendants were thought to be punished by becoming 'hewers of wood and drawers of water' for his sin in seeing his father Noah drunk and naked, but instead from the more innocent Cush.[6] (In fact it is Canaan, 'brother' of Cush and 'son' of Ham whom Genesis regards as cursed.) Wilberforce, Sharp and Clarkson, and many in the anti-slavery movement, could be hostile to the French revolution and to calls for other egalitarian causes. None the less, the anti-slavery movement in itself attracted more libertarian elements among radical and working-class groups: 'Fryer describes a mass meeting in Sheffield in 1794, in which thousands of workers unanimously called for the end of the slave trade and emancipation of the slaves.'[7] The most undeviatingly consistent group actively working to abolish the institution of slavery, from the early 1700s and throughout the century, were the Quakers, and although they had little political power in the state, yet they commanded more respect than other nonconformist Protestant religious groups. They were the first to take action against the trade, as early as 1727, by censuring any involvement by Friends.[8] It should be said that it is remarkable how often Quakers, or those brought up as Quakers, have appeared in this book as campaigners for natural rights broadly defined. Because of its impeccable social pedigree, the movement kept winning the moral campaign ever since it began work in earnest in the 1770s, but losing the succession of parliamentary battles, mainly because it was directly opposed by the huge and growing power of commerce and capital,[9] and secondarily because in the early 1790s the government, and mainly its most eloquent spokesmen like Pitt and Burke, were distracted by a perception that the French Revolution posed a social and political threat to England. The disparity between mass support and disappointing results in Parliament must have tangentially helped persuade many among the middle class that their views were not being represented in that institution. The final abolition of the slave trade was not to come in Britain until the Abolition of Slavery in the British Dominions Act in 1833, significantly soon after the 1832 Reform Act, and as Eric Williams has argued in *Capitalism and Slavery*,[10] it did not happen entirely as a consequence of altruistic activism but, rather, economic circumstances. The whole enterprise was becoming less lucrative because of the steadily increasing insurrectionary activity by slaves themselves, the quelling of which was necessarily paid for by the government. However, the terms on which abolition occurred in 1833 compensated plantation owners to the tune of 20 million pounds.

But there were some victories along the way, and evidence that the tide was turning. Although slavery dated back to Roman times and before, Britain was relatively late in adopting it. Portugal was first in 1444 to transport slaves from the West Coast of Africa back to Lisbon, but it was the opening-up of the New World that drew other European countries in, during the sixteenth century and beyond. Queen Elizabeth strongly disapproved, and it was not until after 1713 that England led the way, sending boats from Liverpool and Bristol to Africa, then to America to provide slave labour, while the sugar, tobacco and rum which resulted were brought back to England. It was not only the slaves who had a hard time – the sailors were ill-treated and actively deterred from returning to England since they were no longer needed. Parliamentary awareness was raised by a damning report augmented with the petitions collected by Clarkson, followed by the shocking news of the captain of the slave boat the *Zong* who threw 132 plague-ridden slaves into shark-infested waters in 1781. From 1788 Wilberforce introduced a bill every year in the House of Commons, gradually chipping away at the majority.[11]

It should be said, however, that not all arguments for abolition were mounted on the principle that enslavement violated a natural right to liberty of action based on the fact of being human, or even on grounds of equality. This was inevitable, since the whole doctrine of natural rights was so controversial and officially unaccepted that to invoke it could have jeopardised the case. The Earl of Abingdon in parliament recognised with some horror the full implications of abolishing slavery, and rejected them: 'what does the abolition of the slave trade mean more or less, than liberty and equality? What more or less than the rights of man?'[12] For the same reason, Burke withdrew his support from the abolition movement. The formal arguments usually focused on the sheer cruelty of conditions, shamed English consumers of luxury goods, and advanced economic reasons, as well as addressing the opposition argument that if Britain abolished the trade then rival nations, especially the hated France, would jump into the profitable vacuum. (Ironically, the French were more serious about abolition than the English, even before the revolution in 1789.) Wilberforce's exemplary speech in the debate in 1789, praised by Burke, Pitt and Fox, mentions only fleetingly that the trade itself is 'disgraceful to human nature' and concentrates on the atrocious conditions in which slaves were transported and kept.

Creative writers played a significant part in the abolitionist debate, dating back to Aphra Behn's *Oronooko: or, the Royal Slave* (1688), which 'established many of the elements which in the late eighteenth century became the cliches of abolitionist poetry and tales by both women and men'.[13] Although some writers, as we have seen throughout this book, were not embarrassed or hampered by scruples about the unpopularity of natural rights, yet the vast majority who contributed to what became a fashionable middle-class literary genre of anti-slavery fiction and poetry, merely reflected the more limited debate in parliament. Sentimentality and benevolence returned with a vengeance, as hundreds of poems were written, turning on pity and empathetic altruism based on the victims' sufferings. Coleridge in his lecture 'On the Slave Trade', published as a pamphlet (Bristol, 1796),[14] refers to 'Benevolence' which he defines as 'Natural Sympathy made permanent by an acquired Conviction, that the Interests of each and of all are one and the same'. He emphasises that the products of slavery are all unnecessary luxuries, 'Sugars, Rum, Cotton, Logwood, Cocoa, Coffee, Pimento, Ginger, Indigo, Mahogany, and Conserves', none of which justifies the human suffering paid for it, 'which the gloomy Imagination of Dante would scarcely have dared to attribute to the Inhabitants of Hell'. He proceeds by opposing logically the arguments made by anti-abolitionists, 'First, that the Abolition would be useless, since though *we* should not carry it on, other nations would. II. that the Africans are better treated and more happy in the Plantations than in their native Country. III. that the Revenue would be greatly injured. IV. that the Right of Property would be invaded. V. that this is not a fit opportunity.' He calls slave-trading a malevolent occupation in which all are implicated, even the 'lady' who 'sips a beverage sweetened with human blood'. He refers once to 'a usage so unnatural, that [it is] contrary to the universal law of life' adverting to the well-known fact that the slaves' population diminished each year through deaths, and he contrasts the insistence by the French on the rights of man. However, his own argument is not squarely based on an argument for natural rights, but rather abhorrence of the living conditions of slaves. Coleridge had, in fact, been concerned about the slave trade since his first year at Cambridge University, when in 1792 he won the Brown gold Medal for his Sapphic 'Ode on the Slave Trade'.[15] Joan Baum argues that the presence of individual guilt in 'The Rime of the Ancient Mariner' owes much to Coleridge's sense of collective implication in the horrors of slavery, while claiming also that he and Wordsworth, who in turn wrote three anti-slavery sonnets, were like many in their society compromised by their own oblique links with the trade. This may be the result of their emphasising individual sensibility and benevolence as reactions, rather than externalising the problem as one of violation of the rights of man.

It would swell this chapter into disproportionate size, to attempt anything like thoroughness in covering the hundreds of writers who contributed to abolitionism. Whole books have been written on, for example, just the contribution of women, who are estimated to have contributed about one quarter of the output.[16] Poets provided Blake and his age with the richest field of sources for anti-slavery popular propaganda, some of them drawing upon natural rights for their rationale. Most famous of all was William Cowper's short poem, 'The Negro's Complaint' (1788). One of its most significant contributions to Blake's armoury (for he must have known the poem) was its use of a persona, in this case that of the Negro slave who has been 'Forced from home and all its pleasures' in Africa 'To increase the stranger's treasures' as a slave.

> Men from England bought and sold me,
> Paid my price in paltry gold;
> But, though slave they have enroll'd me,
> Minds are never to be sold.
>
> Still in thought as free as ever,
> What are England's rights, I ask,
> Me from my delights to sever,
> Me to torture, me to task?

Cowper's poem turns on all the terms and concepts employed by Paine, for example, in his political analysis – the freedom of the mind, 'rights', the slave owners as 'tyrants' the 'man-degrading mart' of an activity worse only in degree from exploitation of labourers in Britain, and equality:

> Deem our nation brutes no longer,
> Till some reason ye shall find
> Worthier of regard and stronger
> Than the colour of our kind.

He also hints at what will become Blake's overriding concern, the way that a corrupt institution can enthral the mind of the slave owner and alienate him from human feelings:

> Slaves of gold, whose sordid dealings
> Tarnish all your boasted powers,
> Prove that you have human feelings
> Ere you proudly question ours!

Even closer to Blake's use of personae in his *Songs* is Cowper's 'Pity for Poor Africans'. Here the speaker is one who, by not taking a positive stand against slavery, tacitly aids and abets slave owners, and is morally no better than them. Although 'shock'd at the purchase of slaves' and full of 'pity' for the slaves themselves, he feels he 'must be mum' for the reasons that majorities in the Commons kept voting against abolition. He assumes the necessity of luxury products like sugar, rum, coffee and tea, and fears that if Britain abolishes the slave trade, then 'the French, Dutch, and Danes' will leap into the breach and become far more inhumane owners. He then tells a brief tale which in many ways is 'Blakean', about 'A youngster at school, more sedate than the rest'. This boy is at first shocked by his comrades' plot to rob an orchard, but he is met with the answer that the robbery will go ahead whether or not he joins it, the apple owner will lose his apples, and 'Tom' will get no fruit for himself. Tom solemnly reasons that his pity for the owner will not save his fruit, that the loss will not be his responsibility because if it were up to him alone no fruit would be stolen, so finally he can see no injury in benefiting himself from the crime:

> His scruples thus silenced, Tom felt more at ease,
> And went with his comrades the apples to seize;
> He blamed and protested, but join'd in the plan;
> He shared in the plunder, but pitied the man.

While not turning on the concept of natural rights, Cowper's poem antici-pates those *Songs* by Blake that reveal through interior monologue a false reasoning or unconscious hypocrisy that enacts the entrapment of the mind within its own categories, fashioned through expediency and conventional thought. It also anticipates Blake's belief that pity alone is useless.

Other celebrated poets added support to the anti-slavery campaign, and their contribution has been readily acknowledged: Chatterton, whose 'Heccar and Gaia' in *African Eclogues* (1770) was the first worthy anti-slavery poem, George Dyer in several poems, William Bowles in 'The African' (1791), Coleridge in 1792 and 1796, Southey in 'Poems Concerning the Slave Trade' (1797–1810), and Wordsworth, who came on the scene only when the battle was being substantially won, in his sonnets, 'We had a Fellow-Passenger', 'To Toussaint L'Ouverture', and 'To Thomas Clarkson, on the Final Passing of the Bill for the Abolition of the Slave Trade' (1803–07). Robert Merry demon-strated awareness of natural rights in several of his poems, and most perti-nently 'The Slaves: An Elegy':

> Say, that in future *Negroes shall be blest*
> Rank'd e'en as Men, and Men's just rights enjoy;
> Be neither Sold, nor Purchas'd, nor Oppress'd,
> No griefs shall wither, and no stripes destroy!

But just as symptomatic are the dozens if not hundreds of heartfelt poems by writers who nowadays attract only passing mention, if any, in literary histo-ries. In many cases the slavery issue inspired their best and sometimes only poems. Some members of the revolutionary circles who appear in this book also published poems opposing slavery. Helen Maria Williams wrote a poem lamenting Wilberforce's failure to win the parliamentary debate in 1788, as did Anna Laetitia Barbauld in 1791. Thelwall consistently opposed slavery in his works, and published the monologue 'The Negro's Prayer' in 1807, in which he characteristically emphasised the equality of black and white in the eyes of God:

> If black man, as white, is the work of thy hand –
> (And who could create him but Thee?)
> Ah give thy command, –
> Let it spread thro' each land,
> That Afric's sad sons shall be free.

The background of the first two lines of this quotation make it possible to read Blake's 'The Tiger', among other themes, as a statement of racial equality. As already implied, women were in the forefront of the poetic anti-slavery genre, and Mary Birkett's lengthy *A Poem on the African Slave Trade* contains important statements of equality:

> Men must be men, possest with feelings still;
> And little boots a white or sable skin,
> To prove a fair inhabitant within

There are lines showing not only Blakean indignation but also sensitivity to the message that the assumption of racial superiority leads to denial of natural rights:

> To our first parents when th' Almighty Cause
> Reveal'd his holy will – his hallow'd laws;
> When from his lips the wondrous accents broke,
> And mortals listen'd while the Godhead spoke;
> In that mysterious moment did he say? –
> "Man shall his fellow ravage, sell, and slay;
> And one unhappy race shall always be
> Slave to another's pamper'd luxury."

The 'blood-stain'd luxury' is sugar, and Birkett calls for a female boycott of it. The answer to her satirically posed rhetorical question is a resounding 'No', and Birkett points out that 'The beating pulse, the heart that throbs within' is the same in all human beings. She provides the clarion call, 'Oh, let us rise and burst the Negro's chain!' Meanwhile, one of the most powerful poems of all along these lines was written by the now neglected Ann Yearsley ('The Bristol Milkwoman'), 'A Poem on the Inhumanity of the Slave-Trade' (1788?). This lengthy and ambitious work focuses on the particular violation of natural rights represented by the separation of the slave from his African family, and invites the 'seller of mankind' to contemplate his feelings if his own family were thus disrupted:

> Away, thou seller of mankind! Bring on
> Thy daughter to this market! bring thy wife!
> Thine aged mother, though of little worth,
> With all thy ruddy boys! Sell them, thou wretch,
> And swell the price of Luco! Why that start?
> Why gaze as thou wouldst fright me from my challenge
> With look of anguish? Is it *Nature* strains
> Thine heart-strings at the image? Yes, my charge
> Is full against her, and she rends thy soul,
> While I but strike upon thy pityless ear,
> Fearing her rights are violated. –

Yearsley derides the complicity of English law with slavery and against justice and natural law:

> Is this an English law, whose guidance fails
> When crimes are swell'd to magnitude so vast,
> That *Justice* dare not scan them? Or does *Law*
> Bid *Justice* an eternal distance keep
> From England's great tribunal, when the slave
> Calls loud on *Justice only*?

She also yearns for a revolution within the mind of the supporters of the slave trade, when their 'minds' can be changed by 'social love, Thou universal good', to recognise their own emotional alienation and be 'freed' from mental bondage:

> Oh, loose
> The fetters of his mind, enlarge his views,
> Break down for him the bound of avarice, lift
> His feeble faculties beyond a world
> To which he soon must prove a stranger!

The idea that the slave-owner is just as manacled and trapped as the slave is one that Blake will pursue, even if he is less optimistic than Yearsley, who can anticipate a time when wealth will be subservient to 'heart-felt sympathy'.

Alongside the celebrated poets, there were dozens of others who chose slavery as their subject, such as Hugh Mulligan who dedicated to Wilberforce his *Poems Chiefly on Slavery and Oppression* published in 1788. By 1809, the cause was so respectable that a volume edited by James Montgomery (who appears later in this book as advocating outlawing the practice of using boys as chimney sweeps), dedicated *Poems on the Abolition of the Slave Trade* to 'His Royal

Highness the Duke of Gloucester, Patron ... of the Society for Bettering the Condition of the Natives of Africa'.[17] This volume is quite triumphalist in tone, as it appeared the battle for abolition was about to be won, and it opens with glowing encomia of Granville Sharpe, Thomas Clarkson and Wilberforce. Montgomery firmly claims that slavery is an affront to natural rights:

> Nature in all the pomp of beauty reigns,
> In all the pride of freedom. – NATURE FREE
> Proclaims that MAN was born for liberty. (144–6)

Though by no means the last of poets on the long list of those who wrote against slavery, Amelia Opie followed Blake's practice of writing illustrated lyrics for children in *The Negro Boy's Tale* (1802) and *The Black Man's Lament; or, How to Make Sugar* (1826). The latter, in graphic pictures and simple verses, shows the direct line linking the European commodity of sugar with the cruelty and dehumanisation of slaves, moralising,

> Oh! that good Englishmen could know
> How Negroes suffer for their pleasure!

Yearsley had some reason to resent Hannah More who, as her 'protector' refused to allow her access to a trust fund set up with Yearsley's own money, and it is sometimes thought that she wrote her poem in competition with More's *Slavery, A Poem* (1788). However true or false this may be, the content of the poems is in broad agreement, and both are pitched at the level of natural rights. More's work is a polished and powerful celebration of 'the pow'rs of equal thought' in all human beings, and a strong assertion of reason and conscience. 'Horrors of deepest, deadliest, guilt arise' from contemplation of the atrocities being committed in Africa with the enforced and shocking separation of families: 'See the dire victim torn from social life', as either a woman is torn from her children or a man from his family. 'See the fond links of feeling Nature broke!' as the slave is torn from 'HOME and FREEDOM': 'They still are men, and men shou'd still be free.' Reason rejects the lust for gold which turns man into traffic and souls into merchandise. And if reason is defective in some, yet More says 'all mankind can feel', and empathy with the feelings of the deracinated slave must be universally condemned. She challenges Britain to follow conscientiously her own place as a free country claiming to be Christian, and her plea brings into the language, perhaps for the first time, the phrase 'human rights' in its modern sense:

> What page of human annals can record
> A deed so bright as human rights restor'd?

Novelists also reflected the political activity and debate about the slave trade from 1770 onwards, but in ways that develop the sentimental novel rather than the literature of natural rights (although the two are of course intertwined through benevolence). Sentimental novelists were drawn by the manifest victimisation of the slave, often represented in poses of 'mute docil- ity'.[18] As is the case for poetry, a convenient source of texts is the multi- volume collection edited by Peter Kitson and Debbie Lee, *Slavery, Abolition and Emancipation: Writings in the Romantic Period*, in this case volume 6 (Fiction) edited by Srinvas Aravamudan, although this reproduces only a small selection of a considerable body of material. Two works in particular are not reproduced in the volume. One is an anonymous translation from a French novel by Joseph de Lavallée, marquis de Boisrobert, *The Negro Equall'd by Few Europeans*.[19] It purports to be the autobiography of a Senegalese slave, Itanoko, complete with authentic, factual footnotes, but is in fact a picaresque novel which reflects the slavery debate, adopting a Rousseauian basis depicting a noble savage whose eloquence is rationalised:

> And why should they not be eloquent? They possess the three first qualities of oratory: sensibility, memory, and the power of persuasion. Instructed and free, they would have their *Ciceros*.

His oratory often turns on the indignities of both slave owners and slaves: 'and we endure at once the remembrance of their ills, the pangs of our own, and the anguish which, as human beings, we feel for the crimes of our persecutors!' (I, 3), the natural man shaming 'civilised', Christian man:

> And these are men! whole nations of men! who would rather have us for slaves than friends. To what end, then, are they taught by philosophy, by the arts, the sciences? Do they pretend those soften the manners, and elevate the soul? We will shew them our chains, and say to them, what more could barbarians do? To what purpose is the sublime religion they profess? Does it instruct them to love even their enemies? Ah! we are their brethren. (I, 3)

At a moment when he intimidates his persecutors as he defends a fellow-slave, he throws a different light on the argument for natural rights: 'do you never forget, that when you menace a negro you force him to recollect that he is a man' (I, 143). Itanoko encourages the Europeans to emulate his own lack of prejudices and forgiveness of enemies, in order that essential brotherhood can be acknowledged, and he explains the difference between Negroes and Europeans by suggesting 'that, with equal integrity of design, civilised man follows natural inclination less than the savage' (II, 266). While the European is inhibited by 'that crowd of puerile modes, of fictitious duties' as 'the children of false education which almost subdue his energy and extin- guish his natural virtues' (II, 226–7), the Negro directly understands 'the first business of man' is 'Do what is right'. As one of the systematic contrasts in behaviour, the owners behave cruelly in contrast to their slaves: 'They were slaves, but they had feeling minds; and their humanity was a striking contrast to the scene which had lately passed in the apartment of the overseer' (I, 143). Another novel, Anna Maria Mackenzie's *Slavery: Or, the Times*[20] exemplifies the rather embarrassing convention of mimicking slaves' imagined modes of speech in a kind of pidgin, quite the reverse of Itanoko's Ciceronian prose. However, the book shows its heart to be in the right place, proceeding by showing vignettes of heroism and humanity among slaves, again as a lesson to Europeans: 'The beasts of burthen, in your own nation, are considered in a light more humane than the captured negro' (8), writes Zimza, King of Tonouwah to Mr Hamilton, a rare slave trader with a conscience.[21]

Anti-slavery themes are incorporated in many other novels of the period, including Charlotte Smith's *Desmond* and some children's fiction which, alongside Amelia Opie's poems, may have influenced Blake's *Songs*. Dorothy Kilner's *The Rochfords* (1786) narrates the touching story of a Negro boy in England, ill-treated and driven away by his cruel master and rescued by the eponymous family. The boy has been dismissed as a 'lazy *black* dog' by his former owner, highlighting the obliteration of slaves' status as human beings, and the conventional contrast shows the slave to be more morally aware and sensitive than his captors. When he is offered compassionate hospitality by the Rochfords, his presence provides the occasion for edifying discussions about equality: black and white are '*brethren* and *fellow creatures*, created by the same God, susceptible of the same pleasures, the same pains, and equally endowed with souls immortal' (49). The presence of children in the family provides an easy vehicle for didacticism, as the boys are shown the visible proof that the Negro has blood of the same colour as them, enforcing the lesson that his race has the right to being treated as human beings rather than being '*misused, oppressed, enslaved*, and *chastised*, as if they were only beasts of burden' (57). Thomas Day's *The History of Sandford and Merton* (1789), heavily influenced by Rousseau and written specifically for children, employs similar methods to demonstrate not only the humanity but the nobility of enslaved blacks. The violation of natural rights represented by slavery was clearly important to Day, as he co-authored with John Bicknell the poem, *the Dying Negro* (1773), and elsewhere in *Fragment of an Original Letter on the Slavery of the Negroes* (1776), he argues that 'slavery is the absolute dependence of one man upon another; and is, therefore, as inconsistent with all ideas of justice as despotism is with the rights of nature'.[22] Like Blake, he is one of the writers who perceives a link between slavery as a specific institution and political and natural rights in general. Of course from time to time there were insurrections by aggrieved slaves who had reached the end of their tether, and some fictions made reference to these rebellions. Mary Hays's *Emma Courtney* (1796) contains a trenchantly anti-slavery episode at the dinner table.[23] Maria Edgeworth's story 'The Grateful Negro' in *Popular Tales* (1804) turns on such a conspiracy, but her characters are so stereotyped, and the rebels so superstitious, that the treatment of slaves is patronising. However, she adds one element to the link between abolitonism and natural rights by allowing a 'good' white planter to comment to a 'bad' white planter that the law is not consistent with natural rights, by protecting the rich freemen but not the slaves: ' "The law, in our case, seems to make the right; and the very reverse ought to be done – the right should make the law" ' (301), which in itself is a classical natural law formulation. Other novels, such as Bage's *Hermsprong, or Man As He Is* and Elizabeth Helme's *The Farmer of Inglewood Forest* (1796) contain inset stories displaying the ill-treatment of slaves and sexual exploitation of black females, and demonstrating the slave's selfless heroism in rescuing his master from death. These are the themes repeated in novel after novel of the period, and even if they do not with any sophistication or complexity raise questions about the existence of natural rights, yet they depend on an overwhelming recognition of shared humanity and of the unnaturalness of slavery. Whereas the law and pro-slavery advocates denied that slaves have any rights, novelists and abolitionists alike asserted that there is no reason in nature for this to be so.

As a poet, then, Blake would have encountered strong contemporary, literary representations of the wrongs of slavery. As an artist, too, he was surrounded by anti-slavery images.[24] The two most famous ones came to carry the same popular currency as modern logos like the symbol for the Campaign for Nuclear Disarmament. Josiah Wedgwood's design for a seal commissioned in 1787, its founding year, by the Society for Effecting the Abolition of the Slave Trade (known for short as The London Society), of a shackled, kneeling and praying slave with the motto 'Am I not a Man and a Brother', was used as a potent image in England and America. At first it was distributed through the industrial middle-class as a medal, handed out, for example, by Clarkson in his investigative travels, sold as a cameo fashion object, sent in numbers to Benjamin Franklin, embroidered by women, and then circulated on a mass scale as trade tokens in the form of small coins. Thomas Spence rather cheekily linked the image and the abolitionist cause with his own propaganda for land reform, issuing coins with the slave on one side and on the other the inscriptions 'Whatsoever ye would that men should do unto you, do ye even unto them' (on the penny coin) and 'May slavery and oppression cease throughout the world'.[25] Like Blake, Spence recognised that the issue of slavery was not isolated or self-sufficient, but was linked with other libertarian causes through the concept of natural rights. As a propaganda campaign, the use of the image was hugely successful and its motto carried a broader, egalitarian message about natural rights through all classes. On the back of one farthing token dated 1795 was the inscription 'Advocates for the Rights of Man: Thos. Spence, Sir Thos More, Thos Paine'. (The linking of the sixteenth-century writer of *Utopia* with Spence and Paine gives an interestingly broad historical link with natural law.) Yet another medal had on its reverse the words 'Humanity is the cause of the people'. Ironically, Wedgwood himself seems not to have been particularly close to the abolitionist movement, as evidenced by his relative non-attendance at the Society's meetings even when invited,[26] and it has been suggested that in his hard-headed, commercial ways he was compromised by his commissions from wealthy, slave-owning patrons.[27] Another powerful and influential image was 'Description of a Slave Ship', known also as 'The Brookes of Liverpool' designed by Clarkson, which was rapidly circulated as a popular poster, and was followed by another version. It raised consciousness of the appalling treatment of slaves on the slave ships plying their triangular path between West Africa, America and Britain, showing 450 individual slaves lying in packed sardine-like formation around the under-decks of *The Brookes* slave-ship, 'crammed into the hold and kept chained each in a space smaller than a coffin'.[28] Cowper was to describe the scene as 'Like sprats on a gridiron, scores in a row', in his poem 'Sweet Meat has Sour Sauce: or, The Slave Trader in the Dumps'. The message about dehumanisation and com-modification of human beings was graphic and unavoidable, and this image, along with Wedgwood's, was the only other one approved officially by the London Committee. Again, it was mainly the middle class which came to own copies, and they were the ones Clarkson mobilised to sign and send petitions to parliament, helping to bring to attention the denial of natural rights to slaves throughout the trade. It was shocking in its unadorned fac-tuality, lacking either the verbal message or pathos of Wedgwood's icon. George Morland between 1788 and 1792 painted pictures such as 'Execrable Human Traffic' and 'African Hospitality' inspired by Collins' poetry, and his approach was being pursued by artists in France, most famously Gericault. Fuseli's painting, *The Negro Revenged* (1788) was commissioned by Blake's publisher, Joseph Johnson, to accompany in engraving form Cowper's *The Negro's Complaint*, although Fuseli himself seems to have been inspired by William Day's 'A Dying Negro'. Other respectable artists such as Thomas Bewick from Northumberland also contributed visual representations of slavery. There were many political cartoons and caricatures by Rowlandson, Cruikshank and Gillray reflecting aspects of the slavery debate, although as satirists their attitudes were opportunistic and mainly designed to ridicule politicians on both sides of the house. Some pictures undoubtedly helped to reinforce the representation of cruelty and sadism, like Gillray's *Barbarities in the West Indias* and Cruikshank's *The Abolition of the Slave Trade*.

William Blake: slavery as metaphor

There have been many studies of Blake's relationship to political events of his time and to radical intellectual movements and traditions. David V. Erdman's *Blake: Prophet Against Empire: A Poet's History of His Own Times*[29] remains central to this approach, linking lines from the poetry with specific historical events such as the American war, the French revolution and English politics of the period. Jon Mee in *Dangerous Enthusiasm: William Blake and the Culture of Radicalism in the 1790s*[30] is more interested in the eclectic range of radical traditions which Blake drew on in a spirit of *bricollage*: popular religious enthusiasm, millenarianism, the revival of Celtic antiquity, and the Bible as interpreted by political radicals like Paine and Spence. E. P. Thompson in *Witness Against the Beast: William Blake and the Moral Law*[31] extends the range of dissenting traditions by tracing them back to the seventeenth century through lines such as the antinomians' and muggletonians'. Christopher Z. Hobson examines in minute detail the various representations of Orc, who is often seen as Blake's central figure dramatising social and sexual rebellion, in *The Chained Boy: Orc and Blake's Idea of Revolution*.[32] My contribution may be little more than a footnote to these detailed studies, and its point may seem over-simple, but it is important in a study of literature of natural rights. I suggest, with rash straightforwardness, that underlying Blake's attitude to particular historical events and cultural, political or religious traditions lies a constant preoccupation with the issue of slavery, generalised to become a paradigm for loss of natural rights. His abiding desire for freedom in all spheres of human endeavour is figured as emancipation from the condition of slavery. The brilliant phrase 'mind forg'd manacles' encapsulates Blake's approach, which is to see slavery as not only an institutional limitation on natural rights but also as a psychological state binding both enslaver and enslaved, and applying at least metaphorically wherever there is a restriction on the natural rights of equality and sexual and political freedom. Love is what 'breaks all chains from every mind' while deceit (secrecy, repression, law and caution) 'forges fetters for the mind'. Even the tyranny of the finished text is resisted by Blake since, as many critics have pointed out, each copy of his engraved poetic works was a 'one-off', different from all others.[33] Whenever Blake invokes rights – of children, adults, nations, and so on – he conceives of the central relationship being one of possessive oppressor and slave, and even the oppressor is seen in this model as in turn enslaved to a system or a *mentalité*. The paradigm is everywhere in Blake's poetry. In fact, so focused, repetitive and sustained is his concentration on the psychology of slavery, that it sometimes seems that he is engaged in a herculean task of understanding and freeing himself from an obsession within his own mind, which simultaneously drives him on and retards him from full and spontaneous mental freedom.

On top of the powerful and popular visual images of slavery described above, came the engraved illustrations to John Gabriel Stedman's *A Narrative of Five Years' Expedition against the Revolted Negroes of Surinam* (1796), also published by Johnson. At least 16 of these are by William Blake, his name engraven below, 'Blake Sculpt'. They were executed in 1791–92. Three extraordinary narrative pictures, 'Negro hung by the Ribs', 'Flagellation of a Female Samboe Slave' and 'The Execution of Breaking on the Rack' represented the degrading and inhuman torture of slaves. Stedman himself was not opposed to the slave trade but was merely documenting it, although he did witness and write with feelings of abhorrence about the torture of slaves. (He himself fell in love with a slave woman.)[34] The moral he draws from them is the wonder of human endurance, an attitude extended by Blake's more outraged depiction of barbaric cruelty. Blake's illustrations are savagely ideological and leave no room for misunderstanding his attitude to slavery. In 'A Negro hung alive by the Ribs to a Gallowes', a male slave hangs from a scaffold, not by the neck but by a meat-hook on a chain nailed to the top of the gibbet, inserted in his side, dripping blood. His hands are tied behind his back and the legs and loin-cloth give the impression that the body is swinging. The head, dangling upside down, indicates the slave is still alive – glowering, a face set into a combination of spiritlessless and silent rage. The haunting eyes are pools of blackness. On the ground lie a skull and bones, including a rib-cage, and in the middle distance two skulls are set on poles. In the distance on the sea's horizon, a tall ship floats in serene indifference. The other picture, 'Flagellation of a Female Samboe Slave' shows a slave woman tied by her hands to a tree in a pose of bondage, her back arched and one foot on the ground. The face this time indicates fear. The scene in the middle distance is ambiguous because of the indeterminate perspective and the uncertain action – it can be seen as two tiny English soldiers dancing around her erotically presented body – while in the background two men who look like slaves but are more likely planters, emerge brandishing whips from a house. Whatever the narrative is exactly, the overall intention is clear, as the woman is cruelly degraded both sexually and psychologically, and even the cloth wrapped around her loins is not so much modest coverings as inadequate bandages. 'The Execution of Breaking on the Rack' is what Erdman describes as a 'bloody document' which Blake shrank from signing. We do not know what Stedman made of Blake's images, but they are unmistakable and viscerally charged statements against the slave trade, harrowing images of the denial of natural rights.

Images of slaves and slavery in varying degrees of expressiveness are scattered throughout Blake's poems and illustrations, and so compact and consistent is his thought that certain patterns can be found almost wherever we look. *America: A Prophecy* provides one example. Although it does chart in very general terms the American War of Independence as the clarion call to the end of Albion's empire, it is in no way an historical or documentary account. Nor is it 'prophecy' in the sense of fore-seeing the future, but rather in the Old Testament, visionary sense of seeing through to the essential process driving the War. At this level, the crucial event, as Blake sees it, is the freeing of a prisoner whose condition is likened to that of a slave, and this gives the poem a central cluster of imagery.

> thy father stern abhorr'd,
> Rivets my tenfold chains
>   ...
> For chaind beneath, I rend these caverns
>   [Plate 1]
>
> The hairy shoulders rend the links, free are the wrists of fire
> Thou art the image of God who dwells in darkness of Africa
>   [Plate 2]

The moment of liberation comes in a spellbinding passage where Blake lets his most rhapsodic poetic vein flow freely:

> The morning comes, the night decays, the watchmen leave
>   their stations;
> The grave is burst, the spices shed, the linen wrapped up;
> The bones of death, the covring clay, the sinews shrunk & dry'd
> Reviving shake, inspiring move, breathing! awakening!
> Spring like redeemed captives when their bonds and bars are burst;
> Let the slave grinding at the mill, run out into the field:
> Let him look up into the heavens & laugh in the bright air;
> Let the inchained soul shut up in darkness and in sighing,
> Whose face has never seen a smile in thirty weary years,
> Rise and look out, his chains are loose, his dungeon doors are open
> And let his wife and children return from the oppressors scourge,
> They look behind at every step & believe it is a dream,
> Singing. The Sun has left his blackness & has found a fresher morning
> And the fair Moon rejoices in the clear & cloudless night;
> For Empire is no more, and now the Lion and the Wolf shall cease.
>   [Plate 6]

The undoubted power of this sequence, comparable in many ways to the scene of liberation of prisoners in Shelley's *Prometheus Unbound*, derives, I believe, from its centrality to the whole mythological and psychological basis of Blake's poetic vision. It enacts the process of liberating the prisoner/slave – perhaps of abolition of the whole slave trade – in poetry which, in its movement from 'breathing! awakening!' to 'Spring like redeemed captives', plays out rhythmically the process it is describing. Its visionary climax is the end of repressive 'Empire' and the reinstatement of an original innocence in which equality reigns. Hierarchies are dismantled for all creatures through an obliteration of difference: 'and now the Lion and the Wolf shall cease'.

Blake's work reveals a lifelong series of re-creations of a personal and in some ways eccentric myth which dynamically explains the process by which the human world entered its state of enslavement, losing its links with nature and with even an awareness of natural rights. The process is most succinctly encapsulated in five lines of *Africa* (1795):

> Thus the terrible race of Los and Enitharmon gave
> Laws and religions to the sons of Har, binding them more
> And more to earth, closing and restraining,
> Till a philosophy of five senses was complete.
> Urizen wept and gave it into the hands of Newton
>   and Locke. [ll. 44–8]

While details of narrative, character and significance differ from work to work, the overall pattern is the same. Man-made laws, institutions and religious dogma increasingly repress human wholeness of existence by separating experience into material categories ('closing and restraining'), such as mind and body and five separate senses. The final stage is the canonisation of the reductive and divisive view of the world embraced by science (Newton) and philosophy (Locke), so that imprisonment in the system is mentalised and internalised. The 'mind-forg'd manacles' are firmly in place and no alternative is available beyond the intellectual horizon.

Many, if not most, of Blake's poems presuppose this myth and work from a tacit assumption that physical and mental enslavement of human beings is complete. But the one which spells out the narrative in most detail is *Urizen*, a kind of serious parody or personal reconstruction of the creation myth in Genesis. This fable or parable tells the story of how human beings came into existence, and how they were enchained and denied natural rights.[35] In Blake's equivalent of the Australian Aboriginals' dreamtime, there was 'eternity', without temporal or spatial dimensions, without earth and sky, without death, presided over by 'the eternals'. Urizen, like Milton's Satan, is a disaffected eternal, banished to solitude. He is egotistical and individualistic (a point which carries a political and commercial point), 'Self-closd, all-repelling'. He destroys the oneness of eternity irrevocably, and sets in train the process that leads to the 'fallen' world of infinitely diverse bodies. The moment of his 'big bang'[36] can appear to us unnervingly like the initial splitting of the atom which led inevitably to the nuclear bomb. It is effected by Urizen in exactly this act of splitting eternity: 'Eternity roll'd wide apart', followed by an ever-increasing binary multiplication of divisions and distinctions in a self-perpetuating spiral. The stars are separated from the earth (or rather, earth is created as a separate sphere), light and darkness appear, fire and ice, life and death, and the whole seismic event is 'Like a human heart struggling & beating' into existence. Boundaries and measurement come into existence, as do the seven deadly sins. The plethora of new entities will lead to the necessity for man to make choices of just 'One King. One God. One Law',[37] thus leading to institutionalised repression, tyranny and dogma. Los is an 'eternal prophet' who in some ways figures Blake's own bardic self-representation. Mee describes his role as 'a residual link with primitive liberty in a world of Urizenic oppression',[38] although we should add that he is more implicated in the disaster than 'residual' suggests. Los becomes tragically an unwilling accomplice to the fall even as he tries to stop it, just as a poet like Blake, seeking to represent timeless unity of spirit and matter must descend to using words, which are implicitly divisive, material, and time-bound. For Los, the compromising medium is the metal chain made from individual rivets. By using it in his attempt to stop Urizen, he lucklessly compounds division and becomes himself despairingly enchained in the whole process. At first Los throws 'nets and gins' around Urizen and his creations, then chains:

> He watch'd in shuddering fear
> The dark changes & bound every change
> With rivets of iron & brass;
>   ...
> Beating still on his rivets of iron
> Pouring sodor of iron; dividing
> The horrible night he watches
>   ...
> The Eternal Prophet heavd the dark bellows
> And turn'd restless the tongs; and the hammer
> Incessant beat; forging chains new & new
> Numb'ring with links hours and days.

The imagery of 'fetters of iron' is relentlessly sustained by Blake in this part of the poem, and the 'linked infernal chain' reminds us of nothing so much as the manacled slave. The illustrations depict chains and leg irons (Plates 10, 19, 20, 26). At first it seems odd that Urizen is placed in the position of slave as victim while Los, who is effectively now Urizen's hapless slave, is placed in the position of oppressor. The solution to these contradictions comes from abolitionist thought in the 1790s as it was canvassed earlier in this chapter. Many writers, such as Cowper and Yearsley, strongly suggest that slavery begins with the mentality of the slave-owner, whose mind is closed and his humanity alienated to profit. Blake is writing in this sense when he describes Urizen as 'In chains of the mind locked up'. In his initial action of breaking eternity into two he has within himself acquired the central fact of slavery – extreme restriction of thought and action – and the fact that his enslavement is internal and to a system rather than externally imposed on him, does not alter this position. He sleeps as if he is dead, 'In a horrible dreamful slumber; / Like the linked infernal chain', and yet the process he has generated goes on and on around him. Second, Los's position as simultaneous slave and oppressor is explained by another contemporary idea on natural rights shared by Blake, which we discovered in the writing of Wollstonecraft and other anti-sentimental writers of the 1790s: the idea that 'pity' for a victim is not just politically ineffectual but also may be radically misplaced. Thus Blake presents the birth of pity into the world as a disastrous event, when Los, against morality but following his emotions, pities the sleeping Urizen simply because he is now chained:

> 6. Los wept obscur'd with mourning
> His bosom earthquak'd with sighs
> He saw Urizen deadly black
> In his chains bound & Pity began
>
> 7. In anguish dividing & dividing
> For pity divides the soul
> In pangs of eternity on eternity

For Blake, pity would have been hopelessly associated with the ideologies of benevolence and sentimentality, weakly ineffectual in dealing with issues of injustice, and retarding rather than helping the cause of social change. Los's self-division, caught between fearful vigilance and inappropriate sentimentality, is given an image, for his pity breaks off from him and becomes an independent 'round globe of blood', a 'globe of life blood trembling', which is the embryo of 'the first female now separate' from the man. She is born as Enitharmon, but 'they call'd her Pity'. Los continues his job of quarantining the damage done by Urizen so that it cannot contaminate all eternity, but in so doing he himself becomes locked within a circle which prevents him from seeing outside. In Blake's thought, an instinct to protect is fatally close to a kind of predatory possessiveness. In order to protect the woman, he makes 'a Tent with strong curtains' and he and Enitharmon go inside the 'curtains of darkness' never to escape, and they are at this point the equivalents of Milton's Adam and Eve, giving birth later to 'a man Child' named Orc. In later poems Orc at times becomes the principle of revolution for Blake, but in this poem he is yet another slave to Urizen's system. He is born energetically bursting girdles only to find that 'another girdle Oppressd his bosom' for they are being created by day and burst by night. The first parents,

> chain'd his young limbs to the rock
> With the Chain of Jealousy
> Beneath Urizens deathful shadow

Hobson sums up his argument about the centrality of Orc as revolutionary figure in this way:

> he represents not a cyclic upsurge but the energy that is bound with the repression of sexuality and the creation of oppressed populations and classes. No doubt, this energy has been partially released in many failed historical revolutions, but Blake does not use Orc to represent these prior upheavals; the Orc who breaks his chains at the start of *America* has been bound since the rise of civilisation.[39]

In the context of this book, we can recognise that the three male figures represent the three processes in slavery: Urizen creates the binary ideological framework which makes slavery inevitable through inequality, Los ambiguously applies manacles and chains even as he desperately tries to contain the evil principle, and Orc is the one imprisoned who will eventually break his chains in rebellion. However, it is necessary constantly when reading Blake to insist that no single formulation catches the multiple dimensions of his thinking, and also to add that he is inconsistent and opportunistic from book to book, as deliberately destabilising of his own mythologies as he is of others'. Enitharmon goes on to bear 'an enormous race' of children, but all the race is doomed to live within the blinkered canopy, both mentally and physically imprisoned. The poem goes on to chart the inevitable development of repressive social systems like 'The Net of Religion', 'woven hypocrisy', laws and so on, all these the product of division 'In form of a human heart' which leads to 'their narrowing perceptions' and a closed world of binary opposites. On this dark note, Blake ends 'the first book of Urizen', though to our knowledge he never wrote a second. His fable of the creation and enslavement of human society is complete, and we must look to other poems for the possibility of escape.

Once we understand the process charted in *The Book of Urizen* we find aspects of it repeated and varied throughout his works, and we can notice the recurrence of the theme of incarceration and slavery, mental and physical, as the setting for deprivation of rights. Enitharmon in *Europe: A Prophecy* 'laugh'd in her sleep' to see her subjects incarcerated, 'the windows wove over with curses of iron'; 'With bands of iron round their necks fasten'd into the walls The citizens'. In *America* we see men 'Shaking their mental chains they rush in fury to the sea To quench their anguish'. Erdman, who confidently says that 'Blake's acquaintance with the abolition debate is evident',[40] tracks it through *Visions of the Daughters of Albion* which he reads alongside Blake's engravings for Stedman, in particular the ones depicting torture of female slaves. (We can only guess at the tone of conversation at a dinner party attended in June 1794 by, among others, Stedman, Blake and a former planter.)[41] Erdman mentions the reading of *Daughters* as a moral allegory of 'oppressed womanhood' (S. Foster Damon's phrase) showing that all daughters remain slaves while possessive morality prevails, but he reads it much more specifically as Blake's response to the parliamentary debates on abolition from 1789 to 1793: 'the frustrated lover, for example, being analogous to the wavering abolitionist who cannot bring himself openly to condemn slavery although he deplores the *trade*'.[42] He sees Bromion as 'Blake's thundering ... caricature' of the slave agent and their spokesmen in parliament.

But rather than pursue the slavery theme in the prophetic works, we can turn our attention to a poetry which seems so different and yet presupposes the same general world-view, in the *Songs*.[43] The most directly relevant is in *Songs of Innocence* (1789), 'The Little Black Boy'. For such a short and linguistically clear poem, it has generated a surprising amount of controversy.[44] Peter Kitson sketches the 'problem' when he asks, 'Does it rehearse, exploit, or criticise the conventions of African pastoral, and does its presentation in the form and style of a children's poem imply a commentary on the didactic designs of much anti-slavery writing, a humanitarian appeal to the English child reader, or both'.[45] Given all we know of Blake's beliefs, it is difficult to accept that he would condone the colonialist discourse that the black boy is really 'white' in purity under the skin or that the white race is superior and to be aspired to. It seems much more plausible to read the lyric as spoken by a persona rather than a mouthpiece. In other words, the black boy is an example of one at first unknowingly trapped within the 'fetters of the mind' set by Urizen, his thought dominated by a false consciousness when he says,

> My mother bore me in the southern wild,
> And I am black, but O! my soul is white,
> White as an angel is the English child:
> But I am black as if bereav'd of light.

However, the poem and its speaker do not stay in this position. The boy's mother teaches through a parable that, if anything, black skin indicates that the boy was born and able immediately to have a direct relationship with God, protected from the heat and light, able 'to bear the beams of love' more immediately than the unprepared white-skinned. When the *souls* 'have learn'd the heat to bear', then colour of skin is meaningless and irrelevant. The conclusion the boy draws is that he is given the senior role of sheltering the vulnerable white boy until he too is able to bear the heat of God's love, at which time true equality can exist:

> I'll shade him from the heat till he can bear,
> To lean in joy upon our fathers knee.
> And then I'll stand and stroke his silver hair,
> And be like him and he will then love me.

To 'be like him' and to want the love of the 'little English boy' does not need to imply a current sense of inferiority or lack, but rather a recognition that they will 'be alike' in God's eyes. There is also a hint that it is the English child who must *learn* to love, while the black boy already has this capacity. The poem traces a gentle unfettering of the mind of the boy into a more enlightened view, and what began as a poem stimulated by the existence of the slave trade, ends as a much more general statement of the natural right of equality.

'The Little Black Boy' is the only poem that directly raises the issue of race, but the rest of the *Songs* exemplify differing degrees of enslavement, whether of the mind or body. Most, if not all, can be read as the statements of *personae* located at different points along a spectrum from insouciant innocence which is easily exploited but also sheltered from pain by lack of awareness, through experience which can be double-edged causing either bitterness or the desire to enslave others, to something like post-experience, an ability to retrieve and understand innocence from a postlapsarian stance where the chains have loosened, or at least they are recognised for what they are. As well, of course, the engraved illustrations can be interpreted as providing commentary and critique on the words. The positions are not neatly segregated, for there are 'experienced' voices in *Innocence* and 'inno-cent' ones in *Experience*. All seem to prove Hamlet's contention that 'There is nothing either good or bad, but thinking makes it so'. Even where we seem to recognise an unmediated authorial voice, it could still be a more limited persona speaking. 'London' uses the phrase 'the mind-forg'd mana-cles', which, interestingly, are not seen but 'heard' clinking through the streets of London. This comes as the voice of clear-seeing experience, angrily lamenting the visible social evils causing misery around him. Characteristically, human pain is linked causally with institutions like 'Every blackning Church', blood-soaked 'Palace walls' and the blighted 'Marriage hearse'. But even here there is no reason to think such anger and pity provide 'the whole story' since, as we know from *Urizen*, even these emotions are ineffectual as social reform. There is no real hope expressed through 'London', merely a rejection. Taken as a whole, the sequence of *Songs of Innocence* and *Songs of Experience* has a meaning which is greater than the sum of its parts. By understanding the ways in which the fettering occurs in society, and by clearly recognising the violation of natural rights which occurs, for example, in the exploitation of children forced into labour or adolescents forced into sexual repression by jealous hypocrisy of church elders, one can potentially dismantle both internal and external chains in order to create a world where natural rights are respected and observed. The operative word, however, is *potentially*. Even the song which ends the cycle, 'the Voice of the Ancient Bard', which starts with the promise to 'Youth of delight' in 'the opening dawn' and with an 'Image of truth new born', closes back on those who are not enlightened, instead of opening out the vision to those who are:

> Folly is an endless maze.
> Tangled roots perplex her ways,
> How many have fallen there!
> They stumble all night over bones of the dead:
> And feel they know not what but care:
> And wish to lead others when they should be led.

It is tempting to read this as an indictment of a public figure like Burke, as perceived through Paineite eyes, his mind fettered by clinging to the past, by intellectual confusion, and by self-aggrandisement. They are as manacled as slaves, but without knowing it.

It is clear that Blake did not work in the intellectual vacuum that used to be assumed, weaving his myths in splendid isolation. He was clearly involved in contemporary events, and as Marilyn Butler says, his views, at least up to the Treason Trials of 1794, were the standard ones shared by libertarians.[46] Moreover, he refers in his writings to others like Rousseau and Paine, and their ideas are reflected at every turn. However, in a sense, Blake was at least different, if not completely isolated. His habitual ways of thought are adversarial and dialectic (despite his rejection of binarism), so that even people we would assume he broadly agreed with came in regularly for his trenchant attack and rejection – even Paine and Rousseau. He was always an uneasy member of the publisher Johnson's radical stable of writers, and by the end of the 1790s he had drifted away from this circle to the patronage of Hayley. 'The Johnson circle was at once too secular in its liberalism and not radical enough in its revolutionism to satisfy Blake', concludes Robert N. Essick.[47] Underneath these differences lay a profound methodological gulf, because, while virtually all the other writers we have dealt with in this book – preeminently Paine, Godwin, Wollstonecraft, Thelwall, and Holcroft – believed in reason as the guide to radical and egalitarian change, Blake had difficulty in accepting reason as a route to truth: 'For Paine, the only tongue in which God speaks to "honest Men" is the voice of reason. Yet for Blake "Reasoning is Nothing" '.[48] His brand of natural rights thinking is distinctly revelationist and imaginative, full of an almost evangelical claim to individual, visionary and unmediated insight into truth, whereas the others followed classical natural law theory in believing that political morality is just as susceptible to critical reasoning as is the natural world. It is this crucial factor that placed Blake so much at odds with even those ideologically close to him, including Milton, the arch-rationalist Protestant. Another contemporary so sure of his own genius that he could flout rational method was the painter Fuseli, who was, significantly, among Blake's most respected friends and models.[49] Fuseli in his *Remarks on the Writing and Conduct of J. J. Rousseau* (1767) shows that he agreed with Rousseau's ideas on inequality as the clue to 'the contradictions of the human heart',[50] but his tone is more heated, polemical and Blake-like than the urbane Genevan's. The difference shows us graphically that natural rights are the position of convergence on basic primciples of very different and even antithetical thinking processes and temperaments, which is a part of the convincing strength of natural rights as a body of beliefs. In Blake's case, the omnipresent tactility of the metaphor of slavery with its imagery of chains and manacles, in a sense anchors him to a powerful version of what others said in their various voices.

Jean Paul Marat: *The Chains of Slavery*

In his habit of using the rhetoric of slavery to stand for all forms of political and emotional oppression, and turning the state of slavery into a paradigm of the denial of natural rights, Blake was in powerful company. A youthful proto-revolutionary, Jean Paul Marat, later to become a qualified medical practitioner at Saint Andrews University in Scotland, lived in Newcastle upon Tyne in the early 1770s, probably working as a veterinarian. At 22 he had been forced to flee France for fear of persecution as a Protestant. He was a well-respected figure, even tending the horses of the Duke of Northumberland, but he attracted the scrutiny of state authorities because of his very popularity with the network of political associations agitating for political reform across the north of England from Newcastle to Carlisle. Given the part he was to play in the French revolution some 15 years later, they were right to be worried, and with characteristic forthrightness and honesty he did nothing to conceal his beliefs. The English authorities did everything they could to suppress and, failing that, to delay publication of a book he wrote which was blatantly advertised as,

> An ADDRESS to the ELECTORS of GREAT BRITAIN, in order to draw their TIMELY ATTENTION to the Choice of proper REPRESENTATIVES in the next PARLIAMENT.

The remarkable and substantial book, 259 pages long, was published as *The Chains of Slavery*, two years after the Mansfield judgment.[51] 'The next parliament' was to be elected in November, 1774, and the Newcastle Club did its best to publish the book before this date. However, the government is said to have spent 8000 guineas trying to stop publication, and they did at least succeed in delaying it until it was actually published two days after the election. Marat was clearly popular on the northern political scene, and he was presented with complimentary invitations to 'patriotic clubs' in a gold box which, says a report in the *Weekly Chronicle* a century later (25 October 1873), 'the Minister stole'. The same report says that after Marat was assassinated by Charlotte Corday in 1793, nobody dared mention his association with Newcastle or the north of England. *The Chains of Slavery* was later adapted for publication in France, where it appeared in 1792 as *Les Chaines de l'esclavage*.

The book is certainly a revelation of the revolutionary principles of one of the most clear-sighted and consistent architects of the French revolution.

It is a kind of anti-machiavel volume, disclosing the nefarious strategies used by rulers to hold power, showing 'THE CLANDESTINE AND VILLAIN-OUS ATTEMPTS OF PRINCES TO RUIN LIBERTY' and 'DREADFUL SCENES OF DESPOTISM'. The reason the book forms such an apt analogue for Blake's work is that, coming 20 years earlier, it holds up the model of slavery as the condition of ordinary English people living under a government which denies natural rights, 'when Princes, to become sovereign matters, trample under foot, without shame or remorse, the most sacred rights of the people' [Opening address]. Marat warns the English, 'Your most sacred rights have been flagrantly violated by your representatives', '– a band of disguised traitors, who, under the name of guardians, traffic away the national interests, and the rights of a free-born people: the Prince then becomes absolute, and the people slaves'. Unlike Blake, who takes a long-range and pessimistic perspective, Marat works within the very limited and flawed system of representative democracy available at the time, advocating that men [sic] should vote in the forthcoming elections in such a way that 'the insolent opulent' 'men of pompous titles' be replaced in parliament by 'men who have not been corrupted by the smiles of a court, men whose venerable mature age crowns a spotless life, men who have ever appeared zealous for the public cause, and have had in view only the welfare of their country, and the observance of the laws'. But behind this legitimate advice lies a thinly disguised recognition that the system will not be changed in this way, that the machinery of power is too deeply entrenched in society and institutions, and that the slavery goes so deep as to have become 'mind-forg'd manacles' of acceptance. And where Marat displays the colours which will surface in 1789 Paris lies in his insistent reminder of the fate of Charles I, executed by the English people as a representative of despotism, a gesture which ushered in the ill-fated but symbolically important republican commonwealth. 'To you is left a power to secure the liberty of the people, or enslave the nation' he advises the handful of voters, those who have the power 'to transmit those rights as entire to their children as they had received them from their fathers', or to 'disgrace the names of [their] forefathers'. To these he addresses the rhetorical question, 'Shall your children, bathing their chains with tears, one day say: "These are the fruits of the venality of our fathers?" '.

Marat's whole argument, like Blake's, turns on the fact that people are enslaved at the mental rather than physical level. They are never 'voluntary slaves' because they do not consciously yield up their rights. Instead, princes and despots do not make open attacks on liberty but work in crafty secrecy and through imperceptible changes which are always represented as being in the interests of their subjects or as duties they owe their ruler: 'To enchain their subjects, they begin by setting them asleep' (ch. 1). If their designs were seen by citizens they would be resisted, just as in Blake's cosmos the only ones who can resist mental bondage are those who can somehow see outside their own blinkered minds – the few wise, experienced personae in the *Songs*, or the tragically divided Los. Marat then in exhaustive detail spends many chapters showing how political indoctrination is effected by the cunning ruler, and his analysis is surprisingly similar to the kinds of approaches now used as part of the methodology of cultural studies in examining the workings of ideology. For example, Marat says, princes entertain, distract and intimidate subjects with public pomp and ceremony; they set up and condone places of entertainment, they patronise the arts and insidiously compromise artists into losing sight of 'the rights of mankind'. Marat anticipates postcolonial analysis in describing cultural imperialism, and his examples most often refer back to the Roman empire. In some ways the renowned Augustus is the slyest of all the despots.

> BY encouraging the fine arts and the sciences among the Romans, Augustus subjected them to the yoke; and by the same method, his successors subdued the barbarians they had vanquished *. (ch. vii)[52]

The path which princes lay for us are 'EVER by ways strewed with flowers' (ch. ix):

> THE entrance of Despotism is sometimes pleasing and joyous: plays, feasts, dances and songs being its cheerful attendants *. But in these feasts and plays, the people perceive not the evils prepared for them; they resign themselves to pleasure, and their joy is unbounded. But whilst the inconsiderate multitude is abandoned to joy, the wise foresee the remote calamities threatening their country, and by which it is at last to be overwhelmed: they perceive the chains concealed with flowers, ready to be fixed on the arms of their countrymen. (ch. II)

Marat repeats the metaphor several times: 'By concealing with flowers the chains which are prepared for us, they extinguish in our souls the sense of liberty, and make us in love with servitude' (ch. x). 'False Ideas of liberty' (titleheading of ch. xiii) are instilled, to the point where 'sports, festivals, merriments, shews, entertainments of every kind, engross the mind, people by degrees lose sight of liberty, and think not of it any more. By entirely neglecting to think of liberty, the true idea of it is obliterated, and false notions take place' (ch. xiii). Marat's very chapter-headings indicate how acutely he sees through the gloss and veneer of benign rule to the apparatus of state enslavement beneath: Of turning virtuous Men out of Places (xvii), Of securing the Tools of Power from the Sword of Justice (xxi), Of preventing the Redress of public Grievances (xxxvii), Of suppressing those Offices which share Power (l), Of accustoming the People to military Expeditions (lii), Of securing the Fidelity of the Army (liii), To inspire the Military with Contempt for the Citizens (lv), Of Flattery (lxii), and so on through a long list. Marat suggests that enslavement is not always a matter of external coercion. 'THE people not only suffer themselves to be enchained, but oftentimes offer their necks to the yoke. When a crafty man gains their confidence, he inspires them with what sentiment he pleases, and masters them at will' (lxiii).

> Not satisfied with being dupes, the people run sometimes to servitude, and lend their own hands to forge their chains. Never thinking that in a free country, every subject has a right to inform against the servants of the public, they ever blindly abandon themselves to their zeal for those who have appeared in their defence; and, yielding to gratitude, ever strike at that very liberty, the defender of which they mean to vindicate.

Once again, Marat is anticipating Blake's 'mind-forg'd manacles', although his own political outlook does not extend to seeing oppressors as victims of their own intellectual limitations based on their acceptance and practice of slavery: to him, oppressors are simply seeking and ruthlessly holding power by denying natural rights to others.

As *The Chains of Slavery* proceeds, its intention clearly changes. Instead of merely seeking to influence an English election in order to bring honest men into parliament, Marat is clearly imagining and anticipating every possible government strategy to be used if and when the people at last have their rights eroded to such an extent that they rebel. The book becomes a blueprint for revolution, detailing each danger and each step of the way. Although the authorial 'we' refers to England, with constant reference to former monarchs, to the Glorious Revolution and Bill of Rights which limited the powers of the monarch, yet it is impossible to read without hindsight knowledge of the events to come in France. Constant reference to the word 'insurrection' recalls the revolts of slaves which assailed French plantation owners earlier than English ones, and it maintains the metaphoric connection between the processes of repressive government and tyranny over slaves. Like Blake, Marat sees a fundamental similarity. Just as in the case of governments 'despotism makes its progress, and the chains of slavery become heavier' (xliv), so it happens in the microcosm of an industry built on slavery. Since both systems are built on the denial of natural rights, so both risk the apparently inevitable resistance and revolt of those whose rights are denied. Marat is considerably more optimistic than Blake, for whereas the latter tends to believe that knowledge of rights among the populace has been permanently clouded, to the extent that a revolutionary will is unlikely to be revived, Marat feels that the knowledge of and desire for liberty, however 'precarious', still exists and will lead to change. The last line of *The Chains of Slavery* is, 'As long as this spirit shall prevail, liberty may be enjoyed; we are undone as it becomes extinct'.

7
Rights of Children and Animals

Once the general theory of rights of man was placed on the intellectual map, the issue of slavery had focused many minds on the categories of natural rights, and more specific rights such as those of women had been initially asserted, then a trend was set in process which could reach to embrace other vulnerable groups. If adult human beings had rights by virtue of simple existence, then why not children, and then why not all living things? Even if Spinoza (1632–77) may have been expressing an extreme view in arguing that trees and rocks have rights to continued existence (a proposition which is no longer seen to be absurd in view of current environmental concerns), yet his logic revealed potential extensions of natural rights theory to all animate beings capable of suffering pain and deprivation of liberty. The purpose of this chapter will be to indicate that important arguments for natural rights were spreading into the general fields of education, a new respect for nature, and also animal rights, but it is impossible in one chapter to be at all thorough in documenting these swelling debates.[1] Taken as a whole movement, the call for natural rights was certainly not achieved by the end of the 1790s, but its central positions had been articulated, and were to be developed and drawn upon by the romantic writers who followed.

It may seem demeaning to lump together children and animals as though their status is equal, but there is a connection through the subject of rights within the order of nature, as the ideas developed in the late eighteenth century. Generally speaking, the push for kindness to animals came as an educational principle aimed at children, who were encouraged to treat animals without roughness or cruelty. The very fact that this and other educational principles were being published, was a result of a novel valuing of children as human beings with potential rights, rather than being small adults who would eventually acquire rights, or worse still that they did not exist in the way adults exist. An emerging belief that children should be taught that they shared with animals the capacity to feel pain, by necessary logic led to the argument that children themselves needed the same protection. Linking rights of children and animals depends on the common rights to preservation of life and protection from cruelty. Not surprisingly, these general attitudes were a part of the literature of sensibility, and also the Scottish enlightenment, both of which have loomed large in this book. Writers like Shaftesbury and Hutcheson, although too early to proclaim rights for children and nature, adopted a world-view that pointed inevitably towards later developments. Hutcheson, for example, placed stress on the conditions which would be used as justifications for rights of children at least, when he describes the state of nature as characterised by 'Good-will, Humanity, Compassion, mutual aid, propagating and supporting offspring'.[2] If the last task is seen as an adult responsibility and duty, then it will follow that children have the right to be supported, which itself leads on to more particular forms of support. The cornerstone will be the right to be treated as a vulnerable child and not as a proto-adult.

Locke

As in so many topics in this book, the pioneering and influential thinkers were John Locke and Jean-Jacques Rousseau. By and large, in earlier times dating back to Roman law, children were accorded no rights, and were regarded as having the status of chattels or slaves. Locke rejects these views in *Some thoughts concerning Education* (1693),[3] a publication of letters he wrote to Edward Clarke advising him on how to educate his son. The book may at first sight seem inauspicious, since the word 'rights' hardly appears, while the word 'rules' does. However, there is a substratum of natural rights thinking, not least because few had ever bothered to write a book which is effectively 'the earliest manifesto for a "child-centred" education'.[4] Locke proclaims inalienable rights to continued life and liberty, and to be looked after and protected. Furthermore, the prescriptive structure of the book implicitly develops from a prior set of beliefs that children have the right to good health, comfortable shelter and clothing, a serious education and especially the capacity to read, appropriate recreation, and a preparation for adult sociability. All this is an amplification of Locke's statement in *Two Treatises of Government* that children have a right 'not only to a bare Subsistence but to the conveniences and comforts of Life, as far as the conditions of their Parents can afford it'.[5] Since parents and teachers are the ones responsible for rearing children, the book is written for them. The existence of rules for parents justifies rights and respect for the child's rights. Babies are not to be treated as 'playthings' if they are not to turn into children 'troubled with those ill humours' (139) which parents project onto them when they become recalcitrant children. Education should be age-specific, adapted to the *'due Season'* of the child's development and they should not have adult expectations imposed on them. On particular issues which have always been perennially contentious, Locke is firmly on the side of protecting the child. He is against corporal punishment, for example, arguing that 'Frequent

Beating or *Chiding* is therefore *to be avoided*. Because this sort of Correction never produces any Good' (155). 'The Rod' is regarded by Locke as 'lazy and short way by Chastisement', which is counter-productive. Good behaviour is hardly worth having if it is solely motivated by a fear of whipping, and the offending adults are by their practice teaching that cruelty is acceptable (148–9). It baffles many people that in 2005, more than two hundred years after the debates we are tracing, the issue of corporal punishment for children in Britain has not been humanely resolved.

The point about teaching that cruelty is unacceptable is picked up by Locke later in his book (chapter 116), when at length he justifies kindness to animals as a central educational precept: 'For the Custom of Tormenting and Killing of Beasts, will, by Degrees, harden their Minds even towards Men; and they who delight in the Suffering and Destruction of inferiour Creatures, will not be apt to be very compassionate, or benign to those of their own kind' (226). 'Children', he says, should 'from the beginning be bred up in Abhorrence of *killing*, or tormenting any living Creature', amongst which he includes, for example, 'young Birds, Butterflies and such other poor Animals which fall into their Hands'. From the cradle they should be made 'to be tender to all sensible Creatures'. Even if Locke presents his advice as directed ultimately at making children 'to be very compassionate, or benign to those of their own kind', yet once again the rule presupposes or at least implies a right that animals, by dint of their 'sensible' faculties and their capacity to feel pain, be treated without cruelty. It could be argued that Locke has thus simultaneously initiated rights for children and animals.

As a related point about moral education, Locke anticipates a part of Rousseau's argument, that delight in '*doing of Mischief*' is not natural or inbred, but taught behaviour, 'a foreign or introduced Disposition, an Habit borrowed from Custom and conversation. People teach Children to strike, and laugh, when they hurt, or see harm come to others' (226). This belief may build on his concept expressed in *An Essay Concerning Human Understanding* of the child's mind as a *tabula rasa*, encapsulated in Thomas Traherne's 'An empty book is like an infant's soul, in which anything may be written. It is capable of all things, but containeth nothing';[6] but Locke's *Education* can equally be read as presupposing benign impulses. He is, at least in this book, acknowledging that human beings are born with natural goodness (or, at the very least, without innate 'original sin' or malice) and at least a capacity for reason which parents must nurture and develop by example. (Locke says that 'innocents' and 'madmen' are distinguished from others by their inability to develop into rationality.) The purpose of education and parenting alike is to take advantage of the innate benignity and develop it into adult processes of rational thought. Enlightenment and Reason are words that come to mind in reading through Locke's works and particularly here. If adults are pre-eminently rational and reasonable in their dealings with children, then they will reinforce pre-existing tendencies to be kind and sensitive to others in an increasingly self-aware and rational way. Even if Locke's stance on natural law over many works tends to change, in *Some thoughts concerning Education* he supports the bedrock principles underlying the classical concept, and uses them to build a prototype for the later espousal of natural rights.

It may take the gloss off his achievement to learn that his work was never intended to apply to the poor and the labouring classes, but rather to fashion those destined to become young gentlemen,[7] but taken out of context it can easily be read as a blueprint that has universal application. For example, as early as 1749, Sarah Fielding's novel of education – probably the first such in English – *The Governess: or, Little Female Academy*,[8] applied Locke's principles to the education of nine female pupils. Her book hardly asserts natural rights for either children or women, but rather follows along the lines of conventional conduct books which emphasised social decorum and respectful relationships. However, in broadening the curriculum from narrow accomplishments like needlework to more socially inclined areas, Fielding was extending the right of Lockean educational precepts to girls, and also regarding children as destined to fit into adult society and therefore worthy of education that prepared them for adult rights. Locke's book is written with accessible clarity, and Locke does not expressly exclude other classes, or even suggest they are enemies of civilised values. It would not be the first time by any means that a document arguing for aristocratic rights fell into other hands and provoked demands from other sections of society. Magna Carta is perhaps the most startling example in England. Equally, it need not undermine the influence of Locke to discover that other writers like Erasmus and Montaigne had anticipated him through their humanistic and humane considerations. In many works that allow people and societies to proclaim and defend rights, originality is not the point, but practical influence is, and Locke made a difference. His book on education, less conspicuous than his political writing, arguably helped to cause the sea-change in the history of thought, which became evident a century later in the 1790s. Indeed, by the 1770s, the anonymous writer of *The Laws Respecting Women, As they regard their NATURAL RIGHTS* ...[9], a summary of the law on legal rights published by Joseph Johnson, could speak already of children having rights:

> Parents are considered as bound in duty to maintain their children, both by the law of nature, and their own proper act, in bringing them into the world; by which they enter into a voluntary obligation to endeavour, as far as in them lies, that the life which they have imparted shall be supported and preserved. By which incontrovertible reasoning, children have a right to receive maintenace from their parents. (350)

But it is clear that the reference here is to the obligation of the father to provide financially for his children (the mother having no power but only an entitlement 'to a dutiful and reverential regard'), not a positive right vested in the child. What was needed to establish the latter, was a clearly child-centred perspective, which was given credence in the 1790s.

Locke's educational precepts did indeed become immensely influential in the period under review in this book, through the mediation of books written specifically for children. The huge growth in book publishing,[10] and presumably in the reading public, in the 1780s and 1790s included an increasingly distinctive genre of writing for children, which directly inspired, for example, William Blake's *Songs of Innocence and of Experience* (1794). Alongside the general increase in education, this genre crossed classes, and its underlying assumptions rapidly found their way beyond the privileged few and into the very middle-class households which were devouring books on 'rights of man' and were supporting abolition of slavery. Like a Trojan horse, the increasing body of children's books unloaded many of John Locke's educational precepts into a generation of children and their parents. The story is told by Samuel F. Pickering, Jr. in *John Locke and Children's Books in Eighteenth-Century England*.[11] In his first chapter, 'Our First Philosopher [Locke] and Animal Creation', Pickering traces through the whole eighteenth century a body of didactic literature for children intended to inculcate benevolent attitudes to animals. The three most important influences on these works were Locke himself, his own favourite children's book, *Aesop's Fables*, and nonconformist preachers, and the most important writers included Sarah Trimmer, writing in the later 1780s. Trimmer warned her readers not to become too attached to animals, stating that they are not 'religious beings', which presumably refers to the lack of a soul.[12] Stories anthropomorphised animals in a way disapproved of by Mrs Trimmer, such as Dorothy Kilner's *Life and Perambulation of a Mouse* (1783) and *The Life and Adventures of a Fly* (1789). While none of these asserted a manifesto of rights for either children or animals, they gave recognition to both as distinct groups which were vulnerable and in need of protection, through the sensitisation of public opinion. More illustrious writers like Wollstonecraft and Coleridge also drew on the Lockean connection between children's education and kindness to animals.

Rousseau and Wollstonecraft

The other writer whose influence on the status and rights of children and animals was as wide and deep as Locke's was Rousseau, and both Pickering and Christine Kenyon-Jones, for example, include him as important in changing attitudes towards animals in children's books. For such an apparently unlikeable man, Rousseau exercised a disproportionate influence over the rise of the cult of the child and of nature in the late eighteenth and early nineteenth centuries, as well as over the whole field of progressive liberalism traced in this book. Nothing if not paradoxical, he declared a 'mortal aversion to books', declaring, 'I hate books ... they only teach people to talk about what they don't understand'. And yet he wrote as many books as anybody in his generation, and inspired and influenced hundreds more in the romantic period. Rousseau's quasi-allegorical view of childhood expressed in *Émile ou de l'éducation*,[13] was to be tremendously important for Blake and Wordsworth in particular. In a nutshell, his basic idea is that human beings are born into nature and corrupted by adult prejudice and social conditioning:

[I, 10] Everything is good as it leaves the hands of the author of things, everything degenerates in the hands of man.

He sees mothers as the ones least likely to do damage, and advises them to 'Cultivate and water the young plant before it dies; its fruit will one day be your delight' [12], and to protect the child's soul from the perversities of public education. Not that his view of childhood is sentimental or regards its state as sweet: far from it. Acknowledging that of all the children born at the time, halfdie before their eighth year, he suggests that nature's hardships are designed to strengthen those that survive: 'This is nature's law; why contradict it?'. Pains like teething and colic are given as examples of nature's version of education, enforcing the factuality of existence through the senses of the 'sensitive' child, and providing strength in the course of self-preservation:

[I, 14] We are born weak, we need strength; we are born lacking everything, we need aid; we are born stupid, we need judgment. All that we lack at birth and that we need when we are grown is given by education ... [I, 15] This education comes to us from nature, from men, or from things. The inner growth of our organs and faculties is the education of nature, the use we learn to make of this growth is the education of men, and what we gain by our experience of our surroundings is the education of things.

Sensation schools our reason by making us aware through experience of pleasure and pain and consequentially allows us to discriminate between unpleasantness, happiness and goodness. So long as the processes are left to nature itself, rational enlightenment will follow, 'but once they are constrained by our habits, they become more or less corrupted by our opinions. Before this change they are what I call nature within us' [I, 12]. In a rhapsodic passage, Rousseau extols the state of childhood and the protection it deserves from adults, in a way no other writer had:

[II,13] Men, be humane; that is your first duty. Be humane toward every condition, every age, toward all that is not foreign to humanity. What

wisdom is there for you outside of humanity? Love childhood, promote
its pleasures, its lovable instincts. Who among you has not sometimes
missed that age when laughter was always on our lips, and when the soul
was always at peace? Why take away from these innocent little people the
joys of a time that will escape them so quickly and gifts that could never
cause any harm? Why fill with bitterness the fleeting days of early childhood, days which will no more return for them than for you? Fathers, can
you tell the moment when death awaits your children? Do not prepare
yourself for regrets by robbing them of the few moments which nature
has given them. As soon as they are aware of the pleasure of existence, let
them rejoice in it; make it so that whenever God calls them they will not
die without having tasted life.

At the same time, he warns against idealising children, saying that in itself
this is a breach of the law of nature and that it will make the child develop
as a whimsical tyrant. Like Locke, Rousseau barely mentions rights, but in
even greater measure almost everything he writes about education turns on
one fundamental right, the freedom to grow in the natural condition,
without constraints of adult preconceptions or deprivation of 'things', material circumstances. 'Society has weakened man not only by depriving him of
the right to his own strength, but above all by making his strength insufficient
for his needs' [my italics; 1, 233]. The perpetrators of wrong, as in Blake's
universe, are institutionalised education, books, and religion, and more generally the products of corrupted adult minds, all of which deprive the growing child of the 'school of hard knocks' which is nature. The other right for
children that emerges from *Émile* is the right to be a child and to be provided
by adults only with what is useful to the child's role and stage of development:
'No one, not even his father, has the right to command the child do what is
of no use to him' [2, 235].

According to his 'growth model' of education,[14] Rousseau believes that at
the age of twelve or thirteen, the child (or here, more specifically, the boy)
becomes 'naturally' capable of rational and conceptual thought. It is clear
that there is an evaluative principle of gradations behind the whole theory,
and that reason is the most important and true end of education. Rousseau's
novelty is in delaying this phase of education so late in the process, but for
him it is supremely important. In the terminology of natural rights, the child
has a right to be a child, and also a right to become an adult by a training in
reason. It is this emphasis which initially attracted Wollstonecraft to
Rousseau's analysis. However, to the discredit of his age rather than uniquely
to Rousseau, and as I have mentioned already in dealing with Mary
Wollstonecraft and Eliza Fenwick, his educational principles do not advocate
equality between males and females. Like Locke before him, and all writers
in between, to Rousseau a 'child' is a boy who has rights to a full and rational education. Girls should be educated differently. There are some apparent

concessions: 'The essential thing is to be what nature has made you; women are only too ready to be what men would have them'.[15] However, he goes on, 'The search for abstract and speculative truths, for principles and axioms in a science, for all that tends to wide generalisation, is beyond a woman's grasp; their studies should be thoroughly practical'. In a somewhat odd way, Rousseau colludes with those who would make women 'too ready to be what men would have them', in advocating that as a 'duty', 'A woman's thoughts ... should be directed to the study of men', since men will provide compensation for their inability to understand the sciences, philosophy, and so on. He does his best to attribute positive qualities to females, but even in doing so he reveals a value system which is clearly unequal: 'Woman has more wit, man more genius; woman observes, man reasons' (350). The girl should thus be educated towards living a life of virtuous honour, and motherhood, and to be skilled in specifically female accomplishments, like needlework. Even the fact that Rousseau holds back his sketchy thoughts on female education until the fifth and final Book of *Émile* indicates that for him the whole subject is supplementary to the rights of boys to full educational opportunities. His preconceptions revealed here had been presented already in his novel, *Julie ou la Nouvelle Héloise* (1760). One can fully understand Wollstonecraft's complicated and ambiguous responses to Rousseau's educational theories. She was excited by his emphasis on rational thought and free choice, but indignant that these should be considered inappropriate to females. Despite her own impassioned pleas, the respective arguments for children's rights and women's rights were kept largely separate until the twentieth century, and even now a whole genre of 'popular psychology' would have us still believe that, while educational (and employment) opportunities should be equal, yet somehow women are by nature imaginative, emotional, intuitive, and so on, while men are rational and principled. Like many such generalizations, it invites the retort, some are, some aren't.

As we have seen in an earlier chapter, Mary Wollstonecraft argued strongly for females to be educated into the kind of rationality that would enable them to resist the conditioned emotiveness of conventional, sentimental literature and to challenge conventional expectations of women's subjugation. Although this argument was almost lost to view, some others in the 1790s followed her lead. Besides Eliza Fenwick and Mary Hays, there was Hannah More, whose influence was significant but ambiguous. She wrote several pamphlets on the subject, and her major contribution to the debate came in the two-volume book, *Strictures on the Modern System of Female Education* (1799).[16] More emerges as politically ambiguous, outspoken against slavery but socially conservative. She strongly supported education for the poor, but her motivation was to instill in them 'values that would support the status quo – piety, frugality, and acceptance by the laboring class of their lower station in life'.[17] On the subject of female education, she is said to have refused to read Wollstonecraft's *Vindication*, and the *Strictures* certainly seem to be directed to 'women of rank and fortune' amongst whom she circulated, rather than the populace. She was certainly on the opposite side from Rousseau, since she considered it a 'foundation-truth' that children are not 'innocent beings' but ones tainted by original sin, and in need of correction.[18] However, if perhaps for the wrong reasons, she does advocate education for girls into knowledge and rational thought, to counteract tendencies towards superficiality and vanity. And like Wollstonecraft, she mentions impressionability to sentimental literature as the danger which education should address:

> Those women, in whom the natural defects of temper have been strengthened by an education which fosters their faults, are very dextrous in availing themselves of a hint, when it favours a ruling inclination, soothes vanity, indulges indolence, or gratifies their love of power. They have heard so often from their more flattering male friends, 'that when nature denied them strength, she gave them facinating [sic] graces in compensation; that their strength consists in their weakness;' and that 'they are endowed with arts of persuasion which supply the absence of force, and the place of reason;' that they learn, in time, to pride themselves on that very weakness, and to become vain of their imperfections; till at length they begin to claim for their defects, not only pardon, but admiration. (ii, 123–4)

She does not deny the importance of compassion, but suggests that when it is stimulated self-indulgently by the 'expensive sorrows of the melting novel or the pathetic tragedy' (ii, 125), it may lead to hard-heartedness in the face of real human misery. More's own educational priorities are far more religious in basis than Wollstonecraft's, and the comparison is an interesting example of how different and even opposite arguments could in practice agree on the one point that women had a right to be better educated.

By placing the child so intimately within the condition of nature, and giving nature the all-important function of educating the human being, Rousseau is simultaneously laying the foundations for asserting the rights of children and of nature itself. As an example, Rousseau contributed significantly to the movement in the late eighteenth century to value breastfeeding by the mother as the most natural and beneficial start to life a child deserves.[19] By the 1790s Mary Wollstonecraft was taking it to be the right of the mother and the child, and regarding the arrangement of wet-nursing as reprehensible and designed by men for their own 'voluptuous' purposes. The whole idea of maternal bonding or 'the maternal instinct' which either did not exist before the eighteenth century,[20] or if it did was not acknowledged, was established as important, not for the mother's sake but for the child's, as a kind of right. Alongside the whole ideological shift to revaluing children which was expressed most fully and eloquently by Rousseau, came an equivalent in visual art. Robert Rosenblum in *The Romantic Child: From Runge to Sendak*[21] traces in France and England the rise after Rousseau of paintings and drawings of intensely observed babies and children. The line runs through such artists as Sir Joshua Reynolds, Blake and family portraitists, but found its specialist in the German Philipp Otto Runge who, from the late 1790s onwards, drew and painted children almost exclusively. In his candid, unprecedented pictures of children unaccompanied by adults, Runge demonstrates the 'elevation of the child to Blake-like realms of heavenly, quasi-religious innocence, a creature as unpolluted as the ambient vision of nature'.[22] Characteristically, children are placed within natural imagery such as leaves and flowers, as though growing within and from their source in nature, the general source for their rights.

Wordsworth

William Wordsworth does not figure in this book as prominently as in other works on high romanticism, because his interests were not so focused on rights, and because his poetry is largely autobiographical, tracing 'the growth of a poet's mind' rather than espousing political change (except for a brief period when his circle of friends included Godwin, Wollstonecraft and Paine). However, he comes into his own in the field of the rights of nature in a broad sense, and consequentially the rights of children. He is a true son of Rousseau in his general picture of human development, placing childhood firmly within the environment of nature, and seeing growing up as a growing away from a source of purity into inevitable moral contamination from the world of adult institutions. However, he goes further than Rousseau in idealising and even sentimentalising childhood as a state of joyful oneness with nature rather than a struggle to survive, and in his evaluation that 'the Child is father of the Man'. Since so much of his poetry and thinking have transparent autobiographical roots, it is possible to suggest that the reason for his nostalgia was his enforced estrangement for eight years from his beloved sister Dorothy, when Wordsworth went to Hawkshead grammar school as a boarder in his ninth year. Although he came to love the school, and it did not separate him from the Lakes landscape, yet the transition must have caused a traumatic breach from his childhood with his siblings amidst rural surroundings. Of course, Wordsworth is not alone in creating his own myth of innocence as the happy child's realm – the pattern continues up to and beyond Sigmund Freud, who rather elegiacally saw adult humour as a largely defective way of recapturing 'the mood of our childhood, when we were ignorant of the comic, when we were incapable of jokes and when we had no need of humour to make us feel happy in our life'.[23] Blake, as we shall see, wears his rue with a difference.

In his literary pantheism, Wordsworth is indebted to Rousseau yet again, but not the writer of *The Social Contract* or *Émile*, but the nature-lover in *Julie ou la nouvelle Héloise* (1761), *Reveries of the Solitary Walker,* and the *Promenades*:

> A deep and sweet revery seizes your senses, and you lose yourself with a delicious drunkenness in the immensity of this beautiful system with which you identify yourself. Then all particular objects fall away; you see nothing and feel nothing except in the whole ... I never meditate or dream more delightfully than when I forget my self. I feel indescribable ecstasy, delirium in melting, as it were, into the system of beings, in identifying myself with the whole of nature. [*Seventh promenade*][24]

This is an equivalent to, and perhaps one of several sources for Wordsworth's 'spots of time', associated most closely with childhood memories. He constantly equates childhood and spontaneous oneness with nature, seeing the state as a moral education: 'The Child is father of the Man' ['My heart leaps up']. In the first book of *The Prelude* this developmental stage is emphasised:

> 'mid that giddy bliss
> Which, like a tempest, works along the blood
> And is forgotten; even then I felt
> Gleams like the flashing of a shield; – the earth
> And common face of Nature spake to me
> Remememberable things[25]

Particular occasions are 'forgotten', but something 'rememberable' remains to influence the adult's moral life, just as both Locke and Rousseau believed. *Intimations of immortality from recollections of early childhood* is the most famous of all statements about life being a growing away from the source of light and life in childhood, to be replaced by the more reflective, conscious and morally and aesthetically attuned state of adulthood. Peter Coveney describes the Ode as 'undoubtedly one of the central references for the whole nineteenth century in its attitude to the child'.[26] Something is lost but something is gained in the painful transition:

> There was a time when meadow, grove, and stream,
> The earth, and every common sight,
> To me did seem
> Apparelled in celestial light,
> The glory and the freshness of a dream.

Characteristically, the adult poet cannot relive the reverie:

> It is not now as it hath been of yore; –
> Turn whereso'er I may,

> By night and day,
> The things which I have seen I now can see no more.

The poet knows in leaving childhood 'That there hath past away a glory from the earth', and the 'fugitive' feelings of the 'Child of Joy' can be remembered but not relived. In *Intimations of immortality* Wordsworth reflects upon the realisation in the spirit of Rousseau:

> Heaven lies about us in our infancy!
> Shades of the prison-house begin to close
> Upon the growing Boy.

And at last the connection with 'the clouds of glory' fades 'into the light of common day'. The six-year-old boy observed in this poem is protected, again as Rousseau would advocate, in the parental security which is seen as the state of nature, 'Fretted by sallies of his mother's kisses, With light upon him from his father's eyes!', but as he grows he will leave this state of emotional safety and unity. The regretful poet retrieves from the memories 'thoughts that do often lie too deep for tears', in a gratitude for memory itself:

> What though the radiance which was once so bright
> Be now for ever taken from my sight,
> Though nothing can bring back the hour
> Of splendour in the grass, of glory in the flower;
> We will grieve not, rather find
> Strength in what remains behind;
> In the primal sympathy

Wordsworth groups children with elderly countryfolk and lunatics, as those who live in 'primal sympathy' with nature itself, reminding us that they too have natural rights. To these figures are added the forsaken mother. In the monologue 'Her eyes are wild', Wordsworth contributes in an unbearably painful and fundamentalist fashion to the newly discovered cult of maternal affection, as the mad woman living in nature is left with nothing but that impulse, abandoned as she is by her husband, and cradling the corpse of her dead baby, refusing to believe that his own madness is a genetic inheritance from her:

> Alas! Alas! That look so wild,
> It never, never, came from me;
> If thou art mad, my pretty lad,
> Then I must be for ever sad.

'The Complaint of a forsaken Indian woman' is another poem establishing the life-giving quality of the child, although in this case the mother lives upon nothing but forlorn hope that she will again find her child who was forcibly fostered into a family far away. While these poems have more to do with the strength of the mother–child relationship than with the child alone, except as symbol, other poems place the child's consciousness at the centre. 'There was a boy' is a snapshot of the archetypal Worsworthian child, joined inextricably to nature in the echoes that envelop him in the valley when he shouts, and then in silence, and then laid to rest before he reaches twelve, in the churchyard. A representative presence remains as an instructive force to the 'mute' poet. 'The Idiot Boy', spoken by an adult villager, implies the magical aura that surrounds the mentally ill child who, having ridden his horse away from society on a moonlit night, seems to embody some elemental, exhilarating, but incommunicable connection with nature:

> Perhaps, and no unlikely thought!
> He with his Pony now doth roam
> The cliffs and peaks so high that are,
> To lay his hands upon a star,
> And in his pocket bring it home.

The narrator cannot tell whether the boy's laughing 'burr' is 'in cunning or in joy', something which is 'the very soul of evil' or the cause of the miraculous cure of the ill Susan Gale, but the fabular structure and tone imply that the boy's link with nature, which can be alienating and frightening, is beneficent for the community. In defending his poem later, Wordsworth was to stress as part of the overall design the altruism displayed by 'the lower classes of society' in caring for the insane in their midst:

> I have often applied to idiots, in my own mind, that sublime expression of Scripture, that *their life is hidden with God*. … I have, indeed, often looked upon the conduct of fathers and mothers of the lower classes of society towards idiots as the great triumph of the human heart. It is there that we see the strength, disinterestedness, and grandeur of love; nor have I ever been able to contemplate an object that calls out so many excellent and virtuous sentiments.[27]

The poetic embodiment of childhood, insanity, and nature, is seen as a morally reverberating quantity, which confers the right to be treated as an individual being within nature.

Other Wordsworthian children teach different lessons, even in their stoical avoidance of the adult's reality. In 'We are seven', death itself is denied by the eight-year-old girl who maintains that in her family, even though two of her siblings ' "in the church-yard lie, / Beneath the church-yard tree" ' they are not dead. She sits beside the graves knitting, singing, and eating meals. No matter how hard the poet presses her to acknowledge there are only five children alive,

> 'Twas throwing words away; for still
> The little Maid would have her will,
> And said, 'Nay, we are seven!'

Her unswerving loyalty teaches by example a reverence for the sanctity of human life, in death as in life, and a reciprocal right of the dead to be remembered. Even the dead have rights. Finally, the dotty, associative logic of the five-year-old boy, who prefers the weather-vane of seaside Kilve to the adult's nostalgically recalled Liswyn Farm in 'Anecdote for Fathers', is quite explicitly but in some unspecified way said to 'teach' the poet:

> O, dearest, dearest boy! My heart
> For better lore would seldom yearn,
> Could I but teach the hundredth part
> Of what from thee I learn.

The lesson, presumably, is one that Rousseau would echo, concerning the resolutely fresh independence of the child unencumbered with adult memories, emotional pain, and preconceptions. 'This infant sensibility', Wordsworth wrote in the second book of *The Prelude* is 'Great birthright of our being', the irrecoverable but fundamental font of knowledge in each individual. It is one way of reasserting what Rousseau says in *Émile*, 'Nature wants children to be children before they are men ... Childhood has ways of seeing, thinking, and feeling peculiar to itself'. Even if Wordsworth advanced no specific or polemical rights of children, his sanctification of the state certainly led to such agenda.

It is nature, and its rights, that preoccupy him. 'Nutting', written in 1798, is a brief and haunting epiphany that links Wordsworth's cluster of moral concerns about children and nature. He wrote elsewhere that it was written 'as part of a poem on my own life ... but struck out as not being wanted there', and published only in *Lyrical Ballads*. (In the same statement Wordsworth writes, 'Like most of my school-fellows I was an impassioned nutter', unaware of the meaning the word would later acquire!)[28] The unexpected turn at the end of the poem to address a 'dearest Maiden', 'move along these shades In gentleness of heart; with gentle hand Touch – for there is a spirit in the woods' – is explained by Dorothy Wordsworth's report that the piece is 'the conclusion of a poem of which the beginning is not written', about the speaker gathering hazel-nuts with his 'beloved friend', Lucy. But it stands independently as a poetic statement of a memory from the poet's boyhood. The poem overlays mature reflection upon the 'eagerness of boyish hope', as the child, 'nutting-hook in hand', sets out. He finds 'one dear nook Unvisited' which is untouched and protected, 'a virgin scene!' In an exultation which is 'Voluptuous', the boy desecrates the 'temple' and whimsically pulls down a branch full of hazel nuts. The boy is at first unaware of his action as an act of sacrilege and mutilation, and he turns to go, 'Exulting, rich beyond the wealth of kings'. However, as he turns, the pantheist poet says that as a boy he 'felt a sense of pain when [he] beheld The silent trees, and saw the intruding sky –', and he clearly leaves in an altered mood that includes guilt. It is a cameo of the shadowline crossed from innocence to experience. More pertinently, the episode recalls Locke's idea that teaching children kindness to animals will make them more compassionate towards people. For Wordsworth, nature includes more than animals. 'rolled round in earth's diurnal sphere, With rocks and stones and trees', humans are connected with all things, whether animate or inanimate. The significance is not directly one of rights but of morals, from which rights spring:

> One impulse from a vernal wood
> May teach you more of man,
> Of moral evil and of good,
> Than all the sages can.
> ('The Tables Turned')

Of course, however, morals and rights are closely related, each one presupposing and implying the existence of the other. Wordsworth continually asserts the right of nature itself to be respected and protected, as the benign environment capable of nurturing, healing, recuperating and binding human society. In this sense it is not inaccurate to group Locke, Rousseau and Wordsworth as founders of rights of children, animals and the environment.[29]

Thomas Spence: *The Rights of Infants* (1797)

Thomas Spence's *The Rights of Infants*[30] owes little to Rousseau, and takes the subject into a political dimension, far from Wordsworthian nature in its sentimental guise. It is an extraordinary work for its time, leading us straight to Blake, and also anticipating certain forms of radical feminism and direct-action politics. It is pithy and brief, and its power comes as much from biblical constructions expressing righteous indignation as its direct and unadorned logic. It is in the form of a dialogue between sneering 'Aristocracy' and angry 'Woman'. ' "And pray what are the Rights of Infants?" ' cry the haughty aristocracy, 'sneering and tossing up their noses', to which the Woman replies 'that their rights extend to a full participation of the fruits of the earth' which essentially means proper nourishment of which even beasts are not deprived. Children, however, are here the occasion for an argument rather than the end of the argument. Because they are the most in need of protection and nurturing, the true rights to the produce of the land must be given to mothers, which means they must be given first to their husbands, which returns Spence to his familiar territory: 'Is not this earth our common also, as well as it is the common of brutes?' (114). What is new is the emphasis on women as being the more likely to demand change than men, because of their nurturing role, their traditionally idealised role as forces of nature, and in some ways their less compromised position than men would be within the social and employment system:

> *Aristocracy* (sneering). And is your sex also set up for pleaders of rights?
>
> *Woman.* Yes, Molochs! Our sex were defenders of rights from the beginning. And though men, like other he-brutes, sink calmly into apathy respecting their offspring, you shall find nature, as it never was, so it never shall be extinguished in us. You shall find that we not only know our rights, but have spirit to assert them. (115)

Perhaps liberated by using the fictional persona of a woman, as if it legitimises him pitching the argument at a more emotional level than he would usually do, Spence allows himself the full rhetoric of political invective:

> And so you have the impudence to own yourselves the cursed brood of ruffians, who by slaughter and oppression, usurped the lordship and dominion of the earth, to the exclusion and starvation of weeping infants and their poor mothers? ... now let the blood of the missions of innocent babes who have perished through your vile usurpations be upon your murderous heads! ... Yes, villains! you have treasured up the tears and groans of dumb, helpless, perishing, dying infants. O, you bloody landed interest! (116)

And again, with the cadences of the Bible mingled with corrosive sarcasm:

> Hear me! ye oppressors! ye who live sumptuously every day! ye, for whom the sun seems to shine, and the seasons change, ye for whom alone all human and brute creatures toil, sighing, but in vain, for the crumbs which fall from your overcharged tables; ye, for whom alone the heavens drop fatness, and the earth yields her encrease; hearken to me, I say, ye who are not satisfied with usurping all that nature can yield; ye, who are insatiable as the grave; ye who would deprive every heart of joy but your own, I say hearken to me! Your horrid tyranny, your infanticide is at an end! Your grinding the faces of the poor, and your drinking the blood of infants, is at an end! (117)

The strategy advocated by the Woman is to seize the initiative from the men who are 'woefully negligent and deficient about their own rights', these male 'gallant lock-jawed spouses and paramours' (118), and to give power to a committee of women. She seems to be suggesting an anticipation of the 'rent-strike', whereby rents are withheld from the aristocracy and instead given to the female committee to manage the community's affairs, so that essential material needs are supplied and taxes paid to the government. What it adds up to is revolutionary appropriation of the aristocracy's unjustly acquired income by taking possession of the land: 'we will begin where we mean to end, by depriving you instantaneously, as by an elective shock, of every species of revenue from lands, which will universally, and at once, be given to the parishes, to be disposed of by and for the use of the inhabitants, as said before'. The pamphlet ends with a poem that irresistibly lures us into the territory of William Blake, at least in its use of the infant as the touchstone of innocence and justice:

> The Golden Age, so fam'd by men of yore,
> Shall now be counted fabulous no more.
> The tyrant lion like an ox shall feed,
> And lisping Infants shall tam'd tygers lead:
> With deadly asps shall sportive sucklings play,
> Nor ought obnoxious blight the blithesome day.
> Yes, all that prophets e'er of bliss foretold,
> And all that poets ever feign'd of old,
> As yielding joy to man, shall now be seen,
> And ever flourish like an evergreen.
> Then, Mortals, join to hail great Nature's plan,
> That fully gives to Babes those Rights it gives to Man. (121)

Did Spence know Blake's *Songs of Innocence and Experience*? Is Blake in fact the representative of 'prophets' and 'poets' who will usher in the Golden Age of natural rights?

Child labour

In contrast again to Wordsworth, Blake was irredeemably a city-dweller. In consequence, nature is a minimal presence in his poems, while childhood is a complex and ambiguous state, by turns ignorant, exploited, protected, and blest, containing joy and pain, piercing insight and false consciousness. He may not have known at first hand the scandals of child labour in Spence's industrial north of England, but his London archetype of the chimney-sweeper stands for many victims. After Blake's time and throughout the rest of the nineteenth century, specific abuses were documented in a series of Children's Employment Commissions' reports on particular industries, like factories (1831–33), mills (1840–41), mines (1842), trades and manufacturers (1843), bleach and dye works (1857), lace manufacture (1861), eventually chimney-sweeping (1863–64), and so on. They record what Blake must have known by observation. Children from the age of five upwards (in one case, three), were used for tasks where small size and apparently infinite subservience were advantages – sitting for twelve hours or longer, deep underground in total darkness and solitude, periodically raising a door in the shaft to ventilate the pit; standing ankle deep in water all day, pumping water from the bottom of pits; harnessed like horses to pull coal carriages; carrying coal in baskets on their backs up steep and long ladders. 'Nobody could pretend that an industry of which such a description could be given was conducted with any regard to life, health, humanity, or civilised habit.'[31] Even the minding families themselves refused to allow their children to be used in this way, so the main sufferers came from the poor-houses which Blake clearly knew about. Few would speak for urban children's rights as they would for men's or even women's, or as Wordsworth could speak for rural children – and particularly not for children who to all intents and purposes did not statistically exist, except as a nuisance to the pre-welfare state. It was in virtually everybody's interests to cover up such distasteful facts and with-hold them from the public. Chimney-sweepers, or 'climbing boys' as they were euphemistically called, were most at risk, and ironically their condition was condoned in the name of 'rights of property'. As the Hammonds in the 1930s point out, the mythology of the Englishman's home as his castle made it impossible for the state to prevent people using the boys, even when it was known that machinery was more effective, if more expensive.[32] Boys were thought (wrongly) to leave furniture cleaner than messy machines did! As early as 1773 the children's misery was being pointed out by individual phil-anthropists like Jonas Hanway, 'a lone voice'[33] and an indefatigable letter-writer on behalf of the rights of charity children, publishing in 1785, 'A sentimental history of chimney sweepers, in London & Westminster: shew-ing the necessity of putting them under regulations, to prevent the grossest inhumanity to the climbing boys'. But even after an Act in 1840 forbidding it, there was evidence that the practice was scandalously increasing, despite evidence of frequent accidents, injuries, suffocations, asphyxiation, burns and early cancers. These were on top of the human degradation of being bought and sold like chattels, beaten for misdemeanours, and constantly bullied. Only Shaftesbury's longevity and continuing energy ended it with a Bill which he introduced in 1875, and which finally tapped the nation's con-science in a way which the slave trade had done far earlier. In asserting their rights, Shaftesbury had done for exploited children what Wilberforce had done for slaves. Only a tiny handful of 'major' imaginative writers even mentioned the malpractices – Blake, Dickens in *Oliver Twist*, and Charles Kingsley in *The Water Babies* – but by and large they were much later than the multitude of denunciations against slavery by well-known writers. There were, however, poets in the 1790s who carried the refrain in attempting to awaken a public conscience.

Up to the late eighteenth century, literary references to chimney sweepers, generally speaking, add colourful detail to urban descriptions, mainly in plays. Occasionally the 'sable sweepers' had been seen as blackened but merry, as in Francis Fawkes's 'Epithalamium on the marriage of a cobler and a chimney-sweeper' (1761) and Thomas Ravenscroft's song, 'Who liveth so merry in all this land' (1609), although in these cases the figure is an adult, a 'broom-man' rather than a child:

> The Broom-man maketh his liuing most sweet,
> with carrying of broomes from street to street:
>
> Who would desire a pleasanter thing,
> then all the day long to doe nothing but sing
>
> The Chimney-sweeper all the long day,
> he singeth and sweepeth the soote away:
>
> Yet when he comes home although he be weary,
> with his sweet wife he maketh full merry.

In Fanny Burney's novel, *Cecilia, or Memoirs of an Heiress* (1782), a guest at a masquerade dresses as a chimney-sweep, and although the account is comic and satirical, it seems to reflect middle-class distaste for the grime and expected rogueishness of the boys who were ironically known as 'the lilly-whites', which might explain why protest was not as vocal as in the anti-slavery debate:

> Before this question could be answered, an offensive smell of soot, making every body look around the room, the chimney-sweeper already mentioned by Miss Larolles, was perceived to enter it. Every way he moved, a passage was cleared for him, as the company, with general disgust, retreated wherever he advanced. He was short, and seemed somewhat incommoded by his dress; he held his soot-bag over one arm, and his shovel under the other. As soon as he espied Cecilia, whose situation was such as to prevent her eluding him, he hooted aloud, and came stumping up to her; 'Ah ha', he cried, 'found at last'; then, throwing down his shovel, he opened the mouth of his bag, and pointing waggishly to her head, said "Come, shall I pop you? – A good place for naughty girls; in, I say, poke in! – cram you up the chimney." (199)

The boys in reality were never washed, and were often encouraged to use their demonic appearance as a weapon of fear to intimidate for criminal purposes. Presumably those who survived long enough to grow too big to fit in the chimneys were destined for lives of full-blown crime and other degrading ways to live, with the gallows as their end.[34] For centuries, the grimy urchins with their splayed brooms had been seen to symbolise subversion and unruly sexual desire[35] – the very stuff of middle-class nightmares, whose ambiguity of significatons made them difficult to sentimentalise. At the very least, Burney's vignette reminds us that the chimney-sweepers would not have all looked or sounded as angelically pure as Millais' beggars or Blake's personae, making their plight a less than glamorous social cause. For whatever reason, scandalously few among the better-known writers associated with the romantic movement, apart from Blake, choose to protest in poetry against the inhumane practice, compared to the dozens who wrote on slavery. This was despite the respectability conferred by King George IV being patron of the 'London Society for abolishing the use of Climbing-Boys in sweeping chimneys'. William Lisle Bowles in 'The Villager's Verse-Book', draws on the analogy in a way that became a commonplace, when he appeals to 'English gentlemen!': 'your hearts have bled for the black slave ... Shall *human* wrongs, in *your own* land, call forth no generous tear?'

They sing of the poor sailor-boy, who wanders o'er the deep,
But few there are who think upon the friendless little sweep!

In darkness to his dreary toil, through winter's frost and snows,
When the keen north wind is piping shrill, the shivering urchin goes.

He has no father; and from grief, his mother's eyes are dim,
And none beside, in all the world, awakes to pray for him;

For him no summer Sundays smile, no health is in the breeze;
His mind is dark as his face, a prey to dire disease.

Mary Alcock followed Blake in a small genre of dramatic monologues, in 'The Chimney-Sweeper's Complaint' (1799), and her poem briefly but memorably sketches the shocking condition of the boys. Although still anthologised, it deserves quotation here, since it fuses the various strands of sentimental and benevolent literature, social protest, and a concern for the natural rights of the most minimally acknowledged human being. In a succinct way, Alcock uses the persona to identify amongst the various culprits not only the cruel masters of the boys, but also the complacent, middle-class employers.

> A chimney sweeper's boy am I;
> Pity my wretched fate!
> Ah, turn your eyes; 'twould draw a tear,
> Knew you my helpless state.
>
> Far from my home, no parents I
> Am ever doom'd to see;
> My master, should I sue to him,
> He'd flog the skin from me.

Ah, dearest Madam, dearest Sir,
Have pity on my youth;
Tho' black, and cover'd o'er with rags,
I tell you nought but truth.

My feeble limbs, benumb'd with cold,
Totter beneath the sack,
Which ere the morning dawn appears
Is loaded on my back.

My legs you see are burnt and bruis'd,
My feet are gall'd by stones,
My flesh for lack of food is gone,
I'm little else but bones.

Yet still my master makes me work,
Nor spares me day or night;
His 'prentice boy he says I am,
And he will have his right.

'Up to the highest top', he cries,
There call out chimney-sweep!"
With panting heart and weeping eyes
Trembling I upwards creep.

But stop! no more–I see him come;
Kind Sir, remember me!
Oh, could I hide me under ground,
How thankful should I be!

One unsung hero emerges among poets as champion of the rights of the 'climbing boys' as they were euphemistically called. Though his name is now virtually forgotten (except as the writer of some hymns), James Montgomery has been described as 'the best loved and most respected by his fellow poets of all the major or minor writers who flourished during the [romantic] period'.[36] He began writing in the 1790s, and is a radical child of the decade, having been imprisoned in 1795 and 1796 because the *Sheffield Register*, which he came by default to edit when its editor fled England in fear of political persecution, was considered by the government to be too radical and libellous. He was imprisoned first for reprinting a song commemorating the fall of the Bastille, and secondly for reporting a riot in Sheffield. He began his writing career in prison, and among other things collected and contributed to a volume entitled *Poems on the Abolition of the Slave Trade* (1809), which has been briefly mentioned in Chapter 6. In 1824 Montgomery published a collection which would have been as timely in any year of the industrial revolution, from the 1780s through to the late nineteenth century,

The Chimney-Sweeper's Friend, and Climbing-Boy's Album.[37] It is a remarkable and powerful volume, standing alone in the annals of children's rights for its implicit moral condemnation of inhumane practices. Montgomery had circularised all the well-known contemporary writers, soliciting imaginative writing to bring home to readers in an emotionally pitched medium the atrocities faced by climbing boys – and girls too. He received very few actual contributions, most of them from writers now totally unknown, although letters of support were sent by Scott, Joanna Baillie, Wordsworth, Samuel Rogers and Lamb – the last sending along Blake's first 'The Chimney-Sweeper' from the *Songs of Innocence*, described as 'a very rare and curious little work'. The cult of the child could embrace picturesque rural 'naturals' but not yet filthy and miserable wretches in the industrial cities. Montgomery himself contributed poems which open and close the second half of the book, and apart from Blake's they are the only ones which merit attention as poetry. One cannot help feeling he was disappointed at the rather meagre response, and to make the volume more substantial he opens with official documents and transcriptions of parliamentary debates and reports of committees. The gruesome detail spelt out in these turn the stomach with graphic detail, and the effect of reading the volume as a whole can be likened to anybody today, reading the transcription of evidence given by indigenous Australians about their 'stolen generation' of children, in *Bringing them home*.[38] The cruelty of masters towards the boys, who had been bought and sold like chattels, was notorious, and the discomforts extreme: 'They have their flesh torn by the sharp points of projecting stones or lime; they are frequentlly wedged, unable to move, and almost suffocated with soot, in narrow and crooked flues; they are often falling down those which are too wide for them' (14). The deaths are shocking:

> They have been sent up chimnies while the fire was in the grate, to force their way through the heated soot. They have been scalded by steam arising from water thoughtlessly thrown into the fire below; nay they have not unfrequently been compelled to ascend and descend chimnies when on fire, sometimes perishing in the attempt. They have been precipitated from the tops of high chimnies in the loosened pots, and dashed upon the pavement below. They have been slowly roasted to death in the flue of an oven. They have been dug dead out of the sides of chimnies, in which they have been stuck fast, suffocating for hours. (14–15)

After the impact of the documentary material, the imaginative writings, coming as they do from inferior authors, are an anticlimax and often sentimental, but they provide a more moralised perspective. There are poems both narrative and in monologue, and several ballads, stories, and even a 'sketch' in dramatic dialogue. Continually, the analogy of slavery is

drawn – *'yet we have slaves at home!'* and amidst the appeals to emotions of
pity there are claims of natural rights for the children:

> Say, did kindly HEAVEN intend it?
> Say, does stern NECESSITY?
> Will HUMANITY defend it?
> REASON dare to urge her plea?

Montgomery closes the *The Climbing-Boys' Album* section with his own
poems, the strongest in the book. There are three monologues in his series,
'The Climbing-Boy's Soliloquies', and they give variations on the violation
on the chimney-sweep's natural rights. The first dwells on his deprivation of
human affection or even company, which has robbed him of youthful hope.
Even the dogs snarl and start at him, and they are 'as bad as men'. The children
of beggars or gypsies are seen as privileged by comparison. In a distracting
reverie, he identifies with the quiet life of fish and snails:

> He feeds on fruit, he sleeps on flowers –
> I wish I was a snail!

But he pulls himself back in unsentimental fashion to focus indignantly on
the factors that prevent the self-regard of a human being – the right to be
human:

> No, never; do the worst they can
>   I may be happy still;
> For I was born to be a man,
>   And if I live I will.

It is a minimal hope, the only one left to him, and its assertion is a claim for
self-preservation which lay at the heart of natural law. The second is a longer
poem, which demonstrates Montgomery's almost uncanny imaginative
empathy with the lot of the oppressed victim. Subtitled 'the Dream', it shows
that the chimney-sweeper can attain temporary freedom only in a dream in
which there are eddies of flight in the moonshine, and of cleanliness in the
sun. But reality intrudes even into the dream, ironically emphasising that it
is his real life which is the nightmare. His master continually looms surreal-
istically, beating him and grasping him 'as a butcher lifts the lamb / that
struggles for its life'. His one moment of self-assertion when he stamps,
screams and weeps, sadly reminds him it is no more than a dream:

> For then – which shows I dreamt –
> Methought I ne'er before had made
> The terrible attempt.

The poem ends with a bleak return to the waking world, and a hint that he will live the nightmare every day until the final release into 'blue heaven':

> Like a sea-bubble on the sand;
> Then all fell dark. – I woke.

The third Soliloquy, 'Easter-Monday at Sheffield', is Montgomery's version of the events Blake bears witness to in 'Holy Thursday'. It also exposes the social hypocrisy of the Easter parade when children from the orphanage are cleaned, dressed up, ushered through the main street, and given a feast – before returning the next day to the life of grime and exploitation. The boy who narrates the poem does not directly see through the ceremony, but he realises the children's occupation shows through:

> All wash'd and clean as clean could be,
> And yet so dingy, marr'd, and grim,
> A mole with half an eye might see
> Our craft in every look and limb.

He himself sees a young girl sitting beside 'Her mother, – mother but in name!', barely recognisable as the androgynous child whom he had often seen blackened and carrying 'a vile two-bushel sack'. He sees also twins, 'Two toddling five-year olds' who had just begun to climb:

> With cherry-cheeks, and curly hair,
> And skins not yet engrain'd with grime.
>
> I wish'd, I did, that [that] they might die,
> Like 'Babes i' th' Wood,' the little slaves,
> And 'Robin-redbreast' painfully
> Hid them 'with leaves', for want of graves; –
>
> Rather than live, like me, and weep
> To think that ever they were born;
> Toil the long day, and from short sleep
> Wake to fresh miseries every morn.

This unbearably sad poem ends with the sweep pinning his hopes on Christ as the saviour of victims, and yearning for death as a release from the pain of a life in which childhood is allowed on only one day of the year.

Heather Glen shows that the form of Blake's *Songs of Innocence and Experience* was not particularly original in their time, nor was their function as vehicles for social protest:

> Late eighteenth-century children's books contain poems and stories on such subjects as the distresses of poverty, the evils of the slave trade and

the need for kindness to animals: most seek to inculcate a mildly progressive humanitarianism.[39]

However, what is new is the way Blake uses the children's poems as a vehicle for 'a subtley articulated alternative vision' presenting 'points of view very different from the customary controlling one of polite adult rationalism' (31). This operates partly through the use of personae with divergent perspectives, showing the subject matter in radically different lights. As a consequence, the simplicity of the surface poetry is deceptive. The two poems specifically named 'The Chimney Sweeper' can be contextualised in various ways. The speaker in the *Innocence* version seems to be an insouciant boy who optimistically cheers up another with what seem at first to be platitudes.

> When my mother died I was very young,
> > And my father sold me while yet my tongue,
> > Could scarcely cry weep weep weep weep.
> > So your chimneys I sweep & in soot I sleep,
>
> Theres little Tom Dacre, who cried when his head
> That curl'd like a lambs back, was shav'd, so I said.
> > Hush Tom never mind it, for when your head's bare,
> > You know that the soot cannot spoil your white hair.
>
> And so he was quiet, & that very night,
> > As Tom was a sleeping he had such a sight,
> That thousands of sweepers Dick, Joe, Ned & Jack
> > Were all of them lock'd up in coffins of black,
>
> > And by came an Angel who had a bright key,
> > And he open'd the coffins & set them all free.
> > Then down a green plain leaping laughing they run
> And wash in a river and shine in the Sun.
>
> > Then naked & white, all their bags left behind,
> > They rise upon clouds, and sport in the wind.
> > And the Angel told Tom if he'd be a good boy,
> > He'd have God for his father & never want joy.
>
> > And so Tom awoke and we rose in the dark
> > And got with our bags & our brushes to work.
> > Tho' the morning was cold, Tom was happy & warm,
> > So if all do their duty, they need not fear harm.[40]

The poem gains a more complex effect when one takes into account the responses of the inevitably experienced reader, who would spot the darker subtext in the reference to being 'sold', the pun on 'weep', the shaved head, the 'cold' morning, and most chillingly of all, Tom's vision of thousands of sweepers 'lock'd up in coffins of black', which bring to mind the chmineys in which so many boys died. These references to the stark realities of the boys' lot makes the speaker's naivety poignant and also somewhat shocking in that he has no insight into his condition. His only perspective comes from passive acceptance, pathetic hopes in Christian angels and an afterlife, and docile obedience. However, another layer is added when we consider that he is speaking *to* another boy, who appears to be younger and at least as naïve and perhaps more so. The motives behind the platitudes might then be re-interpreted not as false consciousness, rationalising awful facts, but as conscious protection of vulnerability, a salvation from despair. It doesn't matter if the speaker believes in his own cheerful advice or not. If it gives reassurance, hope and a benign purpose to Tom Dacre's otherwise intolerable existence and his dreams, then it is saving him from painful knowledge of his utter helplessness and the dreadful pointlessness of his future life. It applies a frame of natural rights even while denying their social acceptance, in dignifying the two boys alike as human beings, who deserve better but who cannot expect improvement in their condition until policy is changed. One feels that at least Tom, and perhaps both the boys are then both mercifully protected against knowledge and insight, with the ability to dignify even the most degrading aspects of their lives, at the cost of endless justification. By focusing on internal shifts in language through officialese to colloquialism to the implied master's warning behind the last line, Heather Glen finds even more ironies in this 'disconcertedly double-edged' poem.

'The Chimney Sweeper' in *Experience* is poetically less complex, but darker in its vision.

> A little black thing among the snow:
>> Crying weep, weep, in notes of woe!
>> Where are thy father & mother? say?
>> They are both gone up to the church to pray.
>
> Because I was happy upon the heath,
> And smil'd among the winter's snow:
> They clothed me in the clothes of death,
>> And taught me to sing the notes of woe.
>
> And because I am happy, & dance & sing,
>> They think they have done me no injury:
>> And are gone to praise God & his Priest & King
>> Who make up a heaven of our misery.

The boy is seen initially as a pathetic figure, silhouetted black against white, the cry of 'weep' more literally the 'note of woe' rather than occupational cry of 'sweep'. After the initial question about the absence of the boy's father and mother, the poem changes into the first person reply. Even the boy himself is aware of the injustice and social scandal of his position, although he refrains from direct blame. The tone is more plaintive than querulous, turning on the word 'because'. To the child's eye, the fact that he was happy outdoors made his parents put him in 'clothes of death' and made him 'sing the notes of woe', both the inevitable result of his occupation. And because he has found some happiness in existence, they do not know the misery they have caused. Of course Blake would have known that in most if not all cases the parents were not entirely blameworthy. Many of the children were orphans, or their parents were paupers and in no position to rear their children. The last line redirects attention to the true culprit – the perversion of Christianity which endorses child labour and pretends that human misery and an institutional denial of natural rights can be redefined as morally justified and a cause for 'praise'.

The occasion for the boy's dancing and singing might have been the annual May Day dance of chimney-sweeps and milkmaids. Or more generally it may have been the London equivalent of Montgomery's Easter Monday in Sheffield, when children from orphanages were dressed up and paraded to Saint Paul's. Blake deals with this socially hypocritical practice in three poems. The two 'Holy Thursday' lyrics need to be read beside each other. In *Innocence*, the scene is described as a celebration of innocence and radiance as 'these flowers of London' become 'multitudes of lambs' accompanied by benign beadles. The hints of restrictiveness lie in the regimented formation and the beadles' 'wands as white as snow' – wands can be canes and snow can be cold – but the perspective is the kind of 'see no evil' attitude of the boy in the first chimney-sweeper poem. The poems bear comparison also because the last lines in both cases can be interpreted as either peacefully accepting or ironically platitudinous:

> Beneath them sit the aged men wise guardians of the poor
> Then cherish pity, lest you drive an angel from your door

As we saw in dealing with slavery, Blake walks a knife-edge in his treatment of 'pity'. The emotion may be necessary as a starting point for imaginative identification with the poor and downtrodden, but if it remains passive and inactive it is merely a sentimental propagandist tool for charity that covers up problems of social injustice and merely salves adult consciences. Pity without action then becomes part of the problem in perpetuating injustices. The *Experience* version of 'Holy Thursday' allows no such leeway. It is one of the most straightforwardly excoriating protest poems written in the period, and resonates across the whole area of child labour which is caused by the existence of poverty. The same procession is viewed in a spirit of angry indictment:

> Is that trembling cry a song?
> Can it be a song of joy?
> And so many children poor?
> It is a land of poverty!

'London' is equally condemnatory. The speaker wanders the streets of a city which prides itself on its 'charters' guaranteeing liberty, taking note of the fetters, material and spiritual, binding the poor:

> In every cry of every Man,
> In every Infants cry of fear,
>   In every voice: in every ban,
>   The mind-forg'd manacles I hear
>
> How the Chimney-sweepers cry
> Every blackning Church appalls,
> And the hapless Soldiers sigh
> Runs in blood down Palace walls

The 'mind-forg'd manacles' so central to Blake's thinking about slavery and what it represents in society, become the ideological weapons of institutions, church and state, persuading people that the absence of natural rights is perfectly justifiable as a part of God's order.

Chimney-sweepers are the most socially visible examples of the denial of children's rights in Blake's poetry, but obviously his work, and particularly the *Songs*, are full of less conspicuous violations. In lyrics like 'The Garden of Love' and 'The Little Vagabond' he singles out for particular condemnation the prescriptions placed on childhood experiences by 'cold, inhuman, joy-less Christianity'.[41] 'The Little Girl Lost', 'The Little Girl Found' and 'Ah, Sunflower' stand alongside *the Book of Thel* and *Visions of the Daughters of Albion* in asserting the right of adolescents to express their burgeoning sexu-ality, against social and psychological repression. (A particular kind of con-temporary 'new age' thinking appropriates Blake as extolling 'free love' in general, but his own monogamous life emphasises that he is referring to 'first love' in adolescents, not the desire for novelty in the middle-aged. His plea is that the young should not be interfered with or be repressed by adults when they first encounter sexual desire.[42] His comments on the responsibil-ities of mature love make it clear he is not advocating free love, or at least not so unqualifiedly as Shelley was to do in *Epipysychidion*.) And so on, through many of his poems, Blake asserts a right of children by condemning its per-ceived violation. His indignation on the subject may have been influenced, or at least confirmed, by his witnessing a circus-boy 'hobbling along with a log tied to his foot, such an one as is put on a horse or ass to prevent their straying'.[43] Blake vehemently protested, and to his credit eventually persuaded the irate circus-owner that 'humane sensibility' made such occurrences as abhorrent as slavery. The cluster of his concerns around slavery, child exploitation and repressive religion that causes adult prurience and hypocrisy, are drawn together in lines from *Visions of the Daughters of Albion*, when he condemns,

> The voice of slaves beneath the sun, and children bought with money,
>
> That shiver in religious caves beneath the burning fires
>
> Of lust that belch incessant from the summits of the earth.

Animal rights

It is sometimes lazily asserted that the cause of animal rights had precedent in Roman law, at least to the extent that humans and animals were included within the order of nature as a whole.[44] This is misleading. At the beginning of Justinian's *Digest* (1.1.1.3–4), specifically ascribed to Ulpian, he distinguished *ius naturale*, which applies to all living creatures, from *ius gentium*, which applies to man alone. *Ius naturale* is what we might call the law of nature (rather than natural law), the impulse to pair and procreate, which ultimately becomes institutionalised in human marriage and child bearing. It is not what we would think of as 'animal rights'; and certainly does not imply that they have any guarantees against abuse by humans.[45] The seventeenth century, if anything, enshrined the opposite of animal rights, with Descartes, for example, justifying vivisection by arguing that ethics do not apply to the human–nature relationship, because of the insensibility and irrationality of animals.[46] Nature was literally at the mercy of humans. The history of modern animal rights thinking perhaps begins with Nathaniel Ward, a seventeenth-century lawyer who in 1634 included in a suggested codification of the new American colony's statutes, the edict that 'no man shall exercise any Tirrany or Crueltie towards any bruite Creature which are usuallie kept for man's use'.[47] Since the fifteenth century in England, there had been spokesmen amongst humanists such as Thomas More and Erasmus, for the view that blood sports are cruel and implicitly breach rights of animals in some sense, but it was once again in the 1790s that steps were taken towards a systematic theory of animal rights.[48]

Christine Kenyon-Jones has written in detail about the romantic poets' attitudes to animals, in *Kindred Brutes: Animals in Romantic-Period Writing*,[49] and it is clear that those central to her book, such as Shelley and Byron, were by their time contributing to a rapidly consolidating movement of thought. Again, however, it was the decade of the 1790s which extended the idea of rights of animals from a few isolated individuals (including the generally seminal Locke and Rousseau) to a wider advocacy. Kenyon-Jones also confirms the argument of this book, that the calls for natural rights in many areas were interlinked. She groups 'women, colonized races, slaves, children and working men without the vote' as the main concerns of the movement to establish natural rights, and to these 'subordinated groups' she adds animals:

> Since animals could be seen to be metonymically or synecdochically linked to these oppressed human groups, they were drawn into the debate, and the continuum of better treatment and rights was also, to some extent, applied to them.[50]

However, with her focus directed to the later romantics, Kenyon-Jones does not elaborate, and more can be said. Behind two classic poetic statements in the 1790s, Blake's 'The Tyger' and Coleridge's *The Ancient Mariner* with its climactic blessing of the water-snakes, lie many writers who clarified and publicised the cause of animal rights. Jeremy Bentham sounded the clarion call in 1789, suggesting that 'the day *may* come, when the rest of the animal creation may acquire those rights which never could have been withholden from them but by the hand of tyranny'.[51] Prose polemics followed in the 1790s, for example by John Lawrence, a farmer who also campaigned for abolitionism and for universal suffrage, and 'was disgusted by the sight of cattle being led into London under appalling conditions to be taken to Smithfield market for slaughter'.[52] John Oswald's *The Cry of Nature* (1791) was influenced by Brahmin philosophy on vegetarianism and argued for sympathetic identification with the 'cry' of suffering animals, a message pursued by Thomas Young in *An Essay on Humanity in Animals* (1798). Lord Erskine in 1809 read a speech on the subject of cruelty to animals to the House of Lords, on the second reading of the bill for preventing malicious and wanton cruelty to animals, and an unnamed 'Clergyman of the Church of England' published in 1824 'A sermon on the unjustifiableness of cruelty to the brute creation and the obligation we are under to treat it with lenity and compassion'. Blake by implication adds his voice in showing that the same God made the lion and the lamb as well as human beings, and he has sharply anthropomorphic images of the lamb which 'forgives the Butcher's Knife' (*Auguries of Innocence*). The gathering movement was even considered threatening enough to warrant attacks through satire and parody, as in Thomas Taylor's *A Vindication of the Rights of Brutes* (1798), which mocks equally the calls for rights of man and rights of animals. However, at least in an institutional sense, some success for rights of animals preceded rights of man, for in 1822–24 the Royal Society for the Protection of Animals (RSPCA) was established. By the Victorian age, as Barbara T. Gates has traced in *Kindred Nature: Victorian and Edwardian Women Embrace the Living World*[53] nature was being viewed in a more benign light altogether, particularly by women scientists. The title of an article by Frances Cobbe, published in *Fraser's Magazine* in 1863, is exemplary: 'The Rights of Man and the Claims of Brutes'.

Like James Montgomery, Samuel Jackson Pratt perhaps deserved a better fate than the posthumous literary oblivion which overtook his reputation. Much of his prolific output appeared under the name Courtney Melmoth, and he was particularly associated with the Della Crusca literary movement. In fictional works such as *Emma Corbett* (1781) and *Family Secrets, Literary and Domestic* (1797), he manifested the sensibility and benevolence associated with that group of writers: '*the tear of Sensibility* is at once the softest and best evidence of the praise which it is my ambition to merit on this occasion'.[54] The works which will occupy us here betray by their very titles the same general approach: *Humanity, or, the rights of Nature, A Poem* (1788), and *Sympathy, or, a Sketch of the Social Passion. A Poem* (1781). Both were reprinted enough times in the 1790s to be influential. Pratt is in many ways one of the prophets of the animal rights movement and vegetarianism. He showed himself to be squeamish on the issue of the French revolution, abhorring its early 'bloody theatre' and hoping for 'milder forms of resistance to authorities',[55] and he seems almost complacently attached to the notion of 'the benevolence of England' as an ideal of justice and liberty, at a time when the British government was notoriously brutal and repressive. But he is vocal on behalf of equality, non-subjugation of the poor, and abolition of slavery. His contradictions show how the struggle for natural rights had diverged from a generalized body of thought close to natural law, to a number of single natural rights that could be contested as separate issues. *Sympathy* establishes Pratt's overall framework of thinking, which links him with the sensibility movement. 'The powers of Universal Sympathy' are 'The cause of Benevolence'. Feeling the lack of company in a neglected landscape where he used to live, the poet muses on 'heav'n's first maxim, BORN TO SHARE', and on 'the bias SOCIAL, man with men must share / The varied benefits of earth and air'.

> Instinct, or sympathy, or what you will,
> The social principle is active still.

Even war is seen as the result of people fighting to defend their innate sociability, and its effect is to bind 'the social links' tighter. The general principle leads him to recognise poverty, for example, as the responsibility of all, capable of stirring conscience through pity:

> Say, can your sordid merchandize deny
> The sacred force of heav'n-born Sympathy?
> Ah, no! the generous spirit takes a part,
> As goodness, glory, pity, move the heart.

What makes Pratt different from the other writers, however, is his extension of sociability to include aspects of nature. In Thoreauvian fashion, the poet claims that even a hermit indulges feelings of sympathy because he can empathise with animals, whose pain elicits the same feelings as human poverty to the person living in society: 'A heart that aches if but a wren expires.' It is this extension of sociability to establish links between the human and animal word that allows him to regard nature not as a backdrop to human activities or as a vehicle for expressing emotions, but a link in the chain binding all living things. This fuels Pratt's lifelong belief in vegetarianism.

> This then is clear, while human kind exist,
> The social principle must still subsist,
> In strict dependency of one on all,
> As run the binding links from great to small.

In *Humanity* he argues that 'Humanity requires that the RIGHTS OF NATURE should be enjoyed by every *Human Being*', and this long poem, intended as a preliminary to a work on 'society' and 'the human race', stresses conscience as the basis of 'Humanity'. He harks back to a golden age before slavery:

> Grac'd with the bow, the Indians harmless ran,
> And undisturb'd enjoy'd the rights of man:
> *The rights of man by nature still are due,*
> *To men of ev'ry clime and ev'ry hue.*

He is to some extent unusual amongst the della Cruscans in showing some resistance to 'enthusiasm', instead extolling 'reason' as the basis of rights thinking: 'His reason sanction'd what his nature taught.' He sees poets and musicians as sometimes culpable, in beguiling us away from awareness of slaves' suffering, pity and sentimentality:

> The sweet enthusiasm ev'ry grief beguiles,
> And the scourg'd Captive even in anguish smiles,
> With thrilling passion ev'ry feature glows,
> So strong the charm it cheats awhile their woes.

The poem *Humanity* ends hopefully in a vision of a new golden age:

> NEGROES ARE MEN, AND MEN ARE SLAVES NO MORE,
> FAIR FREEDOM REIGNS AND TYRANNY IS O'ER.

Pratt's subtitle to *Humanity*, 'The Rights of Nature' points towards a more radical and unusual stance for the times, that all natural creatures, and especially animals, have the right to exist unmolested by man. He attacks the killing of birds and animals with the intention to 'gorge unwholesome food', appealing alike to 'sweet Pity' for their sufferings and also more fundamentally to the argument of necessity: 'FOR HUNGER KILL, BUT NEVER SPORT WITH LIFE.' Blood sports, luxury, and unnecessary carnivorousness are condemned, while the vegetarian Brahmin is praised for his 'blameless life'. The poetry rises in indignation:

> 'Tis not enough that daily slaughter feeds,
> That the fish leaves its stream, the lamb its meads,
> That the reluctant ox is dragg'd along,
> And the bird ravish'd from its tender song
>
> ...
>
> 'Tis not enough, our appetites require
> That on their altars hecatombs expire;
> But cruel man, a savage in his power,
> Must heap fresh horrors on life's parting hour:
> Full many a being that bestows its breath,
> Must prove the pang that waits a *ling'ring* death,
> Here, close pent up, must gorge unwholesome food,
> There render drop by drop the smoking blood;
> The quiv'ring flesh improves as slow it dies,
> And Lux'ry sees th'augmented whiteness rise;
> Some creatures gash'd must feel the torturer's art,
> Writhe in their wounds, tho' sav'd each vital part.
> From the hard bruise the food more tender grows,
> And callous Lux'ry triumphs in the blows:
> Some, yet alive, to raging flames consign'd,
> By piercing shrieks must soothe our taste refin'd!

Timothy Morton, quoting this passage in *Shelley and the Revolution in Taste: The Body and the Natural World*,[56] shows that Pratt's vegetarianism was profoundly influential on Shelley. The slaughter of animals to feed humans is seen by Pratt as 'nature's broken law' which is avenged in the experience of ill health and violated conscience. Shelley, writing in *Queen Mab*, has his preferred utopian end in sight, which returns us to the linking of Locke and Rousseau of children, kindness to animals, and an education into natural rights:

> Little children stretch in friendly sport
> Towards these dreadless partners of their play.
> All things are void of terror; man has lost
> His terrible prerogative, and stands
> An equal amidst equals: happiness

And science dawn, though late upon the earth;
Peace cheers the mind, health renovates the frame.[57]

The reputation of Erasmus Darwin has weathered a little better than
Pratt's, at least to the extent that he is remembered as the grandfather of
Charles Darwin. This in itself has an irony, since it was Erasmus, not Charles,
who originated the fundamental principles behind the theory of evolution
and survival of the fittest,[58] a fact pointed out by Bernard Shaw in his Preface
to *Back to Methuselah*. The grandson was the one who popularised the idea.
Erasmus was yet another writer published by Joseph Johnson, and Blake
illustrated some of his works. He even published a book, printed in a hand-
some edition by Johnson, on education for women: *A Plan for the Conduct of
Female Education in Boarding Schools* (1797),[59] which, although far from
radical in its philosophy, did advocate useful subjects, including geography,
history and natural history, and emphasised physical exercise and good
health. Shelley the vegetarian, for one, appreciated his radical stance in
defending nature. Darwin advances the claims for rights of nature not (simply) by opposing the slaughter of animals and supporting vegetarianism, but
by celebrating the diversity and uniqueness of all species, primarily plants
but also animals and even insects. His works are monuments to wonder at
the simple fact of reproduction, which is in some ways the underpinning
principle of theories of rights which assert the claim to survival of living
things. Even the silkworm is presented with a sensuality worthy of Keats:

> Erewhile the changeful worm with circling head
> Weaves the nice curtains of his silken bed;
> Web within web involves his larva form,
> Alike secured from sunshine and from storm;
> For twelve long days He dreams of blossom'd groves,
> Untasted honey, and ideal loves;
> Wakes from his trance, alarm'd with young Desire,
> Finds his new sex, and feels ecstatic fire;
> From flower to flower with honey'd lip he springs,
> And seeks his velvet loves on silver wings.[60]

This passage is typical of the canto of *The Temple of Nature* (1803) dealing
with 'Reproduction of Life'. It is a kind of love poem set in the natural world,
presenting a riot of reproductive activity that must, Darwin believes, have a
meaning in the wider world of 'Nature's laws' (ii, 446), and which should be
allowed to continue until God should choose to end the process. This might
seem a long way from the subject of rights, but in a sense it is a philosophical prerequisite of the notion that living things have a right to continue
living, and Darwin in the same poem links up his vision to radical ideals by

turning to 'patriot heroes' who advanced the glorious cause[s] 'Of Justice, Mercy, Liberty and Laws' (iv, 273–4). For a work supposedly about the natural world, it has an undertext which links it with the struggle for the rights of man. The work for which Darwin was best known, *The Botanic Garden* (1790), is another work which intersperses detailed descriptions of plants and their growth with digressions extolling philanthropy, equality and social justice. That he was notorious amongst conservatives for what they saw as his combination of radicalism and zealous defence of the botanical world, is neatly proved by an anonymous parody of his work published in 1794, worthy of the *Anti-Jacobin*. It praises the French revolution ('Favourites of freedom, Sons of frisky France') and vegetarianism, and it comically anthropomorphises plants in the style of sentimental poetry:

> See plants, susceptible of joy and woe,
> Feel all we feel, and know whate'er we know!
> View them like us inclin'd to watch or steep,
> Like us to smile, and, ah! Like us to weep![61]

The whole story of the extension of natural rights to include animals (signposted, for example, in the Endangered Species Act of 1973) and current environmental issues, lie outside the scope of this book, but none the less can be placed on a spectrum that includes and began with natural or human rights. It was not until the Hunting Act of 2005 that Britain addressed the most glaring case of animal rights violoations. The change that separated Pufendorf's statement, 'there is no common rights / law between man and brutes' from Pratt's assertion of the right of animals not to be killed or molested by humans marks a cultural shift which was accelerated by the attention to rights thinking at the end of the eighteenth century. As for children, by 1989 the movement culminated in the passing of the United Nations' *Convention on the Rights of the Child*, (UNICEF) which is summarised in these words:

> Built on varied legal systems and cultural traditions, the Convention on the Rights of the Child is a universally agreed set of non-negotiable standards and obligations. It spells out the basic human rights that children – without discrimination – have: the right to survival; to develop to the fullest; to protection from harmful influences, abuse and exploitation; and to participate fully in family, cultural and social life. Every right spelled out in the Convention is inherent to the human dignity and harmonious development of every child. The Convention protects children's rights by setting standards in health care, education and legal, civil and social services ... The Convention on the Rights of the Child is the first legally binding international instrument to incorporate the full range of human rights – civil and political rights as well as economic, social and cultural rights.[62]

The Convention's basic premise is that children are born with fundamental freedoms and the inherent rights of all human beings. The seeds were planted much earlier than the 1790s, and the road was much longer, but once again it was in that decade that thinkers and writers were nurturing the ideas in the popular consciousness which eventually were to find legal sanctions in such statements.

Conclusion

There may be a pattern that occurs in all paradigm shifts. First comes a generalised call for change, usually in the name of freedom. After the impetus builds, and especially if some victories that add fuel to the fire are achieved, then there is a necessary splintering into a set of related but discrete issues. This is what happened after the yeasty days of the 1960s in Paris when workers and students joined hands in a call for liberation, and black activists in America demonstrated against a segregated society and for their civil rights. From then on, for the next 30 years or so, single issues were tackled one by one, as they related separately to political and democratic processes, civil rights, social concerns and living conditions. The same seems to have happened in eastern Europe when in 1989 the Russian style system of soviet imperialism collapsed, to be followed inevitably by calls within independent states for localised changes. It is this pattern, I have suggested, that makes the 1790s in Britain a watershed decade for the cause of natural rights. The revolutions in America and France in the 1780s galvanised an ebbing tradition of natural law which still existed amongst libertarian thinkers among whom were many imaginative writers. The call for change began as a demand for freedom but under the name of 'rights of man' or natural rights – the generalised stage when freedom as an issue dominated over specific instances. As in natural law, the central ethic turned on instincts for self-preservation and for living virtuously, but the shift of emphasis towards rights allowed iniquities and public vices to be singled out and addressed as practical problems turning on individual human survival. That is why, in this book as in the chronology of its material, in the 1790s particular natural rights were not initially spelt out or pursued with single minded rigour, except the cause of abolitionism which was something of a middle-class movement offering a paradigm case for more clearly defined natural rights. When it was clear that the English government was reacting with an equally scatter-gun reaction, seeking to stifle free speech itself, and after some popular victories for liberty showed that the tide was turning, then groups evolved focusing on named natural rights which have emerged in the latter half of this book. Most were not to be officially addressed let alone resolved, for many decades or even centuries, but at least they were placed on public agenda – causes like freedom of speech and publication; freedom of worship for Protestant dissenters; the right to form associations which eventually led to the right to form political parties and trade unions; rights to participate in government through suffrage; women's rights; rights of children and animals. All these movements took legitimacy from 'rights of man', which were encoded as human rights by the United Nations in 1948, in a charter unfortunately more honoured in the breach than the observance. The fact that a writer like Pratt – or for that matter Wordsworth and Coleridge in the 1790s – could believe in some of the rights but not others, showed how different it was as an intellectual system from natural law which was offered as a universal and underlying truth. Literature of the 1790s, and especially the writing of Blake, reflected the dynamic ferment of the process of a revolution in thought, and demonstrated the way that debate on natural rights could filter into a whole range of lived, daily experiences. Those who came in the wake, like Keats, Hazlitt and Shelley, were given the legacy of a clear conceptual framework which had been less evident to their predecessors who were driven more by passion for human freedom than clarity about its detailed implementation. If this book, in trying to find an uncluttered and clear path through mercurial and shifting events, has risked over-simplification of the issues in the earlier period, then it is because I have willingly followed the trajectory of those times. The intellectual shifts from natural law to natural rights, from natural rights to specific campaigns, could not have been predicted in advance, and progressed in waves of uncertainty, victories and defeats, yet in hindsight there does seem a pathway through the material which in the short term led to what we now know as the romantic movement, and in the longer to international acceptance of most of the premises which many thinkers and writers in the 1790s struggled for.

Notes

1 From Natural Law to Natural Rights

1. For a useful overview, see *Human Rights*, eds, J. Roland Pennock and John W. Chapman (New York and London: New York University Press, 1981), esp. Pennock, 'Rights, Natural Rights, and Human Rights – A General View'.
2. John Finnis, *Natural Law and Natural Rights* (Oxford: Clarendon Press, 1980), 198.
3. Lloyd L. Weinreb, 'Natural Law and Rights', in *Natural Law Theory*, ed. Robert P. George (Oxford: Clarendon Press, 1992), 278–305, 280.
4. Peter Jones, *Rights* (Basingstoke: Macmillan, 1994).
5. See, for example, Leo Strauss, *Natural Rights and History* (Chicago: University of Chicago Press, 1953).
6. John Rawls, *A Theory of Justice* (Oxford: Clarendon Press, 1972).
7. Jones, *Rights*, 72–3 credits Ronald Dworkins with drawing the distinction, and suggests that Hobbes is the originator of the 'weak' sense.
8. See, for example, *Poisoning the Minds of the Lower Orders* by Don Herzog (Princeton: Princeton University Press, 1998) and John Barrell, *Imagining the King's Death: Figurative Treason, Fantasies of Regicide 1793–1796* (Oxford: Oxford University Press, 2000).
9. Brendon Bradshaw, 'Transalpine Humanism', in J. H. Burns (ed.), *The Cambridge History of Political Thought 1450–1700* (Cambridge: Cambridge University Press, 1991), 106. I have silently reversed the order of clauses, to suit my own sequence.
10. Eighteenth-century untilitarianism meets unexpected agreement with Freudian psychiatry on the issue of a primal human motivation lying in self-interest and envy: see for example, John Forrester, 'Psychoanalysis and the History of the Passions: The Strange Destiny of Envy', in John O'Neill (ed.), *Freud and the Passions* (University Park, Pennsylvania: Pennsylvania State University Press, 1996), 127–50.
11. It is not impossible that the final couplet, rhyming creature and nature, may be a personal parody of the Geordie accent of Thomas Spence, whom we shall encounter later in the book.
12. Jonathan Bate, *Shakespearean Constitutions: Politics, Theatre, Criticism 1730–1830* (Oxford: Clarendon Press, 1989), 177. Bate's book shows, however, how criticism and cartoons could politicise plays themselves and appropriate them for radical and populist causes.
13. Edward Royle and James Walvin in *English Radicals and Reformers: 1760–1848* (Lexington, KY: University of Kentucky Press, 1982).
14. Paul O'Flinn, ' "Beware of reverence": writing and radicalism in the 1790s', in *Writing and Radicalism*, ed. John Lucas (London and New York: Longman, 1996), 84–101.
15. *An Oxford Companion to the Romantic Age: British Culture 1776–1832*, General Editor Iain McCalman (Oxford: Oxford University Press, 1999), 2–3.
16. See Gale MacLachlan and Ian Reid, *Framing and Interpretation* (Melbourne: Melbourne University Press, 1994) for a systematic summary of 'framing' theory.
17. (London: Macmillan, 1992).
18. Bate, *Shakespearean Constitutions*, 176.

19. See R. S. White, *Natural Law in English Renaissance Literature* (Cambridge: Cambridge University Press, 1996).
20. John Finnis, *Natural Law and Natural Rights* (Oxford: Oxford University Press, 1980).
21. Rawls, *A Theory of Justice*.
22. Richard A. McCabe, *Incest, Drama and Nature's Law* (Cambridge: Cambridge University Press, 1993).
23. Michael J. Lacey and Knud Haakonssen, *A Culture of Rights: The Bill of Rights in Philosophy, Politics, and Law – 1791 and 1991* (Cambridge: Cambridge University Press, 1991), 28.
24. *De Legibus*, transl. C. W. Keyes (Loeb Classical Library), *Cicero* vol. 28 (Cambridge, Mass. and London, 1977), 318–19.
25. *De Re Publica* XXII, 211.
26. See Pina Ford, 'Natural Law Context in Thomas More's "Utopia" ' (unpublished PhD thesis, University of Western Australia, 2001).
27. Aquinas, *Summa Theologica*, 1a 2ae, quae. 91, art. 1 and 2, quoted and transl. by A. P. d'Entrèves, *Natural Law: An historical Survey* (London: Hutchinson, 1951).
28. Aquinas, *Summa*, 1a 2ae, 95, 2.
29. d'Entrèves, *Natural Law*, 43.
30. Quoted by William G. Craven, *Giovanni Pico della Mirandola* (Geneva: Librairie Droz, 1981), 33.
31. White, *Natural Law in English Renaissance Literature*, ch. 9.
32. The next few paragraphs are adapted from the Epilogue to my book, *Natural Law in English Renaissance Literature*, since they form the bridge which makes this book a sequel to the earlier one.
33. Norberto Bobbio, *Thomas Hobbes and the Natural Law Tradition*, transl. Daniela Gobetti (Chicago and London: University of Chicago Press, 1993; first publ. In Italian, 1989), 70.
34. Page references in the text are to Thomas Hobbes, *Leviathan*, ed. C. B. Macpherson (Harmondsworth: Penguin Books, 1968).
35. See, for example, R. E. Ewin, *Virtues and Rights: The Moral Philosophy of Thomas Hobbes* (Boulder, CO: Westview Press, 1991), *passim*, which provides different interpretations of Hobbes's version of natural law.
36. Knud Haakonssen, 'From natural law to the rights of man: a European perspective on American debates' in Lacey and Haakonssen, *A Culture of Rights*, 26.
37. See Jean Hampton, *Hobbes and the Social Contract Tradition* (Cambridge: Cambridge University Press, 1986), 51–7.
38. Haakonssen, 'From natural law to the rights of man', 27.
39. The phrase is from Gregory Claeys, *Thomas Paine: Social and Political Thought* (Boston: Unwin Hyman, 1989), 11–12.
40. Weinreb, 'Natural Law and Rights', 278–305, 278.
41. Haakonssen, 'From natural law to the rights of man', 29.
42. Richard Tuck, *Natural Rights Theories: Their Origin and Development* (Cambridge: Cambridge University Press, 1979). Tuck speaks of a movement from passive rights (to have the right to be given or allowed something by someone else) to active rights (to have the right to do something oneself), but this does not seem very relevant to our period. See also McInerny who notes that 'in the classical sense the right was an external relation to be established between persons on the basis of things', so that the *jus* is the object of justice. However, 'in the modern sense, right has become subjective, it attaches to the individual taken singly as an

instantiation of human nature and amounts to a claim that he can make on the state or on others.' 'Natural Law and Natural Rights', in *Aquinas on Human Action* (Washington DC: Catholic University of America Press, 1992), 213–14.

43. See Tuck, *Natural Rights Theories*, 68–71.

44. For the long and tangled story of the evolution of the Bill of Rights, see Lacey and Haakonssen, *A Culture of Rights*.

45. Dr Bemetzrieder, *A New Code for Gentlemen; in which are Considered God and Man; Man's Natural Rights and Social Duties* ... (London: J. Barfield, 1803).

46. Linda Kirk in *Richard Cumberland and Natural Law: Secularisation of Thought in Seventeenth-Century England* (Cambridge: Cambridge University Press, 1987). I feel justified in using Kirk's paraphrases and quotations from Cumberland, since the original was in Latin. In dealing with such background figures as Cumberland, my book concentrates on ideas rather than niceties of translation.

47. Kirk, *Richard Cumberland*, 24.

48. John Mullan, *Sentiment and Sociability: The Language of Feeling in the Eighteenth Century* (Oxford: Clarendon Press, 1988).

49. Ann Jessie van Sant, *Eighteenth-century Sensibility and the Novel of the Senses in Social Context* (Cambridge: Cambridge University Press, 1993).

50. Locke, *Second Treatise*, 78: see also 80–3 for rights within the family.

51. Quoted in Peter Laslett's edition of *Two Treatises of Government* (Cambridge: Cambridge University Press, 1963), 109. I acknowledge that my views are broadly based on Laslett's in his detailed Introduction, and that I use his edition.

52. For a thorough discussion of this contradiction, see Wayne Glausser, *Locke and Blake: A Conversation across the Eighteenth Century* (Gainesville, Florida: University Press of Florida, 1998), ch. 4, 'Slavery', 63–91.

53. Michael Meehan, *Liberty and Poetics in Eighteenth Century England* (London: Croom Helm, 1986).

54. G. J. Barker-Benfield, *The Culture of Sensibility: Sex and Society in Eighteenth-Century Britain* (Chicago and London: University of Chicago Press, 1992), 105–19.

55. For the key documents, see especially *Divine Right and Democracy: An Anthology of Political Writing in Stuart England*, ed. David Wootton (Harmondsworth: Penguin Books, 1986).

56. Michael Durey, *Transatlantic Radicals and the Early American Republic* (Lawrence, Kansas: University Press of Kansas, 1997), 12–13.

57. Ibid., 13.

58. D. D. Raphael, 'Enlightenment and Revolution', *Enlightenment, Rights and Revolution: Essays in Legal and Social Philosophy* (Aberdeen: Aberdeen University Press, 1989), 11. For the most recent and detailed account of the great changes undergoing England in the Commonwealth period, see David Norbrook, *Writing the English Republic: Poetry, Rhetoric and Politics, 1627–1660* (Cambridge: Cambridge University Press, 1999).

59. See, for example, G. D. H. Cole and Raymond Postgate, *The Common People: 1746–1946* (London: Methuen & Co, fourth edn, 1949), Ch. VII.

60. Barrell, *Imagining the King's Death*.

61. Quoted in Carl B. Cone, *Torchbearer of Freedom: The Influence of Richard Price on Eighteenth Century Thought* (Lexington, KY: University of Kentucky Press, 1952), 183.

62. A. Goodwin, 'The political genesis of Edmund Burke's *Reflections on The Revolution in France*' (Manchester: The John Rylands Library, 1968), 355.

63. (London: Hodder and Stoughton, 1985), 111.

64. E. P. Thompson, *Customs in Common* (London: Merlin Press, 1991).
65. Sir William Holdsworth, *A History of English Law* in 14 vols, ed. A. L. Goodhart and H. G. Hanbury (London: Methuen, 1952), esp. vols XII and XIII.
66. Holdsworth, XIII, 16–33 *passim*.
67. Alan Harding, *A Social History of English Law* (Harmondsworth: Penguin Books, 1966).
68. For an account of law in the early eighteenth century, which stayed in place at least until the 1790s, see Julian Hoppit, *A Land of Liberty? England 1689–1727* (The New Oxford History of England, Oxford: Oxford University Press, 2000), ch. 14.
69. For an almost daily chronicle of these enthralling events, see Barrell, *Imagining the King's Death.*
70. The Human Rights Act passed in 2000 incorporates the European Convention on Human Rights (ECHR) into UK law. It enables violations of the Convention to be overturned in the British courts, without the need for lengthy and expensive appeals to the ECHR in Strasbourg. This was not a particularly radical move, and it can be ignored by governments in making statute law. It is not a bill of rights in, for example, the American sense.
71. See Edmund Blunden, *Keats's Publisher* (London: Jonathan Cape, 1936) and Tim Chilcott, *A Publisher and His Circle, the Life and Work of John Taylor, Keats's Publisher* (London: Routledge and Kegan Paul, 1972).
72. The most recent book on Johnson is by Helen Braithwaite, *Romanticism, Publishing and Dissent: Joseph Johnson and the Cause of Liberty* (Basingstoke and New York: Palgrave Macmillan, 2003). Before that, the standard biography was by Gerald P. Tyson, *Joseph Johnson: A Liberal Publisher* (Iowa City: University of Iowa Press, 1979). Tyson also published an article on Johnson in the 1975 issue of *Studies in Bibliography* and the relevant entry in vol.1 of the *Biographical Dictionary of Modern British Radicals*. Claire Tomalin published a piece in the *Times Literary Supplement* of 2 December 1994, Leslie Chard published an article in *The Library* (1977) and there is also a biographical article by Carol Hall in *The British Literary Book Trade 1700–1820*, vol. 154 of *The Dictionary of National Biography*, ed. James K. Bracken and Joel Silver (Detroit, Washington, DC and London: Gale Research Incorporated, 1995), 159–64. See also Carol Hall's *Blake and Fuseli: A Study in the Transmission of Ideas* (New York and London: Garland, 1985). I am grateful to Ian Gadd of the New Dictionary of National Biography project, and Carol Hall, for leading me to these references.
73. Leslie Chard, 'Joseph Johnson: Father of the Book Trade', *Bulletin of the New York Public Library*, 78 (1975), 51–82. For another appreciation of Johnson written by Leslie Chard, see 'Bookseller to Publisher: Joseph Johnson and the English Book Trade, 1760–1810', *Library*, fifth series, 32 (1977), 138–54.
74. Quoted by Claire Tomalin in *Mary Wollstonecraft* (Harmondsworth: Penguin Books, 1974), 92.
75. For the full story, see Tyson, *Joseph Johnson*, ch. 5, 'Trial and Imprisonment, 1795–1800' and Braithwaite, ch. 4, 'Responses to Revolution'.
76. Robert N. Essick, 'William Blake, Thomas Paine, and Biblical Revolution', *Studies in Romanticism*, 30 (Summer 1991), 189–212, 201.
77. Tomalin, *Mary Wollstonecraft*, 99.
78. Tyson, *A Liberal Publisher*, 138.
79. Braithwaite, *Romanticism, Publishing and Dissent*, 180.

2   The Social Passions: Benevolence and Sentimentality

1. Quoted from *James Thomson: Poetical Works*, ed. J. Logie Robertson (Oxford: The Clarendon Press, 1908). This passage appeared for the first time in the third version, 1730.
2. G. J. Barker-Benfield, *The Culture of Sensibility: Sex and Society in Eighteenth-Century Britain* (Chicago and London: University of Chicago Press, 1992), ch. 5.
3. Samuel Richardson, *Clarissa* (London: Dent, 4 vols, 1932), 4, 559–60 (my italics).
4. Erik Erametsa, 'A study of the word "sentimental" and of other linguistic characteristics of eighteenth century sentimentalism in England' (PhD thesis, Helsinki, 1951).
5. (Cambridge: Cambridge University Press, 1996).
6. (Oxford: Oxford University Press, 1988).
7. Quoted in Leonara Ledwon, *Law and Literature: Text and Theory* (New York and London: Garland Publishing, 1996), 133.
8. Olive D. Rudkin, *Thomas Spence and his Connections* (London: Allen and Unwin, 1927), 17.
9. Barbara M. Benedict in her Introduction to *Framing Feeling: Sentiment and Style in English Prose Fiction* (New York: AMS Press, 1994), mentions the influence of Locke, Shaftesbury, Hutcheson and Hume, although the emphasis of her book is on the evocation of 'feeling' through language rather than the moral or political significances of the genre.
10. Page numbers refer to the facsimile edition with Introduction by Paul McReynolds (Gainesville, Florida: University of Florida Press, 1969) which reproduces Hutcheson's third edn (1742), 308–9.
11. Francis Hutcheson, *On Human Nature: Reflections on our Common Systems of Morality on the Social Nature of Man*, ed. Thomas Mautner (Cambridge: Cambridge University Press, 1993), 113.
12. Ibid., 114. Mautner points out that both Gottlieb Gerhard Titius (1661–1714) and Jean Barbeyrace (1674–1744) offered precedents for this view which was otherwise controversial since most commentators agreed that the worst 'sort of polity' is anarchy.
13. Mautner, ibid., 122.
14. Ibid.
15. Ibid., 74.
16. R. F. Brissenden, *Virtue in Distress: Studies in the Novel of Sentiment from Richardson to Sade* (London: Macmillan, 1974).
17. Ibid., 46.
18. Janet Todd, *Sensibility: An Introduction* (London and New York: Metheun, 1986), 23.
19. Chris Jones, *Radical Sensibility: Literature and Ideas in the 1790s* (London: Routledge, 1993), 93.
20. T. D. Campbell, *Adam Smith's Science of Morals* (London: George Allen & Unwin, 1971), 16.
21. Quoted in Campbell, *Adam Smith's Science of Morals*, 17; published posthumously in *Athenaeum*, December 28, 1895.
22. Tom Campbell, *Seven Theories of Human Society* (Oxford: Clarendon Press, 1981), 101.
23. *The Theory of Moral Sentiments*, eds, D. D. Raphael and A. L. Macfie (Oxford: Clarendon Press, 1976), 10.

24. Ibid., 9.
25. David Marshall, *The Surprising Effects of Sympathy: Marivaux, Diderot, Rousseau, and Mary Shelley* (Chicago and London: University of Chicago Press, 1988), 3.
26. Text quoted is *The Tempest*, ed. Stephen Orgel (Oxford: Oxford University Press, 1987).
27. Thomas Wilson, *The Art of Rhetoric*, facsimile ed. R. H. Bowers (Gainesville, Florida: University Press of Florida, 1962) (t 1 v) and (t 1 r).
28. Campbell, *Adam Smith's Science of Morals*, 103.
29. Ibid., 139 fn.
30. Ibid., 147 fn.
31. Ibid., 181.
32. Campbell, *Adam Smith's Science of Morals*, 193.
33. See especially Bernard Harrison, *Henry Fielding's 'Tom Jones': The Novelist as Moral Philosopher* (London: Chatto and Windus for Sussex University Press, 1975); Thomas R. Cleary, *Henry Fielding: Political Writer* (Waterloo, Ontario: Wilfred Laurier University Press, 1984).
34. Todd, *Sensibility: An Introduction*, 81.
35. Quoted from *Thomas Gray*, selected and ed. Robert L. Mack (London: Everyman Poetry Library, 1996).
36. Quotations from Arthur Friedman (ed.), *Collected Works of Oliver Goldsmith*, vol. 4 (Oxford: The Clarendon Press, 1966).
37. It was once thought that Goldsmith was in an autobiographical vein writing of his own youth in Lissoy, Ireland, but the consensus now is that he is speaking more generally of the process occurring in England where he lived from 1761. See *The Poems of Thomas Gray, William Collins, Oliver Goldsmith*, ed. Roger Lonsdale (London: Longmans, 1969), 670, giving the argument for Lissoy.
38. W. G. Hoskins, *English Landscapes* (London: British Broadcasting Corporation, 1973), 78. The book is a condensation of *The Making of the English Landscape* (London, 1955).
39. Quoted in Hoskins, 78.
40. 'Goldmsmith's "Pensive Plain": Re-viewing *The Deserted Village*', in Thomas Woodman (ed.), *Early Romantics: Perspectives in British Poetry from Pope to Wordsworth* (Basingstoke: Macmillan, 1998), 93–116.
41. Raymond Wiliams, *The Country and the City* (London: Chatto and Windus, 1975), 97.
42. John Barrell, *The Dark Side of the Landscape* (Cambridge: Cambridge University Press, 1980), 77.
43. For an excellent account of the general condition of the rural poor during enclosure, as represented in poetry, see John Goodridge, *Rural Life in Eighteenth Century English Poetry* (Cambridge: Cambridge University Press, 1996).
44. *The Vicar of Wakefield*, quoted from Friedman, *Collected Works of Oliver Goldsmith*, vol. 4, 102.
45. See James H. Lehmann, '*The Vicar of Wakefield*: Goldsmith's Sublime, Oriental Job', *English Literary History*, 46 (1979), 97–135.
46. Benedict in her *Framing Feelings* systematically deals with the 'conflicting ideals' of sentimentality and ridicule that run through some sentimental novels, and especially *The Vicar of Wakefield*, see ch. 2, 'Fools of Quality'.
47. Mackenzie has not been kindly treated by literary critics in general, but one relatively sympathetic commentator is Barbara M. Benedict in *Framing Feelings*, ch. 5.

48. John Mullan, *Sentiment and Sociability*: The Language of Feeling in the Eighteenth century (Oxford: Clarendon Press, 1988), 3.
49. It has been argued that Hume's argument is equivocal when examined in detail, though its overall drift is clear: see Philip Mercer, *Sympathy and Ethics: A Study of the Relationship between Sympathy and Morality with Special Reference to Hume's 'Treatise'* (Oxford: Oxford University Press, 1972), 40–3.
50. Quotations from Henry Mackenzie, *The Man of Feeling*, ed. Kenneth C. Slagle (New York: The Norton Library, 1958).
51. John Mullan, 'The Language of Sentiment: Hume, Smith, and Henry Mackenzie', in *The History of Scottish Literature: Volume 2 1660–1800*, ed. Andrew Hook, general ed. Craig Cairns (Aberdeen: Aberdeen University Press, 1987), 286.
52. Chris Jones offers another explanation in arguing that 'Mackenzie's man of feeling is a conservative construction, the picture of one who does not recognise that in this divinely ordered world there are certain inevitable evils', *Radical Sensibility*, 63.
53. Brissenden, *Virtue in Distress*, 81.
54. For a brief survey of a field that has increasingly generated much scholarship, see Jane Spenser, 'Women writers and the eighteenth-century novel', in John Richetti (ed.), *The Cambridge Companion to The Eighteenth-Century Novel* (Cambridge: Cambridge University Press, 1996), 212–35.
55. Nicola J. Watson, *Revolution and the form of the British Novel, 1790–1825: Intercepted Letters, Interrupted Seductions* (Oxford: Clarendon Press, 1994), 3.
56. Ibid., 4. See also James Warner, 'Eighteenth-Century English Reactions to *La Nouvelle Héloise*', *PMLA* (1937), 803–19.
57. Chris Jones, *Radical Sensibility*, 6.
58. Sarah Scott, *The History of Cornelia* (1750; facsimile edn, New York: State University Press of New York, 1974), 148.
59. Margaret Anne Doody, 'George Eliot and the Eighteenth-Century Novel', *Nineteenth-Century Fiction*, 35 (1980), 278.
60. Cheryl Turner, *Living by the Pen: Women Writers in the Eighteenth Century* (London and New York: Routledge, 1992).
61. For a more complex view, see Julia Epstein, *The Iron Pen: Frances Burney and the Politics of Women's Writing* (Madison: University of Wisconsin Press, 1989).
62. *The New Oxford Book of Romantic Period Verse*, ed. Jerome McGann (New York: Oxford University Press, 1993), xx.
63. McGann's anthology and its apparatus seem modest in comparison with *British Women Poets of the Romantic Era*, ed. Paula R. Feldman (Baltimore, MD and London: The Johns Hopkins University Press, 1997) which is extraordinarily thorough and well researched.
64. (Oxford and New York: Clarendon Press, 1996).
65. Quotations taken from the internet, *Literature Online*: http://lion.chadwyck.com/home/home.cgi?source=config2.cfg. Other quotations from Merry taken from original editions in the British Library.
66. For fuller treatment of this subject, see 'Wordsworth and Sensibility', ch. 7 of Chris Jones, *Radical Sensibility*.
67. All quotations are from *Wordsworth: Poetical Works*, ed. Thomas Hutchinson, rev. Ernest de Selincourt (Oxford: Oxford University Press, 1936).
68. *The Complete Works of William Hazlitt*, ed. P. P. Howe after the edition of A. R. Waller and Arnold Glover (21 vols, London: Dent, 1930), I, 1.
69. Ibid., I, 18.

70. Ibid., I, 14.
71. Ibid., I, 49.
72. See R. S. White (ed.), *Hazlitt's Criticism of Shakespeare: A Selection* (Lampeter: The Edwin Mellon Press, 1996), Introduction and *passim*.
73. 'On Good-Nature' in *The Round Table* (1815–17), 101–2.
74. Unfortunately, the well-known book by Christopher Ricks, *Keats and Embarrassment* (Oxford: Oxford University Press, 1976), is a wasted opportunity, since Ricks focuses on the more superficial aspects of the sentimental link. So, I believe, does Marjorie Levinson (without referring to sentimental literature) in *Keats's Life of Allegory: The Origins of a Style* (Oxford: Oxford University Press, 1988).
75. See for example *Letters*, ii.80 where Jesus and Socrates are linked.
76. Ricks, *Keats and Embarrassment*.
77. *Letters*, II, 174.
78. All quotations are taken from *John Keats: The Complete Poems*, ed. John Barnard (second edn, Harmondsworth: Penguin, 1977).
79. 'The Traveller', lines 385–92, 398–9.
80. Unsigned review, *London Magazine* (Baldwin's), Sept. 1820, in *Keats. The Critical Heritage*, ed. G. M. Matthews (London: Routledge and Kegan Paul, 1971), 222.
81. See Janet Todd, *Sensibility*, ch. 8, 'The Attack on Sensibility'.

3 Rights and Wrongs

1. Arthur M. Melzer, *The Natural Goodness of Man: On the System of Rousseau's Thought* (Chicago: University of Chicago Press, 1990), 16.
2. Quotations from Jean-Jacques Rousseau, *A Discourse on Inequality*, transl. Maurice Cranston (London: Penguin Books, 1984).
3. Ibid.
4. Quotations from *The Social Contract*, transl. and ed. Maurice Cranston (Harmondsworth: Penguin Books, 1968), 64.
5. Jean-Jacques Rousseau, *Emile* transl. Barbara Foxley (London: Dent, 1911), 183.
6. Thomas Paine, *Rights of Man*, ed. Henry Collins (Harmondsworth: Penguin Books, 1969), 116. A useful collection of Paine's writings is *Thomas Paine: Political Writings*, ed. Bruce Kuklick (Cambridge: Cambridge University Press, 1989). A recent, excellent biography is by John Keane, *Thomas Paine: A Political Life* (Boston, MA: Little, Brown, 1995).
7. Gregory Claeys, *Thomas Paine: Social and Political Thought* (Boston, MA: Unwin Hyman, 1989), 5.
8. *A Vindication of the Rights of Men* (1790), in *Mary Wollstonecraft: Political Writings*, ed. Janet Todd (London: W. Pickering, 1993).
9. Edmund Burke, *Reflections on the Revolution in France* (1790), ed. Conor Cruise O'Brien (Harmondsworth: Penguin Books, 1968), 98.
10. Thomas Paine, *Rights of Man*, ed. Henry Collins (Harmondsworth: Penguin Books, 1969), 58.
11. Claeys, *Thomas Paine*, 91, quoting from Mordecai Roshwald, 'The concept of human rights', *Philosophy and Phenomenological Research*, 19 (1959), 354–79, 378.
12. See Claeys, *Thomas Paine*, 104ff.
13. See the volume by Maria J. Falco ed., *Feminist Interpretations of Mary Wollstonecraft* (University Park, Pennsylvania: University State University Press, 1996), especially

the contribution by Virginia Sapiro and Penny A. Weiss, 'Jean-Jacques Rousseau and Mary Wollstonecraft', 179–208.

14. Wendy Gunther-Canada argues that 'Wollstonecraft would never have written the celebrated *A Vindication of the Rights of Woman* had she not first authored the little-known *A Vindication of the Rights of Men*': see the chapter, 'Mary Wollstonecraft's "Wild Wish": Confounding Sex in the Discourse on Political Rights', in Falco (ed.), *Feminist Interpretations of Mary Wollstonecraft*, 61–84, 61.

15. Mary Wollstonecraft, *Political Writings*, 7.

16. Gunther-Canada, 'Wollstonecraft's "Wild Wish" ', 63.

17. See Dorothy McBride Stetson, 'Women's Rights and Human Rights: Intersection and Conflict', in Falco (ed.), *Feminist Interpretations of Mary Wollstonecraft*, 165–78.

18. See Virginia Sapiro, 'Wollstonecraft, Feminism, and Democracy: "Being Bastilled" ', in Falco (ed.), *Feminist Interpretations of Mary Wollstonecraft*, 33–46.

19. Quotations from Spence taken from the excellent and now sadly unavailable selection *Pigs' Meat: Selected Writings of Thomas Spence*, ed. with an introductory essay and notes by G. I. Gallop (Nottingham: Spokesman, 1982).

20. See P. M. Kemp-Ashraf, 'Thomas Spence', in P. M. Kemp-Ashraf and Jack Mitchell (eds), *Essays in Honour of William Gallacher* (Berlin: Allen and Unwin, 1966), 280–4, cited by Gallop, *Pigs' Meat*, 48, fn 3.

21. Gallop, *Pigs' Meat*, 12.

22. For more information on Spence's admittedly somewhat eccentric life and ideas, see M. Beer (ed.), *The Pioneers of Land Reform: Thomas Spence, William Ogilvie, Thomas Paine* (London: G. Bell and Sons, 1920).

23. Olive D. Rudkin, *Thomas Spence and his Connections* (London: Allen and Unwin, 1927), 24.

24. This section quotes from and draws upon William Laurence Brown's *An Essay on the Natural Equality of Men: On the Rights that Result from it, and on the Duties which it Imposes*, with new introduction by William Scott (London and Tokyo: Routledge, Thoemmes Press, 1994), History of British Philosophy, The Scottish Enlightenment, Third Series. Page numbers in the text refer to this volume.

4 Manifestoes into Fictions

1. See Marjorie B. Garber, *Shakespeare's Ghost Writers: Literature as Uncanny Causality* (New York: Methuen, 1987).

2. Edition used is *Caleb Williams*, in *Collected Novels* and *Memoirs of William Godwin*, ed. Pamela Clemit (London: William Pickering, 1992), based on the 1st edn, 1794.

3. The edition used here is William Godwin, *Enquiry Concerning Political Justice*, ed. Isaac Kramnick (Harmondsworth: Penguin Books, 1976), second edn, 1798.

4. Gary Kelly, *The English Jacobin Novel 1780–1805* (Oxford: Clarendon Press, 1976), 181.

5. John Middleton Murry, *Heaven and Earth* (London: Cape, 1938).

6. Pamela Clemit, *The Godwinian Novel: The Rational Fictions of Godwin, Brockden Brown, Mary Shelley* (Oxford: Clarendon Press, 1993), 69.

7. For example, George Woodcock, *Anarchism: A History of Libertarian Ideas and Movements* (Cleveland: Meridian Books, 1962).

8. Quoted in Introductory Note by Pamela Clemit in the edition, vi.

9. To the George, 14 October 1818, in *The Letters of John Keats*, ed. Hyder E. Rollins (2 vols, Cambridge, Mass.: Harvard University Press, 1958), I, 397.

10. (London, 1777), consulted in the British Library.

11. Edition used is Mary Wollstonecraft, *Vindication of the Rights of Woman*, ed. Miriam Kramnick (Harmondsworth: Penguin Books, 1975), 91.
12. See 'Jean-Jacques Rousseau and Mary Wollstonecraft: Restoring the Conversation', as recalled by Virginia Sapiro and Penny A. Weiss, in *Feminist Interpretations of Mary Wollstonecraft*, ed. Maria J. Falco (Pennsylvania: Pennsylvania State University Press, 1996), 179–208.
13. See Vivien Jones (ed.), *Women in the Eighteenth Century: Constructions of Femininity* (London: Routledge, 1990), 218.
14. Thoughts on the Education of Daughters, in Janet Todd and Marilyn Butler (eds), *The Works of Mary Wollstonecraft*, vol. 4 (London: William Pickering, 1989), 7. See also Claire Tomalin, *The Life and Death of Mary Wollstonecraft* (London: Weidenfeld and Nicolson, 1974), 139ff.
15. Syndy McMillen Conger, *Mary Wollstonecraft and the Language of Sensibility* (London and Toronto: Associated University Presses, 1994).
16. George Lakoff and Mark Johnson, *Metaphors We Live By* (Chicago: Chicago University Press, 1980). See also Gilbert Ryle, *The Concept of Mind* (London: Hutchinson, 1949) and Eva Feder Kittay, *Metaphor: Its Cognitive Force and Linguistic Structure* (Oxford: Clarendon Press, 1987).
17. Edition used is *'Mary' and The Wrongs of Woman*, ed. James Kinsley and Gary Kelly (Oxford: Oxford University Press, 1980).
18. Eleanor Ty, *Unsex'd Revolutionaries: Five Women Novelists of the 1790s* (Toronto: University of Toronto Press, 1993), 33.
19. Ty, *Unsex'd Revolutionaries*, 45.
20. Elizabeth Inchbald, *A Simple Story*, ed. Pamela Clemit (London: Penguin Books, 1996), 318.
21. On this topic, see Moira Ferguson, 'Mary Wollstonecraft and the Problematic of Slavery', in *Feminist Interpretations of Mary Wollstonecraft*, ed. Falco, 125–50.
22. E. P. Thompson, *The Making of the English Working Class* (Harmondsworth: Penguin Books, 1968 (first publ. 1963)), 172.
23. Donald H. Reiman (ed.), *Ode to Science and other works by John Thelwall* (New York and London: Garland Publishing, 1978), viii.
24. On some of Thelwall's connections to other writers, see Beverly Allen Sprague, 'William Godwin's Influence upon John Thelwall', *PMLA*, 37 (1922), 662–8 and Burton R. Pollin, 'John Thelwall's Marginalia in a Copy of Coleridge's *Biographia Literaria*', *Bulletin of the New York Public Library*, 74 (1970), 73–94.
25. The edition used here is the facsimile, introduced by Donald H. Reiman (New York and London: Garland Publishing, 1978).
26. 'The Natural and Constitutional Right of Britons', reprinted in *The Politics of English Jacobinism:Writings of John Thelwall*, ed. Gregory Claeys (University Park, Pennsylvania: Pennsylvania University Press, 1995), 6.
27. William Hazlitt, *Works*, ed. P. P. Howe, xii, 264–5.
28. 'The Natural and Constitutional Right of Britons', 53.
29. Quoted by Nick Roe in *The Politics of Nature: Wordsworth and Some Contemporaries* (London: Macmillan, 1992), 143.
30. Thompson, *The Making of the English Working Class*, 175.
31. Claeys has dealt in detail with this subject in the Introduction to Thelwall's *Writings*; see esp. 1ff.
32. Claeys (ed.), *The Politics of English Jacobinism*, 457. Subsequent references from this volume are given as page numbers in the text.
33. 'The Natural and Constitutional Right of Britons', Claeys (ed.), 9.

34. Barrell, *Imagining the King's Death* provides full commentary on constructive treason.
35. See Charles Cestre, *John Thelwall: A Pioneer of Democracy and Social Reform in England During the French Revolution* (London: Swan Sonnenschein, 1906), 122ff. for a description of the occasion.
36. Quoted from copy in Goldsmith's Library, University of London, *The Speech of John Thelwall at the Second Meeting of the London Corresponding Society ...* (1795), 2. Further page numbers appear in the text.
37. Edition used is the facsimile, in 3 vols, ed. Donald H. Reiman (New York and London: Garland Publishing, 1978).
38. Gregory Claeys, *Thomas Paine: Social and Political Thought* (Boston: Unwin Hyman, 1989), 7; my italics.
39. Thomas Holcroft, *The Adventures of Hugh Trevor*, ed. Seamus Deane (London and Oxford: Oxford University Press, 1973), 54.
40. Chris Jones, *Radical Sensibility: Literature and ideas in the 1790s* (London: Routledge, 1993), ch. 5.
41. *Letters*, 1793, quoted in Jones, *Radical Sensibility*, 145.
42. *Letters from France* (8 vols, London, 1790–96), vol. 1, Letter II, anthologised in Anne K. Mellor and Richard E. Matlak (eds), *British Literature 1780–1830* (Fort Worth, Texas: Harcourt Brace College Publishers, 1996), 508–529, 511.
43. Ibid., vol. viii (1796), Letter 1, Mellor and Matlak (eds), 529.
44. Quotations from the facsimile edition, *Poems*, Introduction by Caroline Franklin (London: Routledge/Thoemmes Press, 1996).
45. I place this phrase in inverted commas in deference to Clifford Siskin who entitles his interesting essay on 1798 'The Year of the System', in Richard Cronin (ed.), *1798: the Year of the 'Lyrical Ballads'* (Basingstoke and New York: Macmillan and St Martin's Press, 1998), 9–31.

5 Novels of Natural Rights in the 1790s

1. Thomas Holcroft, Review of Bage's *Man As He Is*, *The Monthly Review*, Ser. 10 (March, 1793), 297, quoted in Gary Kelly, *The English Jacobin Novel 1780–1805* (Oxford and New York: Clarendon Press, 1976), 115.
2. See William Hill Brown, *The Power of Sympathy* (London: Penguin Books, 1996).
3. George Walker, *The Vagabond, a Novel* (3rd edn, London: G. Walker, 1799), I, 152–3. Quoted by M. O. Grenlay in *The Anti-Jacobin: Britsish Conservatism and the French Revolution* (Cambridge: Cambridge University Press, 2001), 57.
4. Kelly, *The English Jacobin Novel*, 58.
5. Elizabeth Inchbald, *Nature and Art*, with an introduction by Caroline Franklin, The Romantics: Women Novelists series (London: Routledge, Thoemmes Press, 1995). This is a facsimile of the second edition (1797) and quotations are taken from it.
6. Edition used is Robert Bage, *Hermsprong or Man As He Is Not*, ed. Peter Faulkner (The World's Classics, Oxford: Oxford University Press, 1985).
7. The references are to Sir James Mackintosh, *Vindiciae Gallicae* (1791), Benjamin Flower, *The French Constitution* (1792) and Thomas Christie, *Letters on the Revolution of France* (1791).
8. See Chris Jones, *Radical Sensibility: Literature and Ideas in the 1790s* (London: Routledge, 1993), 161 and generally ch. 6.
9. (London and New York: St Martin's Press, 1998).
10. Quotations from *The Old Manor House*, ed. Anne Henry Ehrenpreis (London: Oxford University Press, 1969), 487.

11. See Rebecca Morgan, 'The gothic in the novels of Charlotte Smith' (unpublished PhD thesis, Newcastle upon Tyne, 1996).
12. The altered quotation ('hunting' to '*taxing*') comes from *The Ballad of Chevy Chase*.
13. The reference is to David Ramsay, *The History of the American Revolution* (Philadelphia, 1789).
14. Rebecca Morgan, 'The gothic in the novels of Charlotte Smith' (unpublished PhD thesis, Newcastle upon Tyne, 1996).
15. Ibid.
16. Charlotte Smith, *Desmond*, eds, Antje Blank and Janet Todd (London: Pickering & Chatto, 1997), 7.
17. This is the main theme of my book, *Natural Law in English Renaissance Literature* (Cambridge: Cambridge University Press, 1996).
18. Fletcher, *Charlotte Smith*: A Critical Biography (London and New York: St Martin's Press, 1998), 150.
19. Charlotte Smith, *The Young Philosopher* (facsimile, 4 vols, New York: Garland, 1974).
20. Morgan, 'The gothic in the novels of Charlotte Smith'.
21. See Fletcher, *Charlotte Smith*, 270ff.
22. Ibid., 280.
23. Sibella cannot be very common as a name, and may have been borrowed as Sybylla by Miles Franklin in *My Brilliant Career* (1901), an early Australian novel about a woman's right to be a writer, which ironically could only have had a chance of publication if it carried a masculine name. There may be a more pervasive debt to Fenwick's novel, published just six years earlier.
24. Eliza Fenwick, *Secresy; or, the Ruin on the Rock*, ed. Isobel Grundy (Peterborough, Ontario: Broadview Press, 1994), 43.
25. See Isobel Grundy's 'Introduction' to *Secresy*, 25–9.
26. Facsimile ed. With an introduction by Gina Lurie (New York: Garland, 1974).
27. Edition quoted is the facsimile, with a new introduction by Caroline Franklin (London: Routledge/Thoemmes Press, 1995).
28. Nicola J. Watson, *Revolution and the Form of the British Novel 1790 1825: Intercepted Letters, Interrupted Seductions* (Oxford: Clarendon Press, 1994), 49–50.
29. Terence Allan Hoagwood, *Politics, Philosophy, and the Production of Romantic Texts* (DeKalb, IL: Northern Illinois University Press, 1996), 123.

6 Slavery as Fact and Metaphor: William Blake and Jean Paul Marat

1. See Moira Ferguson, 'Mary Wollstonecraft and the Problematic of Slavery' in Maria J. Falco (ed.), *Feminist Interpretations of Mary Wollstonecraft* (University Park, Pennsylvania: Pennsylvania State University Press, 1996), 125–50.
2. Markman Ellis, *The Politics of Sensibility: Race, Gender and Commerce in the Sentimental Novel* (Cambridge: Cambridge University Press, 1996), 50.
3. Quoted by Jon Mee, *Dangerous Enthusiasm: William Blake and the Culture of Radicalism in the 1790s* (Oxford: Clarendon Press, 1992), 156.
4. See for example: James Walvin, *England, Slaves and Freedom, 1776–1838* (London: Macmillan, 1986), and James Walvin, *Black Ivory: A History of British Slavery* (London: HarperCollins, 1992), David Brion Davis, *The Problem of Slavery in the Age of Revolution 1770–1823* (Ithaca and London: Cornell University Press, 1975), David Turley, *The Culture of English Antislavery 1780–1860* (London and

New York: Routledge, 1991), Eric Williams, *Capitalism and Slavery* (London: Deutsch, 1964), Barbara L. Solow and Stanley L. Engerman, *British Capitalism and Caribbean Slavery: The Legacy of Eric Williams* (Cambridge: Cambridge University Press, 1987), Peter Hulme, *Colonial Encounters: Europe and the Native Caribbean, 1492–1797* (London and New York: Methuen, 1986), Wylie Sypher *Guinea's Captive Kings: British Anti-slavery Literature of the XVIIIth Century* (New York: Octagon Books, 1969), Kari J. Winter, *Subjects of Slavery: Agents of Change: Women and Power in Gothic Novels and Slave Narratives 1790–1865* (Athens and London: University of Georgia Press, 1992).

5. Ellis, *The Politics of Sensibility*, 51: Ellis cites other writers who have demonstrated this point, for example, Robin Blackburn (1988), Roger Anstey (1975), Christine Bolt and Seymour Drescher (eds) (1980) and James Walvin (1982).

6. Gretchen Gerzina, *Black England: Life before Emancipation* (London: John Murray, 1995), 196–7.

7. Ibid., 201.

8. Robin Furneaux, *William Wilberforce* (London: Hamish Hamilton, 1974), 64.

9. In this context, see Davis, *The Problem of Slavery in the Age of Revolution*, especially ch. 8, 'The Preservation of English Liberty I'.

10. (London: Andre Deutsch, 1964).

11. For further information, see Roger Anstey and P. E. Hair, *Liverpool, the African Slave Trade and Abolition: Essays to Illustrate Current Knowledge* (Liverpool: Western Printing Services, 1976), Seymour Drescher and Stanley L. Engerman, *A Historical Guide to World Slavery* (Oxford: Oxford University Press 1998), J. R. Oldfield, *Popular Politics and British Anti-Slavery: The Mobilisation of Public Opinion Against the Slave Trade, 1787–1807* (London: Frank Cass Publishers, 1998).

12. Quoted by Richardson, xv, from Roger Anstey, *The Atlantic Slave Trade and British Abolition 1760–1810* (London: Macmillan, 1975), 266.

13. Clare Midgley, *Women Against Slavery: The British Campaigns 1780–1870* (London: Routledge, 1992), 29–30. See also Moira Ferguson, 'Oronooko: Birth of a Pardigm', in *Subject to Others: British Women Writers and Colonial Slavery, 1670–1834* (London: Routledge, 1992), ch. 2.

14. Unless otherwise specified, quotations from writers come either from original editions in the British Library or facsimiles of originals reproduced in the invaluable set of volumes edited by Peter J. Kitson and Debbie Lee, *Slavery, Abolition and Emancipation: Writings in the British Romantic Period* (8 vols, London: Pickering and Chatto, 1999), especially vol. 4 'Verse' ed. Alan Richardson, and vol. 6 'Fiction' ed. Srinivas Aravamudan.

15. See Richard Holmes, *Coleridge: Early Visions* (London: Penguin Books, 1989), 43.

16. See the books by Ferguson, *Subject to Others* and Midgley, *Women Against Slavery*.

17. James Montgomery, James Grahame, and E. Benger eds, *Poems on the Abolition of the Slave Trade* (1809), facsimile edition. With an introduction by Donald H. Reimann (New York: Garland Publishers, 1978).

18. Ellis, *The Politics of Sensibility*, 55.

19. (2 vols, Dublin P. Byrne, 1791).

20. (London: G. G. J & J. Robinsons [sic], J. Dennis, 1792).

21. The novel is mentioned in Aravamuden's introduction, but is not reproduced among the documents.

22. Quoted by Aravamuden (ed.), 97.

23. For some analysis see Ferguson, *Subject to Others*, 194–6.

24. For extensive documentation, see Albert Boime, *The Art of Exclusion: Representing Blacks in the Nineteenth Century* (London: Thames and Hudson, 1990), Hugh

Honour, *The Image of the Black in Western Art* (4 vols, Cambridge, Mass.: Harvard University Press, 1989), David Dabydeen, *Hogarth's Blacks: Images of Blacks in Eighteenth-Century English Art* (Manchester: Manchester University Press, 1987). I have benefited from reading Natalie McCreedy, 'Poetry, Print and Persecution: Images of Slavery in Britain' (unpublished BA honours dissertation, University of Newcastle upon Tyne, 2000) and I am grateful to Dr Stephanie Brown for drawing this work to my attention.

25. J. R. Oldfield, *Popular Politics and British Anti-slavery: The Mobilisation of Public Opinion against the Slave Trade, 1787–1807* (London: Frank Cass Publishers, 1998), 159–60.
26. See McCreedy, 'Poetry, Print and Persecution', 18–20. The question of Wilberforce's commitment is disputed, as Oldfield suggests his attendance at meetings was quite considerable – fn 4, p. 180.
27. Joan Baum, *Mind-Forg'd Manacles: Slavery and the English Romantic Poets* (London: Archon Books, 1994), 57.
28. Furneaux, *William Wilberforce*, 61.
29. (Princeton, New Jersey: Princeton University Press, second edn, 1969, third edn, 1977).
30. (Oxford: Clarendon Press, 1992).
31. (Cambridge: Cambridge University Press, 1993).
32. (Lewisburg and London: Bucknell University Press, 1999).
33. Mee *Dangerous Enthusiasm: William Blake and the Culture of Radicalism in the 1790s* (Oxford: Oxford University Press, 1994).
34. On Stedman's experiences, see Mary Louise Pratt, *Imperial Eyes: Travel Writing and Transculturation* (London and New York: Routledge, 1992), ch. 5, 'Eros and Abolition', 86ff.
35. Since this book is a study in the history of ideas and literature, I do not include consideration of the fiendishly difficult variants in Blake's individual copies of his books, although it does become relevant for one detail. Here, I quote from the facsimile edited by David Worrall, *The Urizen Books: The First Book of Urizen, The Book of Ahania, The Book of Los* (London: The William Blake Trust/The Tate Gallery, 1995).
36. Worrall notes that Blake seems to be drawing on Erasmus Darwin's explanation for the beginning of the universe in a 'primal big bang' (130).
37. Here is where the variant texts become relevant: this phrase is from an additional plate, reproduced in Worrall's book although not included in his copy text.
38. Mee, *Dangerous Enthusiasm*, 84.
39. Hobson, *The Chained Boy*, 53.
40. Erdman, *Blake: Prophet Against Empire*.
41. Ibid., 157.
42. Ibid., 228 and ff.
43. Texts quoted from the transcriptions in the facsimile, *Songs of Innocence and of Experience*, ed. Sir Geoffrey Keynes (Oxford: Trainon Press, 1967).
44. My readings of the *Songs* have been influenced, though not directly on this subject, by Heather Glen's *Vision and Disenchantment: Blake's Songs and Wordsworth's Lyrical Ballads* (Cambridge: Cambridge University Press, 1983).
45. Kitson and Lee (eds), *Slavery, Abolition and Emancipation*, v. 4, xiv.
46. Marilyn Butler, *Romantics, Rebels and Reactionaries: English Literature and its Background 1760–1830* (Oxford: Oxford University Press, 1981), 45.
47. Robert N. Essick, 'William Blake, Thomas Paine, and Biblical Revolution', *Studies in Romanticism*, 30 (Summer 1991), 189–212.
48. Ibid., 210.

49. See Carol Louise Hall, *Blake and Fuseli: A Study in the Transmission of Ideas* (New York and London: Garland Publising, 1985).
50. Henry Fuseli, *Remarks on the Writing and Conduct of J. J. Rousseau* (1767), facsimile, ed. Karl S. Guthke (Los Angeles: University of California, 1960), 21.
51. For convenience the text has been quoted from the full reproduction on the internet at http://www.felix2.f2s.com///english/jpmie.html checked against the original copy in the Robert White Collection in the Robinson Library, University of Newcastle upon Tyne. I am grateful to the library for allowing me to work on this material, just as I am grateful to M. J. Pons, President of the Association Jean-Paul Marat, for posting the immaculate text on the internet.
52. Marat's footnote to this reads:

> * It may appear strange, says a celebrated historian, that the progress of the arts and sciences, which among the Greeks and Romans increased every day the number of slaves, became in late times a general source of liberty; and, to clear this phenomenon, he has recourse to a series of vain arguments; whilst a simple distinction is sufficient.
>
> When the rights of mankind are not the subject of our enquiries, study, by fixing the mind on foreign objects, necessarily causes it to lose sight of liberty: but when the sanctuary of learning is opened to a barbarous people, by a natural progression, they must necessarily turn their thoughts to the relations nature and society have established among men. The Romans were acquainted only with matters of war or state, and in order to divert them therefrom, Augustus brought the fine arts into esteem among them. Under feudal government, the people were extremely ignorant; they lost in their fetters even all sense of liberty: but when they had begun to cultivate the sciences, and turn their minds to meditation, they at last reflected their thoughts on themselves, and were made conscious of their rights. (Ch. vii)

7   Rights of Children and Animals

1. For the broader social history of the humanitarian concern for nature and animals, see Keith Thomas, *Man and the natural world: changing attitudes in England 1500–1800* (London: Allen Lane, 1983).
2. Quoted (without reference) by Peter Coveney in *Poor Monkey: The Child in Literature* (London: Rockcliff, 1957), 5.
3. Reprinted in *The Educational Writings of John Locke*, ed. James L. Axtell (Cambridge: Cambridge University Press, 1968).
4. David Archard, *Children: Rights and Childhood* (London and New York: Routledge, 1993), 1. The chapter is called, significantly, 'John Locke's Children'.
5. *Treatises*, I.i.89.
6. 'Centuries of Meditations': I.1 in H. M. Margolioath (ed.), *Thomas Traherene Centuries, Poems and Thanks givings* (London: Oxford at the Clarendon Press), 1965, i.3.
7. 'The *Education* in Context', Axtell (ed.), 51.
8. Sarah Fielding, *The Governess: or, Little Female Academy*, facsimile edition, ed. Jill E. Grey (Oxford: Oxford University Press, 1968).
9. (London, 1777).

10. See F. J. Harvey Darton, *Children's Books in England* (Cambridge: Cambridge University Press, second edn, 1958).
11. (Knoxville: University of Tennessee Press, 1981).
12. See Christine Kenyon-Jones, *Kindred Brutes: Animals in Romantic-Period Writing* (Aldershot: Ashgate, 2001), 64.
13. *Émile*, transl. Barbara Foxley (London, 1911), re-ed. Grace Roosevelt, online text: http://projects.ilt.columbia.edu/pedagogies/rousseau/em_eng_bk1.html.
14. The phrase is used by Leslie F. Claydon, *Rousseau on Education* (London: Collier-Macmillan, 1969), 92.
15. *Émile*, transl. Foxley, 349.
16. Facsimile edn with Introduction by Gina Luria (New York: Garland Publishing, 1974).
17. *British Women Poets of the Romantic Era*, ed. Paula R. Feldman (Baltimore, MD and London: The Johns Hopkins University Press, 1997), 470.
18. *Strictures*, I, 57.
19. Lawrence Stone, *The Family, Sex and Marriage in England 1500–1800* (London: Weidenfeld & Nicolson, rev. edn, 1979), 267–73, See also Philippe Ariès, *L'Enfant et la vie familiale sous l'Ancien Régime* (Paris, 1960).
20. See Elisabeth Badinter, Mother Love: *Motherhood in Modern History* (New York: Macmillan, transl. 1981), especially 'Introduction'.
21. Robert Rosenblum in *The Romantic Child: From Runge to Sendak* (London: Thames and Hudson, 1988).
22. Ibid., 21.
23. Sigmund Freud, *Jokes and their Relation to the Unconscious*, transl. James Strachey (1905; London: Routledge and Kegan Paul, 1960), 302.
24. Transl. Paul Harrison at website http://members.aol.com/Heraklit1/rousseau.htm.
25. Quotations from *William Wordsworth: Selected Poetry*, ed. Mark van Doren (New York: Random House, 1950).
26. Coveney, *Poor Monkey*, 41.
27. *The Early Letters of William and Dorothy Wordsworth (1787–1805)*, ed. E. de Selincourt (Oxford: Clarendon Press, 1935), 296–7.
28. *The Poetical Works of William Wordsworth*, eds. E. de Selincourt and H. Darbishire (5 vols, Oxford: Oxford University Press, 1940–49), ii, 504–6.
29. See Jonathan Bate, *Romantic Ecology: Wordsworth and the Environmental Tradition* (London and New York: Routledge, 1991).
30. Reprinted in G. I. Gallop, *Pigs' Meat: Selected Writings of Thomas Spence* (Nottingham: Spokesman, 1982), 111–26.
31. J. L. Hammond and Barbara Hammond, *Lord Shaftesbury* (London: Constable, 1923, fourth edn, 1936), 73.
32. Ibid., 200–18.
33. Ivy Pinchbeck and Margaret Hewitt, *Children in English Society* (3 vols, London: Routledge and Kegan Paul, 1973), ii, 356.
34. See M. Dorothy George, *London Life in the Eighteenth Century* (Harmondsworth: Penguin Books, 1966), 242.
35. See Heather Glen, *Vision and Disenchantment: Blake's 'Songs' and Wordsworth's 'Lyrical Ballads'* (Cambridge: Cambridge University Press, 1981), 99–101.
36. Donald H. Reiman 'Introduction', in James Grahame and E. Benger (eds), *Poems on the Abolition of the Slave Trade* (New York and London: Garland Publishing, 1978), v; repeated in the identical Introduction to *The Chimney-Sweeper's Friend* ... below, v.

37. Facsimile edn, ed. Donald H. Reiman (New York and London: Garland Publishing, 1978).
38. *Bringing them home: report of the National Inquiry into the Separation of Aboriginal and Torres Strait Islander Children from their Families* [Commissioner: Ronald Wilson] (Sydney: Human Rights and Equal Opportunity Commission, 1997).
39. Glen, *Vision and Disenchantment*, 9.
40. Quotations are from *The Complete Poetry and Prose of William Blake*, ed. David V. Erdman, Electronic Edition, eds, Morris Eaves, Robert Essick, Joseph Viscomi (Charlottesville, Virginia: Institute for Advanced Technology in the Humanities, 2001).
41. Coveney, *Poor Monkey*, 26.
42. On Blake's thinking as it relates to companionate marriage, see generally Stephen Cox, *Love and Logic: The Evolution of Blake's Thought* (Ann Arbor: University of Michigan Press, 1992), 59–61.
43. Coveney, *Poor Monkey*, quotes these words of Tatham on p. 27.
44. Roderick Frazier Nash, *The Rights of Nature: A History of Environmental Ethics* (Leichhardt, NSW: Primavera Press/The Wilderness Society, 1990), 17, which in turn acknowledges Michael J. Cohen, *Prejudice against Nature: A Guidebook for the Liberation of Self and Planet* (Freeport, Maine: Cobblesmith, 1983).
45. My thanks to Brian Bosworth for his help on this point.
46. Nash, *The Rights of Nature*, 17–18.
47. Quoted in Nash, *The Rights of Nature*, 18.
48. For a more thorough and specialist account of the history of animal rights, see Steven M. Wise, *Rattling the Cage: Toward Legal Rights for Animals* (Cambridge, Mass.: Perseus Books, 2000).
49. Kenyon-Jones, *Kindred Brutes*.
50. Ibid., 40.
51. Quoted in Nash, *The Rights of Nature*, 23.
52. Timothy Morton, *Shelley and the Revolution in Taste* (Cambridge: Cambridge University Press, 1994), 15.
53. (Chicago: University of Chicago Press, 1998).
54. *Emma Corbett*, I, vii.
55. *Gleanings through Wales, Holland and Westphalia, with Views of Peace and War at Home and Abroad* (3 vols, 1795).
56. Morton, *Shelley and the Revolution in Taste*, esp. 94–9.
57. Shelley, *Queen Mab*, viii.
58. Erasmus Darwin, *The Golden Age* and *the Temple of Nature or, The Origin of Society*, ed. Donald H. Reiman (New York and London: Garland Publishing, 1978), 'Introduction', x.
59. Facsimile by Johnson Reprint Corporation (Wakefield, 1968).
60. *The Temple of Nature*, Canto II, 296–7.
61. Published with *The Golden Age* and *the Temple of Nature or, The Origin of Society*, ed. Reiman.
62. Official statement by UNICEF online at http://www.unicef.org/crc/crc.htm.

Bibliography

Anstey, Roger, *The Atlantic Slave Trade and British Abolition 1760–1810* (London: Macmillan, 1975).

Anstey, Roger and P. E. Hair, *Liverpool, the African Slave Trade and Abolition: Essays to illustrate current knowledge* (Liverpool: Western Printing Services, 1976).

Archard, David, *Children: Rights and Childhood* (London and New York: Routledge, 1993).

Badinter, Elisabeth, *Mother Love: Motherhood in Modern History* (New york: Macmillan, transl. 1981), especially 'Introduction'.

Bage, Robert, *Hermsprong, or Man As He Is Not*, ed. Peter Faulkner (The World's Classics, Oxford: Oxford University Press, 1985).

Baine, Rodney M., *Thomas Holcroft and the Revolutionary Novel*, University of Georgia Monographs No. 13 (Athens, GA: University of Georgia Press, 1965).

Bamberg, Stanley, 'A Footnote to the Political Theory of John Adams' *Vindiciae contra tryannos'*, *Premise*, 3: 7 (August 1996), 10.

Baring Pemberton, W., *William Cobbett* (Harmondsworth: Penguin Books, 1949).

Barker, Anthony J., *Slavery and Antislavery in Mauritius, 1810–33: The Conflict between Economic Expansion and Humanitarian Reform under British Rule* (London and New York: Macmillan and St Martin's Press, 1996).

Barker-Benfield, G. J., *The Culture of Sensibility: Sex and Society in Eighteenth-Century Britain* (Chicago and London: University of Chicago Press, 1992).

Barrell, John, *The Dark Side of the Landscape* (Cambridge: Cambridge University Press, 1980).

Barrell, John, *Imagining the King's Death: Figurative Treason, Fantasies of Regicide 1793–1796* (Oxford: Oxford University Press, 2000).

Bate, Jonathan, *Shakespearean Constitutions: Politics, Theatre, Criticism 1730–1830* (Oxford: Clarendon Press, 1989).

Bate, Jonathan, *Romantic Ecology: Wordsworth and the Environmental Tradition* (London and New York: Routledge, 1991).

Baum, Joan, *Mind-Forg'd Manacles: Slavery and the English Romantic Poets* (London: Archon Books, 1994).

Beer, M. (ed.), *The Pioneers of Land Reform: Thomas Spence, William Ogilvie, Thomas Paine* (London: G. Bell and Sons, 1920).

Bemetzrieder, Dr, *A New Code for Gentlemen; in which are Considered God and Man; Man's Natural Rights and Social Duties …* (London: J. Barfield, 1803).

Benedict, Barbara M., *Framing Feeling: Sentiment and Style in English Prose Fiction* (New York: AMS Press, 1994).

Blake, William, *Songs of Innocence and of Experience*, ed. Sir Geoffrey Keynes (Oxford: Trainon Press, 1967).

Blake, William, *Blake's 'America: A Prophecy' and 'Europe: A Prophecy'* (New York: Dover Publications, 1983).

Blake, William, *The Urizen Books: The First Book of Urizen, The Book of Ahania, The Book of Los*, ed. David Worrall (London: The William Blake Trust/The Tate Gallery, 1995).

Blake, William, *The Complete Poetry and Prose of William Blake*, ed. David V. Erdman, Electronic Edition, eds Morris Eaves, Robert Essick, Joseph Viscomi (Charlottesville, Virginia: Institute for Advanced Technology in the Humanities, 2001).

Bloch, Ernst, *Natural Law and Human Dignity*, transl. Dennis J. Schmidt (Cambridge, Mass. and London: The MIT Press, 1987).

Blunden, Edmund, *Keats's Publisher* (London: Jonathan Cape, 1936).

Bobbio, Norberto, *Thomas Hobbes and the Natural Law Tradition*, transl. Daniela Gobetti (Chicago and London: University of Chicago Press, 1993; first pub. in Italian, 1989).

Boime, Albert, *The Art of Exclusion: Representing Blacks in the Nineteenth Century* (London: Thames and Hudson,1990).

Bracken, James K. and Joel Silver (eds), *The British Literary Book Trade, 1700–1820, Dictionary of Literary Biography, Volume 154* (Detroit, Washington, DC, and London: Gale Research Incorporated, 1995).

Bradshaw, Brendon, 'Transalpine Humanism', in J. H. Burns (ed.), *The Cambridge History of Political Thought 1450–1700* (Cambridge: Cambridge University Press, 1991), 106.

Braithwaite, Helen, *Romanticism, Publishing and Dissent: Joseph Johnson and the Cause of Liberty* (Basingstoke and New York: Palgrave Macmillan, 2003).

Brissenden, R. F., *Virtue in Distress: Studies in the Novel of Sentiment from Richardson to Sade* (London: Macmilan, 1974).

Brown, Philip Anthony, *The French Revolution in English History* (London: Frank Cass, 1965).

Brown, William Hill, *The Power of Sympathy* (London: Penguin Books, 1996).

Brown, William Laurence, *An Essay on the Natural Equality of Men: On the Rights that Result from it, and on the Duties which it Imposes*, with new introduction by William Scott (London and Tokyo: Routledge/Thoemmes Press, 1994), History of British Philosophy, The Scottish Enlightenment, Third Series.

Burke, Edmund, *Reflections on the Revolution in France*, ed. Conor Cruise O'Brien (Harmondsworth: Penguin Books, 1968).

Butler, Marilyn, *Romantics, Rebels and Reactionaries: English Literature and its Background 1760–1830* (Oxford: Oxford University Press, 1981).

Butler, Marilyn (ed.), *Burke, Paine, Godwin, and the Revolution Controversy* (Cambridge: Cambridge University Press, 1984).

Campbell, T. D., *Adam Smith's Science of Morals* (London: George Allen & Unwin, 1971).

Campbell, Tom D., *Law and Enlightenment in Britain* (Aberdeen: Aberdeen University Press, 1971).

Campbell, Tom, *Seven Theories of Human Society* (Oxford: Clarendon Press, 1981).

Cestre, Charles, *John Thelwall: A Pioneer of Democracy and Social Reform in England during the French Revolution* (London: Swan Sonnenschein, 1906).

Chard, Leslie, 'Joseph Johnson: Father of the Book Trade', *Bulletin of the New York Public Library*, 78 (1975), 51–82.

Chard, Leslie, 'Bookseller to Publisher: Joseph Johnson and the English Book Trade, 1760–1810', *Library*, fifth series, 32 (1977), 138–54.

Chilcott, Tim, *A Publisher and His Circle, the Life and Work of John Taylor, Keats's Publisher* (London: Routledge and Kegan Paul, 1972).

Cicero, *De Legibus*, transl. C. W. Keyes (Loeb Classical Library), *Cicero*, vol. 28 (Cambridge, Mass. and London, 1977).

Claeys, Gregory, *Thomas Paine: Social and Political Thought* (Boston, MA: Unwin Hyman, 1989).

Claydon, Leslie F., *Rousseau on Education* (London: Collier-Macmillan, 1969).

Cleary, Thomas R., *Henry Fielding: Political Writer* (Waterloo, Ontario: Wilfred Laurier University Press, 1984).

Clemit, Pamela, *The Godwinian Novel: The Rational Fictions of Godwin, Brockden Brown, Mary Shelley* (Oxford: Clarendon Press, 1993).

Cohen, Michael J., *Prejudice against Nature: A Guidebook for the Liberation of Self and Planet* (Freeport, Maine: Cobblesmith, 1983).

Cole, G. D. H., and Raymond Postgate, *The Common People: 1746–1946* (London: Methuen & Co, fourth edn, 1949).

Cone, Carl B., *Burke and the Nature of Politics in the Age of the French Revolution* (Lexington, KY: University of Kentucky Press, 1964).

Cone, Carl B., *Torchbearer of Freedom: The Influence of Richard Price on Eighteenth Century Thought* (Lexington, KY: University of Kentucky Press, 1952).

Conger, Syndy McMillen, *Mary Wollstonecraft and the Language of Sensibility* (London and Toronto: Associated University Presses, 1994).

Coveney, Peter, *Poor Monkey: The Child in Literature* (London: Rockcliff, 1957).

Cover, Robert M., *Justice Accused: Antislavery and the Judicial Process* (New Haven, CT and London: Yale University Press, 1975).

Cox, Stephen, *Love and Logic: The Evolution of Blake's Thought* (Ann Arbor: University of Michigan Press, 1992).

Craven, William G., *Giovanni Pico della Mirandola* (Geneva: Librairie Droz, 1981).

Cronin, Richard (ed.), *1798: The Year of the 'Lyrical Ballads'* (Basingstoke and New York: Macmillan and St Martin's Press, 1998).

Dabydeen, David, *Hogarth's Blacks: Images of Blacks in Eighteenth-Century English Art* (Manchester: Manchester University Press, 1987).

Darwin, Erasmus, *A Plan for the Conduct of Female Education in Boarding Schools* (1797), facsimile edn (Wakefield: Johnson Reprint Corporation, 1968).

Darwin, Erasmus, *The Golden Age* and *the Temple of Nature* or, *The Origin of Society*, ed. Donald H. Reiman (New York and London: Garland Publishing, 1978).

Davis, David Brion, *The Problem of Slavery in the Age of Revolution 1770–1823* (Ithaca and London: Cornell University Press, 1975).

d'Entrèves, A. P., *Natural Law: An Historical Survey* (London: Hutchinson, 1951).

Derry, John W., *Reaction and Reform: England in the Early Nineteenth Century* (London: Blandford Press, 1963).

Doody, Margaret Anne, 'George Eliot and the Eighteenth-Century Novel', *Nineteenth-Century Fiction*, 35 (1980), 278.

Drescher, Seymour and Stanley L. Engerman, *A Historical Guide to World Slavery* (Oxford: Oxford University Press, 1998).

Duffy, Edward, *Rousseau in England: The Context for Shelley's Critique of the Enlightenment* (Berkeley, CA: University of California Press, 1979).

Durey, Michael, *Transatlantic Radicals and the Early American Republic* (Lawrence, Kansas: University Press of Kansas, 1997).

Ellis, Markman, *The Politics of Sensibility: Race, Gender and Commerce in the Sentimental Novel* (Cambridge: Cambridge University Press, 1996).

Epstein, James A., *Radical Expression: Political Language, Ritual, and Symbol in England, 1790–1850* (Oxford and New York: Oxford University Press, 1994).

Epstein, Julia, *The Iron Pen: Frances Burney and the Politics of Women's Writing* (Madison: University of Wisconsin Press, 1989).

Erametsa, Erik, 'A study of the word "sentimental" and of other linguistic characteristics of eighteenth century sentimentalism in England' (PhD thesis, Helsinki, 1951).

Erdman, David V., *Blake: Prophet Against Empire: A Poet's History of His Own Time* (Princeton, NJ: Princeton University Press, second edn, 1969; third edn, 1977).

Essick, Robert N., 'William Blake, Thomas Paine, and Biblical Revolution', *Studies in Romanticism*, 30 (Summer 1991), 189–212.

Ewin, R. E., *Virtues and Rights: The Moral Philosophy of Thomas Hobbes* (Boulder, CO: Westview Press, 1991).

Feldman, Paula R. (ed.), *British Women Poets of the Romantic Era: An Anthology* (Baltimore and London: The Johns Hopkins University Press, 1997).

Fenwick, Eliza, *Secresy; or, the Ruin on the Rock*, ed. Isobel Grundy (Peterborough, Ontario: Broadview Press, 1994).

Ferguson, Moira, *Subject to Others: British Women Writers and Colonial Slavery, 1670–1834* (London: Routledge, 1992).

Ferguson, Moira, 'Mary Wollstonecraft and the Problematic of Slavery', in Maria J. Falco (ed.), *Feminist Interpretations of Mary Wollstonecraft* (University Park, Pennsylvania: Pennsylvania State University Press, 1996), 125–50.

Fielding, Sarah, *The Governess: or, Little Female Academy*, facsimile edition, ed. Jill E. Grey (Oxford: Oxford University Press, 1968).

Finnis, John, *Natural Law and Natural Rights* (Oxford: Clarendon Press, 1980).

Fletcher, Loraine, *Charlotte Smith: A Critical Biography* (London and New York: St Martin's Press, 1998).

Ford, Pina, 'Natural Law Context in Thomas More's "Utopia"' (unpublished PhD thesis, University of Western Australia, 2001).

Forrester, John, 'Psychoanalysis and the History of the Passions: The Strange Destiny of Envy', in John O'Neill (ed.), *Freud and the Passions* (University Park, Pennsylvania: Pennsylvania State University Press, 1996), 127–50.

Foster, Hannah Webster, *The Coquette* (London: Penguin Books, 1996).

Freud, Sigmund, *Jokes and their Relation to the Unconscious*, transl. James Strachey (1905; London: Routledge and Kegan Paul, 1960).

Friedman, Geraldine, *The Insistence of History: Revolution in Burke, Wordsworth, Keats, and Baudelaire* (Stanford, CA: Stanford University Press, 1996).

Furneaux, Robin, *William Wilberforce* (London: Hamish Hamilton, 1974).

Fuseli, Henry, *Remarks on the Writing and Conduct of J. J. Rousseau* (1767), facsimile, ed. Karl S. Guthke (Los Angeles: University of California, 1960).

Gallop, Geoffrey, 'Radical Ideology in Late Eighteenth-Century Britain', paper presented at the Australian Political Studies Association Annual Conference, Perth, Western Australia, August 1982.

Gallop, Geoffrey, 'Ideology and the English Jacobins: The Case of John Thelwall', *Enlightenment and Dissent*, 5 (1986), 3–20.

Garber, Marjorie B., *Shakespeare's Ghost Writers: Literature as Uncanny Causality* (New York: Methuen, 1987).

Gates, Barbara T., *Kindred Nature: Victorian and Edwardian Women Embrace the Living World* (Chicago: University of Chicago Press, 1998).

George, M. Dorothy, *London Life in the Eighteenth Century* (Harmondsworth: Penguin Books, 1966).

Gerzina, Gretchen, *Black England: Life before Emancipation* (London: John Murray, 1995).

Glausser, Wayne, *Locke and Blake: A Conversation across the Eighteenth Century* (Gainesville, Florida: University Press of Florida, 1998).

Glen, Heather, *Vision and Disenchantment: Blake's 'Songs' and Wordsworth's 'Lyrical Ballads'* (Cambridge: Cambridge University Press, 1983).

Godwin, William, *Enquiry Concerning Political Justice*, ed. Isaac Kramnick (Harmondsworth: Penguin Books, 1976).

Godwin, William, *Caleb Williams*, in *Collected Novels and Memoirs of William Godwin*, ed. Pamela Clemit (London: William Pickering, 1992).

Goldsmith, Oliver, *Collected Works of Oliver Goldsmith*, ed. Arthur Friedman, vol. 4 (Oxford: The Clarendon Press, 1966).

Goodridge, John, *Rural Life in Eighteenth-Century English Poetry* (Cambridge: Cambridge University Press, 1996).

Goodwin, A., 'The political genesis of Edmund Burke's *Reflections on The Revolution in France*' (Manchester: The John Rylands Library, 1968).

Gray, Thomas, *The Poems of Thomas Gray, William Collins, Oliver Goldsmith*, ed. Roger Lonsdale (London: Longmans, 1969).

Gray, Thomas, *Thomas Gray*, selected and ed. Robert L. Mack (London: Everyman Poetry Library, 1996).

Grenby, M. O., *The Anti-Jacobin: British Conversatism and the French Revolution* (Cambridge: Cambridge University Press, 2001).

Gunther-Canada, Wendy, 'Mary Wollstonecraft's "Wild Wish": Confounding Sex in the Discourse on Political Rights', in Maria J. Falco (ed.), *Feminist Interpretations of Mary Wollstonecraft* (University Park, Pennsylvania: University State University Press, 1996).

Hall, Carol Louise, *Blake and Fuseli: A Study in the Transmission of Ideas* (New York and London: Garland Publishing, 1985).

Hammond, J. L. and Barbara Hammond, *The Village Labourer 1760–1832: A Study in the Government of England before the Reform Bill*, new edn (London: Longmans, 1920).

Hammond, J. L. and Barbara Hammond, *Lord Shaftesbury* (London: Constable, 1923, 4th edn, 1936).

Hammond, J. L. and Barbara Hammond, *The Bleak Age*, rev. edn (Harmondsworth: Penguin Books, 1947).

Hammond, J. L. and Barbara Hammond, *The Town Labourer (1760–1832)*, vol. I (London: Guild Books, 1949).

Hampton, Jean, *Hobbes and the Social Contract Tradition* (Cambridge: Cambridge University Press, 1986).

Harding, Alan, *A Social History of English Law* (Harmondsworth: Penguin Books, 1966).

Harrison, Bernard, *Henry Fielding's 'Tom Jones': The Novelist as Moral Philosopher* (London: Chatto and Windus for Sussex University Press, 1975).

Harvey Darton, F. J., *Children's Books in England* (Cambridge: Cambridge University Press, second edn, 1958).

Hays, Mary, *Appeal to the Men of Great Britain in Behalf of Women* (1798) facsimile edition with an introduction by Gina Lurie (New York: Garland, 1974).

Hays, Mary, *The Victim of Prejudice* (1799) facsimile edition with new introduction by Caroline Franklin (London: Routledge/Thoemmes Press, 1995).

Hazlitt, William, 'On Good-Nature', *The Round Table* (1815–17), 101–2.

Hazlitt, William, *The Complete Works of William Hazlitt*, ed. P. P. Howe after the edition of A. R. Waller and Arnold Glover (21 vols, London: Dent, 1930).

Henkin, Louis, *The Rights of Man Today* (London: Stevens & Sons, 1979).

Herzog, Don, *Poisoning the Minds of the Lower Orders* (Princeton, NJ: Princeton University Press, 1998).

Heywood, Colin, *A History of Childhood: Children and Childhood in the West from Medieval to Modern Times* (Malden, Mass.: Polity Press, 2001).

Hoagwood, Terence Allan, *Politics, Philosophy, and the Production of Romantic Texts* (DeKalb, IL: Northern Illinois University Press, 1996).

Hobbes, Thomas, *Leviathan*, ed. C. B. Macpherson (Harmondsworth: Penguin Books, 1968).

Hobson, Christopher Z., *The Chained Boy: Orc and Blake's Idea of Revolution* (Lewisburg and London: Bucknell University Press, 1999).

Holcroft, Thomas, *A Narrative of Facts, Relating to a Prosecution for High Treason, Including the Address to the Jury, which the Court Refused to Hear*, second edn (London: H. D. Symonds, 1795).

Holcroft, Thomas, *The Adventures of Hugh Trevor*, ed. Seamus Deane (London and Oxford: Oxford University Press, 1973).

Holdsworth, Sir William, *A History of English Law*, eds, A. L. Goodhart and H. G. Hanbury (14 vols, London: Methuen, 1952).

Holmes, Richard, *Footsteps: Adventures of a Romantic Biographer* (London: Hodder and Stoughton, 1985).

Homes, Richard, *Coleridge: Early Visions* (London: Penguin Books, 1989).

Honour, Hugh, *The Image of the Black in Western Art* (4 vols, Cambridge, Mass.: Harvard University Press, 1989).

Hoppit, Julian, *A Land of Liberty? England 1689–1727* (The New Oxford History of England, Oxford: Oxford University Press, 2000).

Hoskins, W. G., *English Landscapes* (London: British Broadcasting Corporation, 1973).

Hulme, Peter, *Colonial Encounters: Europe and the Native Caribbean, 1492–1797* (London and New York: Methuen, 1986).

Human Rights and Equal Opportunity Commission, *Bringing them Home: Report of the National Inquiry into the Separation of Aboriginal and Torres Strait Islander Children from their Families* (Sydney: Human Rights and Equal Opportunity Commission, 1997).

Hutcheson, Francis, *On Human Nature: Reflections on our Common Systems of Morality on the Social Nature of Man*, ed. Thomas Mautner (Cambridge: Cambridge University Press, 1993).

Hutcheson, Francis, *An Essay on the Nature and Conduct of the Passions and Affections* (1728) facsimile edition with introduction by Paul McReynolds (Gainesville, Florida: University Press of Florida, 1969).

Inchbald, Elizabeth, *Nature and Art*, with an introduction by Caroline Franklin, The Romantics: Women Novelists series (London, Routledge/Thoemmes Press, 1995).

Inchbald, Elizabeth, *A Simple Story*, ed. Pamela Clemit (London: Penguin Books, 1996).

Jackson, J. R. de J., *Poetry of the Romantic Period, The Routledge History of English Poetry, Volume 4* (London: Routledge and Kegan Paul, 1980).

Jaffa, Harry V., 'Natural Rights', in David L. Sills (ed.), *International Encyclopedia of the Social Sciences* (London: The Macmillan Company and the Free Press, 1968), 85–9.

Jones, Chris, *Radical Sensibility: Literature and ideas in the 1790s* (London: Routledge, 1993).

Jones, Peter, *Rights* (Basingstoke: Macmillan, 1994).

Jones, Vivien (ed.), *Women in the Eighteenth Century: Constructions of Femininity* (London: Routledge, 1990).

Keats, John, *The Letters of John Keats*, ed. Hyder E. Rollins (2 vols, Cambridge, Mass.: Harvard University Press, 1958).

Keats, John, *Keats: The Critical Heritage*, ed. G. M. Matthews (London: Routledge and Kegan Paul, 1971).

Keats, John, *John Keats: The Complete Poems*, ed. John Barnard (second edn, Harmondsworth: Penguin, 1977).

Keane, John, *Thomas Paine: A Political Life* (Boston, MA: Little, Brown, 1995).

Kelly, Gary, *The English Jacobin Novel 1780–1805* (Oxford and New York: Clarendon Press, 1976).

Kelly, Gary, *Women, Writing, and Revolution 1790–1827* (Oxford: Clarendon Press, 1993).

Kemp-Ashraf, P. M., 'Thomas Spence', in P. M. Kemp-Ashraf and Jack Mitchell (eds), *Essays in Honour of William Gallacher* (Berlin: Humbolt-Universitas, 1966), 280–84.

Kirk, Linda, *Richard Cumberland and Natural Law: Secularisation of Thought in Seventeenth-Century England* (Cambridge: Cambridge University Press, 1987).

Kittay, Eva Feder, *Metaphor: Its Cognitive Force and Linguistic Structure* (Oxford: Clarendon Press, 1987).

Kitson, Peter J. and Debbie Lee (eds), *Slavery, Abolition and Emancipation: Writings in the British Romantic Period* (8 vols, London: Pickering and Chatto, 1999).

Lacey, Michael J. and Knud Haakonssen (eds), *A Culture of Rights: The Bill of Rights in Philosophy, Politics, and Law – 1791 and 1991* (Washington, DC and Cambridge: Woodrow Wilson International Center for Scholars and Cambridge University Press).

Lakoff, George and Mark Johnson, *Metaphors We Live By* (Chicago: Chicago University Press, 1980).

Larrissy, Edward, *William Blake* (Oxford: Basil Blackwell, 1985).

Ledwon, Leonara, *Law and Literature: Text and Theory* (New York and London: Garland Publishing, 1996).

Lehmann, James H., '*The Vicar of Wakefield*: Goldsmith's Sublime, Oriental Job', *English Literary History*, 46 (1979), 97–135..

Levinson, Marjorie, *Keats's Life of Allegory: The Origins of a Style* (Oxford: Oxford University Press, 1988).

Literature Online (http://lion.chadwyck.com/home/home.cgi?source = config2.cfg).

Locke, John, *Two Treatises of Government*, ed. Peter Laslett (Cambridge: Cambridge University Press, 1963).

Locke, John, *The Educational Writings of John Locke*, ed. James L. Axtell (Cambridge: Cambridge University Press, 1968).

Lockridge, Laurence S., *The Ethics of Romanticism* (Cambridge: Cambridge University Press, 1989).

Loncar, Kathleen, *Legal Fiction: Law in the Novels of Nineteenth Century Women Novelists* (London: Minerva Press, 1995).

Mackenzie, Henry, *The Man of Feeling*, ed. Kenneth C. Slagle (New York: The Norton Library, 1958).

MacLachlan, Gale and Ian Reid, *Framing and Interpretation* (Melbourne: Melbourne University Press, 1994).

Marat, J. P., *Les chaines de l'esclavage* (Paris: Union Générale d'Éditions, 1972).

Marshall, David, *The Surprising Effects of Sympathy: Marivaux, Diderot, Rousseau, and Mary Shelley* (Chicago and London: University of Chicago Press, 1988).

McCabe, Richard A., *Incest, Drama and Nature's Law* (Cambridge: Cambridge University Press, 1993).

McCann, Andrew, *Cultural Politics in the 1790s: Literature, Radicalism and the Public Sphere* (Basingstoke and New York: Macmillan and St Martin's Press, 1999).

McCreedy, Natalie, 'Poetry, Print and Persecution: Images of Slavery in Britain' (unpublished BA honours dissertation, University of Newcastle upon Tyne, 2000).

McGann, Jerome, *The Poetics of Sensibility: A Revolution in Literary Style* (Oxford and New York: Clarendon Press, 1996).

McInerny, Ralph M., 'Natural Law and Natural Rights', in *Aquinas on Human Action* (Washington, DC: Catholic University of America Press, 1992), 213–14.

Mee, Jon, *Dangerous Enthusiasm: William Blake and the Culture of Radicalism in the 1790s* (Oxford: Clarendon Press, 1992).

Mee, Jon, *Romanticism, Enthusiasm and Regulation: Poetics and the Policing of Culture in the Romantic Period* (Oxford: Oxford University Press, 2003).

Meehan, Michael, *Liberty and Poetics in Eighteenth Century England* (London: Croom Helm, 1986).

Mellor, Anne K. and Richard E. Matlak, *British Literature 1780–1830* (New York: Harcourt Brace College Publishers, 1996).

Melzer, Arthur M., *The Natural Goodness of Man: On the System of Rousseau's Thought* (Chicago: University of Chicago Press, 1990).

Mercer, Philip, *Sympathy and Ethics: A Study of the Relationship between Sympathy and Morality with Special Reference to Hume's 'Treatise'* (Oxford: Oxford University Press, 1972).

Middleton Murry, John, *Heaven and Earth* (London: Cape, 1938).

Midgley, Clare, *Women Against Slavery: The British Campaigns 1780–1870* (London: Routledge, 1992).

Montgomery, James, *Poems on the Abolition of the Slave Trade* (1809), ed. James Grahame and E. Benger, facsimile edition with an introduction by Donald H. Reimann (New York and London: Garland Publishers, 1978).

Montgomery, James, *The Chimney-Sweeper's Friend, and Climbing-Boy's Album*, facsimile edn, ed. Donald H. Reiman (New York and London: Garland Publishing, 1978).

Moore, Hannah, *Strictures on the Modern System of Female Education* (1799), facsimile edn with introduction by Gina Luria (New York: Garland, 1974).

Morgan, Rebecca, 'The gothic in the novels of Charlotte Smith' (unpublished PhD thesis, Newcastle upon Tyne, 1996).

Morton, Timothy, *Shelley and the Revolution in Taste: The Body and the Natural World* (Cambridge: Cambridge University Press, 1995).

Mullan, John, 'The Language of Sentiment: Hume, Smith, and Henry Mackenzie', in *The History of Scottish Literature: Volume 2 1660–1800*, ed. Andrew Hook, gen. ed. Craig, Cairns (Aberdeen: Aberdeen University Press, 1987).

Mullan, John, *Sentiment and Sociability: The Language of Feeling in the Eighteenth Century* (Oxford: Clarendon Press, 1988).

Nash, Roderick Frazier, *The Rights of Nature: A History of Environmental Ethics* (Leichhardt, NSW: Primavera Press/The Wilderness Society, 1990).

Newey, Vincent, 'Goldsmith's "Pensive Plain": Re-viewing *The Deserted Village*', in Thomas Woodman (ed.), *Early Romantics: Perspectives in British Poetry from Pope to Wordsworth* (Basingstoke: Macmillan, 1998), 93–116.

The New Oxford Book of Romantic Period Verse, ed. Jerome McGann (New York: Oxford University Press, 1993).

Norbrook, David, *Writing the English Republic: Poetry, Rhetoric and Politics, 1627–1660* (Cambridge: Cambridge University Press, 1999).

O'Flinn, Paul, 'Beware of reverence: writing and radicalism in the 1790s', in John Lucas (ed.), *Writing and Radicalism* (London and New York: Longman, 1996), 84–101.

Oldfield, J. R., *Popular Politics and British Anti-Slavery: The Mobilisation of Public Opinion Against the Slave Trade, 1787–1807* (London: Frank Cass Publishers, 1998).

An Oxford Companion to the Romantic Age: British Culture 1776–1832, gen. ed. Iain McCalman (Oxford: Oxford University Press, 1999).

Paine, Thomas, *Rights of Man*, ed. Henry Collins (Harmondsworth: Penguin Books, 1969).

Paine, Thomas, *Thomas Paine: Political Writings*, ed. Bruce Kuklick (Cambridge: Cambridge University Press, 1989).

Pennock, J. Roland, 'Rights, Natural Rights, and Human Rights – A General View', in J. Roland Pennock and John W. Chapman (eds), *Human Rights* (New York and London: New York University Press, 1981), 1–7.

Pickering, Samuel F., Jr, *John Locke and Children's Books in Eighteenth-Century England* (Knoxville: University of Tennessee Press, 1981).

Pinch, Adela, *Strange Fits of Passion: Epistemologies of Emotion, Hume to Austen* (Stanford, CA: Stanford University Press, 1996).

Pinchbeck, Ivy and Margaret Hewitt, *Children in English Society* (3 vols, London: Routledge and Kegan Paul, 1973).

Pollin, Burton R., 'John Thelwall's Marginalia in a Copy of Coleridge's *Biographia Literaria*', *Bulletin of the New York Public Library*, 74 (1970), 73–94.

Pratt, Mary Louise, *Imperial Eyes: Travel Writing and Transculturation* (London and New York: Routledge, 1992).

Raphael, D. D., *Enlightenment, Rights and Revolution: Essays in Legal and Social Philosophy* (Aberdeen: Aberdeen University Press, 1989).

Rawls, John, *A Theory of Justice* (Oxford: Clarendon Press, 1972).

Richardson, Samuel, *Clarissa* (4 vols, London: Dent, 1932).

Ricks, Christopher, *Keats and Embarrassment* (Oxford: Oxford University Press, 1976).

Roe, Nicholas, *The Politics of Nature: Wordsworth and Some Contemporaries* (London: Macmillan, 1992).

Rosenblum, Robert, *The Romantic Child: From Runge to Sendak* (London: Thames and Hudson, 1988).

Ross, Marlon B., 'Configurations of Feminine Reform: The Woman Writer and the Tradition of Dissent', in Carol Shiner Wilson and Joel Haefner (eds), *Re-Visioning Romanticism: British Women Writers, 1776–1837* (Philadelphia, PA: University of Pennsylvania Press, 1994).

Rousseau, Jean-Jacques, *Emile*, transl. Barbara Foxley (London: Dent, 1911).

Rousseau, Jean-Jacques, *The Social Contract*, transl. and ed. Maurice Cranston (Harmondsworth: Penguin Books, 1968).

Rousseau, Jean-Jacques, *A Discourse on Inequality*, transl. and ed. Maurice Cranston (London: Penguin Books, 1984).

Royle, Edward, and James Walvin, *English Radicals and Reformers: 1760–1848* (Lexington, KY: University of Kentucky Press, 1982).

Rudkin, Olive D., *Thomas Spence and his Connections* (London: Allen and Unwin 1927).

Ryle, Gilbert, *The Concept of Mind* (London: Hutchinson, 1949).

Sapiro, Virginia, 'Wollstonecraft, Feminism, and Democracy: "Being Bastilled" ', in Maria J. Falco (ed.), *Feminist Interpretations of Mary Wollstonecraft* (University Park, Pennsylvania: Pennsylvania State University Press, 1996), 33–46.

Sapiro, Virginia and Penny A. Weiss, 'Jean-Jacques Rousseau and Mary Wollstonecraft: Restoring the Conversation', in Maria J. Falco (ed.), *Feminist Interpretations of Mary Wollstonecraft* (University Park, Pennsylvania: Pennsylvania State University Press, 1996), 179–208.

Scrivener, Michael, *Poetry and Reform: Periodical Verse from the English Democratic Press 1792–1824* (Detroit: Wayne State University Press, 1992).

Scott, Sarah, *The History of Cornelia* (1750; facsimile ed., New York: State University Press of New York, 1974).

Shakespeare, William, *The Tempest*, ed. Stephen Orgel (Oxford: Oxford University Press, 1987).

Shaw, Philip (ed.), *Romantic Wars: Studies in Culture and Conflict, 1793–1822* (Aldershot: Ashgate, 2000).

Siskin, Clifford, 'The Year of the System', in Richard Cronin (ed.), *1798: The Year of the 'Lyrical Ballads'* (Basingstoke and New York: Macmillan and St Martin's Press, 1998), 9–31.

Smith, Adam, *The Theory of Moral Sentiments*, eds, D. D. Raphael and A. L. Macfie (Oxford: Clarendon Press, 1976).

Smith, Charlotte, *The Old Manor House*, ed. Anne Henry Ehrenpreis (London: Oxford University Press, 1969).

Smith, Charolotte, *The Young Philosopher* (facsimile, 4 vols, New York: Garland, 1974).

Smith, Charlotte, *The Poems of Charlotte Smith*, ed. Stuart Curran (Oxford and New York: Oxford University Press, 1993).

Smith, Charlotte, *Desmond*, eds, Antje Blank and Janet Todd (London: Pickering & Chatto, 1997).

Solow, Barbara L. and Stanley L. Engerman, *British Capitalism and Caribbean Slavery: The Legacy of Eric Williams* (Cambridge: Cambridge University Press, 1987).

Spence, Thomas, *Pigs' Meat: Selected Writings of Thomas Spence*, ed. G. I. Gallop (Nottingham: Spokesman, 1982).

Spenser, Jane, 'Women writers and the eighteenth-century novel', in John Richetti (ed.), *The Cambridge Companion to the Eighteenth-Century Novel* (Cambridge: Cambridge University Press, 1996), 212–35.

Sprague, Beverly Allen, 'William Godwin's Influence upon John Thelwall', *PMLA*, 37 (1922), 662–8.

Stetson, Dorothy McBride, 'Women's Rights and Human Rights: Intersection and Conflict', in Maria J. Falco (ed.), *Feminist Interpretations of Mary Wollstonecraft* (Pennsylvania, PA: Pennsylvania University Press, 1996).

Stone, Lawrence, *The Family, Sex and Marriage in England 1500–1800*, rev. edn, (London: Weidenfeld & Nicolson, 1979).

Strauss, Leo, *Natural Right and History* (Chicago: University of Chicago Press, 1953).

Sypher, Wylie, *Guinea's captive kings: British anti-slavery literature of the XVIIIth century* (New York: Octagon Books, 1969).

Thelwall, John, *The Speech of John Thelwall at the Second Meeting of the London Corresponding Society, and Other Friends of Reform* (London: J. Thelwall, 1795).

Thelwall, John, *Ode to Science [and other works by John Thelwall]*, ed. Donald H. Reiman (New York and London: Garland Publishing, 1978).

Thelwall, John, *The Poetical Recreations of the Champion* (1822), facsimile, introduced by Donald H. Reiman (New York and London: Garland Publishing, 1978).

Thelwall, John, *The Peripatetic* (1793), facsimile, 3 vols, ed. Donald H. Reiman (New York and London: Garland Publishing, 1978).

Thelwall, John, *The Politics of English Jacobinism: Writings of John Thelwall*, ed. Gregory Claeys (University Park, Pennsylvania: Pennsylvania State University Press, 1995).

Thelwall, John, 'The Natural and Constitutional Right of Britons', in Gregory Claeys (ed.), *The Politics of English Jacobinism: Writings of John Thelwall* (University Park, Pennsylvania: Pennsylvania State University Press, 1995).

Thomas, Keith, *Man and the Natural World: Changing Attitudes in England 1500–1800* (London: Allen Lane, 1983).

Thompson, E. P., *The Making of the English Working Class* (Harmondsworth: Penguin Books, 1968).

Thompson, E. P., *Customs in Common* (London: Merlin Press, 1991).

Thompson, E. P., *Witness Against the Beast: William Blake and the Moral Law* (Cambridge: Cambridge University Press, 1993).

Thompson, E. P., *The Romantics: England in a Revolutionary Age* (New York: The New Press, 1997).

Thompson, James, *Poetical Works*, ed. J. Logie Robertson (Oxford: The Clarendon Press, 1908).

Thompson, James, *Models of Value: Eighteenth-Century Political Economy and the Novel* (Durham and London: Duke University Press, 1996).

Todd, Janet, *Sensibility: An Introduction* (London and New York: Metheun, 1986).
Tomalin, Claire, *The Life and Death of Mary Wollstonecraft* (London: Weidenfeld and Nicolson, 1974).
Tuck, Richard, *Natural Rights Theories: Their Origin and Development* (Cambridge: Cambridge University Press, 1979).
Turley, David, *The Culture of English Antislavery 1780–1860* (London and New York: Routledge, 1991).
Turner, Cheryl, *Living by the Pen: Women Writers in the Eighteenth Century* (London and New York: Routledge, 1992).
Ty, Eleanor, *Unsex'd Revolutionaries: Five Women Novelists of the 1790s* (Toronto: University of Toronto Press, 1993).
Tyson, Gerald P., *Joseph Johnson: A Liberal Publisher* (Iowa City: University of Iowa Press, 1979).
United Nations, *Convention on the Rights of the Child* (UNICEF) (http://www.unicef.org/crc/crc.htm).
van Sant, Ann Jessie, *Eighteenth-century Sensibility and the Novel of the Senses in Social Context* (Cambridge: Cambridge University Press, 1993).
Waldron, Jeremy, 'Rights', in Robert E. Goodin and Philip Pettit (eds), *A Companion to Contemporary Political Philosophy* (Oxford: Blackwell, 1993), 575–85.
Walvin, James, *England, Slaves and Freedom, 1776–1838* (London: Macmillan, 1986).
Walvin, James, *Black Ivory: A History of British Slavery* (London: HarperCollins, 1992).
Warner, James, 'Eighteenth-Century English Reactions to *La Nouvelle Héloise'*, *PMLA* (1937), 803–19.
Watson, Nicola J., *Revolution and the Form of the British Novel 1790–1825: Intercepted Letters, Interrupted Seductions* (Oxford: Clarendon Press, 1994).
Weinreb, Lloyd L., 'Natural Law and Rights', in *Natural Law Theory*, ed. Robert P. George (Oxford: Clarendon Press, 1992), 278–305.
Whale, John, 'Political Prose of the Romantic Period', in Michael O'Neill (ed.), *Literature of the Romantic Period: A Bibliographical Guide* (Oxford: Clarendon Press, 1998), pp. 364–79.
White, R. J., *Waterloo to Peterloo* (Harmondsworth: Penguin Books, 1968).
White, R. S., *Natural Law in English Renaissance Literature* (Cambridge: Cambridge University Press, 1996).
White, R. S. (ed.), *Hazlitt's Criticism of Shakespeare: A Selection* (Lampeter: The Edwin Mellon Press, 1996).
Williams, Eric, *Capitalism and Slavery* (London: Andre Deutsch, 1964).
Williams, Helen Maria, *Julia: A Novel* (New York and London: Garland, 1974).
Williams, Helen Maria, *Letters from France* (8 vols, London, 1790–06), vol 1, Letter II, anthologised in Anne K. Mellor and Richard E. Matlak (eds), *British Literature 1780–1830* (Fort Worth, Texas: Harcourt Brace College Publishers, 1996), 508–29.
Williams, Helen Maria, *Poems*, with an introduction by Caroline Franklin (London: Routledge/Thoemmes Press, 1996).
Wiliams, Raymond, *The Country and the City* (London: Chatto and Windus, 1975).
Wilson, Thomas, *The Art of Rhetoric*, facsimile ed. R. H. Bowers, (Gainesville, Florida: University Press of Florida, 1962).
Winter, Kari J., *Subjects of Slavery: Agents of Change: Women and Power in Gothic Novels and Slave Narratives 1790–1865* (Athens and London: University of Georgia Press, 1992).
Wise, Steven M., *Rattling the Cage: Toward Legal Rights for Animals* (Cambridge, Mass.: Perseus Books, 2000).

Wollstonecraft, Mary, *Vindication of the Rights of Woman*, ed. Miriam Kramnick (Harmondsworth: Penguin Books, 1975).

Wollstonecraft, Mary, *'Mary' and 'The Wrongs of Woman'*, eds, James Kinsley and Gary Kelly (Oxford: Oxford University Press, 1980).

Wollstonecraft, Mary, *Thoughts on the Education of Daughters*, in *The Works of Mary Wollstonecraft*, vol. 4, ed. Janet Todd and Marilyn Butler (London: William Pickering, 1993).

Wollstonecraft, Mary, *Political Writings: A Vindication of the Rights of Men, A Vindication of the Rights of Woman, An Historical and Moral View of the French Revolution*, ed. Janet Todd (Oxford: Oxford University Press, 1994).

Wood, Marcus, 'William Cobbett, John Thelwall, Radicalism, Racism and Slavery: A Study in Burkean Parodics', *Romanticism on the Net*, 15 (August 1999) (http://users.ox.ac.uk/~scat0385/thelwall.html).

Woodcock, George, *Anarchism: A History of Libertarian Ideas and Movements* (Cleveland: Meridian Books, 1962).

Woof, Robert, Stephen Hebron and Claire Tomalin, *Hyenas in Petticoats: Mary Wollstonecraft and Mary Shelley* (Kendal: The Wordsworth Trust, 1997).

Wootton, David (ed.), *Divine Right and Democracy: An Anthology of Political Writing in Stuart England* (Harmondsworth: Penguin Books, 1986).

Wordsworth, Jonathon and Stephen Hebron, *Romantic Women Writers* (Kendal: The Wordsworth Trust, 1994).

Wordsworth, William, *The Early Letters of William and Dorothy Wordsworth (1787–1805)*, ed. E. de Selincourt (Oxford: Clarendon Press, 1935).

Wordsworth, William, *Wordsworth: Poetical Works*, ed. Thomas Hutchinson, rev. Ernest de Selincourt (Oxford: Oxford University Press, 1936).

Wordsworth, William, *The Poetical Works of William Wordsworth*, ed. E. de Selincourt and H. Darbishire (5 vols, Oxford: Oxford University Press, 1940–49).

Wordsworth, William, *William Wordsworth: Selected Poetry*, ed. Mark van Doren (New York: Random House, 1950).

Index

Epstein, Julia 240n61
Erametsa, Erik 42, 238n4
Erdman, David V. 181, 183, 188, 247n40, 250n40
Erskine, Lord 225
Essay Concerning Human Understanding, An 198
Essay on Humane Understanding 28
Essay on Humanity in Animals, An 225
Essay on Inequality of Mankind, The 72
Essay on the Natural Equality of Men: On the Rights that Result from it, and on the Duties which it Imposes, An 96, 242n24
Essay on the Nature and Conduct of the Passions and Affections (1728), *An* 43
Essays in Honour of William Gallacher 242n20
Essick, Robert N. 191, 237n76, 247n47, 250n40
Ethelinde 149
Europe: A Prophecy 188
Ewin, R. E. 235n35
'Execution of Breaking on Rack' 183

Fable of Bees, The 58
Falco, Maria J. 241n13, 242nn14, 17, 18, 243nn12, 21, 245n1
Family Secrets, Literary and Domestic 226
Family, Sex and Marriage in England, The 1500–1800 249n19
'Fancy' 116
Farmer of Inglewood Forest, The 180
'Father of the Book Trade' 39, 237n73
Faulkner, Peter 244n6
Fawkes, Francis 214
Feldman, Paula R. 240n63, 249n17
Feminist Interpretations of Mary Wollstonecraft 241n13, 242nn14, 17, 18, 243nn12, 21, 245n1
Fenwick, Eliza 162–163, 202–203, 245nn23, 24
Ferguson, Moira 243n21, 245n1, 246nn13, 16, 23
Fielding, Henry 239n33
  Tom Jones 98
Fielding, Sarah 199, 248n8
Filmer, Sir Robert 28–29
Finnis, John 2, 10, 13, 234n2, 235n20
'First Principles' 120, 121

'Flagellation of a Female Samboe Slave' 183
Fletcher, Loraine 150, 161–162, 245nn18, 21
Florence Miscellany 63
Flower, Benjamin 244n7
Footsteps: Adventures of a Romantic Biographer 35
Ford, Pina 235n26
Forrester, John 234n10
Fouqier-Tinville 35
Fox 34, 40, 124, 134, 169, 171
Foxley, Barbara 241n5, 249nn13, 15
Fragment of an Original Letter on the Slavery of the Negroes 179
Framing and Interpretation 234n16
Framing Feelings 239nn46, 47
'framing' theory 234n16
France 34, 40, 64, 84, 90, 93, 136, 141, 147, 155–160, 172, 181, 205
  1789 events in 85
  ancien regime in 27
  The Chains of Slavery publication in 192
  pre-revolutionary France 86
  revolutions in 3, 9, 77, 85, 89, 94, 100, 134, 146, 195, 232
  united Irish's expectations from 37
Franklin, Benjamin 180
Franklin, Caroline 244nn5, 43, 245n27
Franklin, Miles 245n23
French Constitution, The 244n7
French revolution 1, 6–7, 31–35, 61, 64–65, 70, 76, 84–86, 89, 92, 95, 117, 121, 135, 138, 143, 154–155, 160–161, 164, 168, 170, 182, 192–193, 226, 230
Freud and the Passions 234n10
Freud, Sigmund 100, 205, 234n10, 249n23
Friedman, Arthur 239nn36, 44
Furneaux, Robin 246n8, 247n28
Fuseli, Henry 39–40, 181, 191, 248n50

Gadd, Ian 237n72
'Gagging Bills' 40, 124
Gale, Susan 208
Gallop, G. I. 242nn19, 20, 21, 249n30
Garber, Marjorie B. 242n1